The Scribe:

A Life in the Time of Medici

Peggy Post

Author's Note

I have written numerous small booklets about my travels, plus two small travel guides and two wildflower guides about the two areas in which I live, Palm City, Florida and Sky Valley, Georgia. I thoroughly enjoyed the writing process while creating all those books, but I never felt I had the imagination to create fiction.

I have read and loved many phases of history. Eleanor of Aquitaine and Henry, Charles Darwin, the Ancient People, Hildegaard von Bingen, Abigail and John Adams, and Cosimo de Medici are but a few of my favorites in the course of my many reading years. Coming back to Cosimo a few years ago, I fell madly in love with all the stories about the birth of the renaissance and his involvement in so many of them.

Last summer I came upon the idea of using fictional characters to tell his story. As I tell all my friends, that way when I am in the nursing home, the attendants can read the book to me all over again every day for the very first time. I tell it as a joke, but it is what motivated me to write the book.

I have done my very best to get the historical facts accurate, then my fictional characters are straight out of thin air, but they were great fun. I laughed and cried with all them as they told me their story.

The writing process made this last year the most rewarding I have had maybe ever, and I can only recommend everyone write something: fiction, a memoir, short stories of excerpts from their life; anything, but write.

In my Cosimo I have conveyed a man suitable for sainthood. Perhaps that is not the character of the true man, but since it is my book and it is fictional, I took the liberty to tell his story in the most favorable light.

I live in two vibrant, supportive communities, and they know of my travails this last year. I thank all of them for their support and encouragement.I think some of them may actually read my book. If others do, I can only say it was written from my heart. Enjoy the journey.

TABLE OF CONTENTS

CAST OF FICTIONAL CHARACTERS

Daughter – Amalia Donterini

    Husband – Marco Valetti

        Turkish friend – Erudius Forzdal – son Rudi

    Daughter – Alessandra

        Son in law – Bernardo

            Grandson – Bernardo

    Son – Giuliano – (Married Teresa)

        Fabio – Giuliano & Teresa's youngest

    Father – Giuliano Donterini / Mother – Margherita

        Son (Amalia's brother) – Stefano

            daughter – Lisabetta

Servant/ Seamstress – Lucrezia

    Husband – Tenor – Ermanno Evangelista

        mother – Anna

            servant – Francia

            servant – Franco

        father's partner – Benedetto

        daughter – Antonia

    Children: Manno/ Anna/ Ugo

        Manno married Eleanora – died

            child Lia

        Anna married Ludovico – carpenter – Manager husband of twin

                Gino & Mariana

    Ugo marries Lucia (Roberto & Rosetta Lamandola are parents)

Errand Boy – Carlo Cavalcanti

        father – Barto

        friends – Jacko (Jacopo Vespucci), Gino & Paolo

    Marries Lisabetta

        Lisa – youngest child of 3

~ ~ ~

Padre – Bernardo at Santa Maria Novella

Attorney – Messer Sacchetti, Marcilio

    Young attorney – Riccardo and Teresa Riccardi – son Rico

Book world – Master Giorgio Manetti – shop boy – Antonio
   – later works for M.Vespasiano di Bisticci (H)
Girl friends – Constance – Hortensia
           Caterina marries Claudio
                daughter-Blanche (Nursemaid – Clara)
Neighbors – Maria & Filippo DeFrancisco – next door neighbors
   Lucia & Luigi – next door neighbor
   Dona Rutia – neighbor across the street
      Deceased husband – Roberto
      old maid – Maddalena
      Rutia's daughter Rosa – Siena
      Maddalena's daughter – Venice
   Juliana & Guido nurse in neighborhood
   Messer D'Alessandro – leader of gonfalons
   Giovanni and Beatrice Volini (across street in new house
          daughter – Gia
          Mother and Father – Cassetti
   Master Ludovici – rich man in gonfalons with largest house
Master Vicenti – cloth merchant – Lucrezia contact
Poggio Braccioilini (H)
   housekeeper – Marta
   male servant – Rudolfo
Federico (Worker in Marco's boddeghe) married Maria
Nursemaid for Lisabetta – Bianca
Helper in Lucrezia's shop – AnnaMaria
Piero – Young orphan taken in by Carlo
Antonio – orphan taken in to help Lisabetta
Bianca helped Lisabetta on her farm
Violetta – Blanca's mother – housekeeper at the big farm house
Tenerife Frise – forerunner of Bichon Frise

ENGLAND
Nextimo Vespucci (Uncle of Jacko, Great-Uncle of Amerigo(H))
Captains Messana & Petrillo
Misters Crawford & Powers

Photo of the front page of *On the Nature of Things* by Lucretius
scribed by Girolamo di Matteo de Tauris in 1483
and given to Pope Sixtus IV

BOOK I

I   *The End and the Beginning*   *1447*

"Wake up, Amalia, Padre Bernardo will be here very soon. We must get you ready to greet him."

"I'm awake."

"Well, then, let me in so we can get you dressed. You can't delay the inevitable."

"Why not, Lucrezia? When the inevitable is the end of my life, why not delay it as long as possible?"

"Amalia, let me in. This is not the end of your life; although, God knows, it may very well seem like it. Please let me in, or I will be blamed if you are not presentable when the padre arrives."

"All right, Lucrezia, but without Papa, my life is over, no matter what you say. I miss him so much, how can I go on without him? And what will happen to me?" Amalia said as she unbolted the door to allow Lucrezia entry. Lucrezia entered with a basin of warmed water so Amalia could wash herself while the young servant went back downstairs to get the dress she had labored on most of the previous evening and well into the night, trying to alter it so it would fit Amalia properly.

A young girl should not be wearing brown, thought Lucrezia, and certainly not twice in only two years. What will happen to her now that her father is dead? And for that matter, what will happen to me, she thought, now that I will not have a position? Surely Amalia will—will what? What will either of us do?

"Lucrezia, what will become of me," cried Amalia as Lucrezia came back into the room carrying the dress Amalia had worn to her mother's funeral just two years ago. "Not that! How can I wear that same dress?" cried Amalia, "Why, oh why, Papa? Lucrezia, he was such a wonderful father. How can I lose him also?

How can I wear that dress? What will become of me? Will I have to go to a convent? I can't do this alone. What will happen? Please help me, Lucrezia."

"Stop now," said Lucrezia softly. "For now there is nothing to do but what must be done today. The padre will be here presently, and everyone will be arriving. You must do this. Whatever else happens after, we must try to get through today together.

"I altered the dress, so I think it will fit you. I let out the hem as far as I could. I hope it will not be too short. I didn't notice how much you have grown since—" Lucrezia didn't finish the sentence because she knew it would only bring on another cascade of tears. "I hope it is not too tight up top. I sewed in two inserts and changed the cut of the bosom. I hope it works. You are not a little girl any longer."

While she was talking, Lucrezia worked to help Amalia get into the dress, and she was quite impressed with the results. The dress was a perfect fit for Amalia. No one would recognize the two-year-old dress she had rescued from the bottom of the large, decorated cassoni in the corner of Amalia's bedroom that had been in Amalia's mother's family for almost one hundred years. She should not be thinking such thoughts now, but she was impressed with her own abilities as a seamstress. The dress, while appropriately modest, and still the dull brown of mourning, was flattering to Amalia's figure, although, understandably, Amalia didn't take notice of any of that.

Amalia was petite, with very light auburn hair cascading down her back. Usually, her bright blue eyes were her best feature, but today they were puffy and red-rimmed from crying. She was a pretty girl but always seemed unaware of her attractiveness. She had a bright mind and preferred to live inside its confines, being much more studious that her several girlfriends.

Lucrezia was taller and darker skinned with browner hair. She, too, was attractive with her brown eyes, quick smile, and quick wit. She might be relegated to being a maid, and, although she was neither subservient nor obedient, she was always kind. She took charge of Amalia's life, and Amalia's father had liked that he could rely on Lucrezia to protect and steer Amalia in the right direction at all times, even if the headstrong adolescent might decide to behave like all young girls and sometimes head into trouble.

They had just completed braiding Amalia's long hair and fastening it into a fashionable but modest style when they heard the rapping on the front door.

They both started, and then Lucrezia ran down as quickly as she could to answer the call she knew would be Padre Bernardo. She did not want him to be greeted by Carlo, the young boy that sometimes ran errands for them, who was there for the day to help with chores.

Lucrezia didn't know if Carlo even had shoes, but whether he had them or not, Carlo would still certainly be wearing his old soiled clothes. She had made him wash his hands and face, but that was when he first arrived shortly after dawn, and they were surely both dirty again by now. She would have to try to keep him in the kitchen so he would not disgrace Amalia and the memory of her father. Today she must see to it that all went as well as possible for the fatherless—and motherless—young girl who was her mistress but also her friend.

She was almost three years older than Amalia, but they had been together since Amalia's mother had brought Lucrezia into their home when Amalia was eight years old. Lucrezia's own mother had died in the plague that had struck the city eight years ago. In the years that followed, Lucrezia had come to love Amalia's parents, Margherita and Giuliano, for though she was a servant, they had always treated her with kindness. Her relationship with Amalia had become more as an older sister than her maid.

What will happen to Amalia? What will happen to me, thought Lucrezia. She didn't know the answers to these questions that now plagued both of them, but as she opened the front door to greet the padre, she knew from this day forward both of their lives would be changed forever.

Padre Bernardo entered as Lucrezia swung the door wide to receive him. He climbed the stairs to the receiving room, and as he glanced around, he saw Amalia descending the stairs, looking as composed as he could have wished, for he knew the young girl was devastated by the loss of her father. No, she was not a young girl any longer. She was of marriageable age—even past it—but without a dowry and with no one to speak for her to make the suitable arrangements, marriage would not be in her future now. He must speak to the bishop and make suitable arrangements for her to enter the convent at Santa Maria Novella or elsewhere. He would see to that tomorrow. Today Padre Bernardo would bury Giuliano, Amalia's father, and his friend.

Padre Bernardo had known Giuliano since they were boys together.

Giuliano had been tall for his age and grew to be a tall man with warm brown eyes and a pleasant smile. Bernardo had been short and tended toward a plumpness that had never left him. But he too had a quick smile, and they had always enjoyed each other's company.

As the padre at Santa Maria Novella, Padre Bernardo had buried many older people. Just two years ago, many had died when the plague swept through the city. Even Margherita, Giuliano's wife, had died that summer. He should be inured to this, he thought, but he did not come to bury an old or a sick man today. This was a healthy, vibrant man killed in a senseless accident—and his oldest and best friend.

As Padre Bernardo climbed the stairs, behind him two of the neighbor women, Dona Maria and Dona Lucia, came bustling up too. Both women had been friends of Amalia's mother for many years, and they had looked after Amalia following her mother's death. Maria was the older of the two; she was Margherita's age, and Lucia was only a few years older than Lucrezia. They were both married, and each had two children, a boy and a girl, but the two families were years apart in their ages. Maria was short and plump with a pretty round face, whereas Lucia was tall and slender with black hair. They appeared opposites, but the padre knew their hearts were united in their love for Amalia, who lived with her father and the maid, Lucrezia, in the house between them.

He also knew that Amalia loved them both as much more than just neighbors. She and Lucrezia were very grateful that the two women had taken charge of everything when Amalia's father was brought home after the accident, and now they were taking care of the arrangements for Giuliano's funeral.

Padre Bernardo had heard that Amalia's father had lived only a short time after they laid him on his bed. He only regained consciousness for a few moments before succumbing to the injuries inflicted on his body when a cart, loaded with heavy barrels, overturned and one of the barrels crushed Giuliano's chest and smashed into his head. The horses drawing the cart had been startled by a passing carriage and had bolted. Yes, it was truly a senseless accident.

Earlier on the day of the accident, Giuliano had delivered a large Cicero manuscript to Master Manetti that he had been copying for almost a month, and he was on his way home carrying a packet, a new manuscript, wrapped in a piece of oiled cloth. He would have placed it on his writing table and then called to the girls, to Amalia and Lucrezia, to take them to the Mercato Vecchio.

He had always enjoyed that part of this day, because it pleasured him to watch Amalia choose the fruits and vegetables, the cheeses and eggs, the dried nuts and fruits, and sometimes meat or fish with such care, like a woman far beyond her years.

Of course, Amalia and Lucrezia could have gone to the old market without him, and oftentimes they did. They would have been safe, and it would have been proper, but his daughter was the only real joy in Giuliano's life now that his wife was gone, and he treasured these moments when, once a week on the main market day, he joined them. Amalia would be very serious about the choices of the food for their table, but then her joy would be boundless when he offered to buy her a special sweet treat. He would always offer, and she would always accept, but it was a game they had played with each other since they first started going to the market together shortly after Margherita died, and they both enjoyed the moment.

When the two strangers laid Giuliano on his bed, Amalia had wrapped her arms around his broken body as gently as she could, had laid her head near his shoulder, and cried. When he had regained consciousness, Giuliano placed his hand on Amalia's head and with great sorrow said, "I am so sorry, child. I have failed you as your father. I should have made arrangements for your marriage, but I did not want to part with you, and now I leave you in such dire circumstances." She had raised her head so she could see his face, and looking into his gentle brown eyes, taking his hand in both of hers, she had said, "No, Papa, no. You have given me all I ever wanted in this world, and I am grateful. I love you, Papa." He smiled at her, but he could not say more, his pain was too great. He slipped into unconsciousness, not to revive again.

Now, Amalia had to gather her courage, with Lucrezia's prodding, and when she finally walked down those stairs to greet the padre, she knew that she must do all she could to honor her father's memory and to be strong, as he would have wished her to be. With the aid of Padre Bernardo and their many friends and neighbors, she would see to it that her father was properly mourned and buried this day, and what tomorrow would bring, she knew not.

Their friends and neighbors had filled their kitchen with a large assortment of foods since her father's death. Thus, she was able to feed all who came to pay their respects to her father, Giuliano Dontarini, the notary for the guilds, the scribe who copied antique manuscripts, the devout churchman and leader of one of the confraternities at their family church, Santa Maria Novella, as well as a most beloved father.

Once everyone arrived, Padre Bernardo would take charge, and he would conduct the service for Giuliano. A committee of the men in the commune had just finished cutting the hole in the wall of the house so they could pass the body through as they began the processional to the church. That way, if Giuliano didn't leave by the front door, his spirit would not be able to find its way back into the house after he was interred. It was an old custom, still honored, although the ghosts weren't feared now as they once had been. The processional of friends and neighbors would carry the casket to <u>Santa Maria Novella</u> for the funeral Mass and then on to the cemetery where Giuliano would be interred beside his beloved wife.

It was easy for Amalia to walk with Lucrezia beside her, but once she was standing quietly in the church for the Mass, her grief was unendurable. She tried to be strong, as her father certainly would have wished, but there were times she was simply overwhelmed by the grief. It was like a knife thrust into her heart, and she felt she couldn't breathe. Then the ritual of the Mass, as the priests went about their routine, calmed her and gave her an opportunity to gather herself.

Lucrezia was by her side, as was Maria, and Lucia stood directly behind her to comfort her, but she was unaware. The anguish of losing her beloved father and the thought of facing a world without his guidance and affection was overwhelming.

She was barely aware of standing by the open grave as her father was laid to his final rest. It all seemed a blur that only ended as the procession returned to Giuliano's home, everyone to visit this one last time to honor his memory, to reminisce about their friend and neighbor, now gone, and to console his daughter. She thought she caught whispers among them about how she was so young and pretty, they wondered what her future would be. Who would marry her with no dowry? Of course, there was the house. Were there debts? Would the house have to be sold?

No one knew the answers, least of all Amalia.

Lucrezia offered only a few words of guidance, and then Maria and Lucia took charge of the kitchen.

"Are you hungry, Amalia?" Lucrezia asked. "You must be."

"Maybe later," answered Amalia, but neither of them had eaten, so Lucrezia fixed a plate for Amalia, and between greeting the many mourners, she tried to get Amalia to eat a few bites. Amalia had several close girl friends, but she was relying on Lucrezia to stay nearby to bolster her courage.

The three of them—Amalia, Lucrezia, and her father—had spent so many companionable evenings together this last winter, the two young women sewing quietly while Giuliano wrote. Sometimes Giuliano read aloud from one of the manuscripts he brought home to copy, and sometimes Amalia took a turn reading aloud from one of the manuscripts.

Her father had been teaching her Latin for the last two years, and she was now quite proficient and could read and write with an expertise that pleased her father immensely. On the occasions when Amalia read from a manuscript, he would sit back and close his eyes as if allowing her voice and the words to wash over him like a gentle breeze on a spring day. Amalia had a soft, pleasant voice that she used to make the words of the old Roman philosophers like Cicero and Marcus Aurelius come alive.

While Amalia was studying her Latin, Lucrezia would be doing her chores, but when her father was instructing her, Amalia noticed that Lucrezia tried to be nearby so she could overhear and learn all she could. She always had some handiwork in her lap, but it was clear that her mind was freely enjoying the moments when Amalia and Master Giuliano were reciting, and she seemed to understand more and more as the winter evenings stretched into the spring.

~ ~ ~

"Lucrezia, is there nothing more important to be done than to stand here staring at Amalia?"

Lucrezia was startled and turned around to come face to face with Madonna Rutia, maybe as old as the house they stood in, bent and wrinkled as a crumpled napkin, with a voice as raspy as an out-of-tune lyre.

"Oh, Madonna Rutia," and she fell into the outstretched arms of this dear old lady whose head barely reached Lucrezia's shoulders. "I was just remembering what our evenings used to be like together. I will miss him so, and I know Amalia's heart is broken."

"There, there, child. I know," said the old crone.

"What will the future hold for her? What will it be for both of us? We are both so scared."

"You are both young and have long lives ahead of you. It's a sad day, to be sure, and your lives will be different from this day on, but don't give up hope. Hush, now, stop crying. You are both young and strong and healthy. Take my handkerchief, dear, and dry your eyes. Right now, the most important thing you need to do is find me a chair so I can sit."

"Oh, yes, yes. I am so sorry. How thoughtless of me."

Lucrezia helped the old lady the few braccia to a comfortable chair and held her arm as Dona Rutia eased herself down with a loud grunt and then a sigh as she settled herself and caught her breath.

"Now, my dear, you can bring me a glass of wine. These old bones can stay erect for only so long, and the walk over here, climbing those stairs, and standing talking to you has stretched my limit. Surely God should have taken me instead of Giuliano. Such a waste."

When Lucrezia returned with the wine, she found Dona Rutia gently snoring with her head resting comfortably on the side of the highback chair with its winged sides. She smiled, placed the glass of wine on the table next to the old lady, and turned to leave her, knowing Dona Rutia would drink every last drop once she roused herself.

When Lucrezia found Amalia again in the crowded room, she was chatting with two of her girl friends and smiling at something Caterina said. Good, she thought. They are both such happy girls, they will lighten Amalia's spirits. She knew then she could leave Amalia for a few minutes to attend to chores. She began gathering up abandoned glasses, cups, mugs, and plates to take to the kitchen to be washed and put back out on the table that was still piled high with slices of roasted meats, fish and meat pies, rice dishes, salamis, pieces of several cheeses, fresh and dried fruits, breads, black pudding, baked goods, and more.

Even when all these people ate as much as they wanted, she knew she and Amalia would be eating well on the leftovers for several days. Whatever else may befall them, they would not go hungry this week.

The next time Lucrezia found Amalia in the room, she was off in a corner talking with Messer Sacchetti, Giuliano's attorney and friend. She wished she could overhear what was being said, not to be nosey, but she was afraid in her present state that Amalia would not remember or understand all he would be saying. Perhaps she should go over. But no, she would have to rely on Amalia.

Old Signori Cartucci, a neighbor, spilled some wine, and Lucrezia got a rag to wipe it up. Dona Marcella, another neighbor, was seated, and Lucrezia brought her a plate of food so she would not need to get up. She looked the picture of health, but Lucrezia knew she was always in pain and was getting thinner and weaker. Dona Vittoria arrived late, hugged Lucrezia, and handed her a bouquet of flowers from her garden with wishes that they might help to cheer her and Amalia.

Messer D'Alessandro asked her if there was anything they needed. She replied that she truly could not think of anything right now, but that neither she nor Amalia could think properly about anything right then, so she hardly knew. He said to tell Amalia he would drop by in a few days to have a talk with her. Messer D'Alessandro was a leader in their gonfalons, and he had certain responsibilities for everyone. He would probably be the one to take charge of selling Giuliano's house—or Amalia's house—and, with the help of Padre Bernardo, get Amalia situated in a convent. Then Lucrezia would be looking for another position as a servant in some large household where there would be endless work. She would have to think about all of that tomorrow. First, she had to get through today.

There were more cups to take away, more food to be served, more people to greet and console and thank. Sometimes she was consoling them; sometimes they were consoling her. She was only the servant, but everyone knew she was really like a member of the family and Amalia's friend. Most importantly, they all knew she loved Giuliano almost as a father.

If it was hard for her to go through this, how much harder was it for Amalia?

She saw Amalia talking to two other friends, but this time she was crying. Constance hugged her, and then Hortensia must have said something funny because all three laughed and hugged again. She could see that Amalia was getting very tired. It had been a long day, and the strain was beginning to show as the day wore on.

Just then Dona Maria came and ushered Amalia into the kitchen, no doubt to sit her down and encourage her to eat something. Lucrezia saw Amalia balk and protest, but Dona Maria managed to steer her firmly. Then Maria's hand was on Lucrezia's back, steering her also to the kitchen to sit and eat.

"Come, dear. You have had a busy day also."

The four ladies—Donas Berta and Cecilia had recently become part of the kitchen group—started telling stories about old times and laughing like it was a party. Before long Amalia was nibbling on a piece of cheese, then some bread and meat. They got her to drink a glass of wine. Yes, thought Lucrezia, these women truly knew about these things.

Now they were all laughing and crying and then laughing again. Donas Claire and Lisa came into the now crowded kitchen area and had fresh stories to tell about Giuliano and even Margherita, and that created new waves of laughter and crying.

After she had eaten a few bites of the delicious food, Lucrezia felt that perhaps she might actually make it through the day. It was then she became aware of a whimpering coming from the corner of the kitchen. When she looked over, she saw it was Carlo. He was huddled into a small ball with his head down on his knees, cap in hand, but his little shoulders were shaking to the beat of his quiet sobs. Lucrezia got up and went to him. He could not speak, but he reached up to put his arms around Lucrezia's neck as she helped him up, brought him back to the table, and sat him by her side. He rested his head on her chest and cried with his arms still wrapped around her.

After he had cried himself out, he noticed the food in front of Lucrezia and reached for a piece of the meat. Then she noticed. "Carlo, your hands are clean. My, your face is clean, and your clothes are clean."

Maria chuckled and patted him on the head.

"He has been toting water up from your well and running errands for us all day, and we couldn't have him looking like a ruffian, so we cleaned him up. What a good boy he is."

Lucrezia said, "We try so hard to keep him clean, but it seems if there's a puddle or a mound of dirt, he manages to find it. Even Master Giuliano tried and tried again, but with no success. He's a good boy and a good worker, but never clean."

They all smiled, even Carlo.

Amalia said, "Until now. Look at you, Carlo, just to honor Papa. Carlo, Papa would be so pleased," and with that, Carlo collapsed again into a gale of tears and buried his head in Lucrezia's chest, but by then there was not a dry eye in the room as Lucrezia, Amalia, and the other ladies in the room all burst into tears as well. Several ladies reached over and patted Carlo on his head. With that, Carlo hiccuped, and that broke the tension. Everyone started to laugh as the tears were running down their faces. Even Carlo.

Maria said to Amalia, "Now, my dear, you must go back inside. Your guests are beginning to leave, and you must thank them for coming and say goodbye. Come, dear."

Amalia performed her task flawlessly, a few tears shed, a few laughs in between, and finally they were all gone. In the meantime, the "kitchen committee" of ladies, all neighbors and friends, had cleared the tables, wrapped up all the food, and given Lucrezia instructions what to eat first: the fish pie, the fresh meats and fruits, the dishes made with milk. They had managed to slip between the last of the lingering guests and clean up the large room, and also they had cleaned the back room that was their kitchen until everything was spotless. Lucrezia tried to help, but she was amazed at the efficiency of these ladies. She was very grateful because she knew she would have struggled to have done it all alone after everyone was gone.

These ladies would now go home knowing they had done their duty for their neighbor and friend, as they should; but now Lucrezia and Amalia had the long evening and night to endure, and it would not be easy.

Tomorrow they would still be mourning the loss of a beloved father and a kind master, respectively, but tomorrow they must also face the rest of their lives: lives without Giuliano, that father and master. What would the morrow bring? Lucrezia did not know, and she knew Amalia did not know either. For now, their exhaustion and deep sorrow tended to take the edge off their great trepidation about facing the decisions of tomorrow and the dreadful times that might be in store for each of them.

Santa Maria del Fiore (The Duomo)

II   *The Attorney*

Lucrezia was sitting in her favorite chair, sewing when Amalia entered the room and sat down in the chair opposite her by the fireplace. Even though it was summertime and there was no fire, it was still their favorite way to sit in the evenings or any time when they weren't up and about doing the multitude of tasks that filled each day.

When Lucrezia first went to sit in her chair, she was upset by the sight of her master's chair, Giuliano's chair, sitting empty. She knew no one would ever sit in it again, so she had dragged it over into the corner of the room near the window. She knew Amalia would be upset when she saw it, but better she be upset with her than that they both stare at the empty chair for the days and months to come.

"I wasn't expecting you to be up so soon. I was hoping you would sleep late."

"No," said Amalia, appearing. "I have been awake for a while but could find no reason to get up. I heard you start down the stairs, but I'm not hungry, so there was no incentive to rush to greet the day."

"I felt the same way, but I got the idea to take one of your mother's old dresses apart and re-design it. You will need another dark dress when you have to go out in public, so I thought I would get a head start. I hope you don't mind."

"Of course not. Am I really going to have to wear brown and dark dresses forever? Well, I guess it won't matter once I go into the convent. I was thinking maybe I could go into the San Marco convent. Then I would ultimately be working in the hospitals and doing something useful. At least we might get to see each other once in a while."

"Yes, every time I get so sick I have to go to the hospital, we will see each other. Thank you so much," said Lucrezia, and they both laughed.

"Well, it was a plan. Maybe Santa Croce and perhaps I would be allowed to do some scribing. It would only be religious books for the church, but it would be so much better than the cloistered nuns at Muratte that never go outside the walls and are silent and pray all the time. I just don't think I could bear that. What about you? Have you thought about whom you would ask to hire you or what you will do?

"I thought about going home and seeing if my father would let me move back in, but the house is already bulging, and I dislike that woman he married. I can't even say her name. I don't think we would survive under the same roof, and her two children are impossible. Then I wondered if I could get my mother's old spinning wheel and spin the wool yarns as she used to do, but she didn't earn very much, just a few lire each week. It would never be enough to support myself. I guess I will have to look to be a servant in another household. I was thinking about asking Dona Rossi to hire me."

"Oh, no," said Amalia, "little Roberto is a holy terror. You would be boxing his ears before the second day was over and then Dona Rossi would throw you out in the street."

"Maybe you're right," Lucrezia sighed, "but those ears do need boxing. How about Dona Elvira? She is due to deliver in a couple of weeks and needs help with the other two since they are, what, about two and four years?"

"You forget, Lucrezia, you are not wild about little children or tending babies. You're going to take on three of them?"

'Well, maybe I could take over the kitchen and old Cecilia could take care of the children."

"You couldn't get her out of that kitchen with a horse whip, and as fat as she is, it would take a horse and a plow. Besides, can you see her running after the two boys with the new infant tucked up under her arm?"

They each got a mental image of that, and they both got the giggles.

"No," said Lucrezia, "I guess that is not going to work. Besides, Master Rinaldo is such a womanizer and too good looking for his own good."

They then had another good laugh envisioning Lucrezia running around the kitchen table with him chasing her.

"I'll be in the kitchen, so at least I'll be able to grab a knife."

"Wonderful, and how do I get out of the convent to come visit you in Le Stinche? Oh, my, what if they hang you?"

"I wouldn't have to kill him. Dona Elvira certainly knew what she was doing when she hired Cecilia. She might not be able to run, but I don't think he bothers chasing her. Well, at this point I still have a job, even if there is no pay, so I think I will get us some breakfast. I just heard Carlo yawn, so I think he'll be up soon. You go get dressed, and I'll get us some cheese and fruit and bread. We have so many delicacies to choose from, we will be eating well for quite a few days. Come down when you get your dress on, and I'll fasten it."

"Did Carlo stay over?" asked Amalia.

"Yes, he was too tired to walk home last night, so I fixed a pallet for him in the storeroom behind the kitchen."

Once they were all three up and ready, they sat down to eat from a platter of delicious treats—dates stuffed with soft cheese, dried apricots, a chunk of bread only one day old, and more.

"What were the two of you laughing about before? You woke me up, you were so loud."

Lucrezia told Carlo about Master Rinaldo, and they had another giggle fit as she told it.

"Don't laugh," said Carlo. "He chases after the boys too." With that, the three of them laughed some more.

"Maybe I should carry a knife the next time Dona Elvira asks me to help her with a chore in her house," Carlo opined.

"Just stay away from the kitchen knives. They're mine," said Lucrezia, and they again convulsed into a fit of laughter.

They were still laughing when there was a knocking on the door.

"Who can that be so early in the day? Messer D'Alessandro said he would drop by, but surely not this early," said Amalia.

"I'll answer it," said Lucrezia. Your hair isn't fixed. You look a sight." Lucrezia ran down, unbolted, and opened the door to face a stranger. "Pardon me, signorina, for intruding so early, but I am on my way to work, and I wanted to deliver this package. Is this the home of the man who was injured the other day?" asked the young man.

"Yes," said Lucrezia, "it is." She glanced up to see that Amalia had come to the top of the stairs. "Please, won't you come in?"

"Oh, no, signorina, as I said, I am on my way to work."

By now, Amalia had descended the stairs and was at the door beside Lucrezia.

"Good morning, signorina. I am sorry to disturb you. I found this package under one of the smashed barrels of grain, and I thought it might have belonged to the man who was injured the other day. It took me some time to find out where he lived. I am sorry it took so long."

"That's no matter," said Amalia. "May I see the package?"

"Of course."

When she had unwrapped the package—a manuscript—she appeared to be shocked. She looked at Lucrezia with her mouth agape. Finally, once she recovered from the shock, she said, "Yes, I believe this does belong to my father. Well, it doesn't belong to him, but it had been entrusted into his care."

"Good, then I'm glad I found its proper home. I could tell it was not something that should be just thrown away."

"You are so right," said Lucrezia. "May I give you a few coins for your effort?"

"No, signorina. I am just glad to get it back to its rightful place. How is your father?"

Lucrezia responded: "Master Dontarini died from his injuries."

"I am sorry for your loss. I was afraid that was the case. Was it your father who was killed?"

"No," said Lucrezia.

"It was my father, signori," said Amalia. "Please, is there some way I can thank you?"

"Oh, no. I came upon the accident just after it had happened, and I stayed to help clean up after your father had been carried away. Again, I am very sorry for your loss. May God be with you, and good day to you both."

With that, he was gone, and they closed the door. Amalia stood there, holding the manuscript in her hands.

"I know where this came from," she said. "I can return it to Master Manetti at his shop as soon as I dress and get ready to leave."

"Strange," said Lucrezia, "that Master Manetti did not come himself to inquire about the manuscript after hearing about the accident."

"Yes," replied Amalia. "It is odd also that he did not come by yesterday to extend his condolences. He liked my father. Well, Florence is a large city. Perhaps he did not hear of the accident or did not hear the name of the victim."

"It is not so large that news like this would escape Master Manetti's ears," commented Lucrezia.

"Well, I will return it as soon as I can get ready to leave. Will you help me, Lucrezia?"

"Of course."

"Do you want me to return it?" asked Carlo.

"Thank you, Carlo, but I think this is something I must do myself."

While Amalia was dressing, with Lucrezia's help, and all the while Lucrezia was fixing her hair, Amalia was silent. At last, Lucrezia was done.

Amalia turned to Lucrezia and said, "What if I don't return it? What if I copy it and bring a copy as well as Master Manetti's manuscript to him? What if he paid me for the new copy as he would have paid Papa? How much money would I get for a copy of this manuscript? What if I could do others? How much could I earn, Lucrezia? Could we survive? Think about it. I have nothing to do. If I work diligently on the copying, I might be able to finish it and get it to Master Manetti quickly. I think I can do—I know I can do this. I have been working on Papa's copies for months now, and my script is just like his. I know Latin. This is another Cicero, so I am familiar with it. Lucrezia, could we survive?"

"Well, I might as well tell you, what got me up early this morning wasn't just to remake your mother's dress for you but to experiment on a new design I have been thinking about. I was thinking that if I could design, make, and sell some dresses along with doing mending and alterations, maybe I could support myself and not have to take a job as a maid in another household."

"What if we joined our resources? Could we survive then?"

"I will run your errands for free," Carlo said. "Will that help? Could I still eat with you sometimes?"

The girls had not even heard Carlo slip into the room, and when they looked over, he was sitting on the floor against the wall just inside the door with his knees pulled to his chest. They looked at each other with a look that said they were both glad they hadn't been sharing a secret.

"Always, Carlo. I think instead of going to Master Manetti's shop, I will go to Messer Sacchetti's office. I know Papa owns the house, but was he free of debt? Is there any money? If there is any, I know it isn't much. How much money do the rental house in the back and the shop downstairs earn? What is the law? Can Messer D'Alessandro and Padre Bernardo force me to go to the convent? Who will own the house then? Messer Sacchetti said I should come by to see him soon. I don't think he meant this soon, but there are so many questions, and I think I need the answers to them before we do any more dreaming about things that probably can never be."

~ ~ ~

Messer Sacchetti's office was only four blocks away, so her walk over and back was quick. Carlo had walked with her and then sat on the steps outside, waiting for her to finish. The visit had taken over an hour, and by the time they got home, Amalia's brain was spinning so fast she was light-headed.

Carlo opened the door for Amalia but then said, "I have errands to do for my customers. Can I come by later?"

"Yes, of course, Carlo. Come by and eat with us. We have all that food."

Carlo smiled a big smile and said, "I know."

She hung her shawl on the peg at the top of the stairs while Lucrezia fixed them each a cup of tea made from the herbs in their garden and a plate of cheese and bread. Lucrezia cut up a pear to split, and then they sat down so Amalia could tell her what happened.

"Lucrezia, I hardly know where to begin. My brother isn't dead, as I thought. Even before Mama died, they never spoke of him, and one time I asked Mama about him. All she said was that he was gone, and I thought she meant he was dead, but he isn't.

"He lives in Milan, the last Papa heard, but before that he lived in Venice and Genoa. He runs up debts, and then he expects Papa to pay off those debts to protect the family name. That is why Papa had to do scribing at night and in his spare time, because the expenses for Stefano were more than he could earn, even as a respected notary, and he didn't want to go into debt.

"Poor Papa. He never told us. I wonder if Mama knew what was happening. Probably. They shared everything. How sad for both of them."

"How terrible for him," said Lucrezia. "I knew there were times he was troubled, but I thought he was just sad about losing your mother. How dreadful."

The two of them sat quietly for a while, trying to recover from the shock of what Amalia had learned.

Finally, Lucrezia asked, "Will Stefano come home once he learns your father is dead?"

"Mr. Sacchetti didn't know, but he told me that father left the house to me only; and he told me if Stefano shows up, not to let him in and to contact him immediately.

"He is the one that has been in contact with Stefano. Father would not speak to him or write to him, but he would not turn his back on his son. Stefano pressured him to pay off his debts, or he said he would have ruined Papa's reputation."

"And your father let him get away with that?"

"I guess so. Messer Sacchetti said he could have caused Papa great harm. It was his son, and he was responsible for him, even if he was an adult and lived in another city. Word would get back to Florence, and Papa's reputation would be damaged.

"Anyway, there is no money except what Papa had in his pocket from Master Manetti. Messer Sacchetti will check at the guild and notary office to see if anything was owed to him. The latest tax bill is paid, so that is not a problem, and the house is mine. I will need a guardian for another five months, but Messer Sacchetti said that was not a problem; he would take care of it. He said he had written Stefano the day after Papa died and, of course, has not heard from him. He told me he would let me know as soon as he did—if he did. He said he told Stefano that Papa had left the house to me and that there was no money for him or for me. He told me he was hoping Stefano would not come to Florence and cause any trouble, that maybe he would just go his way now and not bother us.

"He said that for years he had hopes that Stefano would change his ways and straighten out his life, but that he had given up hope two years ago when Stefano got himself into a serious scrape with the authorities in Venice. He said I did not need to know the details, but that my brother was not to be trusted, that he felt he was not a good or a kind person. I think this is going to take some time before I can understand it all. It's like a bad dream."

"I'm so sorry, Amalia. What a shock. You have lost your father but gained your brother, but unfortunately, it does not sound like he is worth having."

Amalia said, "I did ask Messer Sacchetti if he thought the officials would allow me to keep the house and live here with you, and he said it was not unheard of, but it was very rare. I have no money, no employment, and particularly my age would be against me. If we both had employment and independent incomes, there might be a little hope, being as we are so well-connected in the gonfalons, but otherwise, there would be no hope.

"There is certainly no money for a dowry, and I told Mr. Sacchetti that I was resolved to not being able to marry. I told him I might have the opportunity to be a scribe, that I truly enjoyed the work if I am just allowed to do it, but that I had no wish to become a nun.

"Anyway, we have a roof over our heads and no debts but very little money. We have income from the house in the back of the garden and the shop downstairs, so that will be a big help, but certainly not enough money to live on or for a dowry. But who cares about that now? Can we earn enough to keep the house and live?"

"Now I understand why Messer Sacchetti took you aside and was so serious yesterday."

"Yes, he didn't want to tell me about my brother then, but he wanted me to know as soon as possible. And he didn't want to blurt out that there was no money. I'm glad he didn't tell me then. It took me quite a while to grasp all he was telling me. I couldn't believe it at first.

"Lucrezia, what if he returns? I don't even know him. I was, what, around eight when he left? Did you ever know him?"

"No, I came right after he was gone. Maybe that is why they hired me, so that I would be here for you. Old Maria was working here as a maid then, and they didn't need me. I overheard a couple of conversations between your father and mother, but I was so young myself, I didn't put it together. After a while, I also just assumed he was dead.

"Not meaning to change the subject, but after you left, I remembered that I had overheard Dona Teresa talking last week that she needed a new dress, so I decided now was a good time to start my new business. I went over to see her, and first I offered to do alterations on an old dress she has outgrown, but she said that had already been done, there was nothing left to let out. I showed her a sketch of a dress I did this morning before you got up and asked if she would like me to make it for her. We had a lengthy discussion, but in the end, she will buy the material with my guidance, and she will pay me an excellent price for the dress, plus she will give me a bonus if I can finish it by next Wednesday."

"Lucrezia, how wonderful for you! She is so kind and has many friends. She will spread the word all over the commune."

"Well," said Lucrezia, "only if she likes it."

"She will like it. She will love it, I'm sure. So why are you sitting here? You have work to do!"

"Not so fast. I am to go with her to Signori Vicenti's mercantile shop later this afternoon to pick out the fabric after her meeting of the committee at the church about the decorations for the new side altar dedicated to Our Lady. She said the construction is finally completed. They have only been working on it for two years now. It will be so much better if they would only finish it.

"Anyway, she will come by to get me once they are done. I think I'll use some of that thin cotton that we didn't use last winter for the fitting. Oh, I will probably be late getting home."

"That's fine. Fortunately, we have all this leftover food. Since we are both going to be very busy for the next few days, we won't have to worry about cooking.

"I'm going to finish unwrapping the package Papa should have brought home if only he could, and I'm going to start copying on my very first manuscript. I know Papa won't mind if I take over his scribing desk. The inks and paper and tools are there, and if you take over that end of the room, we can just turn the receiving room into our work room."

When it was time for Lucrezia to leave, Amalia was so absorbed, she hardly heard her say goodbye. She did mutter a response but never lifted her pen from the paper.

When Lucrezia returned a bit before dark with a large package under her arm, Amalia did hear her. She took a well-deserved break, and they sat down to eat some of the tasty leftovers and then topped it off with some of the left-over fresh fruits that had not spoiled yet.

"Oh, Amalia, it went very well. I love the fabric Dona Teresa chose. I'll show it to you when we finish eating. It will be easy to work with, and I think it will make a beautiful dress. It's a thin, fine wool, and we chose two different shades that blended beautifully. She likes my ideas for the design, so I will start right away.

"Master Vicenti—you know him? The owner of the shop where Dona Teresa just bought the fabric—said to bring the dress by for him to see when it's done. If I do a good job, he will recommend me to some of his customers. He said he just lost two of his regular seamstresses, two sisters who were moving to Venice. One of them just married a man from there, and he agreed that the sister could come back to Venice with them."

"How wonderful, Lucrezia, a day, filled with so much promise! Lucrezia, I know I should feel guilty for not mourning Papa properly all day, but I think he would want us to move forward. This is what he would tell us we should be doing if he could, don't you think?"

"Yes, Amalia, I do."

"Lucrezia, to your new dress, your new business as a seamstress, and to my new efforts as a scribe." They raised their cups of watered wine toward each other and smiled.

Each had a feeling of self-satisfaction they couldn't quite comprehend. They knew they were headed into uncharted waters, as Lucrezia's older brother would have said, and maybe their little boat would capsize in the rough waters ahead—and they knew there would be some rough seas—but they were going to try.

Once they had cleaned up the kitchen, they set a plate out for Carlo, and each went to work on their project at opposite ends of the large receiving room. Carlo came in later and tried to talk to them, but all he got in return was a few grunts. He shrugged his shoulders, ate, put his cap back on, and left, but the girls worked long into the night, excited and filled with an energy they couldn't have understood, even if they had bothered to stop to think about it. By the time they each finally slept that night, the early risers of Florence were beginning their next day.

They both worked diligently for the next several days, sleeping only when they couldn't continue working any longer and eating only what they could nibble quickly. They had been fortunate there had been so much food left, but now it was almost gone.

They usually went to Mass every morning, but with their erratic schedule, they missed all but one. Then, of course, they went Sunday morning and afterwards chatted with neighbors and friends in front of the church. Master D'Alessandro asked how they were, said that he was sorry he had not gotten by, but he had some pressing business to attend to. They both told him they were doing very well. Amalia told him she had been to see Messer Sacchetti and that everything was being handled by him. Master D'Alessandro said he would come by in the next few days.

What would he think of the two girls living in the house alone and trying to make a living for themselves? Would he press for Amalia to go into a convent and sell her house and for Lucrezia to seek other employment? Well, they couldn't worry about that now. First they had to see if they could survive by their own wits working at sewing and scribing.

Dona Maria asked how they were doing and if they had enough food. They said they were eating leftovers and still had some left. She told them she was making a stew for dinner, and she would send some over with some fresh fruit her son had brought back from the Mugello just the evening before. She gave each girl a hug.

They thanked her, and as they turned to walk home, Amalia whispered to Lucrezia, "How does she know we wouldn't want her to invite us for dinner but rather she is going to send food over?"

"Carlo," said Lucrezia. "He told them what we are doing, and Dona Alvira doesn't think it is a good idea, but Dona Maria and Dona Lucia think we should be given the chance. Apparently, they are spreading the word that I want to be a seamstress, and they are hoping you can succeed at scribing. Carlo says they haven't talked to Messer D'Alessandro, but they plan to talk to his wife."

"Amalia, Lucrezia, if I may, will you please walk me home?" came the raspy voice of Dona Rutia. As they moved away from the gathered neighbors, Dona Rutia added, "As a matter of fact, since Dona Maria is sending over some of her stew, I am inviting myself for dinner at your house, so perhaps you can just walk me there."

"Of course, Dona Rutia," they both said in unison, but with great inner dismay. Would they each miss an afternoon of working on their projects? Well, there was nothing they could do about that. They could not refuse Dona Rutia's "invitation" for her to spend the afternoon with them, no matter the consequences.

"I am delighted you will spend time with us," said Amalia, and Lucrezia chimed in with small talk about Dona Rutia's daughter in Siena and her grandchildren.

Once home, dear old Dona Rutia was finally settled in the chair in the corner near the window, Giuliano's chair, and after asking for and receiving a glass of wine, she promptly fell asleep.

"It looks like your idea to move the chair has worked out very well. I was upset when I saw you had moved it, but I knew you had done the right thing or I don't think I would have been able to sit by the fireplace anymore. Now it has a new purpose," said Amalia.

The girls smiled at each other, shrugged their shoulders, and each went to the corner of the room where they worked; and for several hours there was much sewing, scribing, and soft snoring in the different areas of the spacious room.

In the afternoon, Carlo arrived with the stew, the fresh fruit, and some freshly baked bread. Rutia awoke at the sound of Carlo coming up the back stairway, and they all went into the kitchen to enjoy a delicious, freshly made meal. Lucrezia went to collect Dona Rutia's wine, and she found the glass empty. When had she emptied it? She smiled and wondered.

By Tuesday late night, Amalia had finished her manuscript. On the street, Carlo had learned that Master Manetti had been visiting a friend in the country since the day her father had been killed over a week ago now, and so he still did not know about the accident. He was due back to his shop tomorrow, and Amalia intended to be his first customer.

Lucrezia still had a lot to do on the dress and was prepared to work a while longer. Working late that night and then getting an early start in the morning, she hoped she would be able to finish the dress and deliver it to Dona Teresa well before mid-day.

Both girls had worked very hard this last week on their projects. Now would come the test. Would Master Manetti buy Amalia's copy of the manuscript? Would Dona Teresa and Master Vicenti like the finished dress Lucrezia had designed? The girls' future hung in the balance.

Or maybe it wouldn't matter; maybe Master D'Alessandro would insist that Amalia go to a convent like Santa Croce and that Lucrezia find another job as a servant. Then he would sell the house, at a high commission for himself, and give the leftover money to the convent to fund Amalia's lifetime of confinement behind the dreaded, isolating convent walls of Muratte.

Was this the Dontarini House?

III   *The Encounter*

Amalia closed the door behind her as she left Master Manetti's shop and had gone no more than twenty braccia before what had been a constant drizzle all day turned into a downpour. She walked quickly as she tried to wrap her manuscript in her shawl to protect it from the rain. This was her most precious possession, her only hope for the future, and Master Manetti had refused to buy it from her. She had returned the manuscript Master Manetti had given to her father for him to copy and showed him the copy she had made over the course of the last week. He responded that it was improper for a girl to be a scribe, and he wouldn't buy her work.

How was she to survive? She would try other book dealers, but she knew if Master Manetti would have nothing to do with her, surely none of the others would either. He liked her father, her father had been a customer for over two years, and Master Manetti knew Amalia well. She had often gone to his shop along with her father when he delivered a manuscript and picked up another one to copy. He suspected she had often copied pages in place of her father. He had teased them that he could not tell where her father's work left off, and hers had begun or ended. Her father would always just smile and say nothing.

One time she asked her father how he knew, and he had told her to look at the fingers of her right hand. The ink stain was a telltale sign, and Giuliano often returned books very quickly even though he spent all day attending to notary business at the guilds' notary offices. Perhaps Master Manetti had guessed the rest.

It was true; often when her father was off attending to business, she would go to his work desk and continue copying pages from a volume of Cicero or whatever he was copying. In the beginning, she had practiced on pieces of discarded paper, working very slowly so that her penmanship was identical to her father's; but now, after a year of diligent practice, she could write fluidly, and even she and her father could barely tell which of them had copied a page.

Giuliano had taught her Latin, even though she was a girl. After Amalia's mother died, she had asked him to teach her so she could read the books in her father's limited library but also so she could read the manuscripts her father brought home to copy.

She and her father had always been close, but then, without her mother, she was lonely. She had hoped this schooling would be something she and her father could do together in the evenings during that first long winter without her mother. She missed her mother, and she knew her father did also. Theirs had been a quiet life, even quieter now without her loving mother with her gentle ways and her happy laughter that used to fill Amalia's ears.

In the early days, once Giuliano returned home from his busy day and the evening meal was over, their evenings were often spent together, just the three of them, before the fire in the winter or enjoying the garden behind their home on a summer evening.

Margherita had always kept a small vegetable garden so they would have some fresh produce during the summer and well into the winter. She also had an extensive herb garden, not only for flavoring the dishes she and Lucrezia prepared but also for the treatment of all sorts of ailments, from a bout of indigestion to a cold or the swelling of a sprained wrist or ankle. In the back of the garden were the trees: pear, apricot, lemon, a couple of olive trees; then along the back wall were the grape vines that yielded more than enough grapes to make the wine for them to drink throughout the year. There was always a market for any extra wine or maybe just the grapes if it was an abundant year, and their vines almost always yielded more than they could cask. They stored as much as they could cask down in the cellar under the house along with the wood that would be brought to town periodically.

The muss was used to make Giuliano's prized grappa. Making grappa had become a hobby for Giuliano many years before. Long ago, Giuliano had decided to open a small notary office in the very small room on the lower level of their house. It had been used as a storage room, and it was full of many years' accumulation of damaged chairs, tables, swords, containers, even a helmet, and other assorted items collected by his father and grandfather who owned the house before him. There was some equipment amidst the debris that Giuliano intended to dispose of, but a neighbor, Filippo next door, suggested Giuliano ask old Guiseppe from around the corner about it before he threw it away. Guiseppe told him what the equipment was for and taught him how to use it; and so, over time, Giuliano became a proficient maker of an excellent grappa prized by all who were privileged to taste it.

It was a very complicated process to take the muss or pomace from the grapes not used to make the wine—the skins, seeds, leaves, pulp, and stems—and ferment them in just the right way to yield the strong drink. As it would age, he had to release the dangerous gases at the right moment, and he would test it for the proper moment of optimum bottling by rubbing some on the back of his hand and smelling it periodically in the processing. When it was ready, it was bottled in small bottles and stored in the cellar with the casks of wine, the winter vegetables, and the firewood.

A small bottle from Giuliano's well-stocked cellar was a prized gift for the host of a dinner party, and Margherita would bring a bouquet of her fresh flowers or herbs from her abundant garden for the hostess.

In those days, Margherita and Giuliano would stroll their garden path arm-in-arm after supper on a summer's evening and eventually find their way to the bench in the back under the old pear tree. Perhaps Margherita would pick a bouquet of flowers to bring back to the house or Giuliano would check his grapes for ripeness or insects. Then Amalia and Lucrezia would join them once their chores were done. It had been the favorite part of the day for all of them. Now Amalia could not bear to go out there, the memories were much too painful, but she did love the old house. She considered that her domain and was glad to turn the garden over to Lucrezia.

It was an attractive house, ample for Giuliano and his family. It had been his father's house before it was his, and his father's before that, and Giuliano loved the house and made sure it was always kept in good repair. It was situated on the Via del Fiore in their beloved walled city of Florence, but it was a bit removed from the center of town, just beyond Santa Maria Novella. Florence was the heart and soul of Tuscany. Many said it was the most vibrant city in all of Europe, and Giuliano had always loved being a part of the action in the busy, rapidly growing city.

The plague of the previous century had decimated the population and left many vacant houses and shops. It had killed an estimated forty percent of the people. Now the city was growing again and filling those empty houses and shops.

Would she now lose her home—her father's home and her grandfather's home and more? Would she be forced to sell it, as Messer Sacchetti had suggested when she went to his office last week? It was an option, but it was one she dreaded. If she had to sell the house and go into a convent, as Messer Sacchetti and Master D'Alessandro said, it would kill her as surely as those barrels had killed her father.

And poor Lucrezia, she thought. She would have to find employment in another household as a servant, and who knew what her future would be. It would be no problem for her to find employment, for she was a good worker and everyone knew it. No, finding the placement would not be hard, but it was not what Lucrezia wanted now that she found she had a talent for designing and making dresses.

They had dared to dream, had grasped onto that dream, even when they were scared, and now it would not—could not—be.

The rain started to come down even harder as Amalia approached the back of the Duomo. She decided she would duck in the back door and go out the front door and escape the rain for at least a part of the walk home. Since she would be in the cathedral, she thought perhaps she would pause and offer a prayer to Our Lady for her father and give the rain a chance to slacken.

She was running as best she could, bent over her bundle trying to protect it from the storm. She pulled the door open, rushed to get inside, and hit a red wall. She was knocked sideways and stumbled and fell to the floor of the church as her package went flying in the other direction and then skidded across the floor.

She had not hit a wall; she had hit a man. She tried to gather herself and stand up. Then the man had her by her arms and was helping her up.

"I am so sorry; I was in such a hurry to escape the rain."

"No," he said. "It was my fault. Let me help you up. Are you hurt? Can you stand?"

"Yes, I think I'm all right," she said, as she got to her feet. "My elbow hurts, but I think—" At that moment she looked into the face of the man helping her. "Oh, messer, I am so sorry. Pardon me. If I had known it was you I would have—"

"What," he laughed, "missed me?"

"But messer, I am so sorry; I should have been more careful. It's just terrible that I—"

"Stop, child; you did nothing wrong. I'm fine. You're the one that's injured. Calm yourself. How badly is your arm hurt?"

"I'm sure it's just bruised. I think I fell on my elbow. Messer, forgive me, I—"

"No more of that. You should check—"

"Oh, where is my manuscript? I hope it's not ruined with the rain and not scattered." She started looking about frantically to find the package. She finally found it under a table in the darkened corner to the side of the door she had just entered, now unwrapped but still in one piece. She hugged it to her chest and tried to brush the rain from the edges of the binding. The scarf wrapping it was soaked, and she didn't want to put it back around the manuscript.

The man had been watching this, startled by the intensity of her search. He asked her what the writing was, and she started to reply but as the words came out, so did her tears—in great profusion. She tried to explain it was a copy of an ancient manuscript, but the dealer wouldn't buy it from her, even though it was a good copy. Her father had taught her well, but she was a girl. It wasn't fair; she would perish now that her father was killed and she couldn't earn any money, she knew—a flood of more words followed and a deluge of more tears.

Cosimo again took hold of the young woman's two arms and urged her to calm herself. He was thinking to himself that a moment ago she was distressed about bumping into him, but now that was forgotten, and her manuscript was far more important to her. What was this manuscript?

"Here, dry your tears with this before we have a different kind of flood inside the cathedral than we have going on outside."

With that, she had to laugh as she choked down the last of her tears.

"Tell me about your package," he said.

"I don't know what I will do, messer. It is a good copy of an ancient Cicero manuscript, but Master Manetti won't buy it from me because I am a girl, but my father trained me well, but now with him gone and without the money from the sale of the manuscript, Mr. Sacchetti says I will have to sell my house and go into a convent because I am so young and I'm not married, and no one will marry me without a dowry."

He had heard most of the story before, but this time it was a little slower and not muddled in her tears. While she was speaking, he had taken the manuscript from her arms and had opened it. Then he turned a page.

"Pardon," he interrupted, "May I look at your manuscript?"

"Of course, messer. It was the one my father had with him when he was killed, so when it was brought to me, I hoped if I copied it, Master Manetti would buy it as he had bought so many others my father had copied for him."

"Child, I am an old man. May we sit down over here? I would like to look at this. As it happens, it is a copy of one of my manuscripts. You say you deal with Master Manetti?"

"Yes, sire, or at least I would like to, but he won't buy it from me. It is a good copy, sire, I know it is. What am I to do? Now I will surely have to go into the—"

"No more of that." He looked up from the manuscript he had been studying page by page, and he turned toward her. "First things first. How is your elbow?"

"It is better, sire. The pain is lessening. By tomorrow, it will be fine, I am sure of it."

"All right, then. Now, as I said, this happens to be a copy of one of my manuscripts, and, as you say, it appears to be a very fine copy. I like the artwork on the title page. That was not in the original or in Mr. Manetti's copy. Did you do that?"

"Yes, sire. Papa had a manuscript a few months ago that had artwork on many of the pages, and I thought it was beautiful. I have been practicing doing it, and I thought I would just put a little on the one page. I am so sorry, messer, I didn't know it was your book."

"No, it is all right. I know Master Manetti, and he has my permission to have additional copies made. Where do you live, child?"

"On the Via del Fiore near Santa Maria Novella in my father's house with my maid, sire."

"What did your father do?"

"He was a notary, usually working with the guilds." She went on to explain what she knew of her father's work and then how he had been killed over a week ago now. She got through the telling without breaking down, and she was glad because she had sensed this man was not comfortable with her tears.

"How are you surviving now? Do you have an income?"

"We are surviving, messer. Father had some money in his pocket at the time of his death. He had just been paid by Master Manetti for a copy of Cicero's Orations; and Lucrezia, my maid—and friend—is selling a dress she designed and made, and there are rents from a house and shop on my property, but we need for me to be able to bring in money and for me to have employment or I will be forced to go into a convent, and we will not be able to go on."

"Yes, yes. Now listen to me well, child: I believe it has stopped raining while we have been having our delightful little talk. I want you to go home and take care of your bruised arm and be certain you have no other injuries. Tomorrow I want you to return to Master Manetti's shop with your manuscript."

"But—"

"No buts. Just do as I say. Your work is excellent. I am quite certain Master Manetti will treat you fairly. I encourage you to continue gracing pages of the manuscripts with your artwork when it's appropriate. It will enhance the value of the copy when it is sold, and it's quite lovely.

"Now, I must be on my way. I'm late for the appointment I was late for when we first met."

Amalia laughed, and he smiled.

"What is your name, girl?"

"Amalia Dontarini, daughter of Giuliano Dontarini. I don't know what to say. Thank you, sire, for—"

"None of that, Senorina Amalia. I am a businessman, and although the sale of these manuscripts is business—and your copy is more valuable because of the artwork you have added—these manuscripts and what they say to us is very special to me, and they have enriched my life in ways you could not possibly understand."

"Papa always read the manuscript to us as he was copying it, and I also would read and understood them then as I do now as I work at copying. So I think I do have an appreciation for what you mean. There is so much to learn from them."

"I'm glad you have an appreciation for what they contain. I wish more people did, but perhaps that is too much to ask for in these times of such political turmoil and life's struggles. They offer us so much if we take the time to seek the ancient knowledge. And now, do as I suggested to you, Signorina Amalia."

"Thank you, sire, for everything. God bless you and keep you safe."

With that, Cosimo rose and exited the cathedral by the door where they had "met," and Amalia found her favorite place in the old cathedral to pray and thank Our Lady for—what? She could hardly fathom what had just happened: from despair one minute to deliverance the next. That collision that she was worried had damaged her manuscript may have just saved her life. Yes, she would thank Our Lady for her fortuitous collision with the leader of Florence and possible—what? Hope.

Now all she wanted to do was to hurry home to tell Lucrezia the good news. And what a story it would be. She had met the man himself. She had seen Cosimo de' Medici from afar on numerous occasions when her father had taken her to festivals and other functions, and at a distance sometimes in the Duomo, but this was different. She tried to remember what he had looked like up close, but all she could remember about his appearance were his gentle but penetrating eyes. There was nothing weak about them, but there was a hint of sadness, particularly when he had spoken of the political struggles. More, she would never forget the sound of his voice, soft and gentle but still commanding. She had a feeling she would be able to hear that voice in her head for the rest of her life.

She ran into her friend, Caterina, on the way home. She agreed to go with Caterina to a meeting later in the day so the six girls could practice their small role in the pageant their church would be staging in a few weeks for the saint's day celebration. That was the farthest thing from Amalia's mind right now, but Caterina was in charge of their part in the production, and she didn't want to disappoint her friend. She told Caterina, yes, to come by later, and they could walk over to the church together. Now, home quickly to tell Lucrezia her news.

IV *Growing Pains* *Months later*

"Get out of bed, you lazy girl. We have work to do, and this is the day to do it—whether you like it or not."

Amalia groaned. She had worked late into the night on the new manuscript Master Manetti had given her yesterday to copy, and she was in no mood to spend her time working in the garden with Lucrezia. She was intrigued by this new Livy manuscript. It was one she had never seen before, and she had been looking forward to working on it today—all day.

She had copied and delivered several manuscripts to Master Manetti over the past several months, and he had seemed well pleased with the workmanship in all of them. He never made any mention of what had happened to change his mind, but when she went back to his shop that next morning after "bumping" into Messer Medici, he had smiled and said he was glad to see her, and did she have with her a copied manuscript for him to buy. She felt he was very generous when he paid her for the copy she handed over to him, and she thanked him. They then chatted again about the death of her father, and Master Manetti expressed how sorry he was for her loss and her predicament.

Now she just had to continue to do a good job on the copies she furnished to him. She realized just how lucky she was to be doing something she actually enjoyed doing. Except today.

Their home life had settled into a pattern of each working on their individual projects most of the day. Carlo would pop in and out between the chores he did for many of the neighbors, and he would generally visit at mealtimes. Dona Rutia made it a habit of visiting almost every afternoon for a glass of wine and her nap. They never knew when she drank her wine or how often she woke up during her nap, but by the time Carlo finally came back to eat with them in the late afternoon, the wine was gone. They would all eat dinner together, and then Carlo would see to it that Dona Rutia got home safely on his way home to his father's house or to do a late errand for some neighbor.

Besides being torn from working on her new manuscript, she didn't like working in the garden. She left that to Lucrezia and only went out there kicking and screaming when Lucrezia really needed her help to plant or harvest or weed. There were too many memories for her. Her mother had loved her time in the garden; the vegetables, herbs, flowers, fruit trees, all of it; the weeding, planting, harvesting, and even killing the bugs.

Lucrezia understood Amalia's feelings, and since she truly enjoyed whatever time she got to spend in the garden, she didn't ask for help very often. But when she did ask, Amalia knew there was no alternative but to obey, or the consequences would be dire. Lucrezia's wrath could be difficult to bear.

Now that they were living together basically as equals, sharing expenses, sharing the lean times as well as the good times when one of them got paid for the completion of a project, Lucrezia no longer bit her tongue, though sometimes Amalia wished she would. She knew Lucrezia was usually right, but sometimes she just didn't want to hear it.

Amalia knew Lucrezia was smarter than she was, not only because she was three years older, but because she was wise about the ways of the world. Amalia had book sense, but Lucrezia had street sense. But then, she also enjoyed the books. Amalia still read to the two of them or the three of them and sometimes the four of them in the evenings, as she and her father used to do, particularly now that they were deep into winter. They all enjoyed that, and it would come to be one of their favorite ways to spend an evening: Lucrezia sewing, Amalia reading, Carlo fixing or sharpening something, and Dona Rutia listening—or not. Then they got to discuss the manuscript during the ensuing days and weeks.

But this was to be a work day in the garden, whether she liked it or not; even whether Lucrezia liked it or not, because she had a number of orders for dresses she needed to attend to and also some mending and altering she wanted to do on their own clothes.

Carlo was going to come by to help, but Lucrezia wanted to get an early start so there would be enough for him to start sawing and chopping on the branches to be stacked up on the wood pile. Papa usually hired a man to cut out the dead wood from the fruit trees, but they couldn't afford that now. The only reason they could afford Carlo's help was because they paid him by sharing their meals with him, whatever the meal was. They would have shared their meals with him anyway, no matter how little he did or how little they had, so it all worked out very well for the three of them.

At one point they were out of money and out of food. They had a couple of crusts of bread, one small piece of cheese, some dried fruit to share, plus they always could prepare a meal of polenta, but there was nothing else. They both had an errand to run around mid-day, and when they returned, they found Dona Rutia asleep in her chair, and there were a roasted chicken and a bowl of vegetable stew in the middle of the kitchen table. They knew it was Maria who had made the stew for them because they recognized the bowl, and they suspected Dona Rutia had Maddalena, her servant, cook the chicken. Then another time Dona Rutia had sent Carlo to the fishmonger for a piece of fish, and she had Maddalena cook it for all of them while the girls were busy.

Amalia knew Maria's old winter gloves were more holes than gloves, and now deep in winter, she had taken some time and knitted her a new pair from some of the old yarn her mother had stored away years before. Carlo delivered them when he returned the bowl, and nothing was ever said.

Lucia had given Lucrezia six eggs yesterday for some mending she had done for her. They didn't always know where the next meal would be coming from, but somehow, either they bought food, or something appeared from Dona Rutia or one of their kind neighbors. Food was not their problem today. Lucrezia had started cooking a vegetable stew with a meaty pork shank when she first got up so it would be there for them to have after their labors in the garden.

Several cold blasts of winter had passed through in the last few weeks, but today was a sunny, windless day, and it had the promise of being quite warm. This is why Lucrezia had called for Amalia to get up. Who knew if they would get another day so accommodating for their labors?

By the time Amalia got to the back of the garden, Lucrezia was already trimming the lower, reachable branches on one of the trees that had to be pruned back to make it grow in the shape she wanted. Amalia took the ladder and started to climb up and trim out the dead limbs of the tree. It hadn't been but a short time before she had gotten her dress caught several times—really every time she tried to move.

"Oh, this is just too much. I've had enough," she said, and, climbing down, she stomped into the house. Some of the stomping was her exasperation, and some was to get the dirt off her shoes before going up into the house.

When she came back out, she was in a pair of her father's old pants. They were too big, but she had rolled up the cuffs and belted in the waist. Lucrezia took one look at her and doubled over laughing.

"What a sight you are!"

"Well, at least I won't get my dress all snagged up in that tree. I thought I would have to be trapped there forever. Anyway, no one can see us. Do you like it?" Amalia did a little pirouette as if it were her favorite fancy dress.

"Oh, it's lovely. Can I borrow it for our poetry reading confraternity tomorrow?"

"Of course, but you have to promise to not spill anything on it," Amalia retorted as she climbed up on the step stool.

After that, the climbing was much easier. Amalia used to climb these trees for fun, but now it was in earnest. She was as high as she could get in one of the trees, and she could see across the garden wall to the Duomo.

"Oh," she said, "What a beautiful sight. I remember Papa saying that years ago when he was young, he would climb up in these trees and look across, and there was no dome to be seen, just a big hole in the roof of the Duomo. The cathedral had been built over a hundred years before, but no one knew how to build the dome. They had built the church leaving the huge hole hoping in the future someone would know how to construct the dome. "One man wanted to fill the entire cathedral with sand with coins in it. They could stand on the sand and build the dome, and then have children remove the sand with buckets to get to the coins. How silly. Another man wanted to build a huge scaffold to do the work, but there weren't enough trees in all of Tuscany to construct a structure that enormous.

"Then Brunelleschi started to build it, one row of bricks at a time. Papa said Brunelleschi studied the ancient Pantheon in Rome because there hadn't been a large dome built since those times.

"There were many delays, but the city wanted it done if it was possible, and the Medici were in favor of it. Cosimo's father was still alive then, and Papa said the story was that Giovanni and Cosimo pushed for it, so they helped pay for it. No one was sure it would stay up. They say that when Cosimo agreed to build it and pay for it, Brunelleschi told him it was an act of faith because he couldn't be sure it would not collapse.

"You know, there are really two domes, one inside the other, and they say the view from the top is beautiful. You can see all the way to the hills behind Fiesole and across the river to San Miniato al Monte and on to all of Tuscany.

"Remember when Brunelleschi died last year? Papa said he used to come to help us build the stagings for the festival celebrations on the saints' days. He would do some of the carpentry work for the plays, particularly the big pageants, the way all the artists still do. Isn't it remarkable how the artists and writers and musicians worked right next to the carpenters and neighborhood helpers? They were all one during the old days, even if someone was quite famous, and it's the same way today.

"Papa said Brunelleschi was the ugliest man he had ever seen. He was very short and very quiet until his services were needed. Then he became a bundle of energy and ordered everyone around until the job was done exactly to his specifications.

"I saw him on the street a couple of years ago, and I have to agree with Papa; by then he was old and shrunken and really ugly. But what a genius, and what great things he designed. You know he built a beautiful panel when he competed for the commission to make the Baptistry Doors before we were born. Papa saw it once at the exhibition. Of course, Ghiberti won the contest for the commission to build all sixteen panels for the doors, but Papa said Brunelleschi's panel was very beautiful. He liked it better and thought Brunelleschi should have won, but his was solid metal and Ghiberti casted a shell, so his method would be a lot cheaper for the city. They say he gave his panel to Cosimo.

"I love his architecture, the simple, graceful lines over at the chapel at Santa Croce and Santo Spirito and the L'Ospedale degli Innocenti, and especially San Lorenzo. They say he was inspired by the graceful lines of the old Greek and Roman architecture for the wonderful pillars he uses in his buildings. Did you know he designed those but also the—"

"Amalia, if you keep talking and staring over at the Duomo, we will be trimming these trees tonight in the dark. A little less talk and a little more work, if you don't mind."

"Oh, all right," Amalia sighed. "But it is a lovely sight. How about we take your stew up to the loggia tonight so we can enjoy the view of the city one last time before winter settles in for keeps?"

"The loggia is a mess from the storm the other day, and I haven't had time to clean it up," responded Lucrezia.

"Well, maybe we can work quickly and get done with this, and then I'll help you clean it up."

Lucrezia laughed and said, "First I'd like to see the 'work quickly' part right now before we head to the roof."

They both laughed and went back to clipping and cutting.

It was hard work, more than two girls should be doing, but they were strong. Lucrezia wanted the trees kept in good condition with no dead wood or shaggy branches so they would bear more fruit the next year.

If their neighbors could see them, they would be the gossip of the neighborhood, but they knew the only ones who could see down into their walled garden were Lucia on one side and Maria on the other, from their upper windows. They knew neither of them would say one word to anyone that would cause either of the girls embarrassment.

Amalia knew they were very lucky because several of the women in the neighborhood were terrible gossips. Two were quite spiteful, but Lucia and Maria were good, kind women and very dear to her and to Lucrezia as well. Maria, being older, had been wonderful to her after her mother had died. Lucia was younger and more like a much older sister. She and Lucrezia had become closer in the recent months now that Lucrezia was no longer thought of as a servant. They both enjoyed sewing and would walk together to the sewing confraternity every Thursday afternoon. Now that she was not considered a servant, Lucrezia had been invited to join that group. She had always gone along with Amalia and been a welcome help when they all worked on the pageants, but this was different. Now she belonged on her own merit.

After a couple of hours of work, the two girls had taken a quick break to eat a piece of fruit and some cheese with bread. Then they worked into the afternoon. Carlo had not shown up, and they were disappointed, because the debris from the trimming was all around them on the ground, and they had to stumble through it and kick it out of their way.

The apricot and plum trees were smaller and easier to trim, and Lucrezia could reach most of the branches. Amalia had finished the last small olive tree and had walked back to start pruning the grape vines along the back wall. Lucrezia was beginning to pile up all the cuttings by the left wall where one tree had died last year. They had not gotten a chance to replace it before Giuliano was killed. Now they couldn't afford to replace it.

"Well, at least this bare space will come in handy for something," Lucrezia said to Amalia, as she carried a bundle of trimmings over there and dropped them.

Just then Carlo appeared at the back of the house, and they both called to him to come help them. Where had he been? Lucrezia was teasing him about sleeping late. Had he been playing a game of calcio with the boys? She was just teasing him, because he was such a good helper for them and worked so hard for his young years, they wouldn't dream of reprimanding him harshly.

Carlo didn't say anything in response, but when he bent down to pick up some of the clippings, he grunted, and then he groaned. That caught the attention of both girls, and then they saw immediately that he was injured.

"Carlo, how badly are you hurt? How did you get that cut?"

"How did you get this bruise? How did this happen to you? Carlo, can you stand up straight? Can't you straighten up? Does it hurt when I press here?"

"Were you injured in a calcio game?"

Both girls were firing questions at him, but Carlo was in too much pain to answer. He was hugging himself and slumped forward, and the girls could see tears running down his cheeks.

Lucrezia tried to help him straighten up, but he cried out with an anguished, "Noooo."

They looked at each other over Carlo's head with a look of panic in their eyes. What could have happened? What should they do?

Very slowly, with each girl almost lifting him by one arm, one on each side, they steered him, half carrying him as much as Carlo could bear the movement, toward the house. As they got closer to the overhang near the back of the house, Lucrezia held Carlo while Amalia ran back and got the step stool she had been using to climb the trees. She ran back with it, and Carlo used it to slowly and carefully climb up to sit on the table with the girls' help.

The two girls looked at each other. What to do? Carlo was being so brave, but they knew he was hurting with each movement.

"I'm going to get Maria," said Lucrezia.

"Go, go," said Amalia. While Lucrezia was gone, Amalia kept trying to help Carlo to lie back slowly on the table. He cried out once, but finally he was on his back, and then his breathing became a little more regular. She pressed on his ribs, and by his reaction, she was sure at least one rib was broken. Carlo was so thin, she could see his little ribs clearly, and she thought she could actually see where one rib didn't line up properly.

By the time Lucrezia got back with Maria, Carlo was breathing easier and had stopped gasping for each breath.

Maria took one look at him, and she said, "Oh, my poor Carlo. My dear boy."

"Amalia, do you have any more of your mother's theriaca?"

"Yes, Maria, we always keep a small supply in case of an emergency."

"Good. Brew up a weak small cup. Amalia, we will need Dona Juliana. I hope she is home from the hospital. Hurry. If she is not home, go by and ask Dona Vittoria to come. No, wait, Lucrezia, you go for Dona Juliana and Amalia, you brew the pain killer."

"Carlo, child, you are doing just fine. We will have you comfortable very soon. Just try to breathe. You are doing very well." Maria patted Carlo on his shoulder and smoothed his hair back, to calm him. Lucrezia and Amalia were gone in a flash to their appointed tasks. They knew Carlo was in the most capable hands in their gonfalons.

Fortunately, Juliana was home, and the two of them arrived by the time Amalia had the brew ready that would alleviate Carlo's pain.

Juliana asked Carlo several questions and went over his body to determine if there were any injuries other than the ones that were obvious to all of them. Then she used Amalia's brew to ease Carlo's pain as they got him to raise his arms over his head and tried to push the rib back into place. It was painful for Carlo, but he only cried out one time, thanks to the painkiller. Then they wrapped his chest and cleaned his worst cuts and bandaged them.

They found a small chair and moved Carlo onto it so they could get him upstairs and onto the pallet they kept for him in the storeroom behind the kitchen.

They gave Carlo a few more sips of the sedative, and soon he was sleeping, mercifully out of pain.

"Who did this?" asked Maria, "What happened?" she asked once the four of them were back outside the storeroom and seated at the kitchen table.

Lucrezia said, "We don't know. He was supposed to help us this morning pruning the fruit trees, and he just arrived a few minutes ago—just before we came to get you—and he could barely stand up. What could have happened? Was he in a brawl with some of the older boys?"

"Perhaps," said Juliana, "but I have a bad feeling about this. Can you girls handle him when he wakes up? I need to get home to prepare our meal, as does Maria, and the baby is fussing. For the next few hours, just give him a small sip of the theriaca if he rouses. I will come back later tonight to check on him. Mainly just keep him calm, and don't let him move around. You know how to administer it, Lucrezia?"

"Of course, Dona Juliana. Thank you for your help. We will do as you say."

"We can't keep using that. Do you have any willow bark?"

"Yes we have a large supply, and we have valerian and several other herbs. I will brew up a concoction right away."

"Good. And when this is over, I can't wait to hear the story of your outfit, Amalia. Is this Lucrezia's idea of the newest fashion?"

Amalia looked down at herself, realizing she was still in her father's pants.

They all had a good laugh as Maria and Juliana left.

Lucrezia and Amalia did as they were instructed, and Carlo was a good patient. He was very quiet, and the girls assumed he was still hurting a great deal, but they also suspected Carlo was scared, and they didn't know why.

The next morning early, Maria's husband, Signore Filippo, knocked on their door and asked how Carlo was doing and if he could speak with him. Since he was one of the leaders of their gonfalons, their neighborhood, they could not refuse him; nor would they have wanted to, for they knew him to be a kind man and knew that his only interest was the well-being of Carlo. He sat in the room and talked with Carlo for a long time, but the girls could not hear anything that was said. They heard Carlo crying once, but they didn't dare go in.

When Signore Filippo came out of the storage room where Carlo's pallet was, Filippo said, "He is a good boy. We will do what we can. Can Carlo stay here a little longer? Can you care for him and feed him?"

"Yes, Signore Filippo. Carlo often eats with us and even sleeps over sometimes if it gets too late for him to go home. Yes, of course, he can stay with us," said Amalia. "Will he be all right? Is there anything we should know or something we can do?"

"Not right now," said Filippo. "This is a serious matter, and I will be bringing it to the attention of the authorities. I will let you know what is to be done."

Lucrezia and Amalia looked at each other with surprise and concern. If the authorities were involved, what would happen to Carlo? And how might this affect them?

After Amalia showed Signore Filippo down to the door, she returned to find Lucrezia already in with Carlo, and she joined them. He was crying, but they didn't think his pain was that severe anymore. Nor did they think the pain was the real reason for his tears.

"Carlo, what is wrong? What has happened? Is there anything you can tell us?" asked Amalia.

"I am so sorry, Amalia. I did not want anyone to know, but Signore Filippo insisted I tell him. My father drinks sometimes, and two nights ago, he got very drunk and got angry with me because I didn't have any coins for him. He didn't mean it; I know he didn't. He is so sad since Mama left. He cares for me the best he can, I know he does. He didn't mean to hurt me; I know he didn't." And when he started to cry again, both girls tried to soothe him and calm him so he wouldn't irritate his broken and no doubt very sore ribs.

Once Carlo had cried himself to sleep, the girls left his side. While they had been in with Carlo, Lucia had brought over a platter of dried fruit and meats and a nice, large chunk of freshly baked bread. Carlo's share could wait until he awakened, but the girls were overwhelmed by the good smells. They sat down at the table right away to eat. The stew Lucrezia had made could wait until later.

While they were eating, they debated what to do. Amalia remembered there was an old bed and mattress in a storeroom on the ground floor, and Lucrezia remembered a spare chest and chair they no longer used that was stored in a room upstairs. They decided they would clean out the storage room behind the room that was their kitchen that afternoon and set it up as a room especially for Carlo. He could not go home. They had to convince him to stay with them.

As it turned out, that was not difficult. Carlo didn't want to burden them, but he also didn't want to go home. Over the next few days, they learned this was not the first time Carlo's father had beaten him. The other times Carlo had been able to hide it. No, they decided, he could not go home, and he now had a room of his own in the Dontarini home. They just had to convince Maria and Filippo—and maybe the officials.

At Maria's urging, Filippo intervened, and everything was handled quietly. Everyone knew Barto, as he was known, had a drinking problem, but no one wanted to cause him any trouble. Barto wanted Carlo to come home, but then he lost his job because he didn't show up for work. It wasn't the first time, and his employer at the building site was tired of his backtalk. Barto disappeared the next day, and the rumors were that he had left town when his landlord threw him out for not paying his rent. He left without seeing Carlo, and it would be years before Carlo heard from him again.

Carlo was very upset by all of this, but he was a smart little boy, and he realized that his lot with Amalia and Lucrezia was far better than it would have been with his father, now that his mother was gone. Lately, his father had been beating him more often and harder with each assault.

Things really didn't change much for Amalia, Lucrezia, and Carlo. Carlo's ribs mended quickly, and the various cuts and bruises healed even quicker. They had already been eating most meals together, and Carlo was soon able to again do errands for other people in the gonfalons and even out in the commune to earn a few coins to contribute to their household fund. Dona Rutia had some men's clothes that had belonged to her long-deceased husband, Roberto, and Lucrezia cut them up and used the material to keep Carlo in pants and a shirt as he grew, as young boys do.

He was good company, always full of tales and gossip he picked up on the streets while running errands and doing chores for them and for many of their neighbors. The girls told him that he was now the man of the house, which pleased him immensely.

Ghiberti's and Brunelleschi's competition panels for the Baptistry Doors

V *The Meeting* *February 1448*

It was late in winter, and their autumn pageant was behind them, as were the large pageants staged by the several other churches for Christmas and Epiphany.

Their lives had settled into a winter pattern. Amalia liked to start her copying early in the morning. Lucrezia settled into her sewing or planning her day as soon as she came downstairs. They would take a break to go to Mass most days. When they got back, Lucrezia fixed them a light breakfast, and Amalia would do whatever chores needed to be done in the house.

Carlo would always grab his cap and winter wrap and leave shortly after he ate to run an errand for them or for someone who had hired him. If he didn't have anything to do, he would go out to try to find whatever work he could. He had a lot of customers, because everyone in the gonfalons liked him. They knew any task assigned to him would be done swiftly and properly, and he never tried to overcharge them.

He had recovered from his injuries, so now one of his main tasks was to carry the firewood from the cellar and water from the well up to the kitchen for that day. He had a routine he followed, going from house to house to do this for several customers. Then, if they had anything else they needed done, he would do it. Now, in the middle of winter, his hands would get raw from the cold, so Amalia had knitted him a pair of gloves he wore under the old pair of leather gloves his father had discarded.

Lucrezia liked to get her household tasks done early. She would go to the market right after their breakfast and get whatever they needed in the way of food for the day. All three of them were in charge of their own lives now and did a good job of not leaving messes behind, so there was not much for them to do on a daily basis. For special tasks, they all three joined in to get it done as swiftly as possible. Carlo always complained that doing housework was beneath him. He always said he had a career to pursue with his customers, and he needed to be attending to business. One of the girls would cuff him, laugh, and say, "Get busy and do your part or no dinner tonight."

Each girl wore her hair in a simple style unless she was leaving the house for some special reason. Then they would do each other's hair. This was a new adventure for Amalia, but one she came to enjoy; and she found she was quite creative.

Lately, Amalia was the one to fix their big meal for later in the day. She found she liked cooking, and Lucrezia did not mind relinquishing her kitchen duties at all. She often criticized Amalia's seasoning of the meat or fish, but Amalia took her suggestions to heart. Finally, she became an excellent cook. Dona Rutia would also make suggestions, but it was usually that the stew needed more wine added to it.

Whatever time Carlo came home at night, either Amalia or Lucrezia would work with him on his lessons. He worked hard at his reading. Then every once in a while, Filippo next door would work with him on his numbers. He was a fast learner, and before long he would know all that Filippo could teach him.

Who would they find to teach him then? They could not afford to send him to a school. Well, when the time came, they hoped they would find a solution.

Once her chores were done, Lucrezia settled down to her sewing. She might be working at cutting out a garment or basting it together or maybe sketching a new design on the back of a scrap of Amalia's discarded paper.

One day Carlo came home with a supply of scrap paper. He said he had run an errand for Messer Ludovici, who lived in the big house on the corner. He had gone to the workshop of some artist named Donatello in the middle of town near the Duomo. He spotted a pile of trash in the corner of the boddeghe with some sheets of paper in it, and he asked if he could have them. The men in the workshop all laughed and joked that he wanted their trash: Sure, he could have it all. No, he said, he only wanted the paper for drawing. Then he thanked them and left.

Lucrezia was thrilled. She said now she had paper for a lifetime. But she was doing more and more sketching of the designs she had been keeping stored in her head, and the paper would in fact be gone by spring.

They liked their evenings best. Lucrezia would do her easier sewing on a dress, shirt, skirt, cape, or pants; Amalia would be back at her copying; and Carlo would be practicing his reading or writing on a slate he had found at a construction site or maybe sharpening a tool or twining a rope. They might chat about some gossip Carlo had heard in his travels about town or that Lucrezia had heard at the market or Amalia at her poetry confraternity meeting. They genuinely liked each other and were very companionable. Dona Rutia might be there or she might have spent the day at her home, but she was an often-present part of their lives. They all quite enjoyed her company, her raspy voice, and her sharp tongue.

Carlo said, "Lucrezia, if I sharpen your scissors, will you cut my hair? It has gotten so long. Today Roberto and Piero called me a girl."

"Of course, Carlo. Now or tomorrow?"

"Give me your scissors. I will sharpen them now, and you can cut it tomorrow."

The next day began with Carlo and Lucrezia arguing about how short to cut Carlo's hair. Amalia was glad she had an errand to run to Master Manetti's shop on the other side of town. That meant she could escape the furor. She hadn't finished the manuscript she was working on, and although it seemed to be a nice day, everyone was saying there was a big storm coming. She wanted to have enough work in case they became housebound. Plus, she needed more paper and ink.

As soon as Carlo's hair was cut, Lucrezia was going to the market to stock up on food in preparation for the possible storm. Carlo would have a long day bringing in extra wood and water for them and for neighbors, as well as his other errands. Lucrezia had an appointment with Madonna Cavaletti, who lived three blocks away, and she hoped it would not have to be postponed. She was to deliver the new dress she had just finished. This would be the final fitting; and if all went well, Madonna would take the delivery and pay Lucrezia for the dress. Madonna Cavaletti was not an easy woman to please, and Lucrezia hoped she would be happy this time with the bodice that Lucrezia had changed three times now. Hopefully, the weather would hold until they all three got home later in the day.

Once Amalia stepped out the door, she instantly regretted she could not stay home by the warm fire. The wind was in her face and had picked up since she had gotten up several hours ago. She was glad when she finally reached Master Manetti's shop. As she opened the door, the wind blew her and the door into the shop with a great gust. Master Manetti looked up, and the man sitting near him at a table on the far side of the room turned in response to the tumult. Amalia managed to get the door closed with the help of the young man, Antonio, who came around the table to assist. He helped her secure the latch on the door as the two older men went back to their conversation.

"Good morning. Is there anything I can help you with, Signorina Amalia?"

"Good morning, Antonio. Yes, please. I need a supply of paper and also some fresh ink. Then, when Master Manetti is free, I would like to speak with him briefly."

"Yes, signorina. In the meantime, I will get what you wish. It looks like the storm is starting."

"Yes," Amalia said. "How is your sister doing, Antonio?"

"She is better, but now my brother has the same fever and cough. I hope I don't get it. Mama relies on me for everything."

"I think Lucrezia will be brewing up a new batch of the cough medicine while we are housebound. Let Carlo know if you need more of it."

"Thank you, signorina, I will. Carlo came by yesterday and brought us extra wood. Thank him for me. I won't see him if our calcio game gets canceled because of the weather."

"I will, Antonio." Amalia went over by the window and looked out at the gusty conditions on the street. Hats were blowing off heads, and scarfs were flying though the air like giant birds. It was a funny sight, but not so funny when she considered she had to get back home in the teeth of that wind. The only good thing about it, she realized, was it would be at her back as she went home.

Mr. Manetti called to her. "Signorina Amalia, I would like you to meet someone. This is Messer Poggio Bracciolini. I think you are probably familiar with him and his work."

"Oh, yes, sire. It is a great honor to meet you. About a year ago, my father scribed a copy of *On The Nature of Things* by Lucretius. When he was finished, he read it to us. Then he told us there was a wonderful story about how you found the book, but he didn't know all the details; only that it had started our great quest to find the ancient books."

"Mr. Manetti tells me you are one of his finest scribes, but you work at home," Messer Bracciolini said, coughing slightly.

"Yes, sire. I'm sure I would not be allowed to work in a scriptorium, being a girl, but I am really happier working at home anyway."

"Have you done any of the Greek plays?" He was coughing again a little more this time.

"No, sire. I don't know Greek, so I only work on the Latin manuscripts and those to be copied in the volgare, but that is enough."

Poggio said, "So many of the Greek works are being uncovered right now. It is a true treasure trove. Cosimo has agents all throughout the Mediterranean, looking for books. Messer Rucellai recently got a shipment from his agent in the Levant, a number of volumes that—" he coughed again and could not speak for a moment.

"Well, if Master Manetti gets any of them, perhaps I could glance at one." She smiled over at Mr. Manetti, and he nodded in return. "Pardon me, sire, but are you doing anything for your cough?"

"My doctor gave me medicine for it, but it's a waste. I think it is mostly alcohol with a few herbs added, so I'm enjoying it very much, but it isn't doing a thing for my cough." He again fell victim to a siege of coughing.

"Sire, if I may, if you will write down your address, I will have my errand boy deliver some elixir to you. It might help, and it won't hurt. I'm sorry, though, there isn't any alcohol in it."

The three of them laughed as Antonio walked over.

He said, "Sire, Signorina Lucrezia gave me some for my sister, and she is much better since she started taking it."

"Lucrezia?"

"She was my maid and lives with me. She learned all the old herbal cures from my mother. Of course, they don't always work, but very often they do. May I send some over?

"Yes, yes. Here is my address." He barely got the words out before a coughing fit seized him that made Amalia wish she had some of the elixir with her.

"I will have Carlo deliver some as soon as Lucrezia gets it prepared. She was going to start making it as soon as she got home this afternoon. With this weather, we figured there might be a big need for it."

"I will see you—" Messer Poggio started to say, but another coughing spell seized him. He covered his face with his scarf and headed for the door, waving back at Master Manetti.

"Don't worry about that delivery. I will see you next week, and I will take care of it," said Master Manetti.

Messer Poggio turned to give a slight bow to Amalia, and waved a thanks to Master Manetti. He needed Antonio's help to manage the door. He clapped Antonio on the back of his shoulder as he exited.

"This is the weather for sickness. I don't know which is worse: the winter sicknesses or the fevers in the summer," said Master Manetti.

"The fevers," said Amalia. "Sometimes these winter sicknesses kill, but the fevers of typhoid, malaria, cholera and more almost always do."

"Yes, of course, you are so right," Master Manetti said as he smiled at her.

You are wise beyond your years, he thought.

It seemed he had not begrudged Cosimo's intervention on her behalf. He seemed to like her, and she knew he had liked her father. He seemed glad she was a scribe for him. Perhaps he didn't know what the connection was between her and Cosimo, and he didn't ask, but he had complimented her work many times, saying it was excellent and that her artwork on the title pages enhanced her work and made it more salable. He had once muttered that if another woman presented herself at his shop in the future and she was as capable as this waif of a girl, he would consider hiring her.

"Here is what you require, signorina," said Antonio.

"Thank you, Antonio."

"Now, Master Manetti," Amalia said, "since we may be housebound for the duration of this storm, I was wondering if I might have another manuscript to copy. I'm almost done with the one I'm working on, and I don't want to be left with time on my hands and no work to do."

"Of course," said Mr. Manetti. "I have this large Livy manuscript here, but also I have this small one. I think you might enjoy it. If you have extra time, I suggest you make a copy for yourself if you wish. I think you'll enjoy working on the larger manuscript. It is another one Messer Bracciolini found on a recent trip across the Alps. He found another monastery with a large library. Apparently, many of his finds are psalters and gospels, but a couple were new Greek plays and a new Quintilian manuscript. I just received this copy from the scriptorium of this Livy.

"He is truly amazing. He says he is too old now to go trekking into those hinterlands and leaving his wife and all his children behind. He said this was the last such trip he would make, he wanted to devote his time to his writing, but what he has achieved is truly remarkable. Do you know his story?"

"No, sire. Papa said it was very interesting, but he never did tell me. I would love to hear it."

"You know he was working for the Papal Curia for Pope John XXIII as a secretary at the time of the Great Schism. We had the three competing popes: one in Avignon, one in Naples, and Pope John in Rome. The Holy Roman Emperor decided to call the Council of Constance to resolve the issue and return to just one pope in Rome. Pope John and one of the other popes agreed. They both agreed to step down, and they excommunicated the third pope who would not agree. The Medici were the bankers for Pope John, so Giovanni sent his son, a very young Cosimo, to accompany Pope John to represent the interests of the bank. Poggio, being the secretary for Pope John, also went along. That is how the two of them, Cosimo and Poggio, met.

"Pope Martin V was finally elected, and John was unthroned as an anti-pope. They were accusing him of all kinds of things—heresy, simony, schism—so he fled down the Rhine disguised as a postman. Cosimo and Poggio also decided it was time for them to get out of town since they didn't know how far the net would spread. There weren't any charges brought against either of them, but they weren't too sure of their footing with Pope John on the run. Finally, the church officials caught up with John and put him in prison. They threatened to bring charges of piracy, simony, tyranny, heresy, sodomy, rape, murder, incest, and fornication with two hundred women."

"My, that is quite a list," said Amalia, and she almost chuckled.

Master Minetti did chuckle. "Yes, to say the least. Once John was captured, Giovanni de' Medici stepped in to start negotiating for his release. It took him months before he was able to ransom Baldassarre Cossa, as he was now again known, and gain his release. Giovanni was able to offer Cossa asylum in Florence, and then he prevailed upon the new pope, Martin V, to appoint Cossa Bishop of Tusculum so he would have an income.

"In the meantime, young Cosimo and Poggio traveled north. They first went to Cluny, and in the monastery there they found a forgotten Cicero book. After a while, they split up, and Cosimo went north to visit the Medici banks in Northern Europe. Poggio headed to the Monastery in Fulda. He had heard it had a lot of old, ignored manuscripts.

"The rest you probably know. Poggio returned from Fulda with Lucretius's book, the one that changed our entire concept of the ancient world. It started his and others' quests to find even more books in the monasteries throughout Europe and gathered from the entire Mediterranean world.

"You probably know that the monks spend their time making copies of the old books just as you do. Many books were sent to other monasteries, but some were just stored for hundreds of years and forgotten, particularly if they didn't care for the subject matter, like the old Greek teachings of Socrates or Plato and certainly the old plays, or even the early Romans.

"These manuscripts have increased our scanty knowledge of the Greek and Roman worlds of long ago, but there is more. Because of their teachings, they have opened our eyes to nature and the world around us. Even Cosimo himself went on a couple of expeditions into some of the monasteries and old storage buildings in quest of the ancient manuscripts. Cosimo and Poggio went down to Ostia outside of Rome together and explored the ruins there. Cosimo found some ancient marble sculptures he brought back to Florence, but they didn't find any manuscripts.

"Now that we have so much more information, the humanists have had a real impact on Florence and other cities in Italy. Of course, since Florence was an early outpost of the Roman Empire, we have always considered ourselves Romans, so in the beginning we just felt we were digging up our history, like digging up the old bones, broken statues, or broken vases they find in the hills all the time. This was our people, our history. But then it began to be more. This was a new learning, a new way of looking at the world around us that had been previously dominated by the church for all the centuries since Roman times.

"There are agents all over Europe and throughout the Mediterranean looking for manuscripts now. Several of them work for me, and when they bring me a book that is worthwhile, I usually take it to Messer Medici. That's why he allows me to copy outside his scriptorium and why I can employ you to copy books that I can then sell. In addition to his many agents out scouring the entire Mediterranean, the directors at all of his banks are authorized to buy whatever comes their way. He isn't the only one, obviously. Niccolo Niccoli did it for years, and Messer Rucellai and Vespasiano da Bisticci are also deeply committed to the movement. It is all very exciting.

"There had been manuscripts found earlier, but when Poggio found the complete manuscript of *On The Nature of Things* by Lucretius, it just caught everyone's imagination. People started thinking in a different way, living in the here and now for the pleasure of life instead of only seeking the hereafter through the Church.

"It led many of us to begin to study those old philosophers as they talk about a life that is different from the church's teachings. It doesn't necessarily contradict the church; it just enhances our lives and gives people a different perspective, as you know from reading the books you have copied. More of Socrates, Plato, and Aristotle came to light in recent years in addition to the Greek plays, as well as the Roman writings of Cicero, Sallust, Livy, Quintillian, Marcus Aurelius and so many more. Vespasiano told me Poggio found six orations of Cicero in a heap of waste paper at one monastery.

"What an exciting time we live in, Amalia, and you have a window to it all through the many books you copy."

Just then Carlo burst, almost flying, into the shop.

"Ohhh," he said, as the door blew open. "I am so sorry. The wind is getting worse. Pardon me, but, Amalia, Lucrezia sent me to bring you home before the storm gets any worse. It's just beginning to snow, so we should leave as soon as possible."

"Thank you, Carlo. And thank you, Master Manetti, most sincerely. What a wonderful story. Thank you for sharing it with me. I appreciate your kindness."

"Go, child, quickly, and God go with you. Be careful. Enjoy that little treasure in your bundle."

They were out the door with no further ado and on their short but rather perilous journey home. It was only eight blocks, but the streets were freezing over, and the wind seemed to get worse with each block.

They were cold and miserable by the time they reached their front door, but Lucrezia had some hot herbal tea ready for them once they climbed the stairs and were out of their wet winter wraps, gloves, hats, scarfs, and heaviest leather shoes.

"Before I forget, I promised some of your elixir to a gentleman I met at Master Manetti's shop. It was Poggio Bracciolini, the man who brought *On The Nature of Things* back to Florence many years ago. He has a dreadful cough, and his medicine isn't doing a thing to help him."

"It is just about ready. I started it as soon as I got home from Madonna Cavaletti's. She paid me, Amalia." Lucrezia sang out and laughed. "It is done."

"Oh, how wonderful, Lucrezia," said Amalia. "She is a trial, but the money is good. You earned every lira she paid you. Did she seem happy in the end?"

"Yes, I think so. She says she wants another dress for Easter."

They both groaned. Even Carlo groaned. Then he said, "Leave a pin in it."

They all laughed but they also agreed that the money was good although hard-earned.

"Oh, let me tell you. There is more," said Lucrezia. "On my way home, I passed Master Vicenti's shop. He called me inside. He wants me to go to the fulling mills and a couple of the weaving shops so I understand the differences in the qualities of the fabrics I am using. He said he has heard from several sources that my work is good, and if I am going to work for him in the future, I will need to understand these things. He wants me to come to his shop soon after the storm abates. Can you imagine?"

"Lucrezia, that is wonderful. Your reputation is growing every day. Soon you will need a shop," said Amalia.

"Oh, don't be silly. I'm just grateful that the ladies like my designs. I have some new ideas that are very different. I can't wait to see if Madonna Cavaletti will like one of them."

"Lucrezia—"

"I know. I have to stay within the bounds of the Sumptuary Laws, but I'm only pushing them a little bit, and I think I can justify it. Sometimes they are too strict, and they keep all of Florence looking so austere. Actually, I got the ideas when I saw the dress on that French woman we saw at the market last week."

"Lucrezia," piped up Carlo, "Giorgio told me she was a prostitute."

"Maybe so, but she was a French prostitute, and I don't have to mention the second part. You know perfectly well that if it is a foreign idea, they let it go unless it is really outrageous, and it certainly isn't. It's just a different type of the sleeve with trimming in the same fabric and the same color, just different shades. There won't be a single button on the entire dress. What can they complain about?"

Lucrezia had finished up the elixir as they were talking, and she poured some in a bottle and gave it to Carlo.

Amalia said, "Carlo, here is Messer Bracciolini's address. Be certain his maid can read the directions Lucrezia wrote out. I hate to ask you to go back out into the storm, but it isn't too far away, is it?"

"No, Amalia, and I'll stop at Gino's on my way back. His mother will offer me a hot drink, and this time, I'll accept. They live around the corner from Messer Bracciolini," he said as he struggled back into his winter clothes.

"That's fine, but hurry. Don't be gone any longer than necessary; the storm seems to be getting worse."

"I'm gone," said Carlo. He waved his cap, pulled it down on his head as far as he could, and dashed out the front door.

Lucrezia stirred what she was brewing on the large stove, and then the two of them sat down to have another cup of the tea. They exchanged more about Madonna Cavaletti, Master Manetti, Messer Bracciolini, and Master Vicenti, and so on.

Lucrezia told Amalia she intended to use a portion of her money from the dress for the purchase of a pair of leather shoes for herself.

"My first pair of real shoes, not the clogs or sandals of a servant. I am so excited."

"That is wonderful, Lucrezia."

"It was worth waiting for. I went into the leather shop, and Master Brunelli measured my feet and said to come back next week for a fitting. I can't wait. I want to take my clogs down to the river, throw them in, and watch them float away like two little wood boats to the sea. Instead I'll probably give them to that girl Dora down the street. Master Capponi keeps that poor girl in rags. I am so grateful your father never treated me like that."

"And now you are doing something for someone else. Your first step up the ladder of success! I wish I had been able to give you my old shoes when I outgrew them."

"They never would have fit my big feet, plus I would have been arrested if I went out in the streets in shoes like that. This will be such a statement."

They would be working diligently for the next couple of days on sewing and scribing respectively, but for just these few minutes, they sat and enjoyed each other's company and celebrated their achievements.

Much later that same afternoon, Carlo returned, exhausted and miserably cold. He curled up on the floor by the fire on some pillows, taking a well-deserved nap. Lucrezia had bottled all her brews and had settled down to do some sewing. Amalia was writing at her desk.

"Oh, I just remembered," she cried. "Master Manetti sent me home with a large manuscript to copy but also something else. Carlo arrived at the shop to walk me home, and I never saw what it was. It's here bundled with the manuscript. Oh, look, Lucrezia, it is a small book of poetry."

She thumbed through a few pages as she walked over to where Lucrezia was working.

"Lucrezia, how beautiful; this is a book of the poetry of Lucrezia de' Medici, Messer Piero's wife. Remember last year when they recited some of her poems at the confraternity, and then we read more of them at our devotional confraternity this fall? Also, she wrote that beautiful song everyone was singing last year. Her poems are so lovely and inspiring. She's so talented."

"Let me look at it since I am her namesake. I love this poem about devotion to Our Lady. I memorized it for the confraternity meeting you mentioned," said Lucrezia.

As they both looked through the small book, Amalia told Lucrezia that Master Manetti had given her permission to make a copy of it for herself.

"I can't wait to start on it, and I'll do a lot of artwork if I have the time. How wonderful. After our talk this morning, I'm beginning to think maybe Master Manetti actually likes me a little now that he's over the shock of having to deal with a female. Lucrezia, I think we're going to enjoy this storm."

VI   *Poggio*

The storm raged on for three days, and though she and Lucrezia had plenty of work to do to fill the time, Carlo was like a caged lion. If the storm had not finally broken, they joked they were going to throw him out in the wind and snow and lock the door behind him.

Once the storm had ended, Amalia asked Carlo to drop by Messer Bracciolini's home if he was in that gonfalons to see how he was faring. The word Carlo brought home was not good. Poggio was in bed with a fever, and the cough was still severe. The person he talked to told Carlo that Messer Bracciolini was out of the elixir.

Amalia decided to take some fresh elixir to his home herself. She didn't know if he would receive her, but she felt she had to try. Carlo had been told that Poggio's wife was at the house in Fiesole with the children. The woman that had received Carlo when he went by was his housekeeper at the small house he kept in town.

The housekeeper was not happy about receiving this young girl who wished to visit Messer Poggio, but when she told him who was calling, he was most insistent she show Amalia up to his bedroom.

As she approached the room, Amalia heard Poggio fuming, "How absurd! I am at death's door, and my housekeeper is worried about proprieties!"

Before going in the room, Amalia asked the woman, Marta, to prepare a pot of hot tea with the packet she handed her.

"Just empty the packet into a pot, add the hot water, and bring it to the room with a cup. Thank you, Signora Marta."

When she walked into Poggio's room, it felt very cold. The fire had died out, and the housekeeper hadn't bothered to re-ignite it. Amalia went immediately to Poggio's bedside. Before he could even speak to her, he was seized by a coughing fit. She told him to relax and not to try to speak to her.

She said she knew he was glad to see her and that she would do what she could for him. She urged him to try to calm himself. She wrung out the rag in the bowl and started to wipe his face, but the water and the room were so cold, she feared she would give him a chill.

Finally, Marta arrived with the pot of tea and the cup. While Amalia poured some tea in the cup and began trying to get Poggio to sip it, she asked Marta to rekindle the fire. Then she asked her to please get a fresh bowl of hot water and a clean piece of toweling. Marta left, and it was clear she was not pleased about this girl coming in giving her orders, even though Amalia had spoken as sweetly as she could. In the meantime, Amalia tried to get more of the tea into Poggio.

When Marta returned with the fresh bowl of water, Amalia asked her for another pot of the brew. Now the woman was really exasperated, but Poggio gave her a hard stare that clearly ordered: Do it! She left tight-lipped and unhappy, but it was clear she would not argue with this man.

"Ornery as a bear he is, when he wants to be," she muttered to herself but audibly enough for them to get the idea as she left the room, "but he might be dying, and if this snip of a girl can help him, I will do what she says."

The ornery bear and the snip of a girl smiled at each other. By the time Amalia left an hour later, the room was cozy and Messer Poggio was resting more comfortably. His coughing had abated, and he was able to speak a few words without starting to cough again.

She told Marta to give Poggio another cup of the concoction from the pot later in the evening, and if it was all right with her, Amalia said she would return in the morning. By the time Amalia left, she could tell Marta had come to like her. For one thing, it was clear that her master was resting more comfortably than he had for some time, and Marta expressed her relief at that. What was more, Marta informed Amalia that Poggio had quite a reputation with the young ladies, and that with his wife in Fiesole, there was no telling what he might be up to; however, she could see that Amalia was not that kind of a person, and it seemed that Poggio had a regard for her that placed her in a separate category.

"I'm not sure even a nun is in a separate category in his mind, though, or would be safe from his flirtations and advances. You just be careful around him, now. I don't want anything shameful to happen for which his wife will blame me."

"Of course not," said Amalia with such conviction that Marta seemed satisfied.

When Amalia returned the next morning, Poggio was doing only a little bit better. His cough had abated some, but he still had a fever. Amalia handed Marta another packet of herbs to boil and bring to Poggio's room, and she made him drink a full cup of it even though it had a very bitter taste.

"I'm sure you would like it much more if it was mostly alcohol, but the results would only be a headache, not a cure," she said with a giggle in her voice. He smiled and nodded, and then he drank the rest of the brew down, grimacing at the bad taste but without complaint.

The next day when she returned, the servant, Rudolfo, let her in. When she got upstairs, Poggio was sitting up and Marta was arguing with him that he had to stay in bed. His fever had broken, and while he didn't have the strength to get out of bed, he did have the will.

"Perhaps we can compromise," said Amalia. "Perhaps we can get you up if you promise to just sit by the fire."

Between Marta and Amalia. they managed to get Poggio to the chair by the fire. Marta fussed over him, got the blanket from the bed to put around him, placed another cup of the tea on the table, and another blanket for around his feet. She then looked around as if wondering what else she could do.

Finally, Poggio said, "Enough. Stop fussing. Thank you, Marta, but I am fine."

His cough seemed to be gone now, but Amalia didn't want to take any chances. She asked Marta to prepare another packet with boiling water. Poggio started to raised an objection, but she told him that this one would have a pleasant flavor.

Amalia sat in the chair opposite Poggio by the fire. Poggio was exhausted from the exertion of getting out of bed and into the chair, and he had closed his eyes and rested his head back on the chair. She thought he might doze off, so she remained silent.

After a few minutes, he roused himself and he said, "You know, I haven't been this sick since I returned from the Monastery at Fulda almost thirty years ago."

Marta returned with the tea, and Poggio sipped it until it was gone. Amalia poured a second cup, but Poggio only sipped a small amount.

Marta asked Amalia if it would be all right if she went out to attend to some chores for just a short time. Amalia said that would be fine, that she and Messer Poggio would just sit by the fire for a while.

After Marta left, Poggio said, "It would appear you have won a fan. She thought I was going to die, and she would have had to answer to my wife. I wouldn't have wanted to be in her shoes." They both laughed, and Amalia knew he was feeling better if he was now concerned about other people's feelings and could make a joke.

"I thought I was going to die."

At first, Amalia thought Poggio was talking about his present illness, but he had slipped back to thirty years before.

"When I got back to Florence with that manuscript, among the others, in my bags, we weren't even sure exactly what I had found. I knew it was old, and I knew it wasn't a psalter, but it took us months to sort out what it was. Nobody remembered who Lucretius was, and no one had any knowledge about the book itself. They had both been lost from all memory over the intervening fifteen hundred years.

"I was out at Niccolo Niccoli's summer home in Fiesole with him as we were trying to sort it all out when I got sick. It was a full month before I could ride back into Florence. By then, Niccolo, Cosimo, and Marsuppino had figured out what we had and had started making copies of it so they could all read it and it could be disseminated to the group of people that would come to be called the humanists, who were searching for these old books.

"I read a little of it while I was traveling back from Fulda, but a few sections were very fragile, and I didn't want to do any damage. I thoroughly enjoyed reading the first copy Niccolò gave me, and I started to appreciate what we had uncovered.

"Lucretius' works had been lost for so long, nobody even remembered who he was. Not just *On The Nature of Things,* but I also had from that trip Vitruvius's book on architecture. Brunelleschi and the others went crazy when we got it copied. Do you know of them?"

"Only *On The Nature of Things.* My father scribed it over a year before he was killed. It is almost two years ago now that he read it to us, so I was very young. There were things I didn't understand, but I did enjoy most of it. I'm sure I would enjoy it much more now that I'm so worldly."

That gave Poggio a hearty laugh, and she was very pleased that it didn't start a coughing attack.

"I understand from Master Manetti that Cosimo has befriended you."

She didn't know what to say or how to respond to this, so she said nothing. Poggio took it in stride and continued.

"You know we were together in Constance at the Council when Cossa was declared the anti-pope. Cosimo was only a little over twenty years old then, but his father sent him to protect the interests of the Medici Bank. When Cossa had been elected pope, he made the Medicis the papal bankers. The word is that a deal was struck between the old man and Cossa long before he became Pope John XXIII. Giovanni gave Cossa what he needed so Cossa could bribe and blackmail whoever could be bought or threatened, in order to swing the election, but that is the way those things were done back then—and they're still done that way today.

"Cossa actually did want to purify the church, and he probably had the most legitimate claim to the papacy, but the entrenched bureaucracy of the Curia wanted him out. Since at the time they had three popes, the Council decided all three had to go, and there would be a new pope, Pope Martin V.

"What a time we had in Constance! Cossa was a rascal, to say the least, and even though he was older than Cosimo and me, we had a hard time keeping up with him. There were threats by the Council to bring charges against him for various things. Finally, when they gave the order for his arrest, he came up with a disguise as a postman and escaped down the Rhine. They eventually caught up with him and threatened to charge him with a long list of things. Not all of them were fabrications. Cosimo and I decided it was time to leave town. His father took over, and we made our way north. We travelled together for a while to Cluny and a couple other monasteries. Then Cosimo went up to visit the northern Medici banks. He wanted also to investigate the industry in Bruges, the weavers producing the tapestries they're so famous for, and he had a few contacts. I headed to the Monastery at Fulda.

"Cosimo did his best for Cossa, but finally his father stepped in to bribe whoever had to be bribed. Cossa was declared an anti-pope, but finally, after months, Giovanni got him back to Florence where he could protect him. When he died, just six months later, he left everything to Giovanni in thanks for all he had done for him. This included the relic he always kept on his person, the finger of St. John the Baptist. His was quite a story. Giovanni and Cosimo were good friends to him, but I can tell you, Cosimo wasn't too happy about some of those early dealings. As I say, Cossa was a rascal and then some.

"Giovanni gave the finger to be preserved at the Baptistry, and Cosimo hired Donatello to design a crypt to be installed in the Baptistry and hired Michelozzo to build it. The pope was against it, so very strict parameters were set down by the Church. It had to stay between the pillars and couldn't stick out farther than the pillars into the church. They forgot to say how high, so up it went." Poggio chuckled at the memory. "You've seen it. The pope was furious, but since it was the Medici, there was nothing he could do about it.

"The next time I saw Cosimo was after my sickness, when I returned to Florence. He does what he has to do politically, but he is a true humanist. I understand he once said if he could have all the money he could possible want by waving a magic wand, he would still want to be a banker. Maybe that's so, but I think he would like it best if he could spend his days studying the manuscripts with Marcilio Ficino, Bruni, Traversari, and other scholars who truly understand the meaning of the writings in those books."

Amalia thought for a minute, and then she said, "You know, he said something like that to me the day I met him, but I was so wrapped up in my own problems at the time, I didn't understand his meaning. I think you may be right."

Poggio continued, "I've been on a lot of adventures since then, in search of books and manuscripts and other things, but I think that journey with Cosimo was the best time I ever had. We were young, and there were enemies to be outwitted, and he was very good at that. He couldn't save the papacy for Cossa, but I think it was lost before any of us ever got to Constance. We even had some good times after we left Constance before we decided to go our different paths.

"Now, young lady, I just heard Marta return. I suggest you call her so I can relieve myself, and then you need to get me back to bed. This has been most enjoyable, but I am very tired now and need to rest."

Amalia called Marta, and they did what had to be done. Once Poggio was again settled in his bed, Amalia knew he would sleep. She kissed him on the cheek.

He said, "Thank you, my angel. This has been most enjoyable, but I thank you for much more than that. Come back again and I will tell you more tales."

"Messer Bracciolini, I can't think of anything I would enjoy more."

By the time she got home, it was mid-afternoon. She had a lot of catching up to do on her scribing, but she knew the time had been well spent, and not only in regard to Poggio's health. She couldn't think of a more enjoyable way to spend an hour.

Yes, she would go back. She liked the irascible old man, and she hoped there would be more tales.

San Lorenzo – The Medici Church

Manuscript written by Poggio Bracciolini in 1440

VII   *The Storm After the Storm*

There was a lot of damage throughout the city after the storm finally passed. Trees were down all over town, and buildings were damaged everywhere. The old house across the street from the Dontarini house was damaged beyond repair. The roof had caved in and caused one wall to be damaged. No one was injured when it happened. The young couple, Giovanni and Beatrice Volini, and their daughter, who had been living there, moved in with her parents in their much larger house next door.

Giovanni Volini was a guildsman. He had risen in the ranks of the Lara guild, the wool guild, in recent years. He told Maria and Filippo that he intended to tear the house down and build a bigger, better house. Everyone was pleased for them. They were a nice young couple, and they were well-liked in the gonfalons.

An older couple was renting a house about a block away, and it too was damaged beyond repair. The landlord said he would probably rebuild, but in the meantime, the couple was going to move to Siena where his brother had a house they could live in and knew of a job for the older gentleman, Caesar.

Lucrezia had come in from the back yard the morning after the storm to report that the pear tree was blown over, and they would need help to try to right it.

Filippo told her that from his upstairs window he could see some tiles were missing from their roof. He said he would come over and check on it, Lucrezia had told Amalia, and now, they talked about it.

"We're lucky to have him as a neighbor to help us when we need it," said Amalia. "I saw some wagons finally arriving at the market on my way home. I think we may finally be able to get some grain and maybe some decent meat if we go right away."

"Let's wait until Carlo gets back," said Lucrezia. "I'll ask him to bring up some wood, and I'll bake some fresh bread."

"He already brought it in. It's in the back corner, and there is more by the fireplace," said Amalia.

Just then, there was a knock at the door.

Lucrezia got up to answer it, saying, "I hadn't noticed. I should have known he would stock us up before heading off on his errands. Then we should go right away," she said as she went down the stairs. Amalia heard her open the door and say, "Yes, may I help you?"

"You are not Amalia Dontarini," he said.

"No, I am Lucrezia. May I help you?"

"I wish to speak with Amalia," he said, and Amalia heard a slight cry from Lucrezia. He must have pushed his way past her. Amalia got up from her work table and moved to the stairs. He was up the full flight in a flash. She came to a sudden stop when she saw the man's face. It was the face of her father—a much younger and shorter man and, well, not quite like her father, but—

"Hello, Amalia. I am your brother, Stefano. Did you think I was dead?"

"Oh, Stefano." She paused, gathering her thoughts. "Hello. No, Mr. Sacchetti told me you were alive. What are you doing here? Why have you come?"

"Is that any way to welcome your brother? This is my home, so I've come home. I've had a long journey in terrible weather. How about some wine? And what do you have in the way of food?" he asked as he took his winter clothing off and threw everything across the bench nearest the top of the stairs.

"We have very little food. The storm depleted our stores. We were just talking about going shopping for whatever might be at the market. We don't even have any bread left."

"Well, then, just get me some wine for now."

Amalia gave Lucrezia a look, asking her to get some wine for her brother.

Lucrezia did.

"So, little sister, what are you doing living here? Shouldn't you be in a convent? You certainly will make a pretty nun; what a waste. You were just a scrawny little kid when I left."

"I live here with Lucrezia, and this is my house. Papa left the house to me."

"Well, we'll see about that. No girl can live on her own. You belong in a convent, and you, Lucrezia, whoever you are, need to leave.

"But, as I said, I had a bad trip from Milan, so I'm going upstairs to bed. You girls can start making your plans to move out, because tomorrow, you are both gone: you to a convent, and you, out," he said as he pointed to each of the girls in turn with a look between a smile and a smirk. "Right now I'm retiring to my father's bedroom, my new room."

"No," said Amalia. "That is Papa's bed. You can't do that."

"It's my room now, little sister—little nun." He laughed as he walked up the stairs carrying the glass of wine Lucrezia had handed him.

As Stefano slammed the bedroom door, each girl jumped at the shock of the noise. Then they stood still, looking to the top of the stairs, both frozen in place. Slowly, they both turned to look at each other. What had just happened? It had all been so fast, they couldn't comprehend it. After a moment, Lucrezia took Amalia's hand in hers and indicated for them to go into the kitchen.

They sat down at the table. Now what?

Amalia whispered to Lucrezia, "Messer Sacchetti told me not to let him in the house if he showed up. What should I do? He told me to let him know if he came back."

"Well, then, one of us should go over to his office right now."

"I don't want to stay here alone with him in the house. He frightens me." Amalia shivered to think that her own brother scared her.

"I know," admitted Lucrezia. "Me too. I don't want to leave you alone. What can we do? Who will help us? Where is Carlo? What about Maria and Filippo?"

"What about Messer D'Alessandro? Once he agreed to let us live here, he said if there was anything we needed, to be sure to let him know."

"Well, he never really agreed to let us stay, he just stopped talking about it. I don't know," said Lucrezia. "Is this what he had in mind? I don't think so. I still think he would like us gone, and he might just like the idea of the son coming back. I think somehow we have to get word to Messer Sacchetti."

"I agree," said Amalia.

"I'm going to go next door to Maria and Filippo's. You unlock the back door and stay in the kitchen. If he comes down the stairs, go down into the back yard and call me. What do you think? Will that work?"

"Should we involve Maria and Filippo?" asked Amalia.

"We don't have any choice," said Lucrezia. "I need time to get to Messer Sacchetti's, and you can't be here alone. We have to ask someone for help. If they don't want to, then—"

"All right," said Amalia. "I agree. Where is my cape? I want it by the back door." Amalia went into the front room and grabbed her winter wrap and came back into the kitchen. She put it on a chair by the back stairway. "Go, before I lose my courage."

Lucrezia put on her wrap and slipped down the front stairs and out the front door as quietly as she could. Amalia moved a chair so she could sit on it and see the stairway from the kitchen. She was shaking so much, she was sure she would fall down if she didn't sit. How much time passed? It seemed like an eternity as she sat there, staring at the stairs and listening for any noise from the bedroom above.

Where are they? She wondered. What is she doing? Don't panic, she told herself. It's all right; he is not coming down yet. Maybe he's asleep and I don't have to worry. Maybe.

Finally, there was a knock at the front door. Amalia ran down and pulled the door open.

"Hello, Signorina Amalia. I was talking to Lucrezia and we need to check on those roof tiles damaged in the storm." Filippo was talking in a loud voice. "But Filippo, my brother is here. He is asleep in my father's bedroom. I don't think—"

"That's all right. We don't have to go in the bedroom. We won't disturb him, but I want to know how many tiles we need to order. Let's go upstairs. Put on your wrap so you don't get cold out there."

Filippo climbed up on the roof from the loggia so he could examine all of it. He went all along the front edge of the roof, wiggling every tile, and then he went around again. Amalia finally figured out that he was stalling as much as he could and not trying to be quiet about it. He dropped a couple pieces of broken tiles and stomped in a patch of snow, a remnant of the storm, in one corner of the loggia.

"Amalia, I think everything is in good shape. You will need to replace about eight tiles. Shall we go downstairs now? Come along. You can fix some tea, and I'll have a little wine while we talk about how to go about the repair."

"Thank you, Filippo," she said heartily.

They headed down the upper stairway. Then they were in the hallway between the bedrooms, starting to head down to the kitchen and receiving room.

"What's the noise out here?" demanded Stefano as he wrenched open the door of his father's bedroom.

"Well, good day, Stefano. Is that really you? I wouldn't have known except you look so much like your father did as a young man. Remember me? Filippo DeFrancisco. I still live next door to your father's house—well, Amalia's house." Filippo reached out his hand to shake hands with Stefano.

"The storm damaged some of the tiles on the roof, so I just finished checking them to see how many have to be repaired or replaced. I was just going to draw up a contract for Amalia to sign to do the repairs. It isn't extensive damage, but I want to be sure she finds a good tile man to do the repairs."

"She won't be doing the repairs. This is my house now."

"Well, then, who will pay for them? Are you going to assume responsibility for the repairs?"

"No, I'm not paying for anything. Amalia will be going to a convent, and that other one, Lucrezia, will be gone too."

"Come on downstairs, Stefano, and we can talk about it. You've been away a long time. Things change."

"Things are changed, all right. I'm living here now, and I don't need any neighbor sticking his nose in my business."

"Come on downstairs, and we can talk." Filippo took Amalia by the elbow and steered her downstairs and into the kitchen. He reached to get two glasses for wine and said, "Go ahead, Amalia. Fix some tea."

Eventually, Stefano sauntered into the kitchen and took one of the empty chairs. Amalia stayed busy by the stove, revitalizing the fire and preparing to make the tea. Filippo poured some wine for Stefano and himself and sat down.

Maria knocked and came in the front door and came up the stairs, not waiting for Amalia to answer her knock.

"Stefano!" she cried. "I just heard you are back. Let me look at you. Where have you been? You look a lot like your father. How have you been?" She stood before Stefano, inviting him to stand up so she could hug him. Finally he did, but he was obviously not pleased by this gesture.

Stefano sat back down and reached for his wine. Maria sat on the other side of the table still talking, asking questions about where he had been, how he was, and chattering on about what had happened in the gonfalons with all the neighbors since he had left. She went on and on.

Again, the front door opened—no knock this time—and Lucrezia came up the stairs just ahead of Messer Sacchetti. No one saw him, but Carlo had slipped in before the door was closed.

Lucrezia stepped aside, but Messer Sacchetti moved straight forward, approaching the table where Stefano was seated.

"You are Stefano? You look a lot like your father. I am Marcilio Sacchetti, your father's lawyer, and he was also my good friend. You and I have been corresponding over the years but, of course, we haven't met in many years—since you were a child. It's surprising to meet you after all this time. I wrote you about your father's untimely death and that there was no money in his estate. What brings you to Florence?"

"Maybe there isn't any money, but there is the house and property. Knowing Father, it is not indebted in any way."

"I told you in my letter that your father left the house to Amalia, and since she is now of age, she owns it outright."

"Well, I don't agree," said Stefano. "My dear little sister should be in a convent, and I'm here to claim the house as mine."

Again, the front door opened, and Lucia's husband, Luigi, and Giovanni from across the street came in. They strolled over and leaned against the archway between the front room and the kitchen. Lucrezia must have run into them on her way back with Messer Sacchetti, thought Amalia, going on their way to work. They had come to give support to her.

Messer Sacchetti had paused while Luigi and Giovanni came into the room.

Now he said, "No, Stefano, the house is not yours. It is Amalia's, and you are going to have to leave. Now. Perhaps you didn't understand. If you would like to come by my office, I will show you the will, but your father was very explicit."

"I don't care about that. I'm the son, and the house should come to me. She needs to go to a convent where she belongs, and I'm making claim to my dead father's house."

Lucrezia had quietly moved to Amalia's side by the stove and reached now to hold her hand.

Filippo said, "No, Stefano, you need to leave right now. Please, let's not have a scene. We are all here to see to it you leave the house. We don't want anyone to get hurt, so please."

No one wanted to lay hands on Stefano, so everyone just waited, obviously hoping he would get up and walk out the front door. They appeared to be in no hurry, ready to wait, particularly if they could avoid a physical confrontation. If Messer D'Alessandro had been there, he had authority to act as an enforcer, but these were just neighbors. As a lawyer, Messer Sacchetti could say what the law was, but he had no authority to physically remove Stefano. Filippo stood up and Giovanni and Luigi moved forward until the four men surrounded Stefano.

Finally, he stood up, walked over to pick up his heavy wrap and some other belongings there, and then he walked down the stairs. Messer Sacchetti walked him to the door.

As he left, Stefano shouted to Messer Sacchetti, "This isn't the end of this. I want the house, and that girl goes to a convent." With that he turned and walked away.

When Messer Sacchetti reappeared upstairs, he was greeted by laughter and the sound of men slapping each other on their backs. Maria had gone over and was hugging both Amalia and Lucrezia as both girls fell into her embracing arms. Amalia started to go over to Messer Sacchetti, but she found her legs wouldn't work properly. Maria quickly found a chair for her. Messer Sacchetti sat in the chair facing her.

"Thank you, Messer Sacchetti, for your help. I have my house back, but for how long? Surely he will try again."

"Yes, I think he will."

Everyone sat back down to discuss what they had to do to keep Amalia and Lucrezia safe and to keep Stefano out of the house. They would notify the gonfalons authorities, and there would be a watch put on the house. In addition, Carlo announced he had no intention of leaving the house or Amalia until Stefano was no longer a threat to them. Stefano didn't even know about him, and he could be invisible because he was so small, but everyone knew he had the heart of a lion.

No one had heard her enter, but when they finally went back into the front room, Dona Rutia was in her favorite chair, sound asleep and snoring softly. From now on, she was to become a permanent visitor all day, every day, for as long as Stefano's threat lasted.

Life was going to be different now. They thought it would be difficult to concentrate on their sewing and scribing, but it didn't take long to settle into the new pattern. Dona Rutia's presence brought a calm that helped both girls to work. Lucrezia went to the market with a couple of neighbor ladies, and twice, when Amalia had to go to Master Manetti's shop, Giovanni went with her. They never left the house unattended or unlocked, and no one ever left the house without an escort.

Dona Rutia had always enjoyed sitting in what was now her chair in the corner, dozing and watching the girls do their work, but now she had them move her chair closer to the window so she could see the street. She was never inclined to be a nosy neighbor, but she decided that watching the activities on the street might be an enjoyable entertainment for her.

They didn't have to wait long for word from Stefano. In only a couple days, Messer Sacchetti was advised that Stefano was contesting his father's will and was claiming ownership of his father's house. He had hired a lawyer, and his claim was filed with the Podesta, the department of the Florence court system that dealt with wills, lawsuits, and other problems of the popolo. Messer Sacchetti felt that Amalia was safer now that the courts were involved. He felt Stefano probably wouldn't want to do anything to jeopardize his legal claim. Messer Sacchetti petitioned the courts for an early hearing. Amalia would probably be called into court since she was in possession of the house, but Messer Sacchetti did not think she would be allowed to testify.

The waiting time had been excruciating for all of them, especially for Amalia, Lucrezia, and Carlo. This was their home, after all. The day of the hearing finally arrived. The morning Amalia was due to go to the Palazzo del Popolo to meet Messer Sacchetti at the Podesta she was very nervous, mainly because she would have to face her brother again. What could have gone wrong with him that he became so mean-spirited? Why did he dislike her so? She didn't know the answer, but she did know she wanted him out of her life. He had been away for over ten years, so it was no great loss, and she had to admit she was afraid of him.

Lucrezia and Amalia were both puttering around the house, trying to stay busy but not really accomplishing much when there was a knock on the door. Both of them froze. At first, they agreed not to answer to door at all. But what if it was Messer Sacchetti or Giovanni? What to do? The problem was solved for them when Carlo, who had been out running errands for clients, unlocked the door and came up followed by a stranger with a large package that appeared to be quite heavy.

Carlo said, "Amalia, this is Signore Rudolfo. He works for Messer Bracciolini, and he has a delivery for you from Messer Poggio."

"Yes, I met Rudolfo when I visited Messer when he was ill. What can this be?" she said to Rudolfo, "How is Messer Bracciolini? I'm sorry, I haven't been able to come by lately to visit him."

"Carlo comes by regularly to check on things, and Messer Bracciolini is very grateful for your assistance when he was so sick. He is much better now and is leaving tomorrow to join his wife and family in Fiesole. He feels he is finally well enough to travel, thanks to you, and he has concluded his business. He also wants to thank Carlo for the many errands he ran for him while he was still too sick to get out."

While Rudolfo had been talking, Amalia had unwrapped what turned out to be a large fresh ham.

"Oh, my, this is too much. What will we do with all this? How kind of Messer Bracciolini."

Carlo said, "That will be wonderful for the party tonight. Oops."

Lucrezia said, "Carlo, you weren't supposed to say anything."

"I'm sorry. I forgot."

"What 'party'?" asked Amalia, aghast. Rudolfo took the opportunity to exit.

"Well, I'll be going," he said. "Messer Bracciolini said to wish you well and to assure you that all would be fine. Those were his words, whatever it might mean for you." Rudolfo left after Amalia told him to please thank Messer for her.

She turned to the others. "Now what is going on?"

"It's all right, Amalia. The enforcers are planning a small party tonight to celebrate."

"Celebrate what? What if I lose? What can you be thinking? This is crazy. Who are the 'enforcers'?"

Lucrezia said, "Amalia, stop. Everyone wants you to prevail, so they figure they will just act as if you have won. Then nothing can go wrong; you will have to win and keep your house."

"Who else knows about this? How did Messer Poggio know? What 'enforcers'?"

Carlo said, "Everyone knows, of course, and they all wanted to have the party. I guess I might have mentioned it to Marta, and she told Messer Poggio."

"What if I lose? They don't like women owning property. What if they give my house to Stefano?"

Carlo said, "No one wants that to happen."

"That's fine, and I appreciate the thought, but the judges may feel quite differently about it."

Carlo just shrugged and hung his head. Lucrezia had managed to escape into the other room.

"And I didn't know you were going to his house," Amalia admonished Carlo.

"Whenever I'm in that neighborhood, I go by. I know he's a friend of yours, so I just check with Marta to find out how he is doing. You have been busy with other things, but I would have told you if he was sick again. Then he often needs messages delivered, and Rudolfo doesn't know the streets of Florence and isn't always there anyway. He just got back to town yesterday to take Messer Poggio back to Fiesole."

"Yes, Rudolfo said just now he's leaving. I'm sorry I won't get to see him. I didn't know he was leaving."

"Messer Poggio said for me to tell you he will be back in a few months, and he will send word to you then. He knew you were busy, but he says he is sure it will all go well for you. He's a grumpy old man, but Marta said he is actually a good man. I'll take her word for it. He is usually a grump."

"He has been very ill, so be kind."

Carlo patted the huge ham and said, "I'll be kind." They both smiled, and Amalia shook her head at Carlo.

As she walked back into the kitchen, Lucrezia said, "What should we do with it? I guess it can just sit here on the table for now. I'll ask Filippo if he will cook it on his large spit or in that huge oven."

Now it was time to leave. Messer Sacchetti had told Amalia that Lucrezia would not be allowed in the hearing chamber, but he would meet Amalia in the anteroom when the bells rang the tenth hour. Giovanni from across the street said he would walk with Amalia to the Podesta. Messer Sacchetti said he would see her home after the hearing.

That way Giovanni was able to go to work after he checked one last time on the building of his house. He had hired a crew for the actual construction, but he was overseeing the entire project to be sure it was all constructed as he wished. His father-in-law helped whenever Giovanni had to be at the guild office, and between the two of them, they were seeing to it that a fine new house was being built that Giovanni and Beatrice could be proud of.

Over the last few months, the four of them, Amalia and Lucrezia and Giovanni and Beatrice had become good friends. The couple was living with Beatrice's parents in a house smaller than Amalia's house, so things were a little tight. A couple of evenings each week, Giovanni and Beatrice would come by and visit with Amalia, Lucrezia, Carlo, and often Dona Rutia. Beatrice was an excellent baker and would often bring a delicious fruit torte for them to share. Dona Rutia would contribute a fine bottle of wine, much nicer than the Dontarini house wine that they watered down for their everyday drink.

Amalia didn't want to take Giovanni away from his work, but he had insisted upon accompanying her to the Podesta, and she was grateful. Carlo was dedicated to her and would do his best to protect her, but he was just a boy and would be no match if Stefano decided to keep her from the hearing. She was frightened Stefano might even hire some thugs to do his work for him, or even have her assaulted. Yes, she was that afraid of him. She knew she had good cause to fear him, but in the intervening time since he had left her house, she had allowed her imagination to build her brother into a fearsome ogre.

VIII   *The Trial*

Giovanni might walk by Amalia's side to the Podesta for the hearing, but nothing would keep Carlo from her other side. Amalia was glad to have him walking along with them. She was still very nervous, but Carlo's antics kept her and Giovanni laughing. He told them, jokingly, that he saw Stefano coming toward them from around the corner. Then he pantomimed how he would kick Stefano in the shins and punch him, then jump on his back when he fell to the ground. Over and over, each corner they came to, he would meet Stefano all over again and beat him into submission.

By the time the three of them reached the Podesta, Carlo was exhausted from his pretend-fighting, but Amalia had laughed her nerves away. It had all left Giovanni free to keep a good watch against the real Stefano.

Carlo said, "I'll be right here when you come out, and we will walk home. God be with you, Amalia." With that, he sat down on the bottom step against the wall of the Podesta and pulled his cap down over his eyes to wait.

Giovanni went up with Amalia. Messer Sacchetti had given him instructions how to find him, and they had no problem finding the anteroom of the hearing chamber.

"Thank you, Giovanni," said Amalia effusively. "You have been so kind. I'm fine now, I don't want to keep you from work. There is Messer Sacchetti."

"I'm staying with you until you go into the hearing room. Stefano is by the wall at the end of the room, and if Messer Sacchetti were to be called away, I wouldn't want you to be alone. Don't turn around."

"Thank you, Giovanni. I know it will upset me if I have to speak with him. I hope he stays away from me."

"I don't know if you know it, but Lucrezia invited us over for dinner tonight. She is planning a quiet celebration. She has invited all of the 'enforcers' and their wives."

Amalia laughed and said, "Yes, I heard, and I finally figured out who the 'enforcers' were. I think it has grown into a few more than just the 'enforcers.' Leave it to Lucrezia to come up with such a thing. What if it turns out that it's Stefano's house? Is she planning to invite him?"

"No, because that won't happen, so don't even think it."

While he was talking, Giovanni could see that Stefano's lawyer had just restrained him from coming toward them, and he was very glad when Messer Sacchetti joined them.

"Hello, Amalia. How are you feeling today?"

"I'm fine. A little nervous. Messer Sacchetti, you met my neighbor, Giovanni Volini, at my house."

"Yes, I remember the day well," and he smiled at both of them. Thank you for escorting Amalia here."

"I didn't mind at all. Sire, I just noticed that—"

"Yes," said Messer Sacchetti, "I noticed also. Don't worry. I have two men with me, and they will intercede if need be. For his sake, I hope Stefano doesn't cause a scene, but don't worry, Amalia, you are safe."

"Thank you, Messer."

"In that case," said Giovanni, "I will leave. God be with you, Amalia. I will see you tonight."

"Thank you, Giovanni, for everything."

Messer Sacchetti took Amalia's elbow and ushered her into the hearing chamber. This was the trial chamber for the Podesta, the court of the popolo. He showed her where to sit. Since she was a female, she could not sit at the hearing table, but she would be right behind Messer Sacchetti on one side of the room. The judges would be behind the large, wood, raised dais, seated in the three chairs there. When Stefano and his attorney arrived, it looked as though they would be on the other side of the room from her, and she was glad for that.

It was a large room with beautifully carved wood tables, chairs, benches, and carved wood trim. The walls were all painted with battle scenes of old wars fought by Florence before Cosimo had found ways to avoid having to fight wars with Milan, Venice, or Lucca. He had brought peace to Florence. She was very impressed and wondered who had painted them.

Just then Stefano walked into the room without his attorney. He came and sat right next to Amalia, staring at her as he approached her.

"No, Stefano, get up right now and go over to the other side of the room where your attorney will join you."

"Why can't I just sit here next to my sister?"

"Move immediately, Stefano, or I will call the guards, and they will remove you."

"Signore Dontarini, come over here at once," ordered Stefano's attorney in a very commanding voice as he entered the room. With that, Stefano stood up in a leisurely manner, bumping Amalia in the process, and finally made his way to the other side of the room.

"Are you all right, Amalia?" asked Messer Sacchetti.

"Yes," replied Amalia.

"I apologize, I should have known he would try something."

Just then the three judges entered the room and sat in their chairs on the raised dais. After some preliminary discussions and announcements, they asked each attorney to present his case. Stefano Dontarini's attorney would speak first since his client was the one making the claim before the court.

His attorney spoke of how Signore Dontarini had left home at an early age and had not returned until two weeks ago. When he went to his father's house to move back in and live there, his sister had some neighborhood thugs gang up on him and force him to leave. He was his father's only son, and by all rights, he should be the heir to the property that had been in the family for four generations. The law shouldn't allow an underaged, unwed girl with no means of support to inherit, even if she was named as the heir in the father's will. There was sufficient legal precedent in the law that a legitimate son should not be disinherited, and any property, by rights, should come only to him.

Now it was Messer Sacchetti's turn. He told the judges that Signorina Amalia Dontarini was no longer a minor but was now of age and was financially capable of maintaining the house. Indeed, she was employed and earned an income as a scribe for Master Giorgio Manetti. She was capable of supporting herself in an independent manner.

He explained to the judges that Stefano had left home at an early age and had never returned during his father's lifetime; that during his lifetime, his father would have nothing to do with him and that he, Messer Sacchetti, was the sole contact between the two men. He could call witnesses to swear that Signore Dontarini had been drunk on numerous occasions as a young man before leaving Florence and had left Florence owing numerous people considerable sums of money. Further, in his travels to Genoa, Venice, and most recently Milan, he was arrested on numerous occasions for drunkenness. In each city, he had left, owing considerable sums of money to various people. Stefano had told all of these people to look to his father for payment of those debts. Messer Sacchetti presented a paper listing the dates, the people, and the amounts owed by Stefano and amounts paid by his father on his behalf in an effort to keep young Dontarini out of jail and to protect their family name.

Then he presented the will, which stated that those sums of money, plus sums that had been spent when Stefano had gotten in legal difficulties, amounted to over half the value of the house. Those monies, then, should be considered Stefano's inheritance. Nothing more should be paid to him. It also clearly stated in the will that Giuliano left the house solely to Signorina Amalia Dontarini.

Stefano stood up and said, "That isn't true. I never asked my father to pay my debts. He didn't care about me; he was just protecting himself and his reputation. What did I care about that? The house should be mine. I'm his son."

The middle judge said, "Sit down, signore. Allow your attorney to present your case."

Messer Sacchetti continued. He pulled out a stack of papers from his carry case and presented them to the judges, saying that he could prove that Signore Dontarini did demand that his father pay the bills. He reminded them that it was the custom in Florence for a father to be responsible for the actions of his children. He expressed the opinion that although property usually was left to a son, he felt in this case Signore Dontarini had forfeited his claim to all rights by his conduct, as well as the fact that so much money had been paid out in his behalf. The young girl was entitled to inherit enough to maintain herself, and the only thing Messer Dontarini had left to give her was the house, since his son had continually drained him of all cash funds and savings. Most regrettably, Messer Sacchetti expressed to the judges, this son was neither fit nor worthy to inherit the house, the last possession of his father.

The middle judge said that it was usual for a son to inherit the family property, and there was much precedent for a will to be overturned if it was felt by the proper authorities that the son was entitled. Certainly, it was customary that property stay in the hands of male heirs.

The judge was interrupted by a man coughing in the back corner of the room. Amalia glanced around at him; she had not been aware that anyone was sitting back there.

There was a lengthy pause. Then the middle judge looked at the other two judges, and they both nodded.

The judge said, "While there is precedent, we do not feel in this case that

Signore Dontarini is fit to inherit the house. We see no reason to overturn Master Giuliano Dontarini's will. Further, the sums paid out in the son's behalf over the last nine years should be considered as his equitable inheritance, and he shall have no further claim against the estate. This claim is therefore dismissed by this court."

"No, that isn't fair! That house should come to me!" yelled Stefano. "I'm entitled to it!" But by this time, the judges had left the room. Turning to Amalia, he continued yelling, "You have no right to that house. It's mine."

"Stop this, Stefano," said Messer Sacchetti. "It will gain you nothing. The hearing is over, and I suspect even your attorney will now tell you that you have no further claim against the house or Amalia."

His attorney said, "If you had told me the extent of your indebtednesses, I would never have brought a claim of this nature. You lied to me."

"I did not. He's lying. Most of what he said isn't true."

"Yes, it is, Stefano," said Messer Sacchetti. "Your father had me get sworn proof of all the debts and copies of the legal proceedings in each of the cities. I have everything here, everything is documented. I thought your father was acting excessively, but it appears he understood exactly the type of person you had become.

"Stefano, I will ask the judges to demand you stay away from the house, so if you cause any trouble, you will be back in the courts but as the responder next time. Please, let this be the end of this matter. Go your way and start a new, better life. You are on your own now, with no one to fall back on. If you keep living the life you have been leading, you will wind up back here but in Le Stinche, and no one wants that for you."

"What do you care? You're here for HER," yelled Stefano.

"Stefano, I was your father's friend, and I tell you these things as his friend. I've known you since you were a boy, and I don't want to see you go down this terrible path. Your father can't help you any longer."

"I just want my house!" Stefano yelled, and then he stormed out of the hearing room.

The door slammed as he left, and there was a heavy silence in the room. Stefano's attorney then left in disgust. The man who had been sitting in the back corner was nowhere to be seen, and now it was just Amalia and Messer Sacchetti. Amalia could barely breathe. She began to tremble from head to foot. She hugged herself to try to make it stop, but it wouldn't.

When Messer Sacchetti turned and came to lead her out, she said, "I don't think I can stand or walk right now. I'm sorry. How foolish of me, but I can't."

Messer Sacchetti sat down next to her and took her two hands in his.

They just sat there for several moments.

"What happened to him, Messer Sacchetti? How could he have been the son of my dear mother and father? They were both so gentle and kind, and he is so hateful and filled with anger. How could that happen?"

"I don't know, Amalia. You can well imagine what a great disappointment it was for your father and for your mother while she was still alive. They were committed to trying to help him in every way in hopes that he would change his ways and come home, but it never happened, and I think you can understand that now.

"As I told you previously, your father would have nothing to do with him directly, but he would not abandon him either. That's why he had me intervene. Your father did all he could. He did the scribing in order to earn the extra money it cost him to rescue your brother each time he got in debt. He had already run through all their savings, part of which should have been your dowry.

"You have to understand, Stefano drinks a great deal and has for all these years he has been gone, wherever he lived. Perhaps that caused the other problems: the gambling and sordid lifestyle. He was drinking even before he left Florence. That is what caused the rift between your father and mother and Stefano, the drinking and the gambling."

"Messer Sacchetti, I never knew any of this. Stefano is nine years older than I am, so I guess I was maybe eight or nine when he left, but I barely remember him. Even what I do remember, it seems he was never at home, at least to my knowledge."

"Your mother and father tried to shield you from it as best they could. With so many years between the two of you, they just didn't want you hurt by it all. And there were other problems as well. I don't know if you are aware, but your mother suffered several miscarriages before and after Stefano and a stillborn birth. Your birth was a very difficult one, and your mother almost died. They knew there would be no chance of any more children, so you became that much more precious to them."

"I had no idea." Amalia sat in silence for a moment. Then she said, "Messer Sacchetti, I owe you a great deal for helping me. I don't know what I would have done if you hadn't stepped in and taken care of all of this." She waved her arm around the room. "I must owe you a great deal of money."

"Amalia, your father was older than I was, and when I was a young lawyer, he helped me a great deal. He was very active with several of the guilds as a notary, and he would recommend me whenever it came to his attention that one of his clients or acquaintances needed an attorney. I have made a great deal of money, and made many excellent contacts, thanks to your father, so money was never an object between your father and me, I am indebted to him in other ways, not just money. He was a good and true friend and helped me in many ways over the years.

"Money will never be an object between us either. You are a fine girl, and your father was very proud of you. He would be very proud and pleased with what you are doing now, I am sure of that. I will always be there for you if you need me.

"And now, let me see if I can get a moment of the judge's time and secure the document I spoke of to prevent Stefano from bothering you in the future in case he chooses to stay in Florence."

At that, Amalia froze with a renewed sense of panic, but Messer Sacchetti said, "Don't worry. Stay here, and I will send my young associate in to sit with you until I return. You will be safe, and I'm confident Stefano is gone by now, at least from the building, if not from Florence."

Messer Sacchetti left, and after a short time, a young man who seemed not too much older than Amalia came in and said, "Good day, Signorina Amalia. My name is Riccardo de Riccardi. I work with Messer Sacchetti. May I sit?"

"Of course, sire. You say you work with Messer Sacchetti. Are you an attorney? You seem very young."

Riccardo laughed. "I am one of those people with a baby face. I am almost thirty, but I know I look to be twenty. I am married and have a son over a year old. His name is also Riccardo, but we call him Rico. My wife, Teresa, is only a little older than you."

They chatted for several minutes, just making small talk to pass the time. Then Riccardo mentioned that although he liked being a lawyer very much, he loved architecture and had always climbed all over any construction sites going on in Florence. Of course, there were many. Many of the rich bankers were following the Medici lead and building large palazzos for themselves, each outdoing the other, using the Medici design: Rucellai, Strozzi, Guido, and so many more.

He chuckled, then said, "Once they were doing an addition on the Signoria, I had been watching the progress. The architect was one I was friendly with. I was only seventeen, and he kept telling me I should become an architect rather than waste my time studying to be a lawyer. He warned me that I was going to be stuck inside four walls all the time instead of outside in the open air on construction sites. I told him my heart was set on being a lawyer, but I could still enjoy his construction sites. On this particular day, I decided to go up the tower of the Signoria and take in the view of all of Florence, and the guard stopped me.

"'No, Messer Riccardo,' he said, 'you can't go up there now. We have a special prisoner in the Alberghetto, and no one is allowed to go up.'

"I had forgotten that this was where they were holding Cosimo de' Medici, in what they called the 'Little Inn,' the cell up in the top of the tower. He was there on charges of treason for contributing to the failure of the war against the Pisans. They were trumped up charges, but Cosimo wasn't in favor of the war, and Signore Rinaldo degli Albizzi was. Cosimo was the rising star in Florentine politics, and Rinaldo wanted to eliminate him. Cosimo was in favor of trade and commerce, the production of wool and silk cloth, leather and gold—all the things that were making Florence very rich and the center of the trading routes between the Mediterranean world and all of Europe. Signore Rinaldo degli Albizzi was head of one of the old noble families, and they liked to keep their condotierre and mercenary armies busy making war against Pisa, Siena, Lucca, or Milan—wherever they could trump up a reason for a battle. Cosimo was opposed to the wars because they cost a lot of money for the city causing taxes to be levied on all the people, including the poor. Plus, they interfered with trade and manufacturing. Albizzi had a lot of the old noble families on his side, so he brought charges against Cosimo. They were calling for Cosimo's execution, but the monk, Ambrosio Traversiri—you've heard of him, I'm sure—was at the height of his influence then, and he said no, that would not happen.

"Well, now what was Albizzi to do with him? They knew they could not imprison him here in the Le Stinche forever. One of the guards told me that Cosimo would not eat or drink anything the guards provided, only food and drink brought to him by his own family. He was that afraid that Albizzi would try to poison him. Finally, one of the guards started sharing meals with him so he would know it wasn't poisoned.

"Even from that prison, Cosimo was able to exercise his influence. He used his money to buy support all over town, and eventually it was decided he would go into exile from Florence. "The problem for Florence was that when Cosimo was driven out, he took his bank and all its money with him to Venice. Trade dwindled to nothing in Florence, and the merchants starved. There was no manufacturing, because there was no importing of the raw materials or exporting of the finished goods. Signore Albizzi was taking the whole of Florence back into the darkness of the ways of the past, but the people had seen the light of a better way. Everyone cried out against Rinaldo's oppressive measures, and after a year, the Signoria voted to invite Cosimo to return.

"Within a year, Florence was prosperous again, and Rinaldo degli Albizzi and his entire family and all his friends were sent into exile. Cosimo wasn't taking any chances. Little by little, he filled the Signoria with his people and established committees full of his people to do a lot of the work of the city.

"The Signoria is still powerful and governs the day to day affairs of the city, but it is said all the important decisions are made in the Medici palazzo. That is where the real power of Florence rests. Even when foreign dignitaries come to town, their first stop is the Medici home. That is why he needs that new palazzo he is building. Have you seen it?"

"I accidentally went near there a couple weeks ago, and it was chaos. I will avoid that part of town in the future, if possible. It looked as if the entire block— more than just the one block—was disrupted."

"Well, between the palazzo and the gardens, yes. It's going to be magnificent when it's finished. Michelozzo is the architect."

"From what I saw, it didn't look very special. It was huge and very imposing, to be sure, but not very attractive."

Riccardo smiled. "That's Cosimo. He doesn't want it to appear that he is rich. Powerful, yes, but he doesn't feel there should be an outward display of wealth. The Sumptuary Laws would give people grounds to frown on an ostentatious building. I understand his father had always warned Cosimo not to flaunt their wealth.

"That is actually what caused his falling-out with Brunelleschi. They were good friends, and Cosimo had commissioned Brunelleschi to construct or redo several buildings in Florence and even outside the city—Fiesole and elsewhere. Brunelleschi had designed a beautiful palazzo, but Cosimo felt it was too ostentatious, so he hired Michelozzo. He is using a lot of Brunelleschi's ideas on the inside, but the outside is very austere.

"I could take you in to see it if you like. Not right now while things are so hectic, but in a few months, when things will be more finished, and it will be safe."

"I would love to see it. That would be wonderful. Can just anyone walk in there?"

"No, but as I said, I have been visiting these construction sites for so long, all the builders and guildsmen and architects know me. I know Michelozzo quite well. I sometimes wonder if I did make the wrong choice, but I love what I'm doing and can't imagine not being a lawyer.

It's funny, though, most of my clients are in the building trade, and I understand the technical problems when they have a legal issue about something. I think they like that I understand when they are talking about construction, so maybe I have joined my two worlds."

"Riccardo, have you ever met Cosimo?"

"Oh, no. Whenever he is there, no one is allowed in."

"This may be very inappropriate, but my friends have arranged for a gathering tonight to celebrate my victory. Of course, I told them I didn't know if I would prevail, but they were confident, and so there is to be a party. I would like to invite you and your wife to join us if you would like."

"Thank you for the kind invitation. I will check with my wife to see whether she has any plans for us. May I let you know later?"

"I think they have invited most of the neighbors, so there will be plenty of food and drink. Just come if you are able. And bring Rico also. There will be children there. Of course, I don't have any, but several of my neighbors do. I don't know what they would have done if we had lost the case. I asked them if they would have the party anyway to welcome their new neighbor, Stefano."

They both laughed.

"I'm glad it didn't turn out that way. I don't think I would have been invited to attend.

"Ah, here is Messer Sacchetti."

He had good news. The judge had issued the order that Stefano could not come on the property of the house nor attempt to enter the house. He instructed Riccardo to take the paper downstairs to the office where it had to be filed, and he and Amalia left the Podesta.

Messer Sacchetti was in a hurry to get Amalia home, and she was in a hurry to get home. Carlo was waiting where he'd promised to be. With just a quick look at Amalia, he tossed his cap in the air and smiled a victory smile that lit up his face. Then the three of them wended their way as quickly as they could through the crowded streets of Florence. Messer Sacchetti made some small talk along the way, but he was keeping an eye out for Stefano or any ruffians looking for trouble, as was Carlo from his much lower vantage point. As soon as they were away from the Piazza della Signoria and in their own gonfalons, Carlo knew who were strangers and who belonged there. His vantage point might have been lower, but it was probably better.

Once she was home and inside the house, Amalia was greeted by Lucrezia, who came over and hugged her. Lucrezia thanked Messer Sacchetti for all he had done for them, because she was also the beneficiary of his legal services.

Dona Rutia harrumphed, roused herself, took a sip of wine, and smiled at the three of them.

"My dear, I knew it would turn out this way. Otherwise, where would I spend my afternoons? I don't think Stefano would have left the door open with the chair in the corner just for me."

They all laughed, and Messer Sacchetti said he would leave.

"When your next tax bill is published, we will talk. We will probably want to apply for a reduction. In the meantime, if there is anything further you need, just let me know."

Amalia thanked him profusely, and he left.

"Now we can start working on the party," said Carlo.

They all laughed and did just that, except Dona Rutia, who had nodded off again.

This was the Podesta, the court of the popolo, the people,
and Le Stinche, the prison for men. Now it is the Bargello

IX   *The Party*

The night of the party was behind them now, but what a night it was. All their neighbors came and everyone brought a dish, each rivaling the other. The party had started out in their large receiving room, but since the night was mild, it had overflowed down into the loggia and even back into the garden. The wine flowed all evening; some bottles and jugs were from other areas of Italy that everyone enjoyed sampling, for Florentines did love their wine.

Beatrice brought one of her delicious tortes, and her parents came with her and Giovanni. Giovanni brought a friend along who played his lute and sang for everyone in a beautiful tenor voice. Amalia was wishing it had been a different setting and not so crowded and noisy, because he truly had a beautiful voice. She would like to have been able to enjoy it in a proper setting. He and Lucrezia talked several times in the course of the evening, and whenever he played a tune and sang, Lucrezia would wander over to listen. As it turned out, they spent a good bit of the evening together, either with others or off in the garden talking to each other.

Lucia brought a lamb stew, Maria a risotto with cheese and vegetables, Vittoria, Claire, Juliana, Lisa each prepared something delicious, and their husbands brought fiascos of wine. Filippo had cooked the haunch of pork that Poggio had sent to them all afternoon, and the enthusiastic guests ate the fresh roast right down to the bone. From that bone, the next day Lucrezia made a delicious soup they would share with several of the neighbors.

Amalia's friends, Caterina, Costanza, and Hortensia came. Costanza was with her husband, but Hortensia was alone because her husband was in Lucca on business. Caterina came with her two friends, but she had arranged for the young man she was seeing to come. They were both hoping their families would come to an agreement about their marriage.

Riccardo and his wife Teresa did come and formed an immediate friendship with Giovanni and Beatrice. Architecture and building were the common interests of the two men, and one-year-old babies the bond for the two young women.

Messer D'Alessandro even came by and wished Amalia well now that the legalities were over. He spoke at length with Messer Riccardi, then chatted with several of the other men. Two of the ladies who had bought dresses from Lucrezia came with their husbands, as did Master Vicenti. He thought that the following Monday might be a good time to go to the fulling mills and weaving shops, now that they weren't preoccupied with other matters, and the weather had improved. Lucrezia couldn't have been happier.

Dona Rutia, in her raspy voice that was somewhere between metal scraping and an owl screeching, managed to get herself out of her chair and click her glass to get everyone's attention.

"I have known both these girls for many years and have visited with them over the past year almost every day. We have eaten together and laughed together and—now what was I going to say—oh, yes, I need another glass of wine." She sat back down, holding the glass out for someone to fill.

Everyone laughed and said it was the best toast ever. Filippo said he agreed it was a great toast, but he just wanted to add for everyone to enjoy this wonderful night celebrating Amalia's well-deserved good fortune.

"Let God's grace fall upon all under this roof," he finished, and everyone cheered. Several wine jugs were passed around again and then again.

Padre Bernardo was there early on and chatted with Amalia. "I am so glad I was called to Rome and wasn't here during the months following your father's death. Once I got to Rome and remembered, I berated myself for not getting you settled into a convent before I left Florence. And I had also forgotten to mention it to Padre Piero. I couldn't be happier for you and for your success. You and Lucrezia are making lives for yourselves that seem to suit both of you. I think I would have been forcing you to do something that would have been against your nature."

"Thank you, Padre Bernardo. I agree with you. I am quite sure I would have been very unhappy in a cloistered convent. I didn't know what else I could do, but as things turned out, I think Papa would be pleased with what I am doing. He loved scribing, and I always feel it brings me closer to him when I do it. I ask him to guide my hand before I start each new manuscript."

"Yes, I do believe your father would not only be pleased with your choices but very proud of you for the way you have conducted yourself. You have certainly gone against some conventions, but you have done it gracefully and without offense. Your lifestyle is certainly against the customs of our city, but you are both good girls, and you and Lucrezia have made a good home for yourselves and little Carlo. God moves in mysterious ways, and I believe you are held in his light.

"I'm going to leave now so I don't inhibit anyone's good time. I am always here for you, child, both of—all three of you."

"Thank you. You were a good friend to my father as well as his religious guide, and I am very glad you are here for me also. Good night, Padre."

The festivities continued, and several people had a bit too much wine in the course of the evening. A man had come with Alfonsina and Franco Lades from down the street, and this man now approached Amalia, commenting on how unusual it was for the Podesta to give property to a woman when there was a man in the family to inherit.

Amalia said it was her father's wish.

The man said that this could only happen in Cosimo's Florence, that he didn't know why he was spending time in this city. The old Republic was dead, and now Florence wasn't fighting wars for her honor anymore. Florence was just a bunch of greedy merchants making money for the even greedier bankers.

Amalia responded that, no, Florence was at peace, and the people prospered. The guilds thrived in ways that wars didn't allow, and trade flourished.

"Now," she said, "with peace and prosperity, we have time to think about many things. We can enjoy the beauty of our world, the beauty of God's creation and His magnificent gift to us. We also have time to appreciate art and music. There is a better life for everyone."

"Hah," he said. "Do you really think that obscene David by that Donatello is art and beauty?"

"I haven't seen the David of which you speak, although, of course, I have heard tell of it. But for well over a thousand years, since the fall of the Roman Empire, we have been buried in darkness and ignorance with famines, plagues, and wars decimating the population. Is that what you would wish for us?"

"It was God's will."

"Well, maybe now it is God's will that we

enjoy His wonderful gift, the beauty of nature all around us, and seek to recreate that in art instead of just trying to recapture the old scenes from the Bible. Those scenes are beautiful, but can we not appreciate and enjoy both? If we are all to go to Dante's Hell and die from the plague that strikes us every few years and never appreciate nature and the beauty around us, if we are never to enjoy happiness, why live at all?"

"Girl, how do you come to these brash opinions?"

"My father read Cicero and Livy and many other books to me, opening my mind. Who could read Lucretius and not appreciate our glorious world?"

"Your father was wrong to teach you these things. You overreach yourself. You are too opinionated for a girl, and those opinions are sacrilegious." The man then turned and immediately went down the stairway and out of the house.

Amalia was trembling with frustration that quickly grew into a fury. She stumbled backward until she fell against the wall to brace herself.

A voice beside her whispered, "You must be more careful when you voice such opinions, not because they are false but because they are new, and your position in the commune is still fragile.

"Fortunately he is a foreigner and of no consequence and will probably be gone tomorrow, but another time it could be dangerous."

She finally gathered herself and turned to confront this voice to see only the back of his cape as he made his exit down the same stairway near where they were standing.

She looked around to find Lucrezia to ask who those men were, but then she remembered that Lucrezia was probably still downstairs in the back of the garden, sitting on the bench under their pear tree with the gentleman with the beautiful voice. She knew Lucrezia had not seen either of those men—and probably hadn't noticed much of anyone else either.

After that night, everyone in the neighborhood agreed it was the best party ever, with lots of good food, good wine, plenty of singing and music, and such a special reason for a party. The person—two—three—persons they all loved and who were so deserving had prevailed. Now the three of them were secure with a roof over their heads, a special roof over three very special heads.

X   *Three Paths*

Once they had cleaned up after the party, they spent the next day getting back into their normal routine of sewing, scribing, and running errands. This was a relaxed and very enjoyable time for all three of them after the emotional turmoil of the last several weeks. They did have an unexpected visitor early on Saturday morning, however. Lucrezia had gone down the back stairs out of the kitchen to take a bucket of scraps down to her compost pile. Amalia was just finishing her breakfast when she heard Lucrezia coming back up the stairs.

"Look what I just found curled up on those sacks at the bottom of the stairs," said Lucrezia.

She handed a little ball of fur to Amalia. The kitten immediately started to purr, even though Amalia could feel it was cold and painfully thin.

"Oh, Lucrezia, do we have any milk left?"

"No, but we have some leftover fish from last night on the last of our ice. It might like a little of that even more. I wonder where it came from. I'm going to go back out and see if I can find the mother."

When she came back, the report wasn't good. The mother had been injured but had made it back into the corner of the shed in the back of their garden, where it had apparently been living with her kits. There she had died, and two other kittens were also dead. She would have to ask Carlo to dig a hole so she could bury them. This appeared to be the only survivor.

In the meantime, Amalia had fed him some of the fish, and he was now curling up in Amalia's lap and making himself very much at home. They didn't know what to do with him, but they knew they didn't have the heart to put him back out in the cold. He would never survive by himself.

"You poor little thing," Amalia said, holding the kitten up in front of her. "Your mama and siblings are all dead. You are the sole survivor. Lucrezia, we should call him Solo."

"So we are keeping him? If you're naming him, you will never be able to part with him."

"Well, when he gets a little bigger he will keep the mice out of the grain. That would be a good thing, don't you think?"

"Amalia, we don't—Oh, he is so cute. Your mother had a cat many years ago that she loved, remember?"

"I do. It was black with white feet, nothing like this little tiger."

Later, when Amalia started to do her scribing, the kitten again curled up in her lap and purred in absolute contentment. It seemed to know it had found its home.

Carlo came tumbling in later in the afternoon, cold from being on the streets for much of the day. Spring was overdue, and the previous evening had been a brief interlude of fine weather that had passed quickly. By morning, the cold had returned. The cold lingered long and hard this year; everyone was tired of it and the sickness it brought with it.

Amalia fixed everyone a cup of warm brew, and Carlo curled up in front of the fireplace after putting another log on the fire. He announced that he had all sorts of gossip, but first he had to tell Amalia that Master Manetti wanted her to come by his shop first thing Monday morning.

"Thank you, Carlo. I just picked up this manuscript the other day. I wonder what he wants."

"I don't know," said Carlo, "but he is going on a trip, so maybe it has something to do with that. He is going to Siena first. Then, if the weather breaks, he and the others are going on to Rome. A couple of the artists working in Gozzoli's shop are going and another book dealer and two merchants. They say the weather is supposed to turn warm next week, but they have been saying that for two weeks now."

He continued with his gossip: "Marta heard that Messer Poggio made it to Fiesole, and Rudolfo is back to do some work on the house now that Messer is gone. Master Ferino died last night, so do we have to go to the funeral?"

"Yes, Carlo," Lucrezia and Amalia said in unison.

"Too bad. I hate them."

"Nobody likes them, Carlo, but it is something we must do to honor Master Ferina and to comfort Dona Maria. You like her, don't you?" asked Lucrezia.

"I guess. What is that in your lap, Amalia?"

"It's a little kitten that Lucrezia found this morning. Its mother and siblings are dead."

Lucrezia said, "That reminds me, Carlo. Before dark, would you dig a hole in the very back of the yard so I can bury the mother and her other kits?"

"Sure. I'll bury her if you want. Oh, and more: Dona Evangelina had her baby. It's a boy, and Master Alberto says to come by next week if you like. Lucia said to come by tomorrow to pick up that cushion, if you still want it, and Signore Castillo said he has the tiles. Once the weather warms up, he and Roberto will fix the roof.

"Is that all?" asked Lucrezia.

"Well, that's all for you. Paolo said he found a wheel for the cart we are building, so if it's okay, I'll go over there after Mass tomorrow. Let me see your kitten."

Carlo took the kitten and snuggled with him. Before long, both were sound asleep, the kitten tucked up under Carlo's chin against his chest in front of the fireplace on Carlo's favorite pillows.

Monday morning came with a gentle drizzle that was usually the forerunner of warmer weather. Lucrezia was off to meet Master Vicenti to go to the fulling mills and the weavers' shops. Their outing had been delayed these several weeks when they had been so preoccupied with the legalities related to Stefano's "visit," but now it was finally going to happen. Amalia was dressed to go across town to Master Manetti's shop, Carlo was heading out for his daily errand rounds that would lead him who knew where, and Solo was curled up in a snug box under the stove in the kitchen, having already taken care of his necessaries in another box in the corner of the back of the room.

In the late afternoon, Amalia was the first one home. She immediately started the fire, as the house was chilled. Then she relit the fire in the stove so she could start their dinner. She had so much to tell and no one to tell it to. She took out some of the meat from the iced box in the storeroom and started a stew, She cut up some vegetables, put them in, seasoned the stew, and put it to simmer. Then she went to change her clothes, as she had worn one of her nicer dresses today to Master Manetti's shop. She was glad that she had.

By the time she came downstairs, Lucrezia and Carlo were both home, standing in the entry to the kitchen and both talking at the same time.

"You can't believe what happened to me today—"

"Wait till you hear what happened—"

Amalia chimed right in, "My day was so exciting—"

They moved to the kitchen table, each telling snippets of their stories.

Finally, Lucrezia said, "No, this is not going to work. One of us has to tell a story, then the next, then the next. We can't all three talk at once or we'll never hear anything."

"All right," said Carlo. "You go first, but hurry up because mine is the best. I know it."

Lucrezia told her story of going to the fulling mills and the Gora Canal down by the River Arno and seeing the men working in the ice cold waters, cleaning the wool that had been shorn from the sheep and purchased in all areas of the world to be brought to Florence. The men couldn't stay in the water very long, even though they had very heavy leather boots on their feet and legs, but the wool had to be cleaned of all the sand and grime before anything more could be done to it. Siena had fulling mills long before Florence started processing wool, but now Florence exceeded all the surrounding towns and cities in cloth production with probably two thousand factories in the city.

Master Vicenti explained to Lucrezia that this was why the guilds had become so important in Florence. The workmen had very hard lives. The guilds made sure they were treated fairly, not only getting paid properly and in a timely way but protected in every possible way from dangerous or unhealthy work. This was the importance of the guilds and why they now had so much power in the politics of Florence.

Back many years ago, the workers had actually revolted and won out over the nobles. That was when they had taken control of the Signoria. It was called the Ciompi, and even though the nobles now had regained their power, each one of the major guilds had a representative in the Signoria. Two men represented the fourteen minor guilds. Much of the city's politics was discussed at the meetings held

weekly in each of the guilds' halls for each of the trades: the wool manufacturers, bankers, goldsmiths, international merchants, butchers, and so on. Within the cloth guild, there were the fullers and millers, the carders and spinners, the dyers, the weavers, the combers, and more.

Master Vicenti explained to Lucrezia that although Cosimo de' Medici was the uncrowned leader of Florence, he worked very closely with the guilds and the people, "Il Popolo." His power came because the poor people appreciated all he did for them. He organized a charity, the Buonomini, through a confraternity at

San Martino of the twelve richest men in Florence to work closely with the guilds for the benefit of workers that needed help. This was a great part of his strength as the leader of Florence.

"Next, Master Vicenti took me to where they do the dying and told me about the plants used, like the desiccated eggs of the tiny Kermes scale, an insect that lives on the sap of the Kermes Oak and is used for the scarlet red cloaks worn by all the bankers. It is so tiny, it takes a large quantity to do the dying, so it is guarded as if it were gold. That is what makes the material so expensive. Only the bankers can afford it. The Murex snail is another one worth more than gold. Master Vicenti showed me one of the snails. It is where we get the purple dyes. Can you imagine? The secrets of creating and processing the dyes are protected because of the cost. Those secrets are kept in the family and only passed on from one generation to another.

"So much of our trading has to do with importing these various dyes into Florence from all around the Mediterranean. Some of them I actually knew, but some I had never heard of.

"Then there are the mordants used to stabilize the dyes, like alum, so the color won't wash out of the garment. For different fabrics, all different mordants are used: tannin, oak galls, salt, sumac, potash, stale urine, ammonia, and more. These are also closely guarded secrets, but I have to be aware of their uses and purposes in order to evaluate different fabrics.

"There is so much to learn, and he arranged for me to go back next week to work with Master Tommasso and learn more about the dying process. It is so complicated but so important for me to understand this, particularly the mordants. The cloth might look good, but if the mordant is not correct, it will fade in no time. I knew we used stale urine, vinegar, and ammonia, but alum is the main mordant now, and it has to be imported from the area of the Black Sea beyond Constantinople.

"Then we went by a carding and then a spinning shop. I was somewhat familiar with these, because my mother had a wheel years ago, and I remembered a lot about it. Next were several weaving shops, with all different grades of wool making different grades of yarn, making different grades of fabrics. I will have to understand how each step contributes to the final fabric and what makes the best fabrics and the poor ones, and how to tell the difference. We didn't finish going to all the places he wanted to take me—we never got to any silk shops. Then we went back to his shop so he could introduce me to a few of his workers and discuss what he wanted to propose to me.

"He has seen some of the dresses made from my original designs, and he gave me a roll of paper. He would like for me to develop more designs, and he would like me to hire a young girl he introduced to me who would work for me just as a seamstress. That will leave me free to do the designing, cutting, and fitting.

"As we know, the merchant moved out of the shop downstairs a week ago. Well, Master Vicenti knows about that, and he thinks I should take over the shop and have customers come there to see my designs. He thinks it would work, and I could have some sample dresses for them to see.

"You know I have been so overwhelmed, orders have been piling up, and I can't catch up, and not only because we have had other things on our minds these past weeks. I was already thinking I had too much work for me to do alone, but he has just come up with a solution before I had the time or the courage to deal with it. I kept pushing away the idea of hiring someone, but he says this is what needs to be done. What do you think?"

"How exciting, Lucrezia! I won't charge you rent for the shop, of course, but it will leave us without that income."

"No, Master Vicenti says with a cloth shop in the front, it will give him an outlet for his fabrics on this side of town, and he will pay the rent. I can display some dresses in the front and do the sewing in the back of the shop. We will only have fabrics appropriate for the type of garments I would be making, and he would change it seasonally. He would store the other fabrics in his warehouse over by Santa Croce. He would own the fabrics but will give me a share of any fabrics sold in my store. Oh, Amalia, it is so exciting! I just can't get the words out fast enough!"

"Does he need someone to cart the fabrics back and forth? I have a cart and can do that! How much will he pay me?" asked Carlo.

With that, they all laughed and poured some more of their watered wine.

Amalia got out some dried fruits and a piece of cheese for them to share. "I don't know, Carlo. I don't even have the shop yet."

"But you will," said Carlo. "I think it sounds like a great idea."

"I do too," said Amalia. "I hadn't realized you were under so much pressure. Is there anything I can do to help you? I can spare a little time. I can do some straight sewing for you."

"That is what he wants me to hire this girl to do, and he said—and she also told me—she can start right away. I told her I would give her an answer tomorrow."

"Well, where do we put her?" asked Amalia. "The front room is large enough, I suppose. She could be over there against the wall."

Lucrezia said, "She would only be here while she is sewing; then we would have the room back to ourselves for the evenings. Do you think Dona Rutia will object?"

"No, of course not; not if it means good things for one of us. Is she a nice girl? Did you get to talk to her at all?"

"Yes, I did. If she weren't pleasant, I wouldn't even consider the idea. And it will only be for a short time, just until I get the shop set up downstairs."

"Of course. Well, then, we are off on a new adventure. When do we start? Master De Giovanni is gone, but we have to get the shop ready."

Carlo jumped up and said, "We can start right away. I can get some of my partners to come and clean out the shop tomorrow. Then we will see what has to be done."

"Partners? Who are your partners?" Lucrezia asked, laughing.

"Paolo, Gino, and Jacko. We own the cart together that we just finished building. Now we need merchandise to cart in it, and we need other things to do. I have responsibilities."

"Do you think I can do this?" asked Lucrezia, a note of self-doubt in her voice.

"Yes!" said Carlo and Amalia together. Another glass of their well-watered wine and a chunk of bread with their cheese, and they were laughing together and clinking their glasses.

Lucrezia said, "All right, enough about me. There is more to tell, but it will keep. I want to hear your adventure, Carlo."

"No, mine is the best so I want to go last. You go, Amalia, and make it shorter than Lucrezia's. I'm getting hungry."

Lucrezia got up and started serving the stew Amalia had fixed earlier.

Carlo walked over and picked up the kitten who had just climbed out of his box and was stretching himself.

"Well, you were right, Carlo," said Amalia. "Master Manetti is going to Rome at the end of this week, and he will be gone for at least several weeks. Antonio will keep the shop open but only for the store and the supplies, not the manuscripts or the scribing. He took me over to meet Messer Vespasiano da Bisticci near San

Marco. He has many copyists working directly for him. He has over forty scribes working on Cosimo's books and manuscripts alone. I am going to be working for him while Master Manetti is away since he really doesn't know how long he will be gone. Messer Bisticci wants me to add more of the artwork on the manuscripts, and he will pay me more. They are also to be done on a finer grade of paper. He seems very nice, although he is very quiet and serious. I'm not sure, but I think I will like the arrangement.

"After that, Master Manetti had Messer Bisticci's permission to take me in to see the library at San Marco and I saw the library where all of Messer Niccolo Niccoli's books are shelved. His books and manuscripts were the start of the library Cosimo has built there where people can come and borrow a book. Well, I can't borrow a book, but Messer Bracciolini or maybe even Master Manetti could. Isn't that wonderful?

Nicolo asked Cosimo to do this for him in his will. Cosimo had been paying his expenses for years, and Niccolo owed him a great deal of money. That is why he left Cosimo his entire library.

"Maybe someday you or I may be able to borrow a book or at least see those wonderful books. Master Manetti said there is nothing like it in the whole world. What a thrill it was just to see such a vast collection of manuscripts.

"Anyway, Mr. Manetti will be gone, and I have a new contact for getting my manuscripts to copy. It will be so exciting. As I said, Messer Bisticci wants a lot more of my artwork in the front and the beginning of the chapters or other places to enhance the sale value of the books to be sent north to France, Germany, and England. I love doing that.

"He told me something very interesting. He told me that all the customers in those northern countries prefer books scribed by Florentine copyists. Apparently, our script is the most legible of all the many scriptoriums."

They were finished with dinner now, and they quickly cleaned up. Then they moved into the receiving room by the fireplace to hear Carlo's story.

"Well, from what I already told you, you know it was one of those days that took me all over town. Late this morning, I was passing Messer Medici's house —not the new palazzo, the old one. I heard people up on the roof arguing, but I didn't pay any attention. I was early to get to Messer Strozzi's palazzo to pick up a box to be delivered near the river, so I was just walking along. Suddenly what turned out to be a statue—a bust of a man—crashed down on the walkway right in front of me. It shattered in many pieces, and I picked up a few of them. Here they are."

He took out from his jacket a large bronze fragment, half the head of a man. It was a little smaller than life size. He also produced two other pieces.

"What happened?" asked Lucrezia.

"Nothing happened right away. I just stood there, holding these pieces, so finally I left and went to see Messer Strozzi. On my way back to San Marco, a guard was out in front of the Medici house. I told him the bust had crashed down in front of me, and he told me what had happened.

"A man had commissioned the sculptor Donatello to do the bust for him, but when Donatello brought it to Cosimo's house to deliver, the man didn't want to pay the full price. He said Donatello should just charge the cost of the materials and a few lire for his time instead of what Donatello wanted to charge as a creative artist. Cosimo suggested they take it up on the roof where there was better light to see the sculpture better.

"The man kept saying it wasn't worth what Donatello wanted, so Donatello went over and pushed it off the roof. That is when it almost hit me. The guard said the man was very upset and wanted to pay Donatello to do another bust, but Donatello said no and left."

Amalia said, "That is quite a story, Carlo. You could have been killed."

"Wow, I hadn't thought of that. I was just excited that the pieces of the statue I have were made by Donatello. He's the one that made that statue of David that everyone talks about. It's in the entry to Cosimo's Palazzo, and if you look to the side, you can see it when they open the door. I met him once when I ran an errand for Gozzoli. He is such a nice man, very quiet and polite. It is hard to believe he got so angry, he destroyed one of his creations.

"He has his own boddeghe right behind the Duomo, and they say he has a pot hanging in the middle of the room. When he gets paid a commission, he pays all his bills, then puts the rest of the money in the pot for anyone to take whatever they need. I want to go by there and see that pot. He will need deliveries to be made, and I want to be the one to do it. Returning the broken bronze pieces may be my foot in the door."

"Carlo, you know everything that is going on in Florence," teased Lucrezia.

"I'm on the streets all day long. What people need done, I do or I learn to do. But I do hear a lot and see a lot. In the future, though, I need to stay away from statues falling from the sky!"

"That's for sure," said Amalia, and they all laughed.

"Amalia, leave the key out for the shop, and I'll go in first thing tomorrow to see what Lucrezia needs to have done in order to move in.

"All right."

Carlo added, "I'm going to bed now. Can I take Solo to bed with me?"

"Of course," they both said. "Let him relieve himself first," said Lucrezia. "It's so early. Are you feeling all right?"

"Feeling great. It's not every day someone has to dodge falling statues. Besides, I have a really busy day tomorrow, thanks to you."

Lucrezia and Amalia sat by the fire until the embers died to ashes and the room grew chilly, each talking more about their day today and then plans for their days tomorrow and tomorrow. The three of them had traveled very different paths today, each of them in their own singular world. Yet threads connected them to each other in ways that always made everything they experienced so much richer, and it seemed everything was appreciated by all three of them in similar and still very different ways.

Amalia mentioned Dona Rutia hadn't shown up and hadn't heard of their adventures.

Lucrezia added, "Well, now she will hear it tomorrow from each of us, and we will each get to enjoy the telling of it all over again."

A year passed, and their lives changed with it even as they stayed much the same. Carlo's business of running errands and doing chores for neighbors picked up clients over the years. Master Manetti and the man in the shop next door to him, a pharmacist, had become his clients; Messers Sacchetti and Riccardi and the other attorneys that were in the same building as Messer Riccardi near the Signoria needed him; even Masaccio and some other of the artists in the boddeghe near where he had gotten the paper for Lucrezia back in their early days were using Carlo's ubiquitous services.

He went by Donatello's boddeghe whenever he was passing by, which was often because the boddeghe was right by the Duomo in the heart of Florence; but so far he had not been asked to run any errands for Donatello or any of the others working at the boddeghe. Everyone was friendly, but he couldn't break through to get any of them to hire him, even after he returned the bronze pieces to Donatello.

Word continued to spread, and in only a short time, though still much too young for his heavy responsibilities, he was busy every day, making deliveries or doing whatever one of his clients wanted or needed. He really did have those business partners. Gino and Paolo couldn't be relied on very often, but he and Jacko shared the bulk of the work and were doing very well. The cart had been a useful addition. Very often the two boys could be seen around town, pulling and pushing the cart loaded with goods to be delivered to someone on one side of town or the other.

Lucrezia and Amalia continued sewing and scribing long hours every day. They shared whatever household chores needed to be done, but now Lucrezia had the shop downstairs too. Carlo and Jacko, and even the other boys, had been a big help cleaning out the shop on the ground floor of their house, and they had all worked to get Lucrezia moved in. Filippo and Giovanni had helped them build a partition so the customers couldn't see back into the workroom in the middle of the shop. Lucrezia had her table in the back under the window where she would have good light to do her designing.

While the men were doing the construction in the downstairs shop, Amalia asked them to build her a slanted desk like the ones in the San Marco Library. Giovanni had a friend build the desk for Amalia to her specifications. It turned out Lucrezia liked Amalia's slanted table, so Carlo had two older boys he knew build one from some scrap lumber he got from a construction site. Amalia and Lucrezia were suspicious about how he came to have the lumber, but Giovanni assured them Michelozzo had given the boards to Carlo in exchange for a favor he had done him. It seemed Carlo knew everyone and worked with and for just about everyone in town!

Lucrezia had two girls working for her in the sewing room now, plus an older woman, AnnaMaria, up in the front of the store to attend to the customers, selling the fabric and accessories. Lucrezia would be called upon only if a lady was interested in having a dress made for her. Then Lucrezia would take the potential client over to the side table to show her the newest designs she had sketched and discuss the best fabrics for each design. One of the seamstresses was young but very aware of fashions, so she would sometimes talk to the younger customers, but the final design and fabric selections were always left to Lucrezia.

After much angst, Amalia re-opened her father's office on the ground floor. It was a very small, one-room office, barely larger than a closet. It was on the opposite side of the entry from Lucrezia's shop, really under the stairs up to their living quarters.

Giuliano had had his regular notary office where he worked for several guilds during the week. It was over near Orsanmichele where the guild offices were, but he had always kept this office just for Saturday mornings when he would see any of the neighbors with problems that he could help solve. Amalia's father had enjoyed doing that work very much. Sometimes it was actual notary work, but often it was reading or writing a letter for a neighbor who couldn't do it for himself either because he was illiterate or had failing eyesight. Literacy was very high in Florence, but the few illiterates were usually also poor, too poor to pay for a scribe's or notary's services.

Amalia couldn't do the notary work, of course, but she could help a neighbor in other ways. Like her father, she only did it on Saturday mornings, but she looked forward to those mornings. She developed a regular clientele, mainly the older people who needed help with their correspondence so they could keep in touch with relatives out of town. She would read a letter to them that had been delivered, and she would pen a response that the neighbor dictated.

Very often, she learned things about these people that was private, and she made certain it always remained private. Like her father before her, she never charged for this, but very often they would leave two or three eggs or a couple fresh tomatoes or an eggplant if they were able. One old man left a wagon axle, and Carlo was thrilled.

During the week, she continued to do her scribing in the receiving room upstairs. It suited her, because now she was doing a lot more artwork, and that required much more concentration to get the colors right. Messer Bisticci was very pleased with her work, and he paid her considerably more than Master Manetti had been able to pay her, although she did still work for Master Manetti on occasion.

Dona Rutia's legs were beginning to fail her, and she had some difficulty climbing the stairs, so oftentimes Amalia visited her in the middle of the day, bringing a nice meal that she or Lucrezia had prepared. Sometimes Lucrezia was able to join them, and once in a while, Carlo dropped by.

If she was having a good day, Dona Rutia would appear at Lucrezia's shop, with Carlo's assistance, and sit in the front room to take in all the action, with customers coming and going and to see the designs being shown to prospective customers. She had spoiled a sale the other day when she told a customer to lose about five kilos before she tried to wear a particular style. AnnaMaria was shocked, but Lucrezia, Amalia, and Carlo had a good laugh about it later that night.

They still loved their quiet evenings, when they got them. They would listen while Amalia read from one of her manuscripts or they would get Carlo to read so they knew he was advancing in his lessons. The actual lessons were now limited by the amount of time he had to devote to them. Carlo had learned all he could from Filippo about his numbers, but Giovanni had now taken over with some advanced studies, and they were all very happy about that, although Carlo was a lot less happy than Amalia and Lucrezia.

During the year, Messer Sacchetti had kept track of Stefano as he moved from city to city. Stefano wasn't going into debt, but he worked menial jobs and spent all his money on wine. Little by little, he was slipping down a slope to total dissolution. Messer Sacchetti didn't give Amalia the details, but he did assure her that Stefano seemed to show no inclination to return to Florence.

They had built good friendships with Giovanni and Beatrice and with other young people in their gonfalons and the commune of Florence. They each had several girl friends, and they had expanded their circle of friends and acquaintances through their work as well as at the church: Lucrezia made friends through the sewing confraternity and Amalia through the reading and poetry confraternity.

They both had recently participated in the preparations for the celebration their church staged on March 25th, the Feast of the Annunciation. Brunelleschi —now gone—Donatello, Manzetti, or other architects would design and build hoists and scaffolds so they could lift the angels up in the air and have them fly through the sky over the stage. Lippi, Ghiberti, Fra Angelico, Verrocchio, or any other of the excellent artists would paint the backdrops. The local carpenters, seamstresses, and a myriad of local workers would all work side by side with the excellent, accomplished artists to present their annual celebration. This year was no exception. Amalia and Lucrezia both worked very hard and thoroughly enjoyed all the excitement.

Their lives were very full, and they were happy.

Neither of the girls had a love interest. Amalia knew that, having no one to speak for her and no dowry, the chances of marriage were very unlikely. Since Lucrezia was in a lower class in the society of Florence, she didn't need to have a dowry or anyone to speak for her—well, her father would speak for her if she chose to ask him—but she had not found anyone whom she cared for in that way. Now her age was making it unlikely she ever would. It might not be exactly what either of them wished for in their hearts, but they knew things could have turned out a lot worse for each of them. The saving grace was that each thoroughly enjoyed her work.

One Saturday, after Amalia finished in the office, she joined Lucrezia in the garden, preparing the soil and planting the seeds Lucrezia had saved from last fall. Amalia was back in her father's pants and an old shirt, but now they fit her properly. Lucrezia had long ago altered them and made a pair for herself as well. No one ever saw them in these outfits, but it was the best part of a gardening day. Just to look at each other, defying all the conventions of fashion and propriety, made them collapse in giggle-fits. The chore might be difficult and not to their liking— well, not to Amalia's liking—but they would at least have some fun while they did it. It was one of the few times they acted like the young girls they still were.

Later in the day, Amalia got herself a glass of wine and walked to the back of the garden to sit on her parent's bench under the old pear tree. It was not so painful to do so anymore. Time had healed the wounds a little, and she could hearken back to the good memories now.

Shortly after the party a year ago, several of the men had come over and pushed the old pear tree up straight again and propped it up in hopes it would survive the abuse of blowing over in the terrible storm and then being righted. It had a lot more new growth coming out this spring, and it looked very healthy. Lucrezia had long since gotten rid of the winter debris from the entire garden. With the planting of the herbs and vegetables that they had just finished, the garden was ready for the new growing season.

As she sat on the bench, Amalia could hear the chirping of the many birds in gardens throughout the neighborhood.

My mother used to have a bird house back here somewhere, she thought as she sat on the bench. Maybe I'll take that old basin and make it into a birdbath. I'll ask Lucrezia if it's okay with her. After all, this is her territory now.

Lucrezia was away at a client's home for the fitting of a new dress she had designed and made, and Amalia had a ribollita simmering on the stove. Carlo would be back shortly, and she was anticipating one of their quiet evenings together.

~ ~ ~

Sunday dawned as a beautiful day, and they were looking forward to the Mass. They heard there was a special singer who was going to sing a solo.

"Won't that be lovely, Carlo?"

"Sure, great. Who cares? Can I go over to Paolo's after Mass? We are building a new cart out of an old wagon."

"Of course." Both Amalia and Lucrezia were always amazed that Carlo would ask about things like that. He was gone all day almost every day, and he went who knew where, but that was business—his business. Sometimes, though, he acted like the boy he still really was.

They stood through the Mass as usual, often distracted by trying to keep Carlo from fidgeting. Finally the organ played the introduction, and then the entire church was filled with the most glorious sounds of a beautiful tenor voice singing a song they had never heard before. It was like a choir of angels, reverberating through the church. Lucrezia reached over and grabbed Amalia's arm. Amalia looked over at her, and their eyes met.

"It's him. From the night of the party. It's Ermanno, I know it," Lucrezia whispered. That was all she said. From then on, she was entranced in a world of her own, enraptured in a sublime state of euphoria.

When Mass was over, Lucrezia said she wanted to stay behind for a minute, so Amalia left the church. Right outside, she ran into Beatrice and Giovanni in a circle of their mutual friends.

"Wasn't he wonderful?" asked Amalia as she joined the group.

"Yes. This is all so exciting. Amalia, I'm glad you are here. We are having some friends over tonight for a special event. Will you and Lucrezia please come?" asked Beatrice.

"Of course. We would love to," said Amalia.

"A friend of Giovanni's is here and we are—"

"Oh, excuse me. I see Lucrezia."

Lucrezia seemed upset. Amalia caught up with her. "Lucrezia, wait for me. What's wrong?"

"Amalia, it was him—Ermanno. I tried to find him in the church after everyone left, but he was gone. I asked one of the padres, and he said he was gone to another church to sing, but he didn't know where and no one else knew either. I'll never find him. I can't go running all over town, looking in every church."

"I'm sorry, Lucrezia. How do you know it was the same person?"

"It was. I know it was."

They walked home in silence, and Dona Rutia greeted them near their door to tell them that her daughter and son-in-law and her grown grandchildren were arriving for a visit. Would they please help her to get ready?

"Of course," they said in unison.

They changed clothes, and then worked the rest of the day at Dona Rutia's house, helping Maddalena cook a fine meal to welcome Rutia's family. It had to be a stew, because Dona Rutia wasn't quite sure when they would arrive. The house was not as clean as it should be. The servant who worked for Dona Rutia was almost as old as she was and had been with her since they were both very young. When they were young, Maddalena had been hired by Dona Rutia, and then later her husband worked in the house of Dona Rutia and her husband, Roberto. Each woman gave birth to a daughter, and they raised them together. Now they were both widowed, and their children had moved away; Rosa, Rutia's daughter, to south of Siena and Maddalena's daughter to Venice. Both were married to hard-working men and got home to visit their mothers when they could, but their husbands and families left them little time for travel.

Lucrezia and Amalia did not want to embarrass either lady, so they tried to be very discreet as they went through the house and tidied and cleaned the cobwebs and dust. Amalia went home and got some of their dried fruit and an extra bottle of wine. Dona Rutia bought her wine from one of the finer wine makers in the area, but her daughter, Rosa, wouldn't have wanted to water that fine wine.

It was late in the day before they got back to their house. "Oh, Lucrezia, I forgot to tell you. We are invited to Beatrice and Giovanni's tonight for some special event. We just have time to change."

"I don't want to go".

"Why not? It will be fun. Their friends are all good company and we know most—"

"No, I'm tired, and I have a headache." With that Lucrezia went up to her room and closed the door.

Amalia decided she would go anyway. She had put on an old dress when they went over to Dona Rutia's, so she changed into the new dress Lucrezia had made for her during the winter. She had been saving it for a special occasion, and this seemed like the perfect time. It was a very lightweight, soft wool, cut slender to show off her figure. It had big, puffy, tie-on sleeves that were the fashion. It was a deep moss green that was quite flattering to her pale skin tone. She wished Lucrezia was going to see it. Well, maybe she would come over after she rested. Lucrezia never got headaches, and she was concerned.

Amalia didn't want to disturb Lucrezia to ask her to help her with her hair, so she fixed it herself and just pulled it back behind her ears and left it flowing down her back. It was the way she liked it best, but it really was irrelevant. She would know everyone there. There was no one she needed to impress, but she did want to show off the dress properly.

She crossed the narrow street and had reached the open front door to Beatrice's parent's house. She was about to walk in, when she noticed a group of people walking toward her from the direction of the center of town. They were laughing and talking loudly but didn't appear drunk. Then they started to sing a favorite Florentine frotella. One voice dominated the group, and as they sang, that voice got louder until it was drowning out all the others. Could it be? It sounded like the voice that sang at the church this morning. Beatrice and Giovanni came rushing out of the house, along with several of the other guests. The two groups gathered right in the street in front of the house. A couple of the men got the singer up on some steps, and she could see him now. It sounded like the man who sang this morning, but it looked like the man who had played the lute and sang at her party over a year ago. Was that possible?

As the singer started a second chorus, Lucrezia came up beside her and grabbed her arm. Amalia turned to look at her, and she knew by the look of Lucrezia's face this was the same man, and it's the one Lucrezia had spoken of this morning, Ermanno. When the song was over, everyone cheered and laughed as they started entering the house. Lucrezia was still in her work dress and her hair was a mess.

"Lucrezia, he is going into the house. This is what Beatrice meant when she said it was a special event. You're a mess. Go home and change and fix your hair. Hurry. He'll be here."

"Yes, yes," Lucrezia said, and she flew back into their house.

It was only a short time before she was again tugging on Amalia's arm, now in the garden behind the Cassetti house.

"Where is he?"

"He's right there talking to Giovanni and Tomasso."

Amalia didn't know how she had done it all so quickly, but Lucrezia was in the new dress she had made for herself last winter, and her hair was loose with a band holding it back from her face. She looked—Amalia couldn't quite describe it—She looked radiant.

Lucrezia was staring at the man named Ermanno. It was almost as if Lucrezia was willing him to look at her. Finally, the three men broke out in laughter, and "he" glanced around the garden. When his eyes met Lucrezia's, they both held the gaze for several moments. He broke off their gaze, said something to Giovanni, and then he came toward Lucrezia.

"Ermanno, it is so nice to see you again. Do you remember my friend, Amalia?"

"Yes, of course. You were the reason for the party at your house last year when I was last here. It is nice to see both of you again. It has been too long. How have you been, Lucrezia?"

With that, Amalia might as well have not existed as far as either of them were concerned. Very soon they moved off to the back of the garden where it was quieter, and they found a bench.

After a while, Amalia brought them some wine, and they thanked her, but they hardly noticed her and didn't even interrupt their conversation with each other.

As she was returning to the house, Amalia bumped into Beatrice.

"Amalia, have you seen Ermanno and Lucrezia in the garden? It's like there is no one else at the party."

"I noticed," said Amalia, totally amazed. She had her glass of wine in hand, and she sat down on a bench to relax for a moment. Then she became aware of a conversation directly behind her between several of the young men that had come with Ermanno:

"But those countries are each united under one leader, a king. Why isn't all of Italy united instead of all these little city-states and republics vying for power and warring with each other? We have so many different leaders in Italy: a condotierre, Francesco Sforza is the Duke of Milan, there is the Doge in Venice, the King of Naples, and the Kingdom of Sicily. The pope rules the papal states, Rome, Bologna, Urbino, and Perugio, the Duke of Ferrara, The Republic of Genoa, The Duchy of Modena, Forli, Ravenna. The Republic of Florence is controlled by the Medici, besides the Republics of Siena, Genoa, and Lucca. We have so many systems of government, and each thinks theirs is best."

Another said, "Who would be the one to take charge and be the leader of a united Italy? Cosimo de' Medici has the money to buy an army and a great condotierre, but he has no interest in the conquest of new territories or ruling them. He just wants peace so the wool and silk production continues and can be sold all over the world, and trade, and thereby Florence can flourish."

The third young man said, "Is that so bad? My mother told me what it was like when her village was sacked by the pope's troops when they invaded Forli. Her mother hid her in a hole under the flooring in the barn. Her mother was raped, and her sister and father were killed. Do we want that for our city? Do we want to do that to others? War is fine for the nobles, but the little man is the one that pays the price."

The second man said, "There is a lot to be said for peace, and that is what we get with Cosimo. Our economy makes a lot of money for his banks, and his banks make a lot of money for him, but when the banks make money, so do we. It seems the only power he wants is what money buys, not conquered lands. I'm better off than my father was at my age, and there is a lot to be said for feeding your family and having a good roof over your head. My sons are learning things in their school with the monks I never learned, and they will do better than I am doing. That is more important to me than being united under some king and having no future for myself or my boys."

The first said, "Well, I think for tonight we should declare Ermanno king and get him to sing another song. Where is he?"

"Back with that girl he is in love with."

"Let him love later; now, he sings. Where is he?"

Off they went, laughing and jostling each other, headed to where Ermanno and Lucrezia were seated.

"Come on, Ermanno give us another song. That church music this morning was wonderful, but now give us a real song."

One of the other men handed Ermanno a lute. He stood up and put one foot on the bench, strumming the lute. Then he started to play a tune, and finally, he sang. As he sang, he looked directly at Lucrezia as though he were singing the song only for her. Her eyes never left his face.

After the song was over, Ermanno was practically dragged away to meet some new arrivals, but before long he found Lucrezia again, and they drifted back to their bench in the garden. The little scene was played out several times in the course of the evening: he would be called away but would soon find his way back to her side. Ermanno sang several more songs that evening, and one of them was a beautiful song from the big production presented the past winter. It was magnificent, and everyone was certain that Ermanno was much better than the tenor in that production.

Those musical productions were a favorite of all Florentines. They had actually begun right there in Florence in the last century. Many of the instruments were developed in Florence to accompany the singers as they sang the different songs that told a story along with the music. Sometimes it was an old folk tale or one written by a songwriter to go along with the music. It was a favorite winter pastime for Florentines of all classes. The poor might not sit in the audience for the productions staged in the grand palazzos, but that did not keep them from singing and enjoying the beautiful music created for those performances. Then, sometimes there was a production on the steps of the Duomo or Santa Croce, and the piazza would be packed by an audience that truly appreciated the talents of the musicians and the singers as well as the dancers.

In the meantime, Amalia was having a wonderful time enjoying her many good friends. Caterina and her husband were there, and they had a chance to catch up. Caterina had given birth to her beautiful daughter, Blanche, a little over a month ago, and this was Caterina's first real outing, certainly her first party. There were several people there Amalia did not know, and she enjoyed meeting and chatting with them as well.

Amalia received several compliments on her dress, and she never failed to tell anyone who noticed that Lucrezia had designed and made it for her. It was late now, and she was ready to go home, but she wanted to wait for Lucrezia. She knew that Lucrezia would not be leaving the party until Ermanno did.

Finally, a group of men made plans to leave, and they wanted Ermanno to leave with them. That broke up the party, and everyone started to leave. Lucrezia found Amalia and asked her if she was ready to go. Amalia laughed and hugged her friend. They left arm in arm to cross the street to their house.

Lucrezia bolted the door while Amalia went ahead upstairs to got a lamp lit; then she checked to see that Carlo was asleep. Lucrezia came skipping up the stairs.

Grabbing her arm and smiling, she said to Amalia, "He asked if he could call on me tomorrow, and I said yes."

The Duomo

XII   *New Beginnings*

The next day, Ermanno came to call on Lucrezia. After greeting him and spending a few moments on pleasantries, Amalia decided she needed to attend to some chores in the garden. She went down the back stairs to clean out some pots and repot some of the flowers they were planning to put in the middle of the garden and in the box by the front door.

After a while, Carlo called down to her, asking where everyone was. She went back upstairs. Lucrezia was not in the receiving room. Carlo said he had just gotten home, and Lucrezia was not there when he came up. Amalia went upstairs to their bedrooms, and found Lucrezia's door closed and locked. Amalia knocked, and Lucrezia said to please leave her alone.

"I'm all right; just please leave me alone," but it was obvious from her voice she was not all right. Amalia didn't know what to do because she had no idea what could have happened.

Later that evening, Lucrezia came downstairs. Amalia was doing some scribing, but one quick glance told her Lucrezia had been crying.

"Is there anything I can do for you, Lucrezia? What happened?"

"I don't want to talk about it. Please don't ask," said Lucrezia, and so Amalia didn't. It was a very quiet week with very little talking. Carlo and Amalia tiptoed around so as not to disturb or upset Lucrezia. Amalia had tried several times in the course of the week to get Lucrezia to talk to her, but to no avail. Lucrezia went to an appointment she had with a customer on Tuesday, and on Wednesday she went to her sewing confraternity at the church. Otherwise, other than chores, she stayed nestled in her corner, sewing, whenever she wasn't in the shop.

AnnaMaria had asked Amalia if everything was all right because Lucrezia stayed in the back in her office all the time, and was so quiet. Amalia didn't have an answer, but she suggested the girls in the shop be patient and give Lucrezia a little time.

They had just gotten home from Mass the following Sunday, and Carlo was heading out to meet his friends for another of his business ventures. He ran down the stairs and opened the door, only to come face to face with a ravaged face he knew only too well and had hoped never to see again: Stefano. Stefano had a bundle in his arms and was leaning against the door frame, barely able to stand. Carlo wasn't sure whether he should call up to Amalia or just push Stefano back into the street and hope he would go away.

Giovanni was just walking into his house and called over to ask Carlo if everything was all right.

When Carlo said "No!," Giovanni immediately crossed the narrow street to see what the problem was.

"Good God, I thought we were rid of you," he said.

"You will be soon," said Stefano, as he coughed up blood into a rag he was carrying.

"Is it the plague?" asked Giovanni.

"No, it's the lung disease. No danger. I need to see my sister."

"She doesn't want to see you."

"Please, let me see my sister. I mean her no harm, I swear it."

By this time, Amalia had heard a commotion at the foot of the stairs and had come down just as her brother started to collapse into Giovanni's arms. At that moment, they heard a faint cry come from the bundle he was carrying, and as he crumbled toward Giovanni and then to the ground, he passed the bundle to Amalia.

With the help of Giovanni's father, they all managed to get Stefano upstairs and seated in the receiving room. Amalia had unwrapped the bundle and found, under several layers of dirty fabric, a baby girl not more than six months old. She was soiled, listless, and very thin but otherwise seemed healthy with large blue eyes staring out at the shocked face of her aunt.

Lucrezia had been upstairs in her room, but she came down to see about the commotion. Stefano started to rouse himself, and Amalia wanted to go to him. She passed the infant to Lucrezia and went over and knelt in front of her brother. Giovanni's father thought they were no longer needed and wanted to leave, but Giovanni wasn't sure.

Amalia said, "Giovanni, I think it is all right for you to leave. I don't think Stefano is any threat to me. I think we are safe. Thank you."

"If you have any further need for me, send Carlo. I'm going to ask Juliana to come over."

"Thank you, Giovanni," said Amalia, as she turned back to Stefano.

"Stefano, what has happened to you? Who's baby is this?"

"Where is the baby?" asked Stefano, "Where is my daughter?"

"She is right here. She is soiled. Lucrezia is cleaning her up. Carlo, can you get him something to drink, please?"

Carlo handed Amalia a cup of wine, and then he was down the stairs and out the door to Caterina's house. Lucrezia had whispered to him to go get clean clothes and necessaries for the baby and ask if Caterina would send her wet nurse to help feed this infant, who looked as though she was starved and dying.

By the time Carlo got back, Juliana was there. First she went to Lucrezia, who was doing her best to get a dribble of watered milk into the mouth of the infant and to clean her up as best she could without distressing her. The poor child was very listless but had no fever.

Juliana said, "I think she is starved. You are doing all we can do for her right now."

Then she turned her attention to Stefano, who was still slouched in the chair, almost slipping to the floor. Amalia was on her knees on the floor in front of him trying to talk to him, but he was in and out of awareness of where he was or who she was. Juliana sent Carlo to get Giovanni back and get her husband, or Filippo, or any other man nearby so they could move Stefano to Amalia's father's bed. She had whispered to Amalia that he was dying, and Amalia had said he must be made comfortable.

Caterina arrived with her wet nurse right behind the two men. Lucrezia moved the two ladies into the kitchen to get them out of the way of the men carrying Stefano upstairs. Juliana said not to give the baby too much at first, and she thanked the wet nurse for doing this. She asked Carlo to bring a pan of water and rags and followed the men upstairs. Once they had Stefano on the bed, she asked everyone but Carlo to leave while she attended to Stefano—and to get Padre Bernardo right away.

It was now that Amalia had the first real opportunity to look at her niece. Juliana had told Lucrezia she wasn't sure the baby would live, but to feed her small amounts often. They could only wait and see. Finally, the baby latched on to the breast of the wet nurse, Clara, and drank in a goodly amount. Then, exhausted from her effort, she seemed to rest peacefully for a while. Everyone took it as a good sign, but they weren't sure. A half hour later, she awoke and again suckled long and hard, and then fell into a sleep that everyone knew was a good sign.

In the meantime, Amalia went back upstairs to see about her brother. She knocked on the door. Carlo opened it and said for her to come in. Juliana had stripped Stefano of his garments and told Carlo to burn them. She and Carlo had then bathed Stefano. Now Carlo left to burn Stefano's clothes and to run to Dona Marina's house to get the salve Juliana wanted right away.

"Run as fast as you can," Juliana begged him. "I can do nothing for Stefano's lungs, but I can ease his pain from the cracking sores on his body."

Carlo returned quickly. Juliana got more watered wine into Stefano, and soon he was resting as comfortably as could be expected.

"He will die soon," she whispered to Amalia. "But I have the feeling he will die content here at home, with his baby delivered to safety. I think he expended the last of his energy getting the baby here, to his father's home."

Stefano was in and out of a restless sleep for several hours, but then he roused himself.

"Amalia, Amalia," Stefano whispered.

"I'm here, Stefano." She had been sitting on the bed beside him. "You are home now, and you are safe. The baby has nursed and is resting."

"Thank you. I am so sorry. I had no one to turn to, and I didn't want the baby to die. Lisabetta is dead over two weeks now. I tried, I swear I did, but there was nothing I could do for her. I deserve to die; but the baby, I didn't want the baby to die because of me. She's a happy baby, like you were. I told Lisabetta that she reminded me of you when you were a baby. I didn't want her to die. Amalia, I'm sorry." Stefano started to cough then, and after a particularly violent spasm, it was over.

Amalia sat there and looked at him, wondering what brought him down this wretched path of self-destruction, wishing they had had more time to talk.

Juliana slowly reached over and wiped the blood from the corner of Stefano's mouth, closed his eyes, and then pulled the bed linen up over his face. Amalia stared at the white cover where his ravaged face had been only a moment ago.

Finally, Juliana whispered, "I'm going downstairs to see what I can do for the baby."

Juliana went into the kitchen and checked on the baby. She was sleeping soundly. Her color was much better, and her skin tone seemed healthier.

Juliana smiled. "I think she has a chance. I will go tell Maria that there is another death here in the Dontarini house. I am sure Amalia will want the funeral to be a very quiet family affair."

She heard Carlo open the door and greet Padre Bernardo, who said breathlessly, "I'm sorry I didn't get here in time. I was with Dona Anastasia."

Juliana had taken her leave, and she passed Padre Barnardo on the staircase. "It is not for me to say, Padre, but I believe Stefano died in God's grace. Please baptize the baby. I am not sure she will make it through the night. She is very weak, but I think she's a fighter."

When Padre Bernardo entered the bedroom, he said to Amalia, "I'm so sorry I couldn't get here in time. I just got word a short time ago."

"Padre, he is gone. I wish we could have been friends. I would have liked to have had a brother, but it seems instead I now have a baby niece."

"Child, we will talk about that later. Right now I am going to take the cover down from Stefano's face. I don't want you to be upset. I'll administer the last rites. Perhaps his soul hasn't left his body yet."

"Oh, Padre, I think his soul left a very long time ago," said Amalia, as she stood up. She took one last look at her brother's face, and walked down to be with Lucrezia, Caterina, and her niece.

"The padre will be down in a few minutes, and we will need to baptize the baby," she told them. "What shall we name her? Stefano said her mother's name was Lisabetta."

"Before Padre went upstairs, he said you might want to put her in the basket for adoption," said the nursemaid. "It is done all the time. There is the wheel. No one would know."

"I would know," said Amalia, as she sat down next to the wet nurse and took the baby in her arms.

Everyone in Florence knew of the wheel. When Brunelleschi had designed and Cosimo had built the magnificent L'Ospedale degli Innocenti, the foundling hospital, a wheel had been installed in an outside wall. Anyone could lay an infant there, then turn the wheel so the infant was rotated inside the building, and then ring the bell. An attendant would come to collect the infant. The baby would be cared for in the hospital. The foundling might be adopted, and many were; but if not, the child would be schooled and trained to be able to make a living after coming of age and moving out into the world.

After a few moments, Amalia said, "Lucrezia, we are a household of orphans. She is the only person left of my family. I want to keep her, but I can't do this alone. I can't do it without your help."

"Amalia, we have travelled a very rocky road together, and we seem to get stronger with each bend in that road. I don't want to see you give her up. I don't know how good we will be at it, but if we are not going to marry and have children of our own, then at least we can devote our efforts to this poor little girl.

"Does Carlo get a say in this?"

"Carlo says 'yes'," said Carlo from the corner of the room where he was sitting on the floor with his knees pulled up under his chin, his cap pulled down over his eyes.

"Then it is decided. Lisabetta Stefania Dontarini. She should be baptized today since she is so frail. If she survives, we will have the celebration next week after we bury her father next to her grandparents."

Caterina had been sitting quietly.

"Amalia, I always hoped we would both marry and have children we could raise together. Then it seemed that wouldn't happen. Now, all of a sudden, it may happen after all. Maybe not in quite the way I was expecting, but I hope we can raise my little Blanche and your little Lisabetta to be the near-sisters that we have been over the years. I would like for us to try. We were both so alone growing up, there were times I would have been lost without your friendship. I hope we can offer that opportunity for friendship to our two girls."

"Thank you, Caterina," said Amalia. Touched, she rose and walked over toward Caterina, who also stood. The two girls embraced with the tiny bundle between them. "Maybe something good will come from my brother's dissolute life after all," Looking down, Amalia said. "We can only hope. I wish we could have learned more about her mother, but I think that door is closed."

"I would like to be her godfather." Carlo spoke in a very small voice. "I know I'm young, but I will be the only man in her life, so I would like to have a title." Then he spoke more firmly: "Little Lisabetta needs a bed and clothes and blankets, but I think I know where I can get a crib at least. It shouldn't take me long. It's only a few blocks away. Can you wait for the baptism until I get back?"

"Yes, Carlo, we'll wait," said Amalia.

Lucrezia had busied herself making some tea, and then they heard Dona Rutia at the front door. Caterina and Clara went down to help her up the stairs that had become very difficult for her lately. She finally walked into the kitchen, struggling to get seated near the table next to Amalia.

"Ah, what is this little package we have here? I heard. I am so sorry about Stefano, Amalia." She said this as she reached to receive Lisabetta from Amalia's arms. "So, what is to be done?"

"I want to keep her, Dona Rutia. She is the only family I have left, and I think Mama and Papa would want me to try to give her a better life than Stefano could have offered her. Who knows? Maybe he would have turned his life around because of her. He seemed to care about her very much."

"Child, it will be a big responsibility, you know that. You will be—"

Just then, Padre Bernardo, having come down the stairs, entered the kitchen. Lucrezia offered him a cup of tea, which he accepted as he sat down next to Dona Rutia.

"It is done. We can have the burial tomorrow if you wish, Amalia. There is no reason to delay."

"That will be fine, Padre. I don't want any fuss. Few people remember him and none with good thoughts. I would like it to be as simple as possible."

"That's fine. I will speak with Dona Maria and Master D'Alessandro, and I'm sure it can be done as you wish. Now what about the little one? Are there arrangements—"

"Padre, I would like to keep her. I am her aunt. Juliana and Giovanni across the street heard him, heard Stefano. There is no question the child was his daughter. We have no proof, but we have his dying statement. That makes her my niece, my only living relative. I am her only relative that we know of too. Padre, I want to do this."

"It is most unusual, Amalia. You know that. You don't have a husband, and your living conditions are unusual, to say the least. There will be much talk. What will Master D'Alessandro say—the neighbors—what will the bishop say?"

"There will be no talk," burst out Dona Rutia in her gruffest raspy voice. "I am here almost every day, and there is nothing that goes on in this house to be talked about by gossipers. I would know. If Amalia wants to raise her brother's child, then it should be so. There will be many to help her, as they have helped her and others in the past. The sins of the father should not be visited on this poor child. We will see that she is given her chance to live a good and godly life. Master D'Alessandro can see me, and the bishop can only want what is best for the child in God's eyes. Surely, to be raised by her blood relative should be his guide. Does the orphanage need one more child?"

No one had ever heard Dona Rutia make such a speech, and no one spoke now.

After a long pause, Padre Bernardo said very quietly, "Well I will take it to the bishop." Then he spoke up: "In the meantime, I think we need to baptize her. I understand she is very weak."

Amalia spoke, "Yes, Padre, we would like that very much. If you could just wait a few more minutes for Carlo to return. He went to try to get a crib we will need for the baby—for Lisabetta."

As if she had heard her name mentioned, little Lisabetta started to awaken and fuss. The wet nurse took her back from the arms of Dona Rutia, and she was soon quieted. She again nursed eagerly and for quite a while, and there was a growing confidence in all present that the worst of her days were behind her. Looking around her, Amalia was sure that, like her, Lucrezia and Dona Rutia, plus Carlo, would see to it that this baby would not go hungry again if any of them had anything to say about it.

By the time Carlo returned, Maria and Filippo, Giovanni and Beatrice, her parents, Lucia and Luigi, Juliana and Guido, Caterina and Clara, plus Rutia had gathered in the receiving room. While the baby was awake, they cleaned her properly. Caterina had run home and gotten one of Blanche's nicest dresses and replacements for the soiled rags used as panties.

Carlo stood as tall as he was able. With Lucrezia by his side, he carried Lisabetta, in her very pretty dress, into the receiving room for the baptism. Everyone agreed they made a perfect pair of godparents for little Lisabetta, and Padre Bernardo performed an excellent ceremony. They all knew the ceremony next week, when they would take her to the Baptistry and register her, would be the proper welcoming of her into God's light and her new life in Florence.

Every child of Florence was taken to the little octagonal church across from the Duomo, and a bean was dropped into a jar: white for a girl and black for a boy.

This was considered the oldest and most sacred place in all of Florence. It had been a church since the earliest of Christian times, and many said it was a religious temple long before that, back into the early Roman times and even before that. It was thought to go back to the times of the Etruscans, the earliest settlers of their city, and back to the days of the pagan gods.

They would set a date and time and take little Lisabetta there, but in the meantime, today's ceremony would allow everyone to rest easier, since her beginning was filled with so much trepidation.

After the emergency baptism ceremony, everyone had enjoyed some wine and snacks several guests had brought. Then most of them went home. It was getting late, and Caterina and Clara, the wet nurse, stayed only long enough to say that they felt Clara would have enough milk for both Blanche and Lisabetta. The wet nurse had been nursing her own son as well as Blanche, but he was older now, and she had already begun weaning him. Carlo agreed to pick up some fresh milk in the morning, and everyone agreed they would have to work out a plan. With that, everyone helped Dona Rutia down the stairs, and Caterina and Clara saw her home.

Carlo brought up the crib and set it down in the kitchen. All he said was "Don't ask."

Nobody did. Lucrezia said she had some perfect light cotton cloth, and she would have some garments made within a day. What else? She would sleep in Amalia's room, and Amalia had enough milk from Clara to get through the night. They joked it would be a very sleepless night for Amalia, and she agreed, but looking down at the tiny baby in its crib, she knew it would be worth it. If little Lisabetta just kept drinking during the night, it would be a sure sign she would survive.

Now it was just the four of them in the kitchen, as it would be from now on.

Lucrezia spoke: "Amalia, after tomorrow when Stefano is buried, we need to talk about making some changes. Your father has been dead now three years, and the room has been despoiled by Stefano twice. It can't stay as a shrine of remembrance any longer. Your father would not want you to do that. We will need the additional space, and changes will have to be made."

Amalia didn't respond but simply looked down at her hands as they rested in her lap. After a long delay, Amalia lifted Lisabetta from the crib and quietly walked upstairs to her father's bedroom to sit by Stefano. Carlo carried the crib up to Amalia's room, and Lucrezia straightened up so things would be ready for tomorrow's funeral. They didn't have any food supplies for after the funeral, but it wouldn't be necessary this time. There would be few mourners and no fond memories to recapture.

When Carlo came downstairs, he walked over to Lucrezia and hugged her. "That was very brave of you to say that, but it did have to be said. Good night, godmother." Lucrezia's eyes followed Carlo as he picked up Solo, then entered and closed the door to his make-shift bedroom. Yes, she thought, things were going to have to change.

Amalia had put Lisabetta to bed in her new crib and came down to sit with Lucrezia. "I agree that changes have to be made," Amalia began, "but there is more to discuss than my father's bedroom. What about you? I don't just mean sleeping arrangements, Lucrezia. I know you are struggling, and I don't want to pry, but does what you are struggling with change or affect our household in any way? I truly don't want to pry, Lucrezia, but as I said earlier, even though I want to do this, I can't do it alone. I need your help."

"I'll be here for you. It is over with Ermanno. I can't talk about it yet, but we have no future. Although I am upset about it, our household won't be changing in that way. But it has to change in many other ways. Carlo can't stay in that small storeroom behind the kitchen. What if we clean out the large upstairs room and give him a proper bedroom? He is getting older and needs to have a room away from us. We never use the room as it is meant to be used, even on the few occasions we do go up to the loggia. We haven't used that proper kitchen in years. Let's see what we can do about that. Then let's tackle your parents' bedroom, redo the drapery and coverlet, and make it over for you and the baby."

Amalia said, "Why don't you move into my room? It's bigger than yours, and let's make your room into a private room for you. There used to be an arch between them. Let's talk to Giovanni and see if he thinks we can break through the wall again. That would be the only thing we would need help with, other than just maybe moving some of the furniture. We have the new stove downstairs, so we could just leave the old stove in Carlo's new room. He could use it for heat."

Lucrezia said, "You do realize that we can't have them breaking down the wall and making noise and waking the baby." She smiled at Amalia.

"Somehow, Lucrezia, I don't think that will be the only new noise in our lives."

They both laughed.

Then Amalia reached over and took Lucrezia's hand and quietly said, "Lucrezia, when you can talk about it, I'm here and ready to listen."

"I know, Amalia. Thank you."

XIII   *Fiesole*

It was several days before Lucrezia talked to Amalia about Ermanno. She had a dress she had to finish and deliver to Signora Albertini, and she was working downstairs in her shop most of every day. Then she would bring the dress up in the evenings to do more work on it. The days of sitting and casually sewing for long hours were gone. There were many interruptions in her day now that she had the shop. The woman she had hired, AnnaMaria, was excellent, according to Lucrezia, and she could handle most of the callers, but if it involved the potential making of a dress, she would have to disturb Lucrezia.

Amalia was busy too. She was working on a special manuscript that required her undivided attention, but that was no longer possible. Carlo would run and get a supply of milk each morning, and then he would bring more home with him in the afternoon. Yet Lisabetta was still weak and required extra attention during the day and the nights. She still slept more than a normal six-month-old baby and was still demanding extra milk. They thought about experimenting by crushing up vegetables and fruits to feed her, but Juliana said not to overdo it until she had gotten a little stronger.

A solution presented itself when a neighbor lady living a block away lost her baby when she was only a month old. The baby had been weak since birth, and Signora Bianca had four older children. Although she was devastated, she was not surprised as the little one just slipped away one morning while she held her in her arms.

Bianca was willing to come in several times during the course of each day to nurse Lisabetta, and this satisfied Lisabetta's immediate needs and gave Amalia more time to work uninterrupted.

Lucrezia would come into Amalia's room in the early morning and take Lisabetta downstairs and let Amalia sleep in. That helped. Carlo, with some instruction from Giovanni, built a small bed for Lisabetta in Lucrezia's private room in the back of the shop. If Amalia had to run an errand, she would leave the baby there. They all shared the marketing, whoever was out on an errand, and Amalia would work anytime the baby slept or Bianca was there. It was a struggle, and they were managing, but the free time they used to have with their friends was now vastly curtailed.

Carlo had found another crib that they put in the receiving room near where Amalia worked. That also helped.

The first couple months were difficult for all three of them, trying to adjust to the new schedules and interruptions, but little by little, they fell into a rhythm. Lisabetta was thriving and gaining strength daily. Once they started giving Lisabetta mashed fruits and vegetables, Carlo liked to do those feedings if he was home. Sometimes he would appear during the day just so he could take over and feed, even change, and amuse little Lisabetta.

In the beginning, Solo would have nothing to do with the baby. Everyone made sure he got his share of attention, but it was obvious he didn't like the intrusion by this bundle of noise and very different smells. Then after a week or so, he could often be found curled up next to Lisabetta, enjoying a companionable nap.

They were very glad the entire garden had been planted before the arrival of little Lisabetta. It was thriving, but nothing had to be picked or processed, so at least that didn't complicate those early days.

On a Tuesday, it rained heavily all day, and things were very slow in Lucrezia's shop, as was predictable. Since AnnaMaria had very little to do, she had kept Lisabetta almost the entire day. It had been wonderful for Amalia to be able to concentrate with no interruptions for such an extended time. She had gotten a lot done and was extremely pleased with what she had produced. The last time she had been to Master Manetti's shop, she had gotten a new color ink and an additional pen to use with it for some innovative designs she was playing with. She didn't use it a lot at first, but she was getting bolder as the week progressed. Now she was actually afraid she had gone too far. She had to admit, she was very pleased with the results, but she was anxious to hear what Messer Bisticci had to say about them when she brought the finished manuscript to him.

When it was time for AnnaMaria to go home, Lucrezia brought Lisabetta upstairs with her.

"I closed the shop," she said as she laid the sleeping baby down in the crib in the corner. Then she and Amalia took the opportunity to sit and drink a cup of tea together. It was an herbal lemon tea Lucrezia had concocted the day before from some of the fresh herbs in their garden.

"What terrible weather. Carlo will be soaked when he comes in. I hope he hasn't been out in it all day," said Lucrezia.

"I think he was helping some artist clean out his boddeghe," said Amalia.

"Good. By the way, I received a note from Signora Albertini, the client who ordered that new dress I have been working on. They have left the city for the summer and have gone to Fiesole. She wants me to deliver the dress and do the final fitting up there. She said I can stay overnight at her home, if necessary, to get the final alterations done. This is going to make things difficult for you with Lisabetta, but I have no choice. I won't get paid until I deliver the dress, and it may need some final adjustments.

"If I go this Thursday, I can get a ride with Master Vicenti's driver. He has a large shipment to send up there and will have to hire a large wagon. He said there is room for me to ride along."

"How did he find out?" asked Amalia.

"He delivered the message from Signora Albertini. He was planning to go tomorrow, but since the dress isn't done, he put off his delivery one day so I could ride with his driver."

"That was certainly nice of him, but you told me the dress was finally done," said Amalia.

"I knew you needed time to prepare since I will be gone for two days, so I lied."

"Oh, Lucrezia, you are a dear," Amalia said, and they both laughed. "I will go to see Messer Bisticci first thing in the morning. Then I will run by Master Manetti's, and then do any shopping for food we will need on my way back home. Carlo can always pick it up if there is something I forget. What would we do without him?"

Lucrezia sat very quietly and just stared at her tea. Amalia didn't know if she should say something or not.

After a long wait, finally Lucrezia said, "Amalia, Beatrice dropped in this afternoon when the rain slackened to tell me they just heard that Ermanno's entire family has been stricken with the plague. He is the only one not afflicted. His little brother has already died, and both of his parents are in a very bad way."

"Oh, Lucrezia, I am so sorry. I heard at the market that the plague has hit Venice and the surrounding areas, but they said it wasn't too bad. I wonder if that is why Signora Albertini left Florence in such a hurry."

"Maybe. I hadn't put the two together," said Lucrezia.

"They are saying they don't think it will reach us, but then who knows? If only there was something we could do, but Ravenna is so far away."

"There is nothing I could do anyway. It is over between us, you knew that. He told me he wants to sing but doesn't know how he can earn a living at it. Only the finest singers can make a livelihood from singing. Anyway, his father wants him to take over his business and has made arrangements for him to marry his partner's daughter. It's all very convenient for the partners, but the two of them are not in love, and they have always disliked each other.

"I told him I had feelings for him but I could not be involved. Amalia, if Messer D'Alessandro heard about this, what would he do to us? Even Dona Rutia couldn't save us. We have already pushed him beyond what he thinks is appropriate. Only the influence of others has kept him from doing what he really wants to do. You know that.

"Amalia, Ermanno told me he has feelings for me also. That is why he had to come and tell me of his situation, and I'm glad he did. If he had just disappeared for another year, I would have been devastated. At least this way I know there is no hope, and I can try to forget about him. Actually, I'm not sure whether I love the man or the voice. I guess now I'll never get to know the man well enough to decide—but I do love the voice." She looked at Amalia with tears in her eyes and smiled just a little bit.

"I'm so sorry, Lucrezia. I thought maybe he was already married, but I knew it was something like that, because it was so obvious the two of you were attracted to each other."

The door downstairs burst open and then was slammed shut and Carlo threw the bolt. Then he came running up the stairs.

"Well, the rain has stopped for now, but it is a mess out there. Every street is still a river. What a day. What are you two doing? Is that the tea you made up yesterday? That was tasty. I would love a cup of it. Is the water hot? Even if I didn't get rained on, I'm wet through. Tea would taste good."

Amalia got up to heat the water and brew some more tea for all three of them. She also heated up the soup from their meal earlier in the day. They filled Carlo in on Lucrezia's plans to go up to Fiesole, and Carlo said he would plan to be around more those two days to help out. He was almost done at the boddeghe and would finish up tomorrow. He told them the cart he had made with his partners had really come in handy hauling the scraps away. He would have to pay Paolo and Jacko something, but that was all right. He had made good money on the job.

Carlo went on, "Those artists are so temperamental. Things got pretty wild at one point when I was dragging a big pile of scraps out to the cart. One of the apprentices was helping me, and he called for another to help, and one of the artists started yelling that he couldn't work in such chaos. He kept it up and finally threw a pot against the wall. Can you imagine?"

"Yes," said Amalia. "Well, I'm not going to throw any pot of ink, but it is difficult to concentrate if there are distractions. When I'm scribing, it doesn't matter so much because I'm just copying; but when I'm doing the artwork, I simply can't do it if there are distractions."

Lucrezia chimed in. "You know, it's the same for me. I can sew anywhere, no matter what's going on, but I can't design unless I am calm and it is quiet and I'm uninterrupted."

"Do we have to beware of flying pins?" said Carlo, laughing.

"No, not to worry!" The three of them laughed. "But I can do complicated stitching with no problem, even with distractions. I guess it takes more thought, more concentration, when you are trying to create something from your imagination."

"I think you're right, Lucrezia," agreed Amalia.

"Well," said Carlo, "the artists all complain that no one appreciates what they do, what they paint or sculpt, and what it takes to do it, like Donatello with the bust he threw off the roof that time. They say the patrons get all the glory, and they do all the work. I guess it's true. But to do that creating, I guess they think in a different way. I think I get it now. Maybe that's what I like about them."

They chatted on through dinner and past it, until it was time to gather up Lisabetta, climb the stairs, and retire for the night. While she was awake, Lisabetta had been passed from lap to lap as the three friends passed the evening together. At the last, she had fallen asleep in Carlo's arms.

~ ~ ~

It was late Friday night, and Carlo wasn't home yet. Amalia was scribing at her desk, waiting for Lucrezia to get home from Fiesole, and Lisabetta had just fallen asleep in her crib next to Amalia's desk.

When Carlo arrived, it was with a loud bang of the door, and Amalia thought he might awaken Lisabetta, but she slept through the noise.

"Good evening, Carlo. You're late. Is everything all right?

"Yes. I had to make a late delivery over by <u>San Miniato al Monte</u> for Riccardo—some legal document, a contract or something. Then, after the man read it and signed it, he asked me to deliver it over to a man near San Marco. I need a horse!

"I also need to stay away from Medici palazzos. You remember a while back, I almost got killed by the falling statue? Well, last tonight I almost got killed by a man falling down on top of me."

"What are you talking about? Did someone fall?"

"No. Well, yes. It was Fra Lippi, and he had tied the bed linens together to escape from the Medici palazzo. The sheets were too short, and he dropped the last few braccia."

"That's crazy. What are you talking about?"

"We walked two blocks together, and he told me he lives at the Medici palazzo, and Cosimo keeps him locked in his room to try to get him to do the painting he hired him to do. When Lippi gets the urges, though, he can't work, and he is no good for anything. So he was on his way to solve one problem, and the problem with Cosimo could wait until today.

"I ran into him just now. Cosimo had relented and told him he could do as he wished, he wouldn't lock him in anymore, but please, to paint. He said he did love living there, was headed to the palazzo with some new raw materials to make some fresh paint, and he was going to paint all night. He was a happy man."

The two of them had a good laugh, and Carlo said he couldn't wait to tell Lucrezia.

"When will she be home?"

"I expected her before dark. I hope nothing has happened."

"She is fine. Franco is a good man. They must have been delayed."

"Have you eaten?"

"Yes, I stopped by Jacko's. He wasn't there, but his uncle was. We chatted for a while, and I am going to do some work for him next week. He had his servant fix me a bowl of their leftover stew. It was good, but not as good as yours. I'm tired. I'm going up. I need to leave early in the morning. Are you all right?"

"Yes, I'm just staying busy while I wait for Lucrezia. Try to get home earlier tomorrow night. You don't want to miss the street party."

"Oh, all right. I did forget about it. Is the little princess asleep?"

"Finally! Good night, Carlo. See you tomorrow night."

With that, Carlo picked up Solo from the foot of the cradle and headed up to his room on the top floor. That was the first part of their rearranging of the living quarters in the house, and they had completed it to everyone's satisfaction. All they had needed to do was move some furniture up and some odd pieces down to clear space and bring the additional kitchen pots and supplies down.

With all of the cooking now being done in the downstairs room they used as their kitchen, as the room was designated, it meant they had the smell of food through the house, but they had long since gotten used to that. The girls were glad this was already their kitchen, because it made it easier for Amalia to keep an eye on things on the stove while trying to tend Lisabetta and still work diligently at her scribing. Most houses had servants to do the cooking on the loggia floor, the top floor of the house. Then they would bring the food down to the piano floor to be served at the table. That way the smells of the food and the cooking didn't permeate the living quarters.

That was all well and good, but even while Master Giuliano was alive, it had been decided to do the cooking downstairs to save Lucrezia having to run up and down stairs.

When old Maria moved to Pisa to live with her son, Lucrezia took over the household chores, and they never hired another live-in servant. A woman had come in to do the regular cleaning, and another woman had done their washing.

Now they didn't even have that, but they were all three young and strong, and they managed to get things done.

Now Carlo had himself a wonderful large room with a beautiful loggia and a lovely view of the city, all his own. Well, not quite his own. Everyone would still use the loggia for evening meals sometimes when the weather and their schedules allowed, but other than that, it was his.

He loved going out on the loggia first thing each morning to look at the sky and determine what the weather was going to be and thereby know what kind of a day he was likely to have.

Amalia would carry Lisabetta up with her when she went up to her room. She was still in her small bedroom simply because there had not been enough time in their busy days to make the new draperies and bed coverlet. Yet they were little by little rearranging the furniture the way Amalia was going to want it, and they had picked out the fabric they would use for the room. All of the old fabric would be recycled into Carlo's room, which did need window coverings and a bed cover, and the same in Lucrezia's sitting room when they got that done.

Lucrezia and Amalia had gone through her parents' cassone and decided what they would do with the fabrics and the garments stored in them. They had found a small cassone of some of Amalia's baby and childhood clothes that they didn't even know were there, so they got them out for Lisabetta.

They also found another smaller decorated cassone of jewelry in her mother's large cassone that Amalia had not known was in there. They decided, since their lifestyle certainly didn't call for such pieces, to leave that cassone in there, knowing they had a small treasure trove to fall back on should they ever need it. They had fun putting the necklaces up to their necks, pretending they were elegant ladies dancing in a large palazzo. They also pretended that Lisabetta would grow up to marry a rich man, and she would use the pieces then.

The worst was over, the emotional stumbling blocks were behind her, but Amalia still did not feel comfortable moving into the room until they re-did the draperies and bed cover.

Amalia heard Lucrezia's key in the door and greeted her as she came upstairs. "How was your trip? It's late. You must be exhausted."

"I am. Everything went fine. We just got a very late start from Fiesole, and there was a wagon broken down not too far from town. Franco stopped to help the man fix it. Amalia, I have so much to tell you! Oh, by the way, Signora Albertini loved the dress, and I have a pocketful of money. She gave me a handsome bonus for delivering the dress and staying up there overnight to complete the final alterations. It was well worth the trip in that respect. Tomorrow, we will dine like kings—or queens—well, three queens and one king!

"You won't believe this, but I saw the Medici villa in Fiesole, the one built by Michelozzo, and I met Messer Bracciolini. He said to say hello and for you to come along next time. I met his wife and several of his children. He looks tired, but I think his wife and all the children wear him down. Maybe he comes into town to rest. He said he is making good progress on his book, because life is quieter up there.

"The Medici villa is beautiful, nothing like the dark, massive Palazzo here in town. It has a spectacular garden. It meanders down the hillside and spills over everywhere. I would have liked to roam around in it, but neither of the men cared about that. None of the Medici were there, of course, but Poggio asked Messer Albertini and me to accompany him to an appointment he had with Messer Marcilio Ficino.

"I understand he usually lives in a small house Cosimo provided for him behind the Careggi villa where he works all the time translating the Greek works into volgare or latin. I don't know why he was in Fiesole, but I think he struggles. He's a very small man, and both shoulders are slightly humped; plus, he has a stammer. I suspect Poggio brought us along to make it easier for him to converse with everyone. He's a strange little man but obviously brilliant, and very pleasant. Once he starts to talk, you forget all the rest. The conversation flew over my head, but Messer Albertini is familiar with the humanist movement, and I was glad to be of help to Poggio.

"Messer Ficino had a manuscript to give to Poggio, and that was a part of why we were there. Poggio wanted me to deliver it to you since I happened to be there. He said it was very fortuitous, because it would save him having to send Rudolfo down with it to Messer Bisticci on Monday. It's a new Greek play Messer Ficino has just finished translating into the volgare, and Cosimo is very anxious to read it."

Amalia said, "I will deliver it to Messer Bisticci tomorrow. Since Careggi is where Messer Ficino lives, whenever Cosimo is there, there are gatherings to discuss one of those Greek plays. Master Manetti told me Cosimo had directed Messer Ficino to form the group they are calling the NeoPlato Academy, based on the old Greek Plato Academy. They are dedicated to the study of the writings and thinking of Plato, Aristotle, and Socrates and the other philosophers, in addition to discussing the Greek plays that are being found." Amalia sighed. "How Papa would have loved to have heard those discussions! So would I, for that matter. Of course, that would never have happened, but still I get to read the manuscripts while I copy them, and then you, Carlo, Rutia, and I get to discuss them. I wonder if our discussions sound anything like theirs."

They both laughed.

"The thinking back then is so far removed from how we think today," commented Amalia. "It's more like Lucretius' *On The Nature of Things*. Remember when we read that?"

"I do. Instead of God and the angels and reading about the lives of the saints, it was about the beauty of God's gift, the wonderful natural world all around us, and man and his place in that world," affirmed Lucrezia. "Messer Albertini stayed with Messer Ficino when Poggio and I left, and Poggio bent my ear about the humanists all the way back to Signora Albertini's home. He knows we've talked about it, and that I understood—sort of.

"You would love the villa. It's not as large as the Palazzo here in town, but it is beautiful, all light colors, and very open and airy inside. All the walls have beautiful frescoes of nature scenes, mountains, valleys, rivers, gardens. I can see why the family likes to spend time there."

Amalia said, "I'm sure I'd love it."

Lucrezia asked, "What has been happening here? I see Lisabetta is sleeping soundly."

"She is fine. We all are. Carlo has gone to bed. I think he is really enjoying his own little castle up there. Tomorrow ask him about men dropping from the sky. He has a wonderful story.

"AnnaMaria came up before she went home to say she had a good day, and she was very busy. Your new seamstress was there all day today and yesterday and got everything done you left for her to sew. AnnaMaria thinks you will be well pleased with her work. Three potential customers came by to see you about dresses, and they each said they will come back next week. She will tell you all about them tomorrow.

"And I have been experimenting with adding more colors to my artwork on some pages, and I am really enjoying it. I told you I was going to take it by Messer Bisticci's to see if he approved, and he said it was excellent! I am excited about doing it. Now I have to be sure I don't get carried away. These are only copies for sale, after all, but he said he can pay me a lot more for each manuscript because of it. That's all I can think of to tell you right now.

"Oh, Lucia thanked you for the pillows and says she wants two more just like them, but AnnaMaria will tell you about it tomorrow when she sees you.

"We had a brief rain last night, so with the downpour in the beginning of the week, the garden is well watered. That saves us all a chore tomorrow. Maybe some weeding is all that is needed."

"Well," said Lucrezia, "then maybe we should call it a night and go to bed. I am exhausted. Will you be in your office tomorrow morning?"

"Yes," said Amalia. "I'll just bring Lisabetta down with me."

"Good, then. I bolted the door when I came in. If you carry Lisabetta, I'll carry the candle."

As they got to the top of the stairs, Amalia turned to Lucrezia. "Lucrezia, Beatrice told me there has been no further news from Ravenna."

"Thank you, Amalia. I was afraid to ask. I guess we have no way of knowing whether that is a good sign or a bad one. It's in God's hands."

"I am so sorry. Good night, Lucrezia. Sleep well," said Amalia as Lucrezia lit the candle on the cassone inside Amalia's door. Then Amalia, carrying the baby, closed the door for the night.

A book scribed by Ambrosio Traversari in 1474 Florence

Amalia came home from Messer Bisticci's with a new manuscript and additional ink, nibs, and paper under one arm and a wrapped up, fresh fish tucked under the other. She knew her dress would smell like the fish by the time she got home, but when one of Donatello's helpers stopped her to ask if she was Carlo's friend, she had no choice but to take it, knowing it was one of Carlo's many deals.

"This will save me having to go to the marketplace to meet him. Please tell him I will meet him tomorrow for our game as usual. Thank you, signora," said the young man as he turned back into the boddeghe.

Well, she thought, it appears we will be having fresh fish for dinner!

She called up the stairs when she came in, but no one answered. She tried the knob and then knocked on the locked door to Lucrezia's shop. She knew Lucrezia was out on a fitting, but where was Lisabetta? She went up and started dinner, knowing Lucrezia would be home shortly. She had no idea what had happened to Lisabetta, and she was worried. Did AnnaMaria take her home with her because no one was here? Certainly Lucrezia would not have taken her with her to a fitting. By the time she heard the door open, she had worked herself into a very anxious state.

Carlo came bounding up the stairs with little Lisabetta on his shoulders, giggling and pulling his hair with one hand while the other was gouging his nose.

Although she was vastly relieved, Amalia wanted to know what had happened.

"Where have you been? Where did you take Lisabetta? What is going on?

"Don't worry, Amalia. She was with me, and we have been having a good time. Haven't we, Lisabetta?"

"Yes. I rode donkey, Ama. It were fun."

Carlo said, "I had to help my new friend, Marco, get a load of lumber to his boddeghe, so I took Lisabetta with me."

"Carlo, you should have let me know. I didn't know where she was."

"Well, she was safe with me. You know I wouldn't let anything happen to her, Amalia."

"I'm sorry, Carlo. Of course, you wouldn't. I was just so worried when no one was here. I didn't know what happened. What does she mean, she rode a donkey?"

"I was wondering when that would come to you. Like I said, I couldn't delay delivering the lumber to Marco at his boddeghe, and AnnaMaria needed to go home early, so I took Lisabetta along. She rode the donkey on the way back."

"Who is your friend, Marco?"

"I told you about him. He is new in town and doesn't know his way around. I knew of this broken down old boddeghe out near the wall toward the Pisa gate that no one used anymore. He is from Ferrara, but he only returned from Turkey a few months ago. He wants to settle in Florence. He works copper, and he thought there might be a market here for his pots, pans, and cauldrons.

"I like him, and I think you will too, but he is very busy trying to get settled in. He had to practically rebuild the boddeghe in order to have a place to store his supplies and equipment, then try to talk to someone at the guild. It has been several weeks now, and they won't give him permission to work."

"You mentioned your new friend, Marco, but I thought he was your age. This sounds like an older man," said Amalia, as Lisabetta climbed up into her lap at the kitchen table where Amalia and Carlo were sitting.

"I see Salvatore sent the fish home with you," noted Carlo. "I went by the market, and he hadn't been there. I'll start fixing it," and as he worked he said, "and, yes, my friend is older, but I like him, and he has paid me well for what I have been doing for him."

Soon they heard Lucrezia calling as she slammed the door downstairs and made her way to the kitchen.

"I smell fish!" she cried. "Do we feast tonight?" She tousled the curls on Lisabetta's head, then bent down and kissed them. By then, Solo had jumped up on an empty chair, so she gave him a quick rub.

The three of them sat at the table with glasses of wine and shared the experiences of their day, while Lisabetta sucked her thumb and cuddled up to Carlo. She was almost three now and usually a bundle of energy, but apparently her afternoon with Carlo had worn her out.

She managed to take the thumb out of her mouth long enough to tell Lucrezia about her donkey ride. Then the thumb went back in her mouth and her head tucked again into Carlo's chest.

"I think it will be an early night for the little donkey rider," said Amalia. "Maybe we should feed her now. I don't think she will last until the fish is cooked."

"I'll fix something to go with the fish for us," said Lucrezia, and so a companionable evening was passed by the three good friends.

~ ~ ~

Two evenings later, they were again sitting at the kitchen table, and Carlo was telling them his friend, Marco, still could not get approval from the guilds to work.

"Will someone come help me up these stairs, or do I have to sit down here on the bottom step by myself?" called Dona Rutia in her raspiest voice. Carlo ran down and carried Rutia up the stairs, swooped her into the kitchen, and gently sat her down on one of the chairs that had a cushion.

"We weren't expecting you, or we would have lit the torch," said Lucrezia.

"I know the way, thank you. Is there any wine in this house, or do I need to bring my own?"

"Here, here," said Amalia, smiling as she poured Dona Rutia a glass.

"Now, what were you discussing before my grand arrival, thanks to Carlo, my chariot?"

"I was just telling the girls about my new friend, Marco." Carlo went on to tell the three of them that Marco was very worried the guilds would lock him out. He could go to another town, but he wanted to settle in Florence. Carlo said Marco had plenty of money, but still, he had to be able to work his trade. His money would not last forever, and a man needs to work. What could he do?

"A sad tale," said Rutia. "Sometimes the guilds wield too much control. They have to let in fresh blood or the trades and crafts will not thrive. Where is he from?"

Carlo told them that he had been raised in Ferrara, his mother and father were dead, and he had traveled a lot around Italy and the Mediterranean. He had been over in Turkey, and now he wanted to settle in Florence, but it appeared Florence didn't want him.

"That is quite a story, Carlo. When do we get to meet this great traveler?" asked Rutia.

"I don't know. He goes every night to socialize with the craftsmen to try to make a friend who will help him get a foot in the door with the guild, but so far all he gets is a hangover. He doesn't like that at all. He has already tried arranging a meeting with the guild leaders at the council, and they won't listen, so he thought he would try the back door. Now he doesn't know what to do. I think he will leave soon, because it just isn't working out for him here."

"He sounds like a good man," said Rutia. "Carlo, you have always been kind to me and a good friend, so I consider you an excellent judge of character. I think I will have a dinner party Saturday night and invite all of you, and your new friend, Carlo. I will ask Beatrice and Giovanni, Maria and Filippo, Juliana and Guido, and maybe Teresa and Riccardo. Carlo, you get us some nice fish, and girls, you fix some extras, and if Beatrice brings one of her desserts, I'll supply the wine. Tell Teresa I liked the rice dish she served last month, and it will go with the fish."

Everyone agreed that would be an excellent idea, and they looked forward to the end-of-the-week party. Carlo informed them that Marco said he would be very pleased to accept. He might be leaving town if nothing good turned up soon, but he could put it off until next week since he had no definite plans.

Carlo was out of town Friday and Saturday, working with Jacko at a nearby farm owned by Jacko's uncle. Lucrezia was reasonably caught up and decided to spend Saturday working in the garden, and once Amalia was done with her letter reading and writing for the neighbors in her downstairs office, she joined Lucrezia to help her do some weeding. They also staked the tomato and zucchini plants in the garden. Lisabetta was over at Caterina's, playing with Blanche. Neither girl was happier than when they were together, and tonight was special because Lisabetta would spend the night at Blanche's house. Both little girls were very excited about that.

Lucrezia and Amalia finished in the garden and had time to fix two vegetable dishes for dinner, before getting ready themselves. Amalia had washed her hair when they had finished the work in the garden, and now Lucrezia asked if she could fix Amalia's hair in a fashion she had seen a few days ago on a lady visiting at a customer's home. Amalia was very pleased with the results, and Lucrezia was well pleased with her efforts, so they were both in an ebullient mood as they set off for Dona Rutia's house.

Seven o'clock was the agreed-upon hour, and when the bells rang, they headed out the door. They had not heard from Carlo. They hoped he remembered that he was supposed to bring the guest of honor and the main course of fish for dinner. The girls joked as they walked over to Dona Rutia's that it would be a sparse meal if all they had were vegetables, dessert, and wine. Well, maybe not so bad after all, they laughed, enjoying the idea.

Months ago, as her legs were failing her, Dona Rutia had moved her bed down to the ground floor along with most of her more comfortable furniture. She lived very comfortably in the much more limited but adequate space. Generally nobody lived on their ground floor but left it to be let out or used for storage. Dona Rutia had not rented out the space for many years, and what was stored in there was just moved elsewhere.

It had been a neighborhood project when it became evident Dona Rutia could no longer deal with the long flights of stairs in her large but now useless home. She could live up there, but she would be a prisoner and would have still been limited to one floor. This way she was free to walk to a friend's home, sit in her garden, and go to church. She liked that feeling of independence. Her daughter begged her to come live with them, but she preferred to stay in her house with Maddalena, who still had strong legs, and to live near her old and young friends.

Her husband had collected many old statues from the old Roman days, a thousand years ago or maybe even more. Such statues were oftentimes found in the countryside. They were always being dug up by the farmers throughout Tuscany, or a cluster of them might be found in an abandoned copse of trees. Some were missing an arm or a head, but her husband would tote them home anyway. He would line them up against the side walls of the traditional vegetable and herb garden that Dona Rutia and Maddalena had maintained behind their house through the years. Then there came a time when neither of them could or wanted to do the heavy work necessary to maintain the garden, so it had been allowed to go wild except for some tomato plants.

Several years ago, Dona Rutia had hired a gardener to come in and redo her entire back garden area into a display garden of all her husband's old statues. The statues were brought, one by one, into the center of the garden and each was placed on a pedestal with boxwoods around it and a stone pathway between each one, with maybe some flowers or herbs inside the boxwoods. In the recent years both she and Maddalena enjoyed walking the pathways around all the old statues, and a gardener came in regularly to maintain the boxwoods and the herbs and flowers.

Now, living on the ground floor, Dona Rutia could sit in her loggia and look at her statuary garden while sipping her glass of wine whenever she was so inclined. She could listen to the birds sing, see them and the butterflies flit from plant to plant, statue to statue, and admire Roberto's old, broken statues. She was old and broken too, so she saw herself in many of them, she had told Amalia and Lucrezia. Well, not the headless one.

Her large loggia space was now maintained beautifully since it was now a major sitting, relaxing, and entertaining area, but tonight Filippo and Giovanni had set up a large table in the middle. As people and platters of food arrived, the area filled with the warm ambiance of good friends. Giovanni and Filippo had carried out Rutia's favorite chair and placed it so she was right in the center of all the conversations. That way she could take her pick which one she wanted to become a part of. Beatrice and Teresa brought their servants, because everyone knew Maddalena could never handle all the work herself.

Everyone had arrived and all were admiring the arrangements, except Carlo and his special friend, Marco. Amalia and Lucrezia had passed several concerned looks between them, but finally, Carlo came with his friend.

Since everyone had already had a glass or two of Dona Rutia's excellent wine, the greeting was quite spirited, but Carlo did manage to introduce his friend to everyone, particularly to Lucrezia and Amalia. Riccardo, an excellent cook, took charge of the fish, but dinner would be delayed a bit because of the late arrival of the entree. That presented no problem, as the conversations were sparked by interest in the new arrival, the guest of honor.

Marco was peppered with many questions since it was obvious by the looks of surprises on all the faces present that he was not at all what anyone had been expecting of a friend of Carlo's. No one had actually voiced it, but everyone was expecting a very young man barely out of his teens, looking for an apprenticeship with one of the guilds. Marco was a tall, well-built man in his late twenties, perhaps even his early thirties, with light brown hair surrounding a handsome face. He had beautiful blue eyes that smiled almost as warmly as did his mouth. When he spoke, he drew everyone's attention just by a natural, easy command.

Amalia was not immune to those good looks, but it was the way he spoke that totally captivated her attention. She was seated across from him when they finally sat to eat, so she could observe him easily without staring. But there were times when she had to gather herself, for she did find herself staring whenever he spoke and sometimes even when he wasn't talking.

He had wonderful tales to tell, and he was not shy. He clearly wanted these people to like him and wanted to be completely open with them. He explained how his mother had died when he was young, and he had worked with his father from a young age whenever he was not in school. His father was not an educated man, but he wanted to be sure Marco had every advantage his hard-earned money could provide for him, so sacrifices were made. Marco appreciated those sacrifices, so he applied himself diligently to his studies. Also, he would help his father at his copper workshop whenever he could.

When his father was stricken with a fever and died, Marco sold their home and his father's shop, except for his father's anvil. Then he had put the money, the anvil, and his few belongings into the care of his uncle.

At that time, the City of Ferrara was overwhelmed by the Council that Pope Eugenius IV had convened to try to resolve the differences between the Roman and the Greek churches and to discuss the many other schisms. Pope Eugenius IV was there, along with the Byzantine emperor, John VIII Palaiologos, John Argyropoulos, a Greek diplomat, and the representatives of the Patriarchal Sees of Antioch, Alexandria, and Jerusalem. Emperor Zara Yaqob from Coptic Ethiopia sent Alberto da Sarteano as an apostolic delegate. Then there was Abram of Souzdal, a Russian bishop, the archbishop of the Serbian Orthodox Church, and representatives from Armenia to Russia, Greece to India. Indeed, religious leaders from all around the Mediterranean had descended on Ferrara.

Each brought with them a large entourage of people—assistants and servants—and animals, including horses, camels, elephants, lions, leopards, tigers, monkeys, giraffes, and more. The animals as well as the people were attired in the finest of silks, brocades, wools, and golden chains. They wore silk coats, magnificent hats, and had elaborate bridles for the animals. There were ornamented cages and golden woven ropes for the monkeys sitting on people's shoulders. There was an endless array of finery in an infinite display of riches from their far-flung countries.

The problem was, before they could even settle down to business, the fever struck the city—the same fever that took Marco's beloved father—and Ferrara was completely unable to cope with the congestion now that the contagion had struck.

Fortunately, Cosimo de' Medici offered the city of Florence as an alternative host city. Everyone was welcome in Florence as his guest and at his personal expense if they would but make the journey—also at his expense.

Not by coincidence, Cosimo had invited the pope to come to Florence for the consecration of the new cathedral now that the dome had been completed by Brunelleschi. The two events would tie in beautifully. All the celebrations and festivals for the one would just spill over into the grand displays of the other.

"And so it was I came to Florence when I was eighteen, with the caravan. I made friends with the Byzantine party from Turkey, the Emperor, John VIII Palaiologos. I left everything behind with my uncle, and began my great adventure."

Lucrezia said, "I remember when that happened. What an exciting time it was!"

Everyone else joined in remembering when all the magnificent animals and their splendid riders and the many walkers paraded through the streets of Florence. The Florentine families that would be hosting the various dignitaries in their homes and providing the many feasts, celebrations, entertainments, and more walked along with the many foreign dignitaries.

"I have never seen such an array of colors and more gold than I thought existed," said Maria.

"It was not just the colors but the styles from all around the Mediterranean: many African nations, so many from the Levant, Turkey, India, Greece. Lucrezia, you would have gone crazy with the fashions from those places," said Juliana.

"I saw that, Juliana, and I remember being amazed, but I was way too young to remember what they looked like. I guess I was about ten or eleven years then.

Maybe I should try to recall some of them. Maria, would you wear those pantaloons the Turkish men wore?"

"I wouldn't have the nerve, but I imagine they would be very comfortable. Maybe you girls should try them as gardening attire." Several of the women collapsed into a fit of laughter, and the rest wondered what was so funny.

Maria just waved them off as she gathered herself and said, "Sorry," but Amalia and Lucrezia exchanged secret smiles with her.

Filippo went on: "They built a raised walkway from Santa Maria Novella all the way to the Duomo for all the dignitaries to walk. A lot of them were housed at the convent there, and then they had the council meetings at the Duomo, Every morning the parade of all of them in their finery was a thrill for the Florentine people. The boardwalk was two braccio high, so everyone got a good look at the men, the attire, the jewels, the hats, and the animals, everything. What a magnificent display it was.

"I remember every once in a while in the night the howls and roars of the animals went on for hours and kept the entire city awake. Now there are only a few lions and a few of the other animals left out at the zoo, but they still get to roaring every once in a while. I heard them about a week ago.

"I remember one story about a lioness getting loose and creating quite an uproar. It is said that while everyone ran, seeking safety, the lioness came upon one small boy sitting in the street near the Church of San Martino. The mother was by her door, but she was too frightened to come out to rescue her son. The lioness picked up the boy as if he were one of her small cubs, carried it over, deposited it at the feet of the mother, and then went on her way."

Everyone laughed, believing or not believing the story, but Dona Rutia said, "It is an old story, and many don't believe it could happen. Back then, though, I knew that mother's mother, and there is no question it happened. Over at the Church of San Martino, it is considered a miracle. They still mark the day every year."

"I can tell you," continued Marco, "many things happened in that time that were marvelous. I was young and impressionable, but the stories about those days were endless, one more unbelievable than the next. I hated to see it all end."

Riccardo said, "I understand it was considered a great success for the church at that time. It went on for several years, but then, within a year, when everyone got back to their countries, it all fell apart. Patriarch Joseph II died shortly after returning to Constantinople, and the Turks changed direction politically.

Filippo said, "Yes, but what a great success for Florence, thanks to Cosimo."

Riccardo said, "Several of the Greeks stayed. One was John Argyropoulos, who actually taught at the Florence Studium and was part of Cosimo's NeoPlatonic Academy for several years until he went up to Pavia to study. I think he first returned to Constantinople, but when it fell to the Turks, he came back at Cosimo's invitation to teach Greek at the university and study with the humanists."

Marco said, "Yes, I was in Constantinople when he left to return here. He is very special. I had made friends with some of the servants for the Greek prelates, and they were not at all surprised when he and some of the others returned to Florence."

Riccardo said, "Cosimo and the many other humanists were very interested in the writings of the Greeks and others, as the old manuscripts were coming to light, but they had no one to translate them. Cosimo offered Argyropoulos a position at the University of Pisa and promised to found a school devoted to the studies of Plato and Socrates, the Florence Studium, if they would return, and so they did."

Amalia chimed in: "I copy some of those manuscripts now that they have been translated into Latin and volgare. Now many people can read them here in Florence, and they are even sent north to France, England, and other places."

Carlo said, "You just read one of those to us this last winter, Amalia. But Marco, you said you went to Turkey, not Greece."

"Yes," Marco said, "I was helping the Emperor's party with the caravan and just generally whatever needed to be done. All the delegations left a lot of the animals behind in Cosimo's zoo, but it was still a large group making our way back east. I was young and eager and smart enough to know this was a chance that didn't come along but once in a person's life. Once the Patriarch, Joseph II, died, things sort of fell apart, but it was exciting and great fun. Then my time in Turkey was quite exciting. I picked up enough of the languages along the way to get by, so then I did a lot of different things and traveled to a lot of different places, just wherever a job or caravan took me.

"Eventually, I decided to make my way to the copper mines in the Caucasus Mountains. I knew about them because that was where my father got his supply of copper. It was very interesting, and I made a good friend in Erudius Forzdal, the manager of one of the mines. It was much harder work than I wanted to do, so after a couple years, I decided I would make my way back to Italy. We still have business dealings and communicate with each other. I received a communication from him just the other day.

"I had loved my time in Florence during the Council, and I felt perhaps it was time for me to settle down. So I thought I would try my father's trade here. I returned to Ferrara first. My uncle had died, and my aunt was glad to return to me my belongings; so here I am: anvil in hand, money in my pocket, a cart load of copper, a boddeghe, thanks to Carlo here, and I can't work!"

Beatrice said, "That is quite a story. I don't know how we will be able to help you, but with Carlo as a friend, you now have a circle of acquaintances who can at least sympathize and offer you encouragement."

"Thank you," said Marco. "That's very much appreciated. I hope to get to know all of you better in the coming weeks and months, if I am able to stay."

Giovanni said, "I don't know how much help we can be, but we do have some friends in the Fabbri, and we will do what we can. Won't we, Filippo?"

"Yes, of course, said Filippo, "I have a good friend in the Fabbri, but besides the guild, we can talk to Messer D'Alessandro. Maybe he will be able to do something."

"Well," said Rutia, "I need some new pots, so as soon as you get the guild's approval, you have your first customer."

Maddalena perked up from her comfortable chair in the corner where she had been nodding off.

She said, "What do you need pots for? You haven't cooked anything in forty years."

"Well, maybe it's time I do. Your cooking has gotten terrible."

With that, everyone laughed and began to get up from the table, calling an end to a long and enjoyable evening. Beatrice went over to help Maddalena out of her chair and give her a tender hug.

Later Beatrice whispered to Teresa and Amalia that Dona Rutia could be unkind at times. Amalia laughed and said that the two of them fought like cats and dogs but were devoted to each other. She added that Dona Rutia almost always had a nip like a feisty terrier, but she had a heart of pure gold.

As she said this, she looked around. Riccardo and Marco were having a private conversation off to the side as everyone began to push chairs against the wall, carry chairs back inside Rutia's apartment, and then gather the empty platters to take home. Juliana, Maria, and the two servants had gathered the plates and washed them all by the time everyone was ready to leave. Marco came over to say

good night to Amalia, and said, "I hope we will have an opportunity to meet again."

Amalia laughed and said, "If you are a friend of Carlo's, I'm certain of it. You will always be welcome in his home. I very much enjoyed meeting you to-night."

Marco said, "May I see you safely home?"

"Thank you, but it is only across the street, and Lucrezia and Carlo are right here."

"Well, good night, then."

As Marco bowed slightly toward her, the three of them left Rutia's front door and walked the few braccia to their front door.

Once they were inside and walking up the stairs, Amalia said, "Carlo, you have the most interesting friends."

Carlo laughed, and said, "Just the one, Amalia, just the one," and the three friends laughed.

The River Arno

XV *Withering on the Vine*

It was just past dawn, and Carlo stood at the railing of his rooftop loggia overlooking the roofs of Florence as he inhaled the fresh breeze of the first cool air of the season. The summer had been a very hot one, and he could only hope that it might finally be over now and cooler weather on its way. It had been a bad summer for many of his friends.

Lucrezia had heard little about Ermanno and what she did hear wasn't good. Giovanni had told her that his young brother had died, and then after a long struggle, his father had also died. His mother had recovered but was left very weak. He was fighting with his father's partner, but nothing was coming of it.

Marco had filed appeal after appeal with the Fabbri guild, the guild for the metal workers of Florence, but there was no positive response. Giovanni and Filippo spoke to everyone they knew, but it was felt there were enough metal workers in Florence, and they didn't need an outsider. It was not exactly a no, but certainly it was not a yes.

Jacko, Carlo's best friend and "partner" in most of his business ventures, broke his leg in a calcio game and was out of action for most of the summer. After the first couple of weeks, they knew it had been a clean break and a good knit. He probably would heal with no deformity or limp, but mobility was still weeks away.

All the wealthy people had abandoned the city for the hot months and gone to their country villas. Commerce had ground to a very slow pace, if not a halt, and this contributed to the lack of response to Marco's many pleas to join the guild and the commune.

Beatrice was pregnant, as were Caterina and Teresa, and all three were quite miserable and foul-tempered. Lucrezia and Amalia, with AnnaMaria's help, took little Blanche off Caterina's hands as often as possible, which pleased the two girls no end. Beatrice had Giovanni's parents right next door, and Teresa's parents were nearby where they lived near Orsanmichele, but still, there was no relief from the sweltering heat and the discomfort it brought to the pregnant women.

Filippo didn't have enough work to keep him busy, so he spent time at home underfoot. Maria said she was ready to pull her hair out.

Juliana was very busy at the hospital where she worked. With the summer heat came many extra cases of malarial fever, and waves of typhoid, so Guido was left home alone, and he complained endlessly to all the neighbors.

Finally, with the weather break, everything would improve, Carlo believed. As the wool and silk merchants came back to town, commerce would start to pick up, money would begin to flow, jobs would be plentiful, and everyone's health and attitudes would improve, except, of course, Teresa, Beatrice, and Catrina, who would be united but singular in their misery as they each approached their time of delivery.

Amalia and Marco had definitely formed an attachment. Marco came by to visit Amalia very often, much more than would be appropriate except Amalia always made sure they were in public. They took walks down by the river, sat on the bench Lucrezia had put outside the window of her shop, or walked over to one of the zoos of the exotic animals maintained by the Signoria and Cosimo out past San Marco. These were remnants of the animals left so many years ago when all the foreign dignitaries from the famous Council went home.

Often times, though, a visiting ambassador brought a new camel, monkey, or lion, and the zoo would be imbued with fresh blood. The zookeeper currently was a man as fearsome as the fiercest of his caged animals, and no one was allowed to tarry too long or to annoy the animals.

They also enjoyed walking by the construction sites of the several palazzos that were being constructed now that Cosimo had set the example of how a rich Florentine banker should live.

Their courtship was so public, everyone joked about it, but Amalia knew there was certainly no chance of privacy. Messer D'Alessandro was aware of their involvement, and Amalia trembled every time she caught him watching them.

There was so much to learn about each other, they were never at a loss for conversation, but the times they could meet were limited. Sometimes they would take Lisabetta with them to a park area where she could run around, but Amalia didn't want to fall behind in her scribing, even if the heat in the house became unbearable sometimes.

Marco reminded her that she had said that he, Marco, was always welcome at Carlo's home, but he never got invited inside. She asked if he was really there to see Carlo. If so, she would take a walk, and he could visit with Carlo. He would laugh and say he'd walk with her instead; that he liked Carlo fine, but he liked her much more.

Marco made a trip to Siena and found he would be able to work if he moved there. By now, though, as the months passed, he was truly in love with Amalia and she with him. Neither of them could stand the thought of him relocating. She told Marco how, on her way home from shopping one morning, Amalia saw Messer D'Alessandro coming toward her, and she stopped him to ask if there was anything he could do on their behalf.

"It is not a matter of money, sire," said Amalia. "Marco Valetti has money, and he has been trained as a coppersmith. He just wishes the opportunity to ply his trade. Sire, is there anything you can do?"

"No, signorina. I have no influence with the guilds, and it is not appropriate for you to come to me about this matter."

"I am sorry, sire, but Signore Valetti will be forced to leave soon if he is not allowed to work. It just seems so unfair."

"There is nothing I can do." Messer D'Alessandro walked on.

That was the last hope. All their friends had tried everything they could think of. They had approached every person they thought might have some influence, and Marco had decided if nothing changed by the new year, he was going to have to move to Siena and hope that maybe in a year or two, the attitude of the Florentine guild would change.

Lucia and Luigi invited Beatrice and Giovanni, Riccardo and Teresa, Amalia, Lucrezia, and Marco for dinner. A discussion came up about the guilds. Marco understood how they were structured, with the major seven guilds representing the seven major industries in Florence: wool manufacturers, silk manufacturers, bankers, wool merchants, notaries and lawyers, pharmacists and physicians, and metal workers. Then there were the fourteen minor guilds: the bakers, butchers, locksmiths, hoteliers, woodworkers, leather workers and furriers, the blacksmiths and bootmakers. Furthermore, he knew they were a force in the Signoria, but why were they being so difficult? Giovanni and Riccardo explained to him how back a hundred years ago, the nobles ran everything, just like in all the other hill towns and cities in Italy, but the guilds rose in power and staged a revolt they call the Ciompi and threw the nobles out. That is when they really got organized. They said unless you were a member of one of the working guilds you couldn't be in the Signoria, so they disenfranchised the nobles.

Now the nobles were back in control by becoming merchants in the wool or silk trade or bankers, but the guilds still made a lot of the rules.

They told him how Cosimo de' Medici was considered to be a man of the people, even though he was very rich. His roots were with the poor people, and he had always espoused the causes of the poor, the popolo. That was the big dispute and why Senore degli Albizzi had Cosimo arrested and imprisoned in the top of the Palazzo Vecchio in the Alberghetto. When he couldn't kill him legally or by subterfuge, he managed to get him exiled. Renaldo degli Albizzi wanted to run the city of Florence the way the nobles had run it one hundred and fifty years before, but when Cosimo was exiled, he took his bank with him, and the all trade and production dried up. There was no work, and the people clambered for Cosimo's return.

When he returned, of course, he exiled the Albizzi's and their supporters, and he saw to it that trade and commerce began again, and he saw to it they continued to flourish in the present day. He respects the guilds and only imposes his will when there was more at stake than the commercial interests of Florence, so the guilds protect their power.

Knowing and understanding why the guilds guarded their power so jealously didn't help Marco any. After the requisite time passed between the submission of applications, Marco submitted one more appeal to the directors of the guild. A hearing was set for December 5th. He was called before them to make his application.

"Signoris, I am skilled at my craft," he told them. "I am not new to your community. I lived here for several years during the time of the Council of Florence.

I wish to settle in Florence and marry a Florentine woman and raise a family. If you do not allow new blood to enter the Fabbri, the guild will wither on the vine and grow stale in the art of copper craft. I have new ideas, and I am young and eager. I don't know—"

"You need say no more, Signori Valetti. We have decided to admit you to the guild on a one-year probation to be certain that there are no valid complaints about your craftsmanship or your character. You may come by to pick up your license on Monday. Welcome to Florence, sir."

Overwhelmed, Marco bowed his head.

"Thank you, signoris. I will do my best to see that your kindness has not been misplaced. Thank you."

With that, he left the room and almost ran to Amalia's house. He couldn't believe his good fortune, and he didn't understand what had changed their mind. It seemed to him their minds had been made up before he ever opened his mouth. He didn't care, he was in, and now—

He banged on the door, but there was no answer. AnnaMaria came out of the shop to tell him that Amalia was out running some errands and would be back shortly.

"Where did she go?" he demanded to know.

"She had several stops: Messer Bisticci. Master Manetti, the butcher, a friend's house to deliver a package, and Padre Bernardo about the festival."

Marco left to try to find her but at each stop he made, she had been there and left, so he wound up sometime later back at her front door. By this time she had returned, and the entire gonfalons had already heard the good news: that Marco had been admitted to the guild and could work and therefore would stay in Florence. Numerous people were gathered outside Amalia's house, wondering what would happen next.

As Amalia flung open the door to Marco, he took both her hands in his and said, "They approved. I can work. I can stay in Florence. Amalia, will you marry me?"

Amalia said, "Yes, yes, a hundred times yes!" The entire cluster of neighbors that had gathered cheered as Marco took Amalia in his arms and swung her around. Then, setting her back down on the ground, he took her face in his two hands and kissed her as all the neighbors cheered again.

Maria said, "Never has a courtship, proposal, and acceptance been such a public event. Isn't it wonderful, Messer D'Alessandro?" She thumped him on the back of his shoulder as he stood in front of her.

Messer D'Alessandro said, "It will be required for people to stand for them since there is no dowry and no parents to arrange these matters."

Maria retorted, "Messer D'Alessandro, this entire gonfalons will stand up for them. No one here will speak against them, and it is a glory in God's eyes. They are so deserving, and it is a joy to behold."

With that, Maria turned to some of the other neighbors. Within a very short time, plans were started for a party to be held that night. They wanted to celebrate an event that brought joy to the hearts of all the neighbors who had known and loved Amalia since she was a little girl, an event they never thought would be possible. She was to marry a man they all now knew and respected, and they could now welcome him into the commune. He had long since been welcomed into their hearts.

Many asked how the approval by the guild could happen after it had been so adamantly refusing Marco for so long. There was no answer except that apparently the directors had reason to change their mind.

No one would know for many years that the reason was because a message had come from Cosimo de' Medici himself through his secretary, Messer Palle. Many years later, one of the directors of the guild asked Messer D'Alessandro what could be Messer Medici's interest in the coppersmith. He said he had no idea, but he later mentioned it to Filippo, and Filippo told Amalia. She knew her indebtedness to Cosimo was now increased to proportions she could never repay. How had he found out about their plight? She was so grateful, and she knew there was no way she could convey that to him for by the time she found out that he had again intervened in her life, Cosimo had already died.

This would not be the most glamorous marriage ever held in the commune of Florence, not the most politically significant marriage, nor the largest wedding, but it would probably be the most joyful marriage, for the couple were certainly in love with each other. Their entire gonfalons of the Unicorn in the Gonfaloni of Santa Maria Novella loved both of them and were thrilled at the prospect of a union they had all watched grow and blossom before their eyes.

This would be one of the happiest days in Padre Bernardo's life, for he would be seeing his dear friend's daughter safely delivered into the hands of a man he liked and respected. He was grateful Marco would be taking charge of a responsibility for which he had carried a heavy burden in his heart.

The couple talked about going away for a few days, maybe over to the coast to the beautiful Cinque Terra. Yet Marco was anxious to get started at his boddeghe, so they decided that perhaps they would wait for the spring when the weather would be better.

Their marriage, which Padre Bernardo performed on the steps in front of their beautiful Santa Maria Novella in the early afternoon, took place shortly before Christmas. The sun was shining brightly on the magnificent marble facade of the church built by Leon Battista Alberti, on the loving couple, and on those gathered to be a part of this happy occasion.

Then the couple walked hand in hand over to the Palazzo Vecchio to register their marriage with the clerk. Many of the party walked with them, making it quite a happy parade through the streets of Florence over to the government center and then back to Amalia—and Marco's—home where still more of the gonfalons and many more friends had already gathered for the start of a wonderful feast.

Poggio had sent another large package of pork that Carlo could barely carry. A whole lamb had arrived the day before, and Filippo thought it had the ear markings of the Medici herd, but he wasn't sure. Amalia was sure, but she said nothing. Filippo and Giovanni took charge to see that all the meats were cooked to perfection for the big event.

Not only their neighbors were there but also their friends and even some friends of friends, for the word had spread beyond their not-so-small circle. Poggio had been invited, of course, but he was still in Fiesole and sent his regrets. Master Manetti came by, and Amalia had the opportunity to meet his wife and adolescent daughter. Messer Bisticci stopped by briefly, and he and Marco chatted for several moments. Master Vicenti and his wife came, Lucrezia's seamstresses, AnnaMaria, and several of Lucrezia's customers came; Carlo's "partners" all came and were even very helpful, carrying some of the heavy platters of meat over from Filippo's big oven in the back of his house to Amalia's loggia. Girlfriends of both girls came and their families, the old couple that rented the house behind Amalia's garden, friends from their confraternities at church, and several men from the guild that Marco had befriended. Amalia was pleased that they all seemed glad for him, even if he might be competition for a couple of them. He was easy to like and hard to dislike, she reasoned, so they no doubt chose the easier path.

This gonfalons had seen many happy gatherings in the past, but this day would be remembered as one of the best and happiest.

Little Lisabetta and Blanche and the many other sons and daughters of their friends ran endlessly through and around all the many legs and gowns, enjoying themselves immensely. They would be lifted high in the air on many occasions, then they would shriek and giggle to the joy of all nearby. Later, Caterina and Claudio would take both girls home with them, and Lisabetta would spend two days with Blanche, to the girls' mutual delight.

Lucrezia planned to spend the next few days with one of her girl friends, and Carlo would be staying over with Jacko's family, although he didn't understand why he had to leave his castle room. Lucrezia had told him that in a year or so he would understand, but for now, "Just do it."

Only Solo was staying, and he would tell no one of the events that went on in the now Dontarini-Valetti house during the next few days. He wasn't happy about being locked out of Amalia's bedroom that first night, but after that, his presence was tolerated although ignored. The murmurings in the room joined with his purring formed into a delightful chorus at various times during the subsequent days and nights, had anyone been there to hear it.

Very often in Florence, the bed in the master's bedroom was huge, often six braccio across. Even though Amalia's bed was only four braccio, she had always felt lost in the large bed compared to the bed she had slept in prior to their rearrangements and redecorating. Now she was no longer lonely or lost.

When Lucrezia moved back home, she said she was very glad they had spent the time and money to break through the wall to give her a private sitting room, because she was now able to make use of it and leave the rest of the house for the newlyweds.

Carlo was a bit disconcerted when Lucrezia would tell him it was his bedtime when it wasn't, and Lisabetta's bed was temporarily moved into Lucrezia's sitting room.

It didn't take long until they were all back in the large receiving room together in the evenings, Marco helping Carlo on a project or vice versa, the girls sewing, scribing, or reading, sometimes aloud, and Lisabetta traveling from lap to lap or amusing herself near the feet of one of her four guardians.

Amalia's mother's beautiful old rug in the entire middle of the large room got well used by the bottom, knees, and the feet of Lisabetta as she grew into a happy but very active young girl.

Lisabetta had her own slate, the one Carlo had used years ago for his studies, and everyone made it a game they played with her as they taught her to write her letters and numbers.

Marco spent a lot of his time during the next couple of months at the boddeghe he had rebuilt. With Carlo's help, he had built his fire pit and made some
samples of what he could do as a coppersmith. Carlo had found a large barrel
Marco would be able to use for the water he needed for the quenching stage in
his production. Marco bought it from the man, and Carlo carted it over to the
boddeghe and helped Marco dig the hole to set it in. Marco spent some time each
day, usually in the late afternoon, socializing with other smiths and tradesmen and
visiting various shops trying to build relationships in hopes they would stock his
pots and pans, cauldrons and bowls, and more.

It took time, as he knew it would, but eventually there began to be an interest in some of the items in his growing inventory. True to her word, Dona Rutia
was his first customer, and Maddalena was thrilled with the new pot and a large
pan she now had for cooking their meals. Yes, things were moving along, but not
as quickly as he would have liked. His patience was not running out entirely, to
be sure, but he was discouraged today and in a bad humor by the time he came
home.

Lisabetta had a bad cold, so she could not go to play with her friends. Since
she was home all day and very cranky, Amalia said she had done very little on the
manuscript she was working on. It was one she had never worked on, so it was
intriguing to her with regard to its content, and she was disappointed not to be
able to devote the attention to it she would have liked.

Carlo took a fall over by the Arno and had tumbled down the embankment
with his small cart. The wheel had broken off the axle, and it would not be usable
until he took the time out of his busy day tomorrow to fix it. Plus, he hurt all over.

By the time Lucrezia came up from the shop, Amalia had a vegetable stew
ready, and she had roasted a chicken for dinner. No one was arguing but everyone
was in such bad humors they were all pouting, sulking, aching, and sniffling.

As soon as she sat down at the table, Lucrezia started talking.

"I heard quite a story today. You know that the mills are struggling because of the cold and terrible rainy weather. No ships have been arriving at Pisa with raw wool since they are stranded in various ports because of high seas. No ships are leaving port either, so production and sales are both low. Well, the men were paid last week with cloth, and a lot of them are really unhappy. It will mean they will have to sell that cloth to the pawnbrokers for dirt cheap just to get rid of it and get however many picciolis they can get. The pawnbrokers know they are desperate, so they offer them very little.

Marco said, "Yes, there was a lot of talk about it on the streets the last few days. A lot of the workers are really upset."

Carlo chimed in: "Signori Scali, Gino's father, is talking about going to Milan to try to get work until the mills get back in full production and taking Gino with him. Gino is excited, but his mother isn't. She says things won't be any better there than in Florence."

"She is probably right," said Amalia.

"Anyway," said Lucrezia, "I have an idea, and I want to know if we have any extra money we can spare without going into our reserve fund."

"What is your idea, Lucrezia?" asked Marco.

"Well, things are slow in the shop, like everywhere else, because people aren't buying new dresses or capes or anything they don't absolutely need. I fear I will have to dismiss two of my seamstresses at the end of the week. What if I bought some of the cloth from some of the workers at a higher price than the pawnbrokers will pay them? It would still be cheaper than what I would pay Master Vicenti or the other cloth merchants. The workers would come out ahead, I would come out ahead, I could keep my seamstresses busy and not have to dismiss anyone, and when the garments sell, we would make a nice little profit.

"Depending on the quality and type of the fabric, I could make men's work garments or common work dresses or something better. Things will improve for everyone once the weather changes and the ships start sailing again. I think I can sell the pre-made garments then. We would just have to wait a couple of months for the return on the money. What do you think of the idea, and do we have any spare money?"

"I think we do," said Amanda, "I have made good money this year and have some extra. I think it's a wonderful idea. Lucia's son and Vittoria's son both got paid in fabric. It would be wonderful if we could help them out. They both have wives and young babies."

Lisabetta climbed up in Lucrezia's lap to tell her about her cold, and Lucrezia gave her lots of sympathy and hugs and rocked her while she continued.

"I just feel if we can help them in some way—"

Marco said, "I have cash, enough reserve until my business gets going. I am just worried, because it hasn't gotten going the way I thought it would, but I'm confident it will eventually."

Carlo said, "It will. I hear more and more talk about you and your pots and pans. I think it's just the weather and no spare cash; nobody is spending. I'm only getting hired when it's things people really have to do and can't put off. That's why Gino wants to go to Milan with his father, and Paolo may go with them."

Amalia said, "Don't you get any ideas. We need you here, and I don't think it's a good idea anyway. Just get whatever jobs you can get here and spend some extra time on your studies. You have to think about your future, Carlo, not just this winter."

Marco said, "I have a reserve, as much money as you need, Lucrezia, but there is something else we need to discuss. I have received a letter from Erudius Forzdal in Turkey, my friend from the copper mines. He is in position to send shipments of alum and copper. When I was still in Turkey, I agreed to take delivery when the ship docks in Ravenna, and then take it to a distributor in Bologna or Milan, I don't know where yet. It would mean I would be gone for probably two weeks, maybe more, and I would have to pay the freightage, then get reimbursed when I get paid in Bologna or Milan or wherever for everything. Erudius has set up an account with the Medici bank in Ravenna for the bill of exchange. It will be a sizable financial expense, but, as I say, I have the reserve cash. I can give you some now, and then when I get back, I'm sure I will have whatever you may need, Lucrezia."

Amalia pretended to cry. "Our first time apart. I hate the idea, but what a wonderful opportunity," she smiled.

"I was afraid of what you would think of the idea, but with everything that was happening here, I had actually forgotten about it until I got the letter today."

"Marco, I will miss you but I would never stand in the way of an opportunity like this for you. And by the time you return, they will be beating down the door of your boddeghe to buy your pots and pans."

Carlo had been sitting quietly, as Lisabetta had gotten down from Lucrezia's lap and climbed up in his.

As he wiped her nose and rubbed her back, he said, "I don't know how to say this, but could I come along? You know I have the cart and the wagon, and I do carting all over Florence and even up to Fiesole and Prato and some of the other nearby towns. I like doing it, and, even though I'm still too young, I can see a future for me in that kind of freighting. I'd like to see what is involved, and my large wagon is strong enough to transport the alum and copper."

Marco said, "It would be fine with me. I'd love the company, Carlo, but it's not for me to say."

Lucrezia said, "Well, I say go. The sooner the better. You have been a pest all winter with not enough to do, so it is a perfect time to go on an adventure."

Amalia said, "I'm definitely not happy about losing both of you, but I agree, it is an adventure and business, Carlo, you can't pass up, and a business deal, Marco, that you can't pass up either. In the meantime, I think we can scrape together enough cash, and, Lucrezia, you should buy as much cloth from the workers as we can afford. We can fall back on Marco's reserve after he gets back until the clothes start to sell.

"I haven't told any of you, but Caterina came by this morning. Several women right on her street have children near the same age as Blanche and Lisabetta, so her husband and she have hired a young girl from the orphanage to move in with them to take care of her two girls full time. She will also be taking care of the other neighborhood children for a few hours every day. She asked if I would want Lisabetta to join the group. I said yes. She needs to be around more children. Beatrice is going to do it also.

"There are plenty of schools at the various monasteries for boys, even at a young age, but almost no schools for girls. This girl from the orphanage can read and knows her rudimentary numbers. Caterina thinks this girl has the ability to run it as a small school as well as for play, and she would like to give it a try. I didn't know what you all would think of the idea, but I love it, plus it would free me up for a few hours. Then if Lisabetta spends a little time down in the shop, as usual, it would give me that much more time to work. It looks like I'm the only one right now with a lot of work and no time, so once Lisabetta is well, I would like to give it a try."

"I think it's a great idea," said Lucrezia. "You need the time, and it will be good for Lisabetta."

"I agree," said Carlo. "I get home when I can, but none of us has the time we used to have, and this will give you more time to work."

"Lisabetta needs the other children. It will be good for her too," said Marco.

While they had been talking, Amalia had served dinner, and now they were almost done. There was a knock at the door. Carlo ran down and let Beatrice in. She joined them at the table, and Marco poured her a glass of wine.

Beatrice handed Lucrezia a letter as she said, "It is from Ermanno. We had one also, so I know some of what he is probably telling you. I'm sorry, it is not good news. He is really struggling and has asked Giovanni for his input. Once you have read the letter, you may want to go over and talk to him."

Lucrezia took the letter and left the table to read it in private where she could concentrate.

Beatrice continued to talk to the rest of them.

"He is in a dispute with his father's partner, now his partner, and he is considering legal action. Also he is troubled about the proposed marriage with the partner's daughter. He doesn't know what to do. Giovanni just got back from talking to Riccardo, and he may be able to help. That is why I delayed bringing Lucrezia's letter over to her. There is more happening than just the letter."

"I am so sorry, Beatrice," said Amalia. "I know he is a good friend of Giovanni's, and you also. I hope Riccardo will be able to help him."

Lucrezia came back into the kitchen only to say she was going over to talk to Giovanni. Beatrice told her she would be along as soon as she finished her wine.

After Lucrezia was gone, Beatrice said, "I am so sorry for both of them. They obviously care about each other. With his father gone, his share of the business falls to Ermanno, but the partner is being very difficult, and Ermanno doesn't want any part of the business or the daughter. What can he do?"

"I don't know," said Amalia, "but it has been very difficult for Lucrezia."

Turning to Marco, she said, "You haven't met Ermanno. He and Lucrezia met here in this house several years ago, and I think Lucrezia fell in love with his beautiful voice before she ever got to know the man. His father made arrangements with his partner years ago for Ermanno to marry the partner's daughter, Antonia is her name, but they don't even like each other—"

"To put it mildly," said Beatrice.

"Then Ermanno's father and brother died a year ago, two of the few victims of the plague that year in Venice and Ravenna. His mother, who survived the plague, has been left very frail. Ermanno is trying to work in the business with the partner, even though he hates it, but he is sure the partner is taking advantage of him, as Beatrice said. What a mess! Ermanno and Lucrezia can't see each other, of course, but he does write Giovanni, and Giovanni tells Lucrezia what is going on. On the one occasion Ermanno got to come over here, we all conspired to give them time together, unbeknownst to Master D'Alessandro or even the other neighbors, but it was risky for us.

"Ermanno would like to pursue a career singing, but he doesn't know how or even if he could make a living doing it. In the meantime, he is tied to this partner. He spent some time in Florence a few years ago and has some friends here, but he just doesn't know what to do." Looking at Beatrice, she said, "It sounds like this might be some sort of crossroads if Giovanni went to talk to Riccardo."

"Maybe," said Beatrice. "Let me get back. I think Gia may need some attention, and I don't want her disturbing Giovanni and Lucrezia. I'll see you tomorrow for confraternity? Have you read the poems?"

"Yes, several times. I really like the third one. It will be an interesting meeting. See you then," said Amalia.

Marco marveled at how the little "family" had all pulled together and cheered up with their plans and aid to one another.

By the time Lucrezia got back, Amalia had cleaned up after dinner, and Carlo had put Lisabetta to bed. She had fallen asleep in his lap, so he just carried her upstairs. Marco had gone next door to ask Filippo if he could borrow some tools from him in the morning, and he returned just ahead of Lucrezia.

"Well," Lucrezia addressed Marco and Amalia, "I hardly know what of it is good or bad. What Beatrice surely told you is what Ermanno wrote to me also. He would like to see me. He is planning somehow to make a trip over as soon as he can without the partner/father, Signori Benedetto, or the daughter knowing, so he will just come when he can and stay with Beatrice and Giovanni.

"In the meantime, Riccardo has to go to Ravenna to settle an estate for a client. He has been putting it off and was going to put it off until the spring, but now he is going to go right away. He doesn't know what he can do, but he agrees with Giovanni that Ermanno needs some legal advice."

"Ermanno is in Ravenna, you say?" asked Marco. "I didn't know that was where he lived. That's where I'll be going next week. Maybe there will be something I can do while we are there. I'll talk to Giovanni tomorrow about it. I think I will go up now and write the shipping company to let them know I will be taking delivery whenever the shipment arrives. Erudius said the shipment was being loaded on a ship that was intending to leave port the next weather break after he sent this letter to me, so I think I should plan to go over as soon as possible."

Carlo walked into the kitchen and said, "I just went upstairs and packed. Next week, you say? I'm ready. I'm not near as sore now as I was when I got home."

"Why are you sore?" asked Amalia.

His tale about his tumble down the embankment was told as they put out the candles and the oil lamp in the middle of the table, and climbed the stairs, each with things to do and things to think about once they closed their bedroom doors, and Carlo climbed the stairs to his castle room.

~ ~ ~

The rest of the week was spent making the many arrangements for Marco's, Carlo's, and Riccardo's travels, Lucrezia's purchases, and Lisabetta's first school days.

Once Lucrezia put out the word she would buy the cloth, many of the workers visited her shop, and she bought all she thought her girls could handle and spent all she felt they could afford to spend without overburdening her shop or their finances. They stacked up all of this cloth on a separate table in Lucrezia's back room, and Lucrezia intended to keep the finances for this venture separate from her usual shop work.

Carlo worked extra hard on getting ahead where he could on deliveries and other jobs and arranged for Jacko to take over and Gino and Paolo to help him, especially if the two of them didn't go to Milan.

Marco managed to get a few pots and pans and other items into a couple shops as samples. He and Carlo brought his large copper reserve home to be stored in the downstairs storage room, as he did not feel it would be safe in the abandoned boddeghe if he was going to be gone from Florence for several weeks.

It was decided it was time for Carlo to buy a horse to save having to borrow one all the time, and Riccardo decided to ride over with them. Using Carlo's wagon would make the trip slower, but it was a trade-off because now Marco wouldn't have to find and buy a wagon in Ravenna. Riccardo even tied his horse to the back of the wagon and rode with them for parts of the long journey over the mountains.

Once word spread throughout the commune of their trip with the wagon to Ravenna, several people asked if Carlo would deliver items to friends, relatives, or businesses in the area, and Carlo, now being a long-distance freighter, took charge of all of those arrangements.

Marco found it difficult to believe how efficient Carlo was and how everyone treated him as if he were a much older man, mature and responsible. Carlo told Marco that once they got to Bologna and Milan, after they delivered Marco's shipment, he would spread the word and would probably be able to make the trip back to Florence a profitable venture also.

Marco told him he was too young to undertake this on his own, and Carlo agreed, but he said he would make a few contacts and see how things were done. In a few years or if he could tie in with some other freighters making the trip, it would be safe for him to get started. Plus, he reminded Marco, Jacko was a couple years older than he was and big for his age instead of being small for his age, as Carlo was. Things would happen.

What a boy, thought Marco.

Once they arrived in Ravenna, Ermanno invited the three of them to stay with him and his mother. Their home was a very nice townhouse in the heart of the city, larger than Amalia and Marco's home.

Once settled in, Carlo left to attend to the deliveries of his shipments and then find a stable to bed down his horse, Traveler, and store the wagon. Once all of that was done, he was free to pursue other things.

Marco got directions from Ermanno and left to go down to the docks and the shipping company's office near the docks. He found out the docks weren't anywhere near the town but a long ride by horseback toward the coast. Riccardo offered him the use of his horse, and he was very grateful. This left Riccardo and Ermanno free to discuss his problems and see if Riccardo had any input to help Ermanno solve them.

Marco got back quite late and Carlo was even later, but finally the four of them sat down for a very late meal. Marco had good news. The weather had improved, which they already knew, and the ships were sailing, presumably in both directions, for the last few days, at least. Marco felt he could expect his ship to arrive in port by the end of the week, surely. Riccardo's horse was in Ermanno's small stable behind his townhouse, but Carlo would bed it down tomorrow at the same place he had found for Traveler.

Riccardo said he had some ideas that he and Ermanno had been discussing, and he was going to try to meet with Signori Benedetto tomorrow.

Carlo waited patiently while they exchanged their information, because he was quite confident his information would put an end to all other discussion.

Finally, he interjected: "Ermanno, I am sorry to tell you, but the woman you are proposed to marry, Antonia, is having an affair with the carpenter, Vittorio, who lives on the other side of town."

"Carlo, how do you know that? Where did you hear that?" chorused Ermanno and Marco.

"While I was making my deliveries, I got familiar with the town. It's not very large, so I knew where I wanted to go once I got Traveler and the emptied wagon taken care of. Then the stable boy was a big help. So I went around, and I heard things.

"She manages to see him three or four times a week, just about every time you and her father go down to the docks. Also, your partner is in deep debt to your suppliers, and at least one of them is getting anxious. If he doesn't get paid soon, he is going to take action. He is your main supplier of the hemp for the lines, ropes, halyards—whatever they are—and the cordage. I don't know what I'm talking about, but he is sick of waiting for his money. I know that."

Ermanno said, "Carlo, how did you find all this out?"

"Everyone ignores a kid. I know where to go and how to listen."

Riccardo said, "It looks like there will be more to discuss with your partner than we had planned. We just might have some leverage now on both counts. I feel a lot better about this. Thank you, Carlo. You just may have helped Ermanno a great deal."

"Also, Marco, the Bologna market is glutted with alum because the bishop is importing from a supplier through Venice. You probably need to find another buyer."

"That's not good news, but at least we won't waste the trip there. Maybe we should just take it back to Florence and find a buyer there. I wonder if the Medicis will buy from me. They have their own ships, and I don't want to run competition with them. I'll do some checking tomorrow. Thanks, Carlo."

With that, everyone was ready to go to bed. It had been several long hard days of traveling, then a lot of business was accomplished once they reached town, and everyone was tired.

The next day, Marco found out Carlo's information was correct, and there was no point in taking their shipment to Bologna. Marco didn't need all the copper, but he knew he could eventually find a market for it and make a good profit for himself and Erudius.

The alum was another story. He wasn't familiar with the market and would have to hope he could dispose of it without running competition with the Medicis.

The best and worst was the news for Ermanno. Signori Benedetto had been pulling all the cash out of the company since Ermanno's father had died. Riccardo had to act swiftly before Signori Benedetto was able to effectively bankrupt the company, for which Ermanno would be one-half responsible.

Once Riccardo threatened legal action to have the courts and creditors step in, Signori Benedetto suddenly found the cash to pay off the creditors. Ermanno's father had been well-liked in the town, and things didn't go well for Signori Benedetto when everyone became aware of what he had been doing.

Venice was rapidly taking over the shipping in the Adriatic, and Ravenna was now a small, withering port. A representative from Venice, acting as an agent for a Venice cordage company, was willing to buy out Ermanno for his share of the company. Signori Benedetto could not argue with it since the courts would certainly rule against him on numerous counts if Ermanno were to pursue a suit against him for his unscrupulous and illegal actions.

Ermanno knew this would be the demise of his father's business, but he had no wish to be in partnership with Signori Benedetto, and this was the best solution. In his heart, he also knew this way he would be out of a business he never wanted to be in.

As for his proposed bride, Carlo's further investigations revealed that she just might be pregnant. Ermanno told Signori Benedetto that he would not renege on his father's commitment, but he would not marry Antonia for six months and would have nothing to do with her. He said that he was leaving town immediately, and if she was pregnant, since he was not the father, he would not marry her.

Antonia admitted to her father that she was pregnant and that Ermanno was not the father. Riccardo and Ermanno needed to hear no more. Whatever Antonia and Vittorio decided to do was not their concern. Now it was time for Ermanno and his mother to pack up and make the journey to Florence to begin a new life. What life had in store for them they weren't sure, but certainly Ravenna was very soon to be behind them.

Ermanno's father's house was very nice and in the nicest part of town, so as soon as word spread that Ermanno and his mother would be moving to Florence, they had several offers from people who wished to rent the house at an excellent price.

His mother was not happy about leaving her childhood home and her many friends, but her son was all she had left in this world. She knew his future lay in Florence. By not selling her home, she felt she was still somehow connected to her previous life, and she was easier about the move.

Also her maid, who had been with her for over ten years now, decided to come with them. Francia had no family and no strong bonds in Ravenna. She was a very shy person, and Anna was so good to her, the relationship was much closer than servant and mistress. Anna was so frail now from her illness last year, Francia couldn't bear to part from her.

Ermanno took three horses and a large wagon from the cordage company as part of his payment, and they loaded it with some of their belongings. Once they found a place to live and the weather improved, another trip would be made by Carlo and Ermanno to bring the rest of what they needed and what his mother didn't want to part with.

Many problems would have to be resolved in the future. Now they just had to find a place for Ermanno and his mother, Anna, to live. Well, first things first. They had to make the perilous, treacherous, rutted, journey across the cold, snow-capped mountains between Ravenna and Florence with their two heavily laden wagons.

The return trip was a lot harder than the trip over, because the wagon was heavily loaded with the alum and copper, much more than Carlo's poor wagon should handle, so they had to go slowly whenever the terrain was rough, which was a lot of the time.

The journey was very difficult for Anna, but the men had placed two chairs in the wagon behind the drivers so Anna and Francia could sit and be padded and cushioned as much as possible from the bounces and bumps on the road. They also were surrounded by a wall of rugs, and covered with blankets and bed coverings when they were in the high mountains and the air was cold.

~ ~ ~

Everyone was pleased to see them back home in Florence safely, and as word spread, the receiving room of Beatrice and Giovanni's home filled with people wanting to welcome Ermanno and his mother and hear what had happened. Ermanno, Marco, and Carlo told the story over and over. Riccardo, who had gone home, changed out of his travel clothes, and brought Teresa and Rico back for what would be quite a gathering.

Anna was given a warm welcome, particularly by the older neighbors, and Dona Rutia invited her and Francia to stay with her in the now unused upstairs portion of her house.

It was to become a very successful arrangement, and the younger Francia and old Maddalena were soon comfortable in the routine of the two older ladies. Many changes would be made under Dona Rutia's roof in the next few months, all with the approval of the now many inhabitants, and to the joy of Dona Rutia who now had no need to visit her neighbors for her daily entertainment.

Lucrezia and Ermanno happily disappeared together for the rest of that first evening once he had told the story of all that had happened in their travels a couple of times. Now he wanted to share his innermost feelings about it all with Lucrezia.

Padre Bernardo was returning from Signori Lagattuta's house back to Santa Maria Novella when he passed by the Volini house. He was called inside by one of the comers or goers, he didn't know which, and once he heard all of the good news, he privately told Amalia he would gladly waive the announcement of the bans of marriage if the couple were so inclined.

Amalia made sure he was introduced to Ermanno's mother, and she told him she was pleased to meet him; that she knew she would need his guidance and was eager to be welcomed into the embrace of the church in order to ease the transition into her new life.

Anna had been exhausted by their journey, and then she was further exhausted by what was a wonderful but tiring welcome. She was very pleased when Dona Rutia suggested they leave to give her a chance to settle in at her new home just two doors away. There would be time tomorrow and the next day for further introductions.

The gathering went on for several hours. Some of Ermanno's friends from the old days arrived expecting to hear him sing, but no one knew where Ermanno was, so they left promising to return soon. If he sang at all this night, it was quietly; it was for one person only, and no one else.

When the gathering finally broke up and everyone had gone home, Marco and Amalia crossed the street and finally climbed the stairs to their bedroom. Amalia had some good news for Marco. She was sure she was pregnant. They were both overjoyed. They spent part of that night in each other's arms planning how life would be with the pleasures of a son in their life, then planning the pleasures if it turned out to be a daughter, and then enjoying the pleasures they could and did bring to each other.

Giotto's Campanile – 414 steps

XVII *Woven Threads*

The years passed. Many things changed, and many things stayed the same. Lucrezia and Amalia were still devoted to each other, but their lives were very different.

The house on the back of Amalia's property that she had rented out to the elderly couple for years had become vacant while the men had been in Ravenna. The man had been ill all winter and then had died, and his wife went to live with her son and his family on the other side of town near San Marco. This left the house free for Lucrezia and Ermanno to move into once they were married by Padre Bernardo.

Both of them were certain they did not want to delay their union one day more than was necessary since they had waited for so long already. They wanted the joy of celebrating the holiday festivities and all the parties and events as a couple as they began their new life together. The winter festivals not only had the productions for the saints' day and the usual parades with the relics and singing, the waving of the special unicorn, lion, ox, adder, and twelve more banners of each one of the sixteen gonfalons. There was also the camaraderie and all the wonderful bonfires in many of the piazzas throughout town that led to music, singing, dancing, and more.

Everyone joined in to clean out and refurbish the house, which was even older than Amalia's house. It was not as big as Amalia's but it had large, open rooms. It didn't have the upper floor, but it was more than large enough for Lucrezia and Ermanno now. They would worry about children and a larger house in the future, even though the first of their children was on its way only months after their marriage. By living in that house, Lucrezia got to keep her garden, situated between the two houses, and she had a very short, delightful walk to and from her shop each day. They simply opened up a small archway through the wall behind the grape arbor.

The garden space right outside the back window of her shop opposite the well was the first play area for Lucrezia's children and Amalia's, plus the older Lisabetta and oftentimes Lisabetta's best friend, Blanche.

Ermanno and his voice were welcomed into the commune of Florence with open arms. He had many engagements that first spring, and his place in the company that performed their delightful musical productions was secure for the entire season of the next winter. The future seemed to hold in store only good things for him, as his talent was appreciated and enjoyed in public and private performances as was his participation in the feast day at their church.

At the close of the performance on the steps of Santa Maria Novella, his voice was then heard through the streets of all of Florence as the performers paraded throughout the city. The drums beat, the trumpets blared, the banners waved as the members of each of the confraternities joined together to walk in their saint's day parade. Then Ermanno sang. This was singular to the Santa Maria Novella, and it drew huge crowds along the streets, in the piazza by Santa Maria Novella, and by the Duomo. Finally, they urged him to go up on the steps of the Duomo to sing. It was quite the event of the entire season, and it boded only good things, as afterward he was hired by many of the rich bankers and merchants whenever they held a large feast in their palazzos and wanted good entertainment.

Franco, the man that had worked for Ermanno's father in Ravenna for many years, came to Florence. He had left when Ermanno's father died, but he had not found anything he enjoyed doing. The families welcomed him with open arms, as his services were badly needed, and he was appreciated. He lived in the lower room at Dona Rutia's house with the four women, now all comfortably situated upstairs, and he took care of whatever chores any of them needed to have done.

Dona Rutia had moved back upstairs to share the good lifestyle created by Anna, Maddalena, and Francia. She still couldn't climb the stairs, but life was now so enjoyable in her receiving room, she rarely asked Franco to help her down except for church.

The neighbors often dropped by to visit and sometimes have a glass of Dona Rutia's excellent wine, and Maddalena and Francia both loved to cook in the beautiful copper pots. The two servants and two mistresses lived in accord with good food, fine wine, and new-found friendship. It was a good life for the four women, who appreciated their benign good fortune.

Dona Rutia's last year was a very happy one that she enjoyed to the fullest, but her ancient body and heart finally just wore out. The only thing that never wore out was the acid tongue and raspy voice that had kept Anna, Maddalena, Francia, and all her visitors laughing until her very last day.

When she was young, she had been considered ornery and sometimes even bossy and a little critical; then in her later years, she had become quite exacting, and even demanding sometimes. At times she was even rude to just about everyone except Roberto and her daughter. In old age, though, she had reached her stride, and as her friends learned how to interpret her, she had become a joy: funny and insightful with her barbed, acidic tongue. She had been an acquired taste very much to the delight of the friends and neighbors on Via del Fiore, and most particularly Lucrezia and Amalia.

When Dona Rutia died quietly one night in her sleep, going much more quietly to her eternal rest than she had lived, the girls were both devastated. They knew how much she had done for them in the early years when their lives and their future hung by a mere thread. Lisabetta kept wanting to go to heaven to visit with "Auntie" and could not and would not be consoled.

Ermanno's mother lived on in the house another year with Maddalena, Francia, and Franco, but then she too died. Maddalena went to live with her daughter in Siena, and Francia came to live with Amalia, Marco, Lisabetta, Carlo, little Giuliano (named for his grandfather, Amalia's beloved father) and baby Alessandra, named for Marco's mother. Rutia's daughter, Rosa, went about selling the old house.

Francia was a welcome addition to the burgeoning family, for she was well-liked, and her services were appreciated. Over the years, she became a bit more outgoing and a big part of the family's life as well as a part of the gonfalons, particularly the activities at the church. Franco moved into the downstairs of Lucrezia and Ermanno's house, and he became the handy man and helper for the two households as well as a helper for Lucrezia in the shop when needed.

Lisabetta was growing into a beautiful young girl. She was active, bright, and happy with blond, curly hair. She excelled at Caterina's school, and was a favorite of the tutors Caterina hired for the older girls because she was so bright and quick.

In addition to her schooling, she loved to spend an evening, particularly in the wintertime, scribing like her aunt. At first Amalia just gave her short poems to copy, but recently she had given her the small book of poems that had been her prized possession for all these years: the book of poems written by Lucrezia de' Medici, Cosimo's daughter-in-law, and the wife of Piero. Amalia had loved that book above all others all the years since Master Manetti had allowed her to make a copy for herself. She wanted Lisabetta to appreciate Lucrezia's book as well as the poetry.

Everyone loved the child, and she loved them all in return, but she was devoted to Carlo. She followed him everywhere and was often a big help—as much as she was able—with his carting and toting. She adored the horses, especially Traveler, and sometimes, returning from a delivery when the cart was empty, Carlo let her ride on Traveler's back.

Once when Carlo was hired to deliver a large statue over to Orsanmichele, Lisabetta was with him. This was the guild church. All around the outside of the church stood large statues of the patron saints of each of one of the twelve major guilds; Ghiberti's St. John the Baptist, Verrocchio's Christ and St. Thomas, Brunelleschi's St. Peter, Donatello's <u>St. George</u> and many more. In its past, the old church had been an open market; then it became a granary. The holes could still be seen where the grain would be shot down to fill a wagon. Now <u>Orsanmichele</u> was this most special but unusual church. It blended the hearts and minds of Florentines, first a business, now the religious center of the guilds, a church of the workers' guilds.

While they were loading and padding the statue to properly secure it for transport, one of the artists sat Lisabetta up on one of the pedestals. A very young boy did a sketch of her and then gave it to her. It was her prized possession, and it hung in her room from that day on.

After that, any time she was passing that boddeghe, she would run in to say hello to the very young Botticelli, kiss him on the cheek, and run back out, to the laughter and calls of all the other artists, students, and workers in the shop. They would want to know where their kisses were, but she would just laugh and wave as she ran out.

Next door at Maria and Filippo's, Filippo's leg had been broken in a fall at work and had not healed properly. He was no longer able to work, so his son moved back in the large house with his wife and family. Maria was delighted since she liked her daughter-in-law very much, but Filippo was not at all happy with the arrangement.

Marco asked him to come to the boddeghe to help with customers and just be there when he had to be gone. That became the routine for the next several years until Filippo's leg developed an infection from which he ultimately died. Maria was devastated, and everyone worked hard to see her through the difficult times.

Riccardo did very well in his law practice, now almost exclusively devoted to the builders and architects of Florence. Riccardo and Teresa lost their next baby

before he was a year old, and then Teresa had a miscarriage, but she was now pregnant again, nearing her time to deliver.

Caterina and Claudio had four children, all healthy, and she was expecting again. She did this all while she was busy running the school that was fast becoming one of the finest in Florence. They had just hired an additional tutor and acquired more space, because the enrollment was growing steadily.

Beatrice and Giovanni across the street had two boys in addition to Gia. Signori and Signora Cassetti, her parents, had both died in an epidemic of cholera a year ago, but until then, both had enjoyed their later years with their young grandchildren.

Carlo's hauling and carting business had continued to grow as he had grown into a tall, gangly young man. He let his beard grow as it started to come in so he would look older, but it annoyed him and didn't last long. Other than the hottest days, he wore an oversized leather jacket so people couldn't see how skinny he was as he tried to make himself seem older. He still worked at jobs far beyond what his years dictated he should be doing, but since he did it all so well, few noticed, and none complained.

He asked Marco to buy a small farm out toward Fiesole. He had saved his money to pay for it and then found that although he was old enough to earn the money, he was not old enough to buy the land. He needed it for the horses and the two mules he bought, plus storage of the carts and wagons he and Jacko had accumulated for all their different ventures. Jacko's uncle was getting far too distracted with his many business ventures to attend to the farm properly, so Carlo bought a small piece of it, the part that contained a small house along with two small barns and a couple of sheds.

He now had shelter and pasture for his horses and mules as well as four other horses he boarded for people in Florence. One of the sheds was a perfect hen house, so he fenced in an area for them and kept their gonfalons well stocked with fresh eggs. The rest of the land he kept in grains. He helped Jacko's uncle seed and harvest his part of the farm, then mill both sections, and then they split the profits.

A stray dog wandered in and earned his keep by keeping the vermin at bay from the chickens and the animals in the barn and pasture. Luppo, as he came to be called, never left the farm, and as long as he was there, no one would dare set foot on the place. He had staked out this plot of land as his domain, and unless Carlo said they were welcome, no one and no critter was tolerated. He bedded down with either Traveler or Boots, the cat that lived in the barn and made a steady diet of the barn mice. When Lisabetta was there, Luppo never left her side. She was part of his domain, and Carlo felt certain he would protect her even to his death.

He had so many business ventures going, Amalia and Marco, as well as Lucrezia and Ermanno, often commented and wondered how Carlo kept track of them all, but he did. Since he had to tend the animals in the evenings and mornings, he often spent his nights in his little house on his farm. He spent a lot of his spare time fixing it up, and Lisabetta often spent her free days there taking care of the animals and helping him to mix plaster or passing tiles up to him for repairs to the roof of the house. Amalia wasn't happy about her doing such chores, but Lisabetta said no one was ever around to see her doing it, and it was what she loved doing.

Sometimes, rather than walk home, Carlo and Lisabetta would ride to town on Traveler, to the consternation of the neighbors. Then Carlo would ride back to the farm after eating with either of the families, where he was always welcome.

Free days to work on his farm were few, because he was almost always busy in town. Florence was flourishing, and everyone's businesses were growing except for those of the truly incompetent or infirm. Carlo's favorite job was helping the artists. It wasn't always the best paying work, but he loved being around the creative men and then seeing the results of their genius. There were so many of them in those days. Donatello was one of Carlo's favorites, and Lippi usually called on him when he needed something done that he knew Carlo could handle. Verrocchio was not his favorite person, but he did love seeing his artwork. The young Botticelli did marvelous drawings. They were nothing like the other artists; even Carlo could see that. Botticelli lived at the Palazzo Medici, but oftentimes he could be found at one or another of the many boddeghe's in town. It seemed great art was being created from the incredible competitive spirit between and among the many artists of Florence.

One night Carlo came home and told them he had helped Michelozzo with a large shipment of timbers. He didn't have enough wagons to transport everything, so Carlo offered to help and then he wouldn't take any payment. Michelozzo asked him why, and he said his family was indebted to Cosimo de' Medici and this was a very small way of thanking him.

"But Carlo, Cosimo won't know of it and even if he did, he wouldn't know who you are," said Amalia.

"No, but I know and you know, and that's all that matters."

"Thank you, Carlo," is all Amalia could say through her tears.

"Don't be sad, Ama," said Lisabetta, "Don't cry."

"Oh, dearest, I'm not sad. These are tears of joy."

The two families, one on each end of their garden, flourished and enjoyed the largesse they created by their hard work, good judgment, and great fortune.

Over the years, Marco expanded his boddeghe and hired men to help him. He was often called over to Ravenna or Venice or Pisa to take delivery of shipments from Erudius in Turkey. As Erudius expanded his export business, Marco's importing and marketing businesses were equally expanded. Carlo would always handle transporting the shipments, but markets had to be found.

One time Carlo and Marco both went on a large delivery, a shipment of two wagons loaded with goods to Rome. They took time to roam the many ruins throughout the ancient city, but they were so disgusted with the filth of the city and the laziness of the people, they couldn't wait to leave.

One of the sites they went to was the old church, the <u>Pantheon</u>. Both of them had heard talk that it was the inspiration for Brunelleschi to build his dome for the Duomo. They joked that he should come back and finish this church because while now the Duomo had a completed dome, this dome in the Pantheon still had the hole in the center.

They looked up at the bright sky through that hole and marveled that here was the oldest dome known in their world, build so long ago. It was so huge, no one had been able to exceed it until the construction of their very own Duomo, thanks to the genius of Brunelleschi.

They wandered all over the city, seeing statues without arms or heads, like those in Dona Rutia's garden, and they marveled at the number of them just standing in open spaces or scattered on the ground. They saw pillars, many still vertical but no longer supporting a roof, and many more horizontal. They saw how Brunelleschi and the other architects of Florence had been inspired by the grace and beauty of those pillars, how they had used the idea of them in the many churches' interiors they had designed in Florence, Fiesole, Siena and elsewhere. They had used the inspiration for the loggia of the L'Ospedale degli Innocenti, and even the interiors of the many palazzos being built in the style of Cosimo's palazzo, designed by Michelozzo.

There were several amphitheaters scattered around Rome, as they were scattered in almost every town in Tuscany and throughout Italy. One was still in use in Fiesole. The one in Florence was buried under the new city. Legend said it was buried under the Palazzo Vecchio and the Forum of Florence, under the Mercato Nuovo.

The ancient Colosseum was the most impressive ruin they visited in Rome, but the stench of the people living in there in abject poverty was repugnant. They climbed up to the top and looked down into and across the entire magnificent ruin, but then, with all the people living on the floor of the Colosseum, down underneath and behind the seats and even up on the seats, Marco commented it was like watching maggots on a corpse.

They made their way to what they had been told was the center of the old city, the ancient Forum. They tried to imagine what it would have looked like over a thousand years ago and knew it must have been glorious. They agreed, though, that while that might have been so, there was nothing glorious about this modern city, and they couldn't wait to get out.

When they were finally done with their deliveries, their pockets were filled with more money than Carlo had ever seen at one time.

Carlo had managed to find some goods to fill part of one of the wagons for the return trip as far as Siena, but they were nervous about being on the roads with the amount of money they were carrying. Marco went to the Medici bank in Rome to see if they could do a bill of exchange rather than carry the florins with them. That worked out well, and then by some connections recommended by the director of the bank, they were able to fill their two wagons with a shipment all the way to Florence, and the director arranged for them to travel with a wagon train as far as Siena.

Sometimes their ventures weren't quite as successful, but little by little, the importing for Marco and the shipping for Carlo increased over the years.

Marco still loved working with copper, and he kept tight control on the caliber of craftsmanship at his boddeghe. He made certain the workmanship was technically excellent. To his delight, it seemed his men were honest and loyal. He kept his men busy, and he always had a handy reserve of various pots, pans, and so much more. When a particular favor was done for him or for any of the family, he would see to it that the wife got one of his pots or pans so that many of the neighbors and all of their friends cooked with the finest cookware available. The wives and their cooks all adored him.

Carlo would always go by to visit Poggio whenever he had a delivery in Fiesole and would report back to Amalia how he was doing. He was definitely slowing down, had a lot of joint pain, and he was still grouchy—Carlo said nothing new there—but his mind was clear, and he always had a good word to send down to Amalia. He still spent his time writing, and was enjoying his life as best he could. One time Poggio sent a copy of a Livy book he knew Amalia particularly liked for her to keep, and he would often send some produce from his garden if there was anything growing at the time. She and Marco would take Lisabetta, and then Giuliano and Alessandra and more in a carriage every summer for a visit, and she always saw him when he was in Florence, but now those times were very rare. What a jewel he had been in her life. She knew she was very fortunate to have actually known and been friends with such a man.

Lucrezia's business flourished as her reputation as an innovative designer grew. The Guards of the Night were mainly patrolling to be sure the prostitutes were kept in check, and they almost never bothered the higher classes of ladies about their fashionable attire or their buttons anymore, so she was freer to be more creative.

She had four girls in the shop in addition to AnnaMaria, and she employed several women who sewed in their own homes. By buying extra fabric on the side whenever she could, she was always able to keep her girls busy, even if the high end part of the business hit a slump. The pre-made garments were sought after almost as fast as she could get them made. She knew her market and didn't over-price the items. She charged a very high price for her specially designed, expertly crafted dresses, shirts, jackets, or capes using the finest brocades, damasks, wools, velvets, silks, cottons, and furs, but she priced the items sold to the working class as low as she could.

A notary moved in on the next block and wanted to open an office to do what Amalia's father had done for the gonfalons for many years. Once he agreed not to charge the poorer people for just reading and writing their letters, Amalia closed her little Saturday writing office. Lucrezia immediately took over the space to stock the pre-made clothing. That way the two classes of her clientele didn't need to rub elbows, to the embarrassment of each.

Master Manetti retired and sold his shop to a man neither she nor Antonio particularly liked. Antonio was soon able to get a job with another book dealer, as he was very good at his job. Finally, she couldn't tolerate the man's rudeness toward her and declined to take the next manuscript home for copying when he begrudgingly offered it to her. She knew he was pleased, and she quickly realized that she was also.

Messer Bisticci kept her as busy as she wanted to be these days. Earning money was no longer a necessity to keep food on their table, but she so loved the work, she did not want to give it up entirely. She spent more time now on each book, doing much more of the artwork she had come to love. During the winter while she was pregnant with Alessandra, Messer Bisticci had given her Lucretius's *On The Nature of Things* to copy. She spent many winter days not only on the text that she loved so much but also an extraordinary amount of time on the artwork. Many years later, Messer Bisticci told her that it was the copy of the book that he kept for himself in his studiolo.

One evening the two couples were together for a late dinner at Lucrezia and Ermanno's home. It had rained and was blustery all day and threatening an early snow. All of the children were in bed. Ermanno said, "I had a strange thing happen last night. You know I was at the Rucellai palazzo to sing, and when I was done, I was in an outer room preparing to leave when one of the guests approached me, a woman. I assumed it was to compliment my singing or ask if I would be available for some occasion in the future. Both of those things were true, but when she introduced herself as Lucrezia de' Medici, I was stunned. I blurted out that my family was greatly indebted to her father-in-law for their well-being in Florence, and I thanked her as a representative on behalf of my wife and her dear friend. I blurted out that you were a scribe, thanks to Cosimo, and you became a seamstress and you were now an excellent designer." He looked at Amalia and Lucrezia in turn.

"Before I realized it, she had led me into a deeper description of what you do, Lucrezia, and then she wanted to know how to contact you. I think you may be hearing from her. It was beyond politeness. Piero finally came out to ask her if she was all right. She said she was and just wanted to chat with the singer. She introduced me to him, and then he led her back inside.

"As they were walking away, she said, 'His family knows Cosimo.' He chuckled and said, "My dear, everyone knows Papa.' She said, 'I don't mean that way, I mean in a special way.' And that is all I heard."

Lucrezia did not hear further from Lucrezia de' Medici, and she never met her, but Madonna Medici sent her daughters and two nieces to see Lucrezia. They, along with some friends and friends of friends, as word of her talents spread, became steady customers for many years.

After seeing Madonna Medici at a religious poetry confraternity meeting a few years later, Lucrezia came to understand why she had never heard from the great lady herself. Although she was a Medici and was very rich and wrote beautiful poetry for which she was famous in her own right, she obviously had no interest in fashion for herself.

Lucrezia would have liked to approach and greet her namesake to thank her, but the room was crowded, and Madonna was ushered out of the room soon after the meeting broke up, the opportunity lost.

Ruins of Rome

XVIII   *Swerve*

The years passed, and they were good years. There were times of sadness: the deaths of friends, children of friends, or parents of friends, to be sure. Yet there were no bad plagues, no ruinous storms or floods, no wars, and there were many births adding new life to the growing city. The economy was excellent, trade was good, employment, and production for export was high.

Cosimo was often criticized in Florence as being a prince or an uncrowned king rather than allowing Florence to be the republic she wanted it to be, but surely the Signoria would have floundered in indecision. It always had in the past. They would have been drawn into costly and useless wars, as had also always happened in the past.

In the old days, once war was declared, a condottiere had to be hired, and paid very well; then the mercenaries had to be hired, and paid very well. To pay them, the city had to tax the people, including the poorest people. Then the mercenaries on both sides would pursue their battles, which were more like jousting contests at festivals. They would joust on one hill, then move to another hill, joust some more, then go back to the first hill. No one wanted to kill anyone, because today's enemy might switch sides and be tomorrow's comrade if the pay was better.

Everyone knew the story of the three-day battle near Lucca. In the three days, three mercenary soldiers died, two by falling off their horses and drowning in the mud, and one by being thrown from his horse and being killed when his horse fell on top of him. The only ones to truly suffer in these times of war were the working people and the poor.

Cosimo brought an end to the wars. He wanted production in the mills and factories and good commerce; he wanted trade of the raw materials for the production of the finished products. Certainly Cosimo de' Medici benefited from the good economy, for he was a banker and a merchant, but he also made certain the people benefited too. He listened to the guilds, he listened to the popolo, and with the ever-growing trade, he and all the people benefited. For this the people called him "Il Popolo," the man of the people, and through the years it would prove to be a great political strength.

For all the talk on the street about Cosimo being too powerful, only those who were jealous of his power because they were hungry for it themselves were truly dissatisfied. He was not interested in taking over any territories beyond Tuscany either for himself or for Florence. It was common knowledge that he bought off foreign powers that wanted wars, because war would be ruinous for the trade and commerce of Florence. He brokered deals, like the Peace of Lodi, between foreign enemies to keep peace and thereby protect trade and commerce, not only for Florence and Tuscany but for much of the rest of Italy. What was there to complain about?

It seemed all Cosimo truly wanted was money and the power and the things that money brought him. He never seemed to want or enjoy the glory. On the contrary, he seemed to avoid that sort of thing, putting forward friends and relatives whenever possible rather than himself. He saw to it that a great deal of his money was spent on the beautification of Florence. He did this through the buildings he built or rebuilt, and then through the art he paid for to decorate those magnificent edifices, giving birth to and nurturing a generation of artists never to be surpassed in history.

The first artists usually continued the old tradition of painting scenes from the Bible, but little by little, they were inculcated by the spirit of Cosimo's humanists, and were opened to the beauty of nature, as well as the glory of God. This was conveyed in their art as the women got longer necks, more defined bodies, with even nipples on their breasts showing under their gown.

There were many more pastoral scenes with a growing concern for perspective and proportion. This was a new concept for the artists. It was first explored by Giotto but then really developed by Brunelleschi and Donatello and then finally thoroughly explored by Leonardo. This idea was to change the look of painting evermore.

The art of that generation and the generation to follow swerved as thinking swerved on the road forward. In the future, the world would look back on Medici Florence as a period in history like no other.

Many accused Cosimo of usury. He certainly felt guilt on this account, because he ultimately petitioned the pope for the means to gain God's forgiveness for this "egregious" sin. Everyone knew the pope passed a special Bull saying that if Cosimo rebuilt the cloistered quarters of San Marco and then the church itself, his sins of usury would be forgiven and the doors of heaven would be opened to him. He built or rebuilt San Marco and many other churches: the Holy Sepulcher in Jerusalem, San Giorgio in Venice, the Badia in Fiesole, his own church of <u>San Lorenzo</u>, and more. Surely later generations would look askance at Cosimo's sin as well as the pope's act of forgiveness, but did not all future generations benefit in a glorious way from his penance?

Amalia heard comments about him in her travels around town, and she would always rise to Cosimo's defense or join in his praise. She would remind people that there were no wars, the economy was almost always good, and jobs were plentiful. Maybe a neighbor's son couldn't find a job immediately, but if he really wanted a job, some neighbor knew some relative who knew some guildsman, and an apprenticeship would be found for him.

If a man was complaining about not finding work, it was usually a man who just wanted an easy ride for very little work or maybe no work at all. Such types wanted and needed to blame someone else for their lots in life. Hasn't every age produced such men? The people in Florence had no time and little patience for this type of person. Truly, it was a society based on work, not titles or status or birth. If you were willing to work, you had a good chance of success.

Florence was a growing, vital city with a good climate, good soil, excellent commerce, and sound leadership. Surely these things contributed to it becoming a center for creativity and ingenuity that tended to leave behind the small and narrow-minded sort. It was the center of humanistic thought that was revolutionizing the minds of men. Thanks to Cosimo and many like patrons, there was a ready market for all that the artists, great and even mediocre, could create. Florence was the envy of all of Europe, and she set the bar for all the principal cities throughout Italy and all of Europe for art but also for thought.

Now, with steady work, food in their stomachs, adequate housing, and a taste for better attire, there was time to think about life and the living of it. Not for the last thousand years were these people able to do that. For a thousand years, life had been lived on little more than the edge of survive or die. This had allowed the church to hold a firm grip on the minds of the people, because through the teachings of the church, they could at least look forward to a glorious afterlife. But then in the 1300's, the plague killed over half the people. Death was everywhere. The church was no longer a refuge, the teachings of the church no longer satisfied their hungry spirit. Minds and thought began to change. If they were going to die soon—and they probably were—why not live a little in the meantime, why not look for something more to enjoy along the road to what was probably an early death?

At this moment in history, the climate became warmer, farming became easier and more productive, and, because of the plague, there were fewer mouths to feed and less competition for resources. Also, at this time, information began to become available, because of Poggio Bracciolini and others like him, about the better life lived in the glory that was Greece and the grandeur that was ancient Rome. The philosophies of life of those people who lived so long ago instructed Florentines. There was much to learn, and learn they did.

This was Medici Florence, situated in a position to develop these ideas and then export them, along with their wool, silk, and leather, to all of Europe, which was ripe for the knowledge, and they too were beginning to have the time to explore and discuss philosophies of life and the living of it.

Throughout history, a farmer's mind had no need to change its basic thought processes about production. A merchant, craftsman, or manufacturer of a product for trade by necessity had to be more adaptable, more inventive and creative. Florence was the perfect environment for this. After over a thousand years in the darkness, it was like waking to the beautiful sunrise of a new and exciting day.

Cosimo's Florence was very austere and conservative in all respects. There were laws, civil and church, for and against many things. In practice, it was a time of great disparity between what was written in the law and what was enforced or tolerated. It was a period of great flux, and there was an overriding pragmatism in dealing with the consequences of sins or the violations of laws.

In Florence there could be no buttons on garments, by law, and ladies' dresses had to be modest and in one color. There were times when the Onesta, the police in charge of enforcing the Sumptuary Laws, would look under a lady's cape to check for buttons or decorations on her dress. Yet poisoning of one's enemy or opponent or competitor was not an uncommon event in Florence and particularly not throughout the rest of Italy.

Sodomy was rampant in these times, and it was prosecuted endlessly by the Onesta. There were over 14,000 trials, and many more charges managed to disappear before trial. If tried, the penalty was usually very light. Surely, all these men were not homosexual. It was a time of great liberation of men's minds and spirits and energy, but the girls and women were kept locked up by their families. So what was a man to do? There were many prostitutes with their bells, but few wanted to or could afford to pay for the privilege.

Even though the girls were locked up, there were a great many illegitimate children born in Florence and throughout Italy during this time. If it was financially realistic, the child would be raised in the father's home by his wife as a part of his family. Cosimo's illegitimate son was raised in his home by Contessina and Madellena, the mother, a Circassian slave woman bought by Cosimo during the year he was in exile. That boy, Carlo, was schooled and trained for the church, and became a cardinal. In the upper classes, these sons were usually trained for the church, visiting sexual chastity upon the product of the promiscuous father. The illegitimate daughters were married off in politically advantageous marriages, as were the legitimate daughters.

Everyone knew the story of Caterina, the illegitimate daughter of Galeazzo Sforza, Duke of Milan. Galeazzo was himself the legitimate son of the illegitimate Francesco, who was a dear friend of Cosimo. Caterina was later married to the nephew—or was it the son?—of the pope, and she later ruled Forli and Imola in her son's behalf, befriended by Lorenzo Il Magnifico, grandson of Cosimo.

In times like these, there were many unwanted babies or babies that just could not be cared for by the parents, so the orphanages were many and full. L'Ospedale degli Innocenti, built by Cosimo, was only one of many, but here the children were schooled and trained until they were adopted or old enough to make their way in the world.

Out of this cauldron, the good and the bad, came Florence's many gifts to the world.

Amalia and all her friends and neighbors were only on the fringe of politics and the artistic world, but it was not a large city and people talked. Even Carlo was on a first-name basis with most of the great artists of the day and did business with many of them or worked shoulder to shoulder with them on the many festival productions. Marco came to know some of the finest artisans and guild leaders. Ermanno sang at the many palazzos and knew their rich owners, and he worked with the finest musicians and entertainers in the city. Lucrezia sold her finest garments to some of the richest ladies and gentlemen in town. Amalia scribed the manuscripts and books that brought them that vast store of ancient knowledge. She read the manuscripts to her family, and they discussed them and then shared the ideas with their friends.

Even if they did not travel in the world of the leaders, they knew them, how they lived, how they thought, and what kind of people they were. They liked and respected some of them, and some they didn't. Yet there were few secrets in a town where private dealings and personal secrets were as much commodities traded for power and influence as silks, wools, and spices were commodities traded in the commercial market.

The leaders of the guilds were active in the Signoria and had a hand in politics, and the leaders of the financial and commercial world were tightly bonded with those guildsmen. By the natural inclinations of people, the information always trickled down from the highest level of leadership to the lowest apprentice.

When the Arno flooded in the fall, as it did every few years, Cosimo would be blamed as the commune struggled to recover from the destruction. If there was a bad crop because of too much rain or too little rain or too much heat, the people grumbled that it was Cosimo's fault, even though he instituted a plan for the storage of grains in the good years. When the plague hit every few years, it was Cosimo's fault because he was a usurer, and he brought God's wrath upon them.

On the other hand, when there were no plagues, good crops, and no floods, then many people felt it was thanks to God's benevolence as well as their own industriousness and good fortune. Truly, such is the nature of man. Cosimo knew and understood human nature, so he did what he chose to do for his own reasons with little thought of return other than the power to enable him to keep on doing more.

Cosimo urged the Signoria—and helped pay for—the reconstruction of the aqueduct from the mountains to bring fresh water back into the city. This contributed significantly to the better health of the people. Of course, no one understood why this water was better for them. All they knew is that there was less sickness when they drank it.

Cosimo urged twelve of the richest men in Florence to form a confraternity at the Church of San Martino called the Buonomini. Although the "Few Good

Men" contributing to this charity were the twelve wealthiest men, Cosimo was known to contribute over half of all that was donated.

This church, the patron church for the saints Damian and Cosmos, was favored by Cosimo, because he and his twin, Damian, had been named after these two saints. They were saints of the medical profession. Cosimo's twin, Damian, had died shortly after his birth. The balls, the "pelle," on the Medici escutcheon were believed to represent the pills administered by doctors. There were rumors the family had descended from doctors, but that was shrouded in the mists of the past. Actually, most believed the gold "pelle" represented the coins of the banker.

Through the Buonomini, bread and wine would be distributed every Wednesday to the poor by six assistants directed by Cosimo's secretary, Palle, working with the guilds. Periodically, flocks of sheep would be driven to the steps of San Martino to be slaughtered and the meat distributed. This was not a charity for the destitute or the infirm. They would be provided for by the Misericordia organized in each of the local churches throughout the city whose mission it was to provide food and clothing for the poor.

The Buonomini was organized with the intent to cooperate with the guilds to provide for a worker who was down on his luck: a man who went bankrupt and hadn't gotten back on his feet; a widow of one of the guildsmen who didn't have family to provide for her or, perhaps, her large family; or an injured worker and his family for the period while he couldn't work.

Marco, Carlo, Ermanno, and Giovanni became active in helping to gather produce when available in the summer and fall and firewood through the cold winter months. Carlo provided two wagons, and the four men would go out to some of the local farms outside the city, load up the wagons, and drive one wagon to the Church of San Martino. The other one they drove to Padre Bernardo at Santa Maria Novella for the poorest of the poor.

Here, they lingered and talked to the men and even the women. Many were so old or sickly there was nothing to do but give them the soup the nuns would prepare in their large cauldrons using the produce the men provided.

But once in a while there would be someone that did want to work. Then they would keep an eye out in their travels to find jobs for those people; probably a menial task, but if they wanted to work, a job was found.

The four men traveled in very different circles throughout Florence, and so they came in contact with people from all parts of the city and all circumstances revealing many opportunities.

Conversely, rarely would one of them be in an area of town where he wouldn't be recognized and greeted by a laborer doing some kind of work: sweeping out a shop, cleaning a debris site in the street, dressed up in livery and leading a rich man's horse through the narrow streets of Florence, or making a delivery with one of Carlo's carts or that of one of his competitors.

Marco had found his best and most loyal worker just this way, a man who had been badly maimed in a fire and was so unsightly, no one would hire him. Marco hired him and let him live at his boddeghe until he could earn enough to afford to rent a room, and then Federico did even better for himself.

The growing Valetti and Evangelista households, joined by a common garden, bonded by a mutual love for their own and for each other as well as for their commune, thrived in these days and appreciated their good fortune.

June 24th

Of the many saints days celebrated in Florence, and there were over one hundred of them each year, June 24th was the biggest and the finest celebration of them all. The Church of the Flower, Santa Maria del Fiore, was the Cathedral of Florence. It was called The Duomo, and it was the heart and center of the town. The Baptistry, old and small, just across the piazza from the Duomo, was the heart of the religious activity for the celebration, since it was actually the church named for St. John the Baptist, and this was his day. The piazza between the <u>Baptistry</u> and the Duomo, though, was the center for much of the other activity connected to the event that actually spanned several days.

A huge tent of a bright, golden-colored fabric was erected surrounding The Baptistry. Under it, on the first day, the merchants would display the finest of wools and silks produced in Florence, and all the beautifully crafted jewelry made from the finest gold and other metals and magnificent gem stones of all kinds. In

addition, the finest products of leather and every craft each guild and merchant had to offer were displayed.

This was not a day for sales; this was a day for exhibiting, a day to awe the visiting dignitaries and merchants from other city-states and duchies throughout Italy. More than that, though, it was a day to let men from other countries see and know that they needed to trade with Florence, buy in Florence, and sell their raw materials to Florence, because this was where it was happening.

Cosimo had only recently brokered a permanent peace, the Peace of Lodi, between Venice, Milan, Naples, and Florence, as well as some of the smaller states. Since travel was now safer, the city was packed with those dignitaries, tradesmen, and merchants.

Contacts were made, deals were brokered, competitors were challenged, but the array of precious stones and metals, fabrics of all sorts, and wares was a parade of the superlative accomplishments of the Florentine guildsmen. It was meant to awe and excite and to advertise to all of Europe the excellence of Florence. For the Florentine workers in these many trades and crafts, seeing this array and rubbing elbows with these dignitaries gave them a sense of pride in their accomplishments and contributions. They saw and understood that Florence was special in a grand way, and this made those workers special, even if only in a small way. The following days of the festivities were for trade and sale of all of these items.

In addition, all the finest produce available from the local farmers was brought into the city on these days. There would be public feasts each of the days, and the produce used was the best Tuscany had to offer. Also, all of the churches, confraternities, and guilds participated in the many parades through town with trumpets, drums, chanting and singing, all the participants dressed in their costumes or in their finest attire, waving the banners of their gonfalons or confraternity.

Then the final day would be more trading and celebrating, but in the afternoon was the paleo, to be run from one end of town at the meadow by the River Arno near the church of Ognissanti right through the Piazza del Duomo in the center of town, then continue along the Via dell' Oriuolo to the other end of town to San Pier Maggiore and the Porto Santa Croce. Much revelry and betting accompanied the running of the race of the finest horses owned by the rich bankers and merchants, and it was the culminating event of the celebrations of the festival.

While all the trading was going on in and around the Piazza del Duomo, Piazza Santa Croce had been covered with sand and straw and would be the arena for endless games of calcio between all the teams of the city. On many years there were even jousting competitions by the young men of prominent families.

Much planning and labor went into the preparation for each of the festivities throughout the year. Stages needed to be built and painted by the excellent artists; platforms had to be erected; plays needed to be written by the best writers of the day, and costumes made for the performers. Practices had to be held for the performances and the many pageants, and these provided the main source of income for artists of all types.

For this festival, there was even more. Tents had to be made and hung around the Baptistry; In addition, the merchants had to prepare and then select for sale the finest wares they could produce.

Carlo, Marco, and Ermanno had each participated in the construction of stages, backdrops, and platforms, carting the lumber into town, arranging the musical productions, and doing many other tasks in the preceding weeks. Plus, Marco was making some special pots, pans, and cauldrons as well as some artistic decorations and ornaments to exhibit as one of the tradesmen.

Ermanno was in charge of the music for their confraternity in the parades, but he would also be singing a solo in the main production on the steps of the Duomo as well as participating in preparation of other musical productions. The finest musical director in Florence was in charge of the production celebrating the life of St. John the Baptist, and it was to be the grand event.

All these preparations brought people from every walk of life together to work on a common project, exchanging ideas, sharing snacks, sharing the labors, and exchanging stories of their families and lives. Surely this broadened people's perspective and contributed toward a universality of the minds of the citizens of Florence.

Lucrezia was planning a great surprise. She, with Master Vicenti's assistance, had secured permission to exhibit her dress and cape designs. Master Vicenti had to act as the man in charge in order to get permission, but he had faith in her and had left her to her own devices to prepare her exhibit. He expected a collection of dresses and shirts, coats and capes jackets and accessories would be laid out on the table in the space he had procured for her. Yet Lucrezia astounded everyone when the time came for her to unfold her "display."

She spent months in the designing, and then her shop was very busy sewing, ripping out, redesigning, resewing, embroidering, and altering each dress until each sleeve, bodice, neckline, and waistline was exactly what Lucrezia wanted. She had secret meetings with several women in town, but no one was the wiser as to her intent, except Amalia.

There was a notary shop down a small alley right off the Piazza del Duomo behind the Baptistry, and it would be closed through the days of the festival.

Lucrezia prevailed upon Marco and Carlo to rent it for her for the first two days. They had to explain to the notary that nothing would be touched, that the space was needed in the front room to store Lucrezia's dresses, capes, and cloaks in order to rotate the exhibit. Since the notary had been a friend of Amalia's father and he knew Carlo slightly, he agreed.

Lisabetta was thrilled by all the excitement, and her lessons were, if not suspended, certainly curtailed. She was to participate in a children's production that Caterina was spearheading, and she was very excited about that. It was simple, so Caterina kept the rehearsals to a minimum, knowing the children would get bored otherwise. She had generated a lot of interest in the project, and it had grown, with the help of many others—particularly the mothers—into quite a production, with each group of children having only a small part in the larger production.

When she could, Lisabetta rode in the wagon bringing in lumber, rode the horses and mules when Carlo allowed, helped Marco in the boddeghe, and helped take care of the animals on the farm when Carlo was too busy to do even the basics that needed to be done for their well-being. Much of it was more play than work, but oftentimes she was a great asset to everyone in the family.

Amalia was the only one not totally emersed in the activities. She had the primary care of Giuliano and Alessandra as well as little Ermanno, called Manno, Lucrezia's son, and Anna, their daughter. She and Francia tried to keep things normal for the younger children. With Franco's help, errands were run, food bought, wood and water toted, meals made, vegetables gathered from the garden, and all the necessaries of life taken care of amid the chaos. What was more, she was everyone's confidante.

Amalia was distracted because of all this and very little scribing got done on any books or manuscripts. She did manage to scribe and deliver a copy of Vitruvius's book on architecture, *Da architectura,* which was new to her. It was one of the earliest books Poggio had brought to Florence, but in all these years, although she had heard talk of it, she had never seen a copy of it. She reveled in every page and came to understand what had stimulated Brunelleschi and Masaccio and later Leonardo to take such an interest in perspective and proportion. She knew this was the book that had contributed to the interest in architecture that had changed the entire appearance of Florence; not only the skyline with the addition of the dome on the Cathedral by Brunelleschi, but the return to the classical thought about rooms and space, entries and facades, and pillars. It had been the most exciting manuscript she had worked on in years. When she delivered her copy along with the copy she had worked from, she asked to speak to Vespasiano himself if he wasn't too busy.

"I just wanted to thank you for the opportunity to copy this manuscript," she said. "It was such a thrill to understand where so many of our current new ideas came from. To think, Vitruvius wrote the original back two hundred years before Christ. It is amazing."

"Yes," said Messer Bisticci, "it is truly amazing. The copy you made is actually for me. Once Cosimo moves to Careggi after the festival, we will be gathering for the NeoPlato Academy sessions whenever we can, and I am hoping this book will be a topic of discussion. It isn't philosophy in the sense of Socrates and Plato, but I feel it has a lot to say on perspective and proportion, and, of course, the use of space can apply to more than just buildings. What do you think?"

"Oh, I agree. So much can apply to values in our lives. Well, I don't want to keep you, but I just wanted to say how much I appreciated the opportunity to read and study Vitruvius's manuscript and make it into a book. Thank you for entrusting me with that task. It was great fun."

"Most scribes would have considered that a burdensome if not impossible task. You think it fun. You are amazing."

"I like the challenge as well as the learning. I had a wonderful discussion with a friend of mine who understands architecture. He came by one evening, and we read several sections together," she said as she smiled.

Messer Vespasiano shook his head and smiled in return. "I see Jacopo has given you another Cicero to copy."

"Yes, I am pleased. I truly love the writings of Cicero, as did my father. He is my favorite because of the wonderful philosophy. I never stop learning from him no matter how many times I copy one of his books. I always come away feeling enriched with a greater appreciation of my life and love for my community."

Vespasiano said, "Cicero is Cosimo's favorite also. He has often said he tries to be guided by Cicero in his guidance of Florentine politics, with the idea of leading for the benefit of the people. I think he tries to be guided by Cicero's virtuous man in the Roman sense in his own life as well. We could all take a little direction from Cicero's writings. Cosimo always says the value of a man is in his deeds, not his words."

"I like that, trying to be the noble leader of the people," said Amalia.

"Cosimo says his father instilled in him the need to contribute to Florence, their city, but Cicero gave him the direction. He says he only wishes he had read Cicero earlier and started spending his money earlier on things to enhance the city.

"Well, young lady, enjoy the Cicero, and come by next week after the festivities. I think I will have a special project I would like you to work on over the summer."

"Thank you, Messer. I will look forward to it."

Amalia had numerous errands to do on her way home, but her mind kept wandering back to Vespasiano, wondering what he had in store for her.

She was anxious to get home and begin work on her new Cicero. Her hand might write the letters and words, but her heart would write the phrases and thoughts. She couldn't wait to share it with everyone. She knew they had their evening entertainment for the next week once the festival was over.

Finally, the 24th arrived. Everything had been constructed by the hundreds of workers from all over the city, including Carlo, Marco, and Ermanno. Rehearsals were over; the tent had been raised all around the Baptistry; and the weather was good. It had the promise of a beautiful and very exciting day.

Francia and Amalia were up very early to prepare breakfast for everyone. Since no one knew when their next meal would be, Amalia wanted to get as much food in everyone as she could.

Carlo had been hired by several of the merchants to help them set up, but first he would help Marco cart all of his wares to be exhibited on a beautiful purple cloth Lucrezia had made for him. Carlo would be busy all day helping those who hired him and also many who didn't.

Ermanno wouldn't be busy with the musical production until much later in the day, so he was going to help Lucrezia and Amalia in anything they needed. Jacko joined the group for the early breakfast because he had brought a cart to the front of Lucrezia's shop to transport all of her creations to the notary's office on the alley near the piazza. In it was a set of wooden steps to be transported along with the garments and the rack to hold them.

Carlo and Marco left first; then the rest left after kissing the children goodbye. Amalia knew Francia would have dinner ready for all of them when the day was over. They still had busy days ahead of them, so they would not be among the revelers in all the piazzas and streets of Florence tonight.

By the time they loaded the cart and got to the notary's office, Marco had already set up the array of his beautiful pots and pans, one of his large cauldrons, and his special ornaments and display pieces. Carlo was off helping other merchants.

Amalia, Lucrezia, Jacko, and AnnaMaria got all the garments inside the notary's office and laid them in order on the large rack Ermanno carried in. Lucrezia started pinning numbers on each garment as she put them in order. On a table off to the side were some other items, also numbered: two hats, three reticules, several scarves, some jewelry, other items, and then a beautiful large purple cape lay across the end of the table.

The piazza was beginning to fill with people from every walk of life, from the lowest peasant and workman to local and foreign dignitaries. The rich and the poor were elbowing for space in order to see the many exhibits by the merchants. One table was still empty, and the nearby merchants glanced at it, as if wondering what had happened to that exhibitor; but they were busy with their own problems, and they felt they would find out soon enough.

Lucrezia waited until there was enough of an audience before commencing her exhibit. Ermanno and Jacko carried the steps out and set them to the side of the large table. Jacko went back to guard the door of the office, and Lucrezia approached the table. She was dressed in a deep blue dress, beautifully tailored in a conservative but flattering design. It was not flashy, by any means, but it was quite exquisite. Perhaps some people noticed that Ermanno's trunk-hose and wrapped jacket were in the same color, and it hung to just below his knees. He was standing behind the steps, and Lucrezia was off slightly to the side of the step as a beautiful young woman wrapped in a long, full, beautiful purple cape approached. She curtsied to Lucrezia, then turned to face the steps. Lucrezia removed the huge cape from the woman's shoulders as the woman stepped up on the first step, took Ermanno's hand, and was guided to stand on top of the table. She wore a startling dress of a brilliant emerald green fabric with sleeves tied on at the shoulder and puffed to the elbow, having three gold inserts in the puffed area on each sleeve, one in a patterned green and gold fabric. There was the same gold and emerald patterned insert to one side on the skirt of the dress. She faced the audience with her arms slightly extended, out away from her sides.

In the meantime, Lucrezia had folded the cape into a ball and handed it to Lisabetta, who ran as fast as she could back to the notary's office—the changing room. Jacko waited for her and opened the door as she approached. Inside, AnnaMaria and Amalia were helping the next young woman into Outfit Number 2. AnnaMarie handed Lisabetta a reticule with the sign Number 2 on it to carry back to Lucrezia.

The first young, very attractive woman was just coming down the steps with the confident assistance of Ermanno's steady hand after she had turned two slow times while standing on the table. As she reached the bottom of the steps, she again curtsied to Lucrezia, and then slowly strolled toward the changing room. If someone wanted to touch the fabric or look closely at the sleeve, the young woman smiled and paused. She was in no hurry but neither did she hesitate to move along.

Once she entered the changing room, Jacko saw to it that the door remained closed for just a moment before another young woman emerged totally enshrouded in the large purple cape. Once she curtsied and Lucrezia had assisted her out of the cape, she was handed the small reticule, and the routine was repeated as it would be again and again throughout the day. This dress had a great deal of beautiful embroidery work all around the neckline and bodice and on the crown of the sleeves, making the top of the dress a beautiful garden of different colored flowers.

There were three young women modeling the dresses, two of whom were twins. Only their hairdos distinguished them one from the other, and each was more beautiful than the other. Then a young man exhibited the men's jackets and capes, long and short, several embroidered or done in a trapunto style, showing a pattern or design on the silk fabrics. Since it was summer, Lucrezia didn't show any of the heavier damask, velvets, furs, or woolen jackets.

It took them two hours to exhibit all of the items, and then they would stop for a half hour before starting the routine all over again. By the time the Campanile rang five hours, they were all exhausted, and it was time to call it a day. The crowd was thinning near the merchants tables as most were heading off toward different types of entertainment, including the food and drink, and the music and dancing which would go on well into the night in the crowded piazzas throughout the town.

By the time the Valetti-Evangelista group left the Piazzo del Duomo, they knew Lucrezia's exhibit had been a huge success. At first, the merchants nearby were upset because as each young woman ascended the steps and stood atop the table for all to see, all interest in their merchandise ceased as the spectators would be drawn to a lady in a beautiful dress. But the merchants soon realized that attention then returned to their wares. In addition, larger crowds were drawn to and tended to linger in their area to see the beautiful garments and girls. These crowds would then view their wares in between. Lucrezia's show was quite an attraction, and although the very beautiful girls were certainly an enticement, the garments were a huge hit that would bring Lucrezia much notoriety and business in the future.

As they all got back to the house, they found that Francia had wine poured for everyone and a good meal had been laid out. Ermanno had gone off to attend to his responsibilities with the musical productions, and Carlo, Marco, and Lucrezia were late arriving. By the time Lucrezia sat down, Lisabetta was already asleep, with her head in Amalia's lap. She had done an excellent job, running back and forth all day. She had taken a nap somewhere in the middle of the day, and AnnaMaria made one trip from the dressing room to Lucrezia and back until Lisabetta awakened, but then she was eager to renew her part in the great fun.

Lucrezia was exhausted from nervous tension as much as from standing most of the day, but she was also thrilled at the way her creative designs had been received by the women as well as the men. She said she assumed the other designers would be quick to copy her ideas.

Since tomorrow would be an early start again, Francia suggested Lucrezia allow little Manno and Anna to spend the night with Giuliano and Alessandra, and soon after, Ermanno and Lucrezia left to walk back to their house. Jacko decided to stay over, and as he and Carlo climbed the stairs to Carlo's castle, Marco lifted the sleeping Lisabetta from Amalia's lap, and headed toward the stairs for an early night of well-deserved sleep.

Amalia said, "Francia, I hate to leave you with such a mess."

"It's all right. I have had an easy day compared to the rest of you, and Franco will help me. Sleep as late as you can. I will have everything ready for tomorrow, don't worry."

"Thank you, Francia. It is such a relief to know I can rely on you. Good night."

The next day Carlo was just as busy helping the various merchants, as was Marco with his own table stacked high with his copper ware, now for sale. Lucrezia posted a sheet on the post by her table, saying when each dress would be exhibited. Each would only be exhibited one time throughout the day, ending at the fourth hour. This was when Caterina's production with the children began and Lisabetta would perform. Lisabetta had stayed home today so she would be rested and dressed for her big performance. Francia would have her ready, and Amalia would come home in time to take her over to the steps of the Cathedral.

Ermanno could only help Lucrezia until the noon hour. He would be busy all afternoon working with the musical director, preparing for the big musical production to begin at the sixth hour at the Cathedral, following the children's production.

Jacko, dressed in an outrageous outfit of many colors and of a most unusual design, filled in for Ermanno and was there to help each young woman ascend and descend the steps. He got quite carried away with his job and added a few flourishes to his simple act. He started walking around the table and eyeing the girls and the garment, feeling the edge of the hem and lifting it an inch or two, clapping and doing a little dance when one of the girls flicked her finger at him, to the delight of all those standing nearby.

Lucrezia warned him not to get bawdy, and he didn't, but he did lighten up the crowd by creating some amusement.

This second day was easier because everyone knew what would be expected of them. Lucrezia had plenty of time to talk to fellow designers and potential customers as each garment was exhibited. She had told the girls she only needed one or maybe two of them, but all three wanted to continue. They had all been very apprehensive when Lucrezia had approached them about doing this, but they had found it had been fun, even if it was actually hard work, and they had become quite the celebrities. They were all three very beautiful, and Lucrezia had chosen them for their looks as well as their slim, excellent figures, so there were often men in the audience who cared not at all about the fashions, only the beautiful girl exhibiting them.

When the Campanile bells rang the fourth hour, AnnaMaria and the girls went their way, Lucrezia was done, and Jacko helped her lock up the shop. They raced across the piazza so they would get a good spot from which to watch the children's production of little vignettes as two, four or maybe six children at a time pantomimed a folk tale, sang a children's song, or girls danced around a May pole with pretty ribbons attached to it while young boys played instruments to accompany them. Each skit was greeted by thunderous applause, generally from the parents, relatives, and neighbors of the children in that skit—or another one. All the relatives and friends in the audience had a wonderful time cheering on the children, who were very nervous prior but then overjoyed after their performance. All in all, it was a total success. Carlo, Jacko, and Marco had found Lucrezia and Amalia in the audience in time to see Lisabetta dance around the May pole in the beautiful dress Lucrezia had made for her. Of course, they believed with all their hearts that Lisabetta was the prettiest and the best dancer of the six girls, but everyone in the group standing nearby firmly believed their daughter had been the best and prettiest, and so they all laughed and applauded. Then the group behind them clapped loudly for their son playing the drum, and on it went.

When it was over, the children came out from the Cathedral to join their families. Beatrice and Giovanni found the group among the huge crowds, and Caterina and her entire family also joined them as they all waited the start of the next event.

The bells of the Campanile sounding the sixth hour was the signal for the commencement of the main performance of the day, a re-enactment of various times in the life of St. John the Baptist, interspersed with the singing or chanting of various hymns and songs. It was a truly splendid performance, all staged and planned by the excellent musical director of their superb musical company. Some of the most talented singers, musicians, and actors took part in this special production each year. Lucrezia could hear Ermanno's voice in several of the group songs, but he made no effort to drown out the other singers.

The last song, after the dramatic presentation was over, was Ermanno's solo performance with the other singers and musicians. Because Ermanno's fame had spread, it was a highly anticipated event of the day. It was a beautiful song, and Ermanno's voice was magnificent. Lucrezia, as usual, was totally enraptured throughout, and the rest of them thoroughly enjoyed it as well. At the end, the audience didn't want him to end. He was very embarrassed, but finally the musical director suggested he sing a beautiful song from one of their productions last winter, since it had religious overtones. The applause was thunderous, but the audience wanted still more. The musical director brought the St. John the Baptist performance to a close, and as he signaled for all the performers and singers to begin exiting to go back inside the Cathedral, he signaled for Ermanno and the musicians to continue. The crowd roared as the musicians began to play another song, not so religiously oriented this time. When Ermanno began to sing, the crowd roared again to the point of drowning him out. They quickly quieted, and a concert commenced like none Florence had seen in many years, for only when there was a man with a superlative voice would a director allow such a performance. Lucrezia was crying now, and when Amalia saw this, she hugged her friend, but Lucrezia was not to be comforted. Eventually, when the next song ended, she whispered to Amalia, "He is no longer my Ermanno, his voice is no longer only mine to love. Now he belongs to the city. It will not be easy to learn to share him and his voice with so many."

"Oh, Lucrezia," was all Amalia could say, and she hugged her friend tightly as they watched Ermanno bow and begin his next song, one the audience knew and loved well. Before long, the entire piazza had joined him.

When it ended and the audience quieted, he started the same song again, and once everyone was singing, Ermanno looked over and bowed toward the musicians and waved, still singing, and then slowly descended the steps of the Cathedral of Santa Maria del Fiore. He embraced Lucrezia, and as he and the entire piazza continued to sing, Ermanno and Lucrezia, hand in hand, led their party across the piazza toward their street and their home, the crowd parting as they slowly proceeded. As they entered their street, it was almost dark, but they could still hear the song being sung in the piazza several blocks behind them.

Beatrice and Giovanni invited everyone in, and soon many of the neighbors joined them. The pleasures of the day continued well into the evening as everyone shared stories of the events of the day.

The next morning, Carlo and Jacko had a calcio match, but they said they were going to get beaten badly and not to come to watch. Marco, Ermanno, and Lucrezia went to the notary's office with two carts. The men loaded the few items Marco had not sold plus the table and wood steps in one cart while Lucrezia and AnnaMaria bundled all the garments; then everyone helped to load them onto the other cart. They brought the garments to Lucrezia's shop, and Marco took the copper goods as well as the table and steps and display rack back to his boddeghe.

Once that was done, Marco and Ermanno went over to watch the boys, but it was not a pretty sight. Although the boys came out of it unscathed, they had been soundly beaten, and nothing more was said about the game by anyone.

Well after midday, now it was time for each of them to dress in their own finery for the parades with their neighbors and friends throughout the city, with the drums and trumpets playing, the flags waving, and everyone singing and chanting.

There would be groups of priests and monks and friars from the various monasteries and churches in their finest vestments or solemn robes. The priests from the San Giovanni Basilica, the Baptistry, first and foremost, paraded in the processional, carrying the sacred relics from the church. Also parading were groups of men from each of the various guilds, groups from each of the separate gonfalons of Florence, groups of men and women from the various confraternities in each of the churches throughout the city. All were parading in their finest attire, all were playing and chanting or singing in their finest voices, waving their banners and flags. No one was in a hurry; it was a time of camaraderie within each group and friendly competition with all the other groups. They paraded through all the streets of Florence for several hours. Someone might start out with their neighbors, and when they ran into their confraternity at an intersection, they might switch to that group, and maybe switch back again a few blocks later.

Even the Medici would parade the streets enacting the "Journey of the Magi." It was said Cosimo had a special sable cape given to him by a Russian dignitary which he kept just for these events. The "Magi" was his favorite theme even for the artwork he commissioned at the various churches.

Once each group ended the day by parading back to their own part of town or their designated destination, each gathered in a large area: sometimes a park, sometimes the loggia of a large palazzo, sometimes in the street. Messer Ludovico's palazzo was the gathering point for Amalia and Lucrezia's neighbors, but in fact, many of the people, drinking and eating the foods prepared for this feast, spilled out into the street. The music, drinking, eating, and revelry went on deep into the night.

The next day was the paleo. The finest horses in all of Tuscany, ran from one end of town to the other right through the heart of the city, the Piazza del Duomo.

Many thought the paleo in <u>Siena, in Il Campo</u>, was better, but it was a very different format. Each of the twelve communes of Siena entered one horse and expected it to win and beat the other gonfalons. There was fierce rivalry, and over the years a lot of animosities had developed between the gonfalons of the city, so feelings always ran high. Because of this, hostilities oftentimes broke out. On the day of the parades, each commune had its group of musicians, drummers, chanters, and flag-wavers dressed in the colors of their commune. When one group met another at some intersection in the town, sometimes things got out of hand.

In Florence, it was different; their paleo was an event everyone looked forward to with great anticipation. Everyone had their favorite horse and jockey, and everyone wagered large or small bets on the "winning horse." It was all run for the fun of it, except for the owners of the horses who, of course, wanted to own the winning horse—and except for the wagerers who had bet and perhaps lost more than they could afford.

The paleo was the final event of the annual celebration of the Feast of St. John the Baptist, the patron saint of Florence.

This particular year, it had rained in the morning, but the race wasn't run until after the midday meal, so all was well. Everyone knew the route taken by the jockeys, and they would be at their favorite viewing spots long before the horses came racing past.

Some wanted to be near the beginning, near the Porta al Prato where there was always a lot of pushing and shoving by the jockeys for a good position at the start. Some wanted to be at one of the sharp turns just prior to the horses entering the Piazza del Duomo, because very often a jockey was unhorsed or a horse would stumble and fall there. Sometimes, there was a pile-up that could prove quite disastrous for horses and jockeys; others along Via dell' Oriuolo, and some wanted to be near the finish line by Porta Santa Croce. Usually, the owners and their supporters and the heavy betters were there.

The Strozzis had a good horse this year, as did the Rucellai family. The Medicis always had an excellent entry and often won the event because Cosimo took great interest in the breeding of his horses out at his villa in the Mugello. The Pandolfini's had an excellent horse this year, and it was expected to win. The Vespucci's had an entry, and Jacko said it was a good horse but the jockey didn't know how to control him. It was his uncle's horse, the same uncle Jacko and Carlo had worked for in the past. There were twelve horses in all, owned by the richest bankers and merchants in Florence.

Ermanno and Marco placed some bets, guided by Carlo and Jacko, who knew most of the jockeys and all of the horses.

Francia wanted no part of the race, preferring to stay home and take care of the babies; and Lisabetta wanted to go over to Caterina's house to be with Blanche. Carlo and Jacko were nowhere to be found, off to do mischief and have fun with their friends. Lucrezia and Ermanno, Marco and Amalia, and Beatrice and Giovanni set off to the other side of town. They had decided they would go behind the Duomo where the track was wide and then narrowed to enter Via dell' Oriuolo, not too far from the end of the race.

The Pandolfini horse won, to no one's great surprise, and the walk home was thoroughly enjoyable. The six of them were gathering at Beatrice and Giovanni's with a few other neighbors, but they wanted no part of the wild celebrating and partying that would go on well into the night throughout the city. Theirs would be a quiet party with excellent food, wine, and laughter with good friends.

Marco knew the two boys, Carlo and Jacko, had no such quiet evening planned, and although apprehensive for their well-being, he knew they could take care of themselves and would stick together and watch out for each other. Jacko, who was quickly becoming quite the ladies' man, probably would not come home with Carlo—if Carlo made it home—or make it back to his uncle's house. Yet they were good boys, and Marco trusted them—sort of.

XX *The Aftermath*

On the day following the horse race, Lucrezia closed her shop so she could unpack everything, clean the garments, and repair a tear that had happened to one of them. Then she would put them on display in her shop. Not all at once, of course, but she planned to rotate the ones that had not been sold or spoken for. Three were a perfect fit for the customers that wanted to buy them, and a couple would need some minor alterations. All of the men's attire had been spoken for. The customers would come by or send someone by later in the week to pay for and pick up the items.

The two younger girls, the twins, that had modeled Lucrezia's garments, were orphans at L'Ospedale degli Innocenti, having been left in the turn basket within days of their birth. Their mother might have been one of the numerous unwed mothers of Florence and had brought them to the turn basket, knowing she could not give them any kind of a life. Or the mother might have been married and, having too many mouths to feed already, had to give her babies up to give them the chance of a better life. Perhaps the mother died or the father died, and the surviving parent could not provide for the two babies.

There were many reasons for a parent to be forced to give up a baby in these difficult times, for sicknesses were rampant, particularly among the poor, and early deaths were common. The plague struck periodically; malaria, typhoid, cholera, and other deadly diseases struck often; tuberculosis was an ever-present threat, and childbirth itself was a life-threatening event for every mother and infant.

When the city saw the need, Cosimo de Medici had commissioned Brunelleschi to design and build L'Ospedale degli Innocenti, mostly at Cosimo's personal expense. Only one other man contributed to its construction. A very rich merchant in Prato left a large sum of money for its construction in his will in 1410. This was a Master Francesco di Marco Datino.

There were other orphanages, but this one, right in the heart of Florence, was founded on the premise that if a child was not adopted, he or she was to be schooled and trained so as to be able to grow up and be able to contribute and survive out in the city—and the world.

These two girls should have been adopted at a very young age, but they had not been healthy, and both had a very difficult beginning. Well into their teen years, they were still sickly and so were passed over by any potential adoptive parents. They were also too frail to be considered as a servant by anyone who might take on a child with a physical potential for hard work.

Then, over a year ago, both had blossomed into beautiful young ladies, now healthy and strong. They had always been happy, particularly when together. Because they both clung to life for so long by such a tenuous thread, they became very reliant on each other and were even closer than most sisters or twins.

In addition to being beautiful, both of them were literate, having been properly schooled in the orphanage. Plus, they had been trained in recent years to work hard as attendants in L'Ospedale. Both wanted to work in Lucrezia's shop. They weren't trained seamstresses but they knew how to sew because every young girl did her share of sewing at L'Ospedale. Both were eager to learn and work hard if it meant an opportunity to leave L'Ospedale permanently and venture out into the city. There, they might have a chance at a life not behind convent walls, a possible destination for both of them in the next year or so if they could not find a better situation.

They had met Lucrezia when she had come with Amalia to volunteer during the winter when so many of the children had been sick, and the three of them had formed an instant friendship.

When Lucrezia asked them to do this posing for her, they were very hesitant. Could they do it physically, was their stamina good enough? Would such a thing be proper to do or would the nuns refuse to allow them to do it? What was more, the crowds, and the thought of being on exhibition, terrified them. Lucrezia understood all they said, and told them it would have to be their decision; they would have to gather their courage to do it, she couldn't do it for them. She assured them she would be there with them every step of the way, but that she was also scared, so she had her own demons to conquer.

Lucrezia brought them to her shop to meet AnnaMaria, then took them over to chat with Maria, her older neighbor who had been like a mother to both her and Amalia. She asked Maria to give them some motherly advice and maybe some encouragement, but she knew that ultimately it was a decision the girls would have to make for themselves.

It did not take them long to decide that this opportunity was being handed to them, and there might not be another one. Thus, they started coming to Lucrezia's shop on Saturday afternoons when they had free time, and AnnaMaria worked with them on how to walk and stand, hold their heads up, smile small, uninviting but friendly smiles, and much more. Plus, in the back room Lucrezia would fit the dresses to the girls figures, so both the girls and the dresses showed to the maximum advantage.

Now that the festivities were over, and they had expressed an interest in working at Lucrezia's shop, and AnnaMaria had agreed to taking on their training as seamstresses and shop workers, they needed a place to live. Once the director of L'Ospedale degli Innocenti learned what they had been doing, although she did not accuse them of any inappropriate conduct or behavior, she told them they would have to leave L'Ospedale.

Fortunately for them, Beatrice and Giovanni had not found an acceptable renter for Beatrice's parents' home after the couple that had been renting it moved back to Milan. Since the house was fully furnished, they agreed to let the girls live in the house for a nominal rent until they could find more appropriate quarters.

Master D'Alessandro would surely have a problem with the arrangements, but they would try to convince him. The quicker the girls were working and settled, the stronger their arguments would be. After all, there was precedent in the gonfalons that had turned out well, and both Lucrezia, Amalia, and Beatrice as well as Maria would all speak up in the twins' behalf, as well as all of the husbands. Master D'Alessandro knew that Amalia—for reasons he could not understand—had a powerful benefactor in Cosimo himself. But if he did object, Maria said she had a large bedroom they could stay in until other arrangements could be made. Somehow, it would all be worked out, but those problems were all for the weeks ahead.

~ ~ ~

Marco had received so many orders for pots and pans plus the wall pieces and ornaments, he feared he actually might run out of copper before Erudius's next shipment arrived. He knew the boddeghe would be busy through the summer into the fall.

The next week he had to make a delivery of alum to Genoa for shipment to Bruges, and it would take some extra time to accomplish. He had to get it loaded onto a good ship and get it insured. Carlo would be in charge of the freighting, of course, but Marco would have to conduct the business in Genoa. Then, once he received word from Erudius on the next shipment, he and Carlo would have to go to Venice to receive delivery. Obviously it was going to be a very busy summer.

Several weeks later, Marco and Carlo left Florence on a clear day which boded well for an easy journey to Venice. Carlo had a large delivery to make in Bologna, and then he hoped to pick up a shipment from Bologna to Venice to make that part of the trip profitable. He was disappointed to find no one knew of any pending shipments, so he and Marco left Bologna with an empty wagon. The only good part of that was it made for a very light, very fast, easy trip for them and for the mules.

They left Padua in the early morning with the sun rising in their faces. If they were lucky, they would be in Spinea late afternoon. Marco had received word the shipment had already been transported from the Venice docks over to Porto Marghera, so they would not have to cross over the water to Venice to receive it.

When they came to the Brenta River, knowing it was the last good freshwater river they would pass before dropping down to the marshes, where the water was brackish, they decided to water the mules. This took some time, but it was going to be an easy day, and although the mules didn't know what a treat they were getting with the good, fresh water, Carlo and Marco did.

Once done, they got the six mules back in harness. Then, just as Marco went to climb back up on the wagon, several riders rounded the bend in the road from Venice at a very fast pace and startled the mules as well as Carlo and Marco. Just as Marco's foot stepped up, the wagon jarred just slightly but enough to unbalance Marco, and he fell backwards. In his fall, he hit his head on a rock and was knocked unconscious.

Carlo tried to bring him around by wiping his face with some water. He managed to wipe the blood from the wound and wrap Marco's head with some clean rags, but they were stranded with the wagon in the middle of the road, with Marco off to the side in the ditch.

After some time, a rider came along who helped Carlo get Marco into the back of the wagon. With that, Carlo headed to Spinea in hopes of finding medical attention for Marco.

By the time they got to Spinea, Marco was rousing, mainly groaning, particularly whenever the wagon hit a rut or rock. The doctor said it was a clean wound and nothing really could be done except for Carlo to let his friend rest and keep him quiet.

Carlo found an inn and got Marco comfortable, but all the next day, Marco was in and out of awareness, conscious but dizzy. All Carlo wanted to do was to get Marco home, but the trip would be too much for him in his present condition, plus they would be leaving the large shipment of alum behind on the docks at Porta Marghera only a mile away.

Three days later, Marco was finally able to stand, and he was insistent they head to the docks to pick up the shipment. When they got downstairs and out to the wagon, the team was all hitched, and the wagon was ready to roll west. Marco looked at the heavily loaded wagon, and said, "What have you done? What is this?"

"Alum. Let's go home"

"But how did you do this?"

"You obviously couldn't go to the docks and complete the deal, so I did. Let's go home. Get in. I made a spot for you behind the seat where you can rest if you need to. Let's go home."

Marco ignored him and climbed up on the bench saying, "Carlo, how did you do this? What about all the papers? The contract? The releases? The money?"

"All done."

"How?"

"Marco, I have been watching you all these years. Do you think I have learned nothing? Fortunately, it was not a complicated delivery. The only tricky part was getting them to actually deal with me."

"Well, how did you manage that?"

"I just told them that you were over in Venice on a much more important negotiation, and you sent me to take delivery of this small, insignificant shipment. I said that if I didn't get it done, you would beat me, probably to death, and then come after them."

"You lied?"

"Well, not really. The deal is done, so there was no need for you to beat me, and who knows whether you would have or not—or gone after them."

"Unbelievable. Do you think I would beat you?"

"Since we have the shipment, we'll never know, and you never can tell about those things, can you?" Carlo flashed a huge grin at Marco, and then they both laughed.

"Now let's get you home. I thought I was going to be bringing you back in a box, and I don't think Amalia would have been too happy with either of us."

April of the next year, Marco received a very large shipment of alum. He had brokered a sale to a company in London willing to pay considerably more than the dealers from Bruges, with whom he had also been negotiating.

Jacko's uncle, Jacopo Vespucci, had a very large shipment of cloth: silk, cotton, a large amount of wool fabrics, some brocades, and more, as well as some gemstones. It was all scheduled to leave Livorno the beginning of May, provided there were no delays with the ship he owned with three partners. Jacopo and Marco had been talking, and since Erudius's shipment had arrived in time, Marco was planning to ship it on Jacopo's ship. Jacopo was sending his factor, Marsilio, who would keep the gemstones safe on his body at all times; and he wanted his nephew, Jacko, to go along as an extra guard. Plus, he thought the experience would be good for the boy, who was certainly a boy no longer.

Marco had been very busy at the boddeghe all winter, and he had a huge stock of his special pans and also the pots. Although still in demand in Florence, Marco knew he was going to have to start looking for additional markets.

One night while the six of them were having a late meal together, Marco was telling them of his concerns and that he was going to have to make some plans soon.

Carlo was very quiet for much longer than usual to the point where Amalia put her hand on his arm and asked: "Are you all right?"

Startled, Carlo looked at her and said, "I am. I was just thinking. Marco, what if I went with Jacko and Marcilio and took a shipment of your pots and pans and sold them in London?"

Amalia said, "Carlo, you can't go with them. You are too young. It's too far, too dangerous."

"I knew you would say that, but I'm not too young. You know I have always lived beyond my years, and I will be with a good friend and an older man who will be a protector for both of us. And, Marco, you know I can sell tomatoes to a tomato farmer. It would be a good experience for me. Who knows where it would lead, and it would be great fun, especially with Jacko. This would be a gift, an adventure. Jacko doesn't want to go, but if Messer Jacopo will let me join them, then I think Jacko would think differently about the trip."

Marco said, "Well, Carlo, it appears you really have been thinking."

Carlo continued, "Until I am a couple years older, the roads of Italy aren't safe for me to do my freighting alone or for far distances. I still think that may be what I want to do in the future, but I'm tired of hauling goods around the city and shipments to nearby towns. It would be a good bridge. Otherwise, I fear I may get bored and idle and fall into bad ways like Jacko and start chasing women or gambling."

Amalia, Lucrezia, and Lisabetta cried out, "No, no."

Then they all laughed when they realized Carlo was only baiting them.

Lisabetta added, "Anyway, you can't start chasing women. You have to wait until I'm old enough for us to marry."

Then they all laughed even more, and Lisabetta giggled.

Carlo was right, though, and Amalia knew it in her heart. Marco and Carlo worked out an arrangement for the sale of the copper ware with Marco pricing each item. It turned out Jacopo was very pleased Carlo was going along.

Amalia had an idea that if Carlo took a chest of books and manuscripts, perhaps he could sell them in London to the book dealers and make some money. She talked to Master Manetti, and he was pleased with the idea. He often shipped books, and always worried about delivery or damage along the way. He told her that last year a small box of books had been delivered but all had been ruined in transit.

Master Manetti took charge of gathering the books and manuscripts to be shipped. He spoke with Messer Bisticci and several other book dealers and scribes. In the end, he had enough books to fill a large chest and several smaller ones, and then he handled the finances for all of them on their end. The value of each book was written on a piece of paper placed inside it, and Carlo would have to become familiar with the value of the English currency in order to be sure to make a profit.

Carlo was anxious about this and didn't want to make a mistake, but Master Manetti assured him that once he was there for a while, this would not be so daunting.

Master Manetti told Carlo who the dealers were and which ones he had had dealings with in the past. If he couldn't find buyers for all of the books, Carlo was to leave the extra ones with a Mister Doggins on High Street. Master Manetti felt he could work out a fair deal later with him for those remaining books.

This was not the usual way he did business and certainly not with this number of books. Usually he sent four or six specific books that had been requested in advance, but he trusted Carlo.

Amalia asked Marco to ask Jacopo to go by Master Manetti's shop and bring Marcilio by to introduce them. Being an older man, she felt it would give Master Manetti comfort that Carlo was not on his own in a strange country, negotiating with foreigners on these business dealings. Master Manetti was grateful to meet Marcilio, but he said he knew Carlo well enough to know he could handle any business dealing better than most adults.

Carlo sold all of the mules and two of the horses in anticipation of being gone until late in the year. He kept only Traveler. Neither he nor Lisabetta could possibly part with him, unless there was no alternative. Lisabetta promised she would go out to the farm regularly and see to him and the chickens plus Boots and Luppo. This would not be burdensome since she spent so much of her free time out there anyway.

Paolo, one of Carlo's old friends, was back in town from Milan where he and Gino had gone almost two years ago, and now he was a little more settled. He had a horse, and he was going to use Carlo and Jacko's small wagon and try to pick up some of Carlo's work and build a business for himself. He promised to look after Lisabetta and give her rides back and forth between the house and the farm.

The farm was only two miles outside of the city wall on the road toward Fiesole, so it was not too far to walk, but it could be dangerous for a young girl outside the wall.

~ ~ ~

Lisabetta hadn't told anyone, but she had already decided she would ride Traveler back and forth and bed him down by Marco's boddeghe. There was a very small plot of open land right beside the boddeghe, and the boddeghe had an extended roof on the side facing the lot. That would give Traveler protection if a sudden storm came up. All he would need would be water and a little feed. She knew she could ask Marco to store a barrel of feed for him, and she would ask Paolo to bring in a load of hay when she needed it. Besides, Traveler would have plenty of time to graze during the time she was at the farm. She had this all planned out, but told no one until it was time for her to execute her plan.

Marco's boddeghe was right near one of the gates to the city, but it was not the Fiesole gate. Lisabetta knew she could not be riding Traveler through the streets of the city without causing a stir and probably getting herself and Amalia in trouble. She had been attentive during those last few weeks before Carlo left whenever she was out with Carlo or Marco on the wagon trips. She was sure she could get from the Fiesole Road around to the Pisa gate on the road that circled the outside of the wall. Once inside the Pisa gate, it was only a hundred braccia to Marco's boddeghe.

No one would question her coming from the boddeghe to their house, since she often walked there and back either with Marco, Carlo, Amalia or oftentimes by herself.

She would execute her plan, and when it was successful, Amalia and Marco would not be able to tell her it wouldn't work.

When the time came for Marco and Carlo to leave with the two wagonloads of alum, the boxes of Marco's pots, and the chests of books, Amalia, Lucrezia, and Lisabetta were devastated. The three of them plus, Ermanno, and several neighbors walked to the Pisa gate to see them off.

Ermanno and Lucrezia carried little Manno and Anna, and Marco carried Alessandra while Amalia carried Giuliano. Alessandra kept saying she was a big girl and she wanted to walk, but after fifty braccia, she would want to be carried. Then she wanted down again and then back up again in Marco's arms. She wanted to go with him, wherever it was he was going, so maybe this was going to be an even more difficult parting than they anticipated. Even though Marco would be back in a week or so, how did you explain time to a four year old? Although usually such an agreeable little girl, she was being extremely difficult and demanding now. She did not understand what was happening, and no one could explain it to her to her satisfaction. She knew from the way the adults were behaving what was happening wasn't good. She didn't like it at all, and she let them all know it.

Amalia was used to Marco and Carlo being gone one or two weeks, even three weeks sometimes, but for Carlo to be gone for seven or eight months or maybe more left a hole in her heart, and Lucrezia felt the same way. They both had the love of a mother for the boy—no, they had to concede, he was no longer a boy, he was a grown man in everyone's eyes but theirs, but it still would not be easy for either of them.

Once the goodbyes were over, hugs were shared, and the tears shed, the little party walked back home in silence, blessed silence as it turned out, because Alessandra had cried herself into such a state she finally fell asleep with her head on her mother's shoulder for the walk home and Lisabetta carried Giuliano.

~ ~ ~

Marco still had a lot of business to conduct once they got to the port in Livorno, including the loading of the shipments and acquiring insurance, but at least the business had been accomplished between Jacopo and him before he ever left Florence.

There had been some repairs to be made to the ship, and it was an extra two days before they could load their shipment. When the time finally came, Carlo and Jacko were helpful when Marco was loading his shipment onto the ship, and then Marco helped Marcilio with Jacopo's shipment.

When Carlo and Jacko sailed away, Marco was as apprehensive as the girls had been when they said their goodbyes back in Florence. He was glad there was no one there with him, because it took forever for the ship to be pulled from the docks, raise some sail to get under way, and then to start raising more sail as the sails began to catch the wind. He watched until the ship was almost out of sight. He loved Carlo deeply, and he knew he might never return. He couldn't bear to think about that, and he could only imagine what such thoughts must be doing to Amalia and Lucrezia.

Carlo had promised he would write when they were in any port in hopes that word would get back to Florence. Marcilio would be writing Jacopo, of course, and Jacko said he would write, but no one held out much hope of that happening.

It was over a month later that word came from both Carlo and Marcilio telling the same story:

Amalia, Lucrezia, Lisabetta, Marco, Ermanno, and all the little ones, We have arrived in Sassari on the island of Corsica and are awaiting favorable winds to head for the strait to pass through and enter the Great Sea. We will then turn north to head for England, passing Spain and Portugal and then France. A ship is leaving tomorrow for Genoa, so Marcilio and I will send what we are each writing in hopes one of them reaches Florence.

The seas have been very calm, and it has been a very slow crossing of the Gulf of Genoa. We were all three sick the first day out, but thankfully, since then, we have been fine. Jacko climbs the riggings like one of the sailors and is having a grand time becoming as one of the crew and manning the lines. Amalia, I am very glad you insisted I bring some books. Marcilio and I have been doing some reading on the many calmer days. Marcilio also brought a bag of books, so between us, I am sure we will have enough to get us through the journey.

I generally go out in the small boat each day with some of the crew to try my luck at fishing with them, and we usually catch something, so we and the crew and the other two passengers have some fresh fish each day.

The other two men traveling with us are Englishmen. One is a merchant from north of London, a place called York, traveling with his shipment, as are we. The other man is a factor for the manufacturers of tapestries in Bruges. He says these tapestries are very special. He is the man you, Marco, were talking to in Florence who was interested in your alum. He says he wants to talk to you again the next time he is in Florence. I suspect by the end of this journey, I will know whether you will want to do business with him or not, but so far he seems nice enough. His Italian is poor but since my English is not to be heard, I cannot fault him. I will try to learn some English from both of them so I can speak the language by the time we land in London.

I can't say I have enjoyed the journey so far. It has been quite boring, except for the time spent watching Jacko climb the riggings like he has been doing it all his life. Maybe he has found his life's ambition. I went up into the crow's nest one time on a calm day, and that was enough for me. I was sick the rest of the day.

I am going to help Captain Messana with some letter-writing soon, so I will give this to Marcilio to post when he posts his letter with the captain of the ship heading for Genoa.

I miss all of you and think of you often. Carlo.

It was another month before they heard from Carlo again.

Amalia, Lucrezia and everyone,

This will be brief but there is a lot to tell. I have been keeping two logs, so I will enclose the one copy.

We ran into an abandoned ship at sea when we were twelve days out of Sassari, not too far from the southeast corner of Spain. Apparently, it had been boarded by pirates, and everyone was either killed and thrown overboard or taken by the pirates as prisoners. Whatever else they took, we have no idea as the captain's log is gone, and we could find no documents, but there is still a lot of the cargo stowed below decks. Since we had favorable winds, the captain wanted to sail it to the Spanish port of Malaga. It was a slow journey, but there will be a considerable reward for him for the recovered cargo, particularly if it is insured.

The authorities came on board and questioned all of us to be sure of the captain's story, but we have hopes of being back under sail as soon as the captain's business with the authorities is concluded. I am told we are close to the strait and will enter it our second day out once we depart here. It looks like a very poor, run-down city so I have not spent any time—

The captain is back and Marcilio just came to get my letter. The dock master is preparing to release us for departure so I must close. I miss you all. Carlo.

It was another two months before they had word. Only Carlo's letter arrived, so his information was passed on to Jacopo and Jacko's father. It would be another four months before Marcilio's letter, mailed on the same day, reached Jacopo.

Everyone,

We have survived a bad time, but are now safely in port in Cadiz, a port in Spain on the Great Sea. I will again enclose the copy of my journal. You will know if all my letters get through by the dating in the log.

We were hit by a terrible storm not half way through the strait, and we nearly foundered on the rocks of the African coast. After it was all over, the captain told us if we had foundered there and managed to survive the rocks, we would have almost certainly all been killed by the uncivilized people inhabiting the coast there.

The worst was yet to come, as once we were free of the African coast, our main mast cracked in the fierce wind and crashed down on the deck, killing one of the crew members. As it happened, it was the man Jacko had made friends with, Guido, and Jacko is still very upset. The ship would certainly have been lost, and we would have all been drowned, except that almost immediately after the mast fell, the winds and the seas abated, giving us time to make some emergency repairs. We could not make any port before we were blown out of the strait and into the Great Sea until we were nowhere near land. We were not in any immediate danger of crashing on a rocky coast but we had very little sail power and we had contrary winds.

Over the next few days, we made what repairs we could to the sails and rigging and managed to remount the main mast and rig it with some abbreviated sail. The captain is very ingenious and is a good sailor who knows his ship and how to sail her in the worst of circumstances. I suspect with a lesser man at the helm, I would now be at the bottom of the sea.

We finally got a favorable wind and managed to limp into Cadiz, a very, busy port with many ships docked port to starboard and still more anchored in the middle of the harbor. We will be here until we are able to make the necessary repairs, and right now we have no idea how long that will be.

Nothing can be done for Jacko. He will have to work through the pain of his loss in his own way and in his own time. This is what Marcilio tells me. We had a formal burial at sea for Guido once we were out of the straits and immediate danger. The service performed by Captain Messana was very moving. Guido was only a few years older than Jacko, and he had been well-liked by the entire crew.

We will be going ashore shortly and will be able to stay ashore for several days once the Captain has some idea about the repairs of the main mast. Marcilio wants to stay aboard the ship during the repairs to protect the cargo in the ship's hold and his personal cargo, but he said Jacko and I should go ashore and explore as long as we have the opportunity. Jacko is not enthusiastic, of course, but I am hoping things will improve for him once we are away from the ship and have an adventure to pursue. I suspect his adventure will be in a dress.

It is the next day, and the captain just advised us the repairs will take at least a week if not more, so he gave the whole crew leave for one week and paid them a small portion of their wages. Marcilio is still determined to stay on board the ship during the repairs, as is Mister Crawford, as he is called. Mister Powers is coming with Jacko and me once we have eaten. I will give this to the dockmaster when we leave, and I will hope to write again just before we depart if it is possible.

I am glad to still be here and able to write to all of you. I miss all of you more than you can possibly know. Pray for me and my safe return. Carlo.

One last thing. I lost my cap in the storm.

It was another ten weeks before they heard from Carlo again. There was a letter from Marcilio mailed from Cadiz almost three weeks after Carlo sent his letter. It was mainly business, but Jacopo sent it over for everyone to read It said the repairs had taken longer than expected, and they were only now ready to depart for England.

Cadiz itself was very small, a walled city only six blocks wide in some places on a hooked peninsular jutting into the sea. One side was the very busy port, and the outer edge was a beautiful white sandy beach. There was a Roman amphitheater near the middle of the town, and they had some events there on festival days. The men had explored all the sights of the town quickly and spent most of their time in the many drinking establishments or walking the beach.

Fortunately, everyone was back on board on the day of departure, being simply bored trying to entertain themselves in the small town. The last of the repairs were supposed to take all that day and the next, but they found the repair to be unnecessary, and they were able to leave a day early.

Marco said that this was probably why Carlo didn't write again, expecting he had that last day to do it. Or maybe this time his letter would be delayed in transit and would arrive after he was already back home.

The next word was over two months later:

To my family, Amalia, Lucrezia, Lisabetta, Marco, Ermanno, little Giuliano, Alessandra, Manno, and Anna,

As I write each of your names, I spend time thinking of you, for I wonder if I will ever see any of you again.

I am well, but again things have not gone well. I enclose the log for safekeeping and for you to read.

We left Cadiz, and the captain was well-pleased with the way the ship was handling with the new mast, some new sails, and some new rigging, and with how the crew was getting familiar with the changes that were made.

We were making excellent time, cruising north with a favorable wind until we were off the coast of southern France where we were blown far out to sea by a contrary wind, currents, and rather foul weather. The captain was distressed because we are losing so much time reaching London, but he was not able to bring the ship into the wind and make any headway.

The weather cleared for a couple hours on the last night of the wind, and the captain was able to get an accurate reckoning of our position, but by dawn, we were becalmed in a fog that was so dense you could not see the bow nor the stern of the ship when standing amidships. It was very eerie. I had a feeling of great fear, although Marcilio and the captain as well as Misters Crawford and Powers said there was nothing to fear. I wasn't actually afraid, if that makes sense, but I couldn't get rid of that terrible feeling of great trepidation.

Obviously, we did survive it all, and I felt foolish afterward for my fears, but I can't say I want to experience that ever again.

That was not the end of our troubles. Once the winds picked up and the fog dissipated, we could make very little headway north toward England. We could travel eastward, but that eventually put us on the coast of France, where we found port in Brest and then Calais and found we were unable to cross the channel between France and England.

It seems we are marooned here until the winds change and allow us crossing. We have all spent all the time we wish to spend in Calais, so we simply live on board reading, playing droughts, and talking. The crew have their games, and Jacko joins them occasionally, but he seems to have lost his enthusiasm for their company without Guido's presence.

Marcilio and I are the least bored since we have a good supply of entertainment with our books. Sometimes one or the other of us will read aloud to anyone who wants to listen.

The only good to come of this is that our English has improved, and we now converse with Misters Crawford and Powers in English. I don't anticipate we will have any language problems once we arrive in London. French in Calais is another matter.

The worst of this is that the captain told us last night that by the time we do cross, there will be no time to conduct our business and find a ship for a return trip, so we will be stranded in London until spring.

Mister Crawford told me this happens very often, and I guess I knew it was a possibility but I just didn't want to think it would really happen. If we get across soon, the captain will try to find cargo ready to load, and he will leave immediately. In that case, we will have to find another ship in the spring for our return shipment of the raw wool both Marcilio and I must still buy.

There will be no way I will have time to contact Marco's man and get the alum transaction completed, complete the dealings with the Medici bank, and then purchase the wool and get it loaded, plus find an outlet for the copper ware, and the books, even with Marcilio's help. Marcilio has his personal items to dispose of too, so I am resigned to spending the winter in London.

If you do not hear anything to the contrary, assume this is what will happen. At least I will have adequate time to find the absolute best sale for the copper ware and books rather than having to rush the deal. Plus, Mister Crawford told Marcilio and me that if we make a trip to the Cotswolds, we can probably make a much better deal for the purchase of the raw wool. I will investigate as soon as we get to London, if we ever do actually get there, which I am beginning to doubt.

I will mail this. Dear family, do not expect to see me again before next fall if I make it then or ever. My love to all of you. Carlo

After another week's delay, they did finally make the crossing and made their way by riding the tide slowly up the Thames to London.

Carlo was grateful Mister Crawford had told them where to stay and where to eat in London, and more importantly, he advised them who to deal with at the wool market, and gave them the name of the director to deal with at the Medici bank. He also knew of a couple farmers and dealers in the Cotswolds, and he told Carlo which was the best warehouse for temporary storage of his smaller items.

XXII   *Merry Olde England*

While they were glad to have arrived in England and were not sorry to be leaving the ship, they were sorry to be saying their goodbyes to Mister Crawford and Mister Powers. They had both been good company. Since they were both experienced travelers, their guidance had been very helpful throughout the journey. Now it seemed their advice would make the introduction to the world of London much easier for the three Florentine travelers.

The sale of Marcilio's cloth was the simplest deal to complete: the usual agent met them at the dock shortly after the ship arrived in London, and he took delivery as soon as the large bundles of cloth were unloaded from the cargo area of the ship. The money was taken to and deposited with the Medici bank they found over on Lombard Street easily enough, thanks to Mister Crawford's excellent directions.

Marcilio went with Carlo shortly after the ship docked to meet with the agent who was supposed to buy the entire shipment of alum to be sure the man didn't take advantage of Carlo's youth. All went well. His office was not far from the dock, and the agent agreed to take delivery the next day as soon as he could arrange for cartage.

On their way back from the alum agent's office, they rented the warehouse space to store Marco's copper ware and the chests of books. Then all three walked into town and found the inn, all thanks again to Mister Crawford.

The next day, once the alum was unloaded from the ship and freighted away by the new owners and they made another trip to the Medici bank, the three men got the copper ware and books transferred to the warehouse. They moved their personal belongings to the inn and said their farewells to Captain Messana.

Their new home away from home was a delightful inn, The Bull and Rooster, run by a Mister and Mistress Murphy in a pleasant, quiet section of town. They had a private room upstairs, and downstairs there was a comfortable sitting room off to the side of the busy pub. They were to learn Mister Crawford's suggestion had been an excellent one, because although the inn was small, they would be hard-pressed to find a better meal in London or in their travels while in England. None of the food was particularly to their liking, being so different from what they were accustomed to eating back home, but nonetheless, they soon were able to tell what was properly prepared and what was not.

One of their first adjustments at mealtime was getting used to the stares of the locals when they would take their forchetta out from their belts to eat their food. Everyone would stare anyway because they were foreigners, but they would be discreet about it; but the forks were apparently too much. They just stared. In Florence, everyone used them, and most households just put them on the table, but whenever away from home, it was part of the traveling equipment in their belts, along with their daggers.

The sitting room had an assortment of comfortable chairs and two small desks for writing, plus it had a fireplace they knew they would appreciate once the cold weather arrived. Although it was still October, the weather was not cold, apparently a reprieve after what had been for the Londoners a cold and very nasty September. The men did not yet realize just how much they would enjoy that cozy fireplace.

Thinking of their horrible voyage, where he felt that everything that could go wrong did go wrong—other than their actual demise to the bottom of the sea—Carlo had expected the worst to happen with his alum deal. When all went smoothly, he transferred his fears to Marcilio's various deals concerning the gemstones.

Until Marcilio was rid of those gemstones, the three of them traveled together any time Marcilio left the ship, or later, the inn. Now they all three went to his meetings concerning the sale of the gems. Again, Carlo's worries were for naught, for all went smoothly; and after three days of negotiations with the various dealers, again the money was safely deposited in the Medici bank.

It had been a very busy week, but now the three of them were free to see the sights of London, and so they did.

They were surprised how small the city was, how narrow the streets were, and how dirty everything was. The sun rarely shone but since the days were still quite warm, they had to bear the fetid stench of human and animal waste that was far worse than in Florence. The people all seemed to rush down the streets and everyone seemed angry all the time. In the inns late in the evenings, things improved a bit and everyone seemed happy, but Carlo remarked to Marcilio that it was just the beer and ale laughing. The next day those same people were as glum, grumpy, and sour-faced as everyone else.

In their travels about town, Carlo visited some craft and artisan shops to get an idea of the copper ware market, and he dropped in on any book shops they passed. Marcilio was always amazed at Carlo's business acumen for a person of his age.

Jacko was starting to enjoy some of the delights of London, but Carlo wasn't interested in spending much time in the brothels liberally distributed throughout the city.

He and Marcilio decided it would be a good idea to make a trip over to the Cotswolds to see if what Mister Crawford had said was true and also to escape the retched stench of the city. They found out they could purchase all the wool they wanted from the London warehouses near the docks, but what was now left in those warehouses was not the finest grade. It would still sell in Florence if they were forced to buy it, but it would not bring top florins. The Cotswolds were reputed to have the finest sheep and therefore the finest wool in all of England, and maybe they could make a deal to purchase finer, freshly sheared wool.

Since they were going to be trapped in England until spring anyway, they had plenty of time to spare, so it was worth a trip over there. Jacko was not anxious to go, but they said they would not leave him to his own devices in London. They needed to go, so he would have to go with them.

They had purchased three horses in London for the venture. Since the King was embroiled in a war, they were told to stay on the main roads and not go north into Northampton. They never did see any troops, but there was a lot of talk about the two royal houses, Lancaster and York, that were warring. Each was nicknamed for a rose, the red and the white. They got directions to Cirencester and instructions as to which inns to stay at and which ones to avoid on the journey. They already had Mister Crawford's suggestions where to stay once they got to Cirencester.

They all three found they enjoyed the English countryside very much. The sun shone brightly almost every day, and now removed from the city, the air was clean and crisp with the growing hint of winter.

The quaint villages with their thatched cottages and the stone and wood shops tucked into the green hills were lovely. Inns were scattered along the way, some larger than others, some in worse repair than others, and some with a clientele to be avoided. With a little discretion, though, those places could be easily skipped.

Thanks to Mister Crawford's and Mister Murphy's suggestions, they almost always found one where the evening was spent in friendly camaraderie with the local folk, who were usually interested in chatting with the Florentine visitors. At one inn, the people seemed cautious of these strangers, so they kept to themselves, and retired to their room, making an early night of it. In general, though, they found the farmers and shop owners affable, and they were enjoying their travels.

Once they reached the Cotswolds, all three were enchanted by the Cotswold villages and the lifestyle there. Although the people weren't rich, they were honest, and they were good farmers who loved the land and understood how to husband their animals. Life was at a much slower pace that made for very pleasurable days, and now, as the land prepared to go to sleep for the winter, it gave its last glorious burst of splendor. The scenery so buoyed their spirits, they sometimes rode along singing a Florentine frottola.

They wished Ermanno were here to lead them, as their voices paled in comparison to his, but without him for comparison, they thought they were quite good. They applauded themselves merrily, sometimes with a laugh and a slap on the back of one or the other.

The three of them traveled throughout the area for over two weeks, talking to many farmers and several agents and looking at a lot of sheep. Actually, Jacko knew more about the sheep than Carlo or Marcilio did because of the time he had spent on his uncle's farm. He educated them as they happened upon good specimens and poor ones.

They soon felt they had enough information to make arrangements to buy and take shipment as soon as the sheep were shorn in late April or early May.

Carlo and Marcilio had soon contracted a deal with the agent in Cirencester to receive shipment at the London wool docks as soon as the wool arrived. A small amount would be paid to the agent's partner in London as soon as the three Florentine men returned to town, and the rest would be paid upon delivery of the wool to the London docks.

Both Carlo and Marcilio felt good about the wool purchase, and they were confident Marco and Jacopo would be very happy with the deals they had made. If Marco and Jacopo had left it for agents to make all the arrangements and take their commissions, a lot of money would have been lost; plus all three felt they would have been getting a lesser grade of wool. All three felt that, once back in Florence, when the wool was sold to the merchants, Marco and Jacopo would make a huge profit on the sale of the wool. The dealings were certainly not completed yet, and they weren't back in Florence, but they had a good feeling about what they had accomplished since arriving in London. Carlo and Marcilio felt that the trip had not been in vain, nor had their time been wasted. The trip home was ahead of them in April, and whether they or the raw wool ever got back to Florence would be in God's hands.

Carlo still had to find a market for Marco's pots and pans and Amalia's books once they got back to Londontown, but there was plenty of time for that. The countryside was truly beautiful and the people so delightful, they decided to stay away from London until the weather drove them back. At least, Marcilio and Carlo decided.

The three went first over to Bristol, and it being a port for the many sailings to and from Ireland, Jacko came alive and was gone all day every day down to the ships, the docks, the pubs, and who knew where else. Sometimes he made it back to their inn for dinner, and sometimes he didn't, but at least when he did make it back, he was in a much better frame of mind than he had been during their time in the Cotswolds. He had not enjoyed, as Carlo and Marcilio had, roaming Stow-on-the-Wold, Broadway, Chipping Norton, Mouton-on-the-Marsh, and all the other quaint villages comprising the Cotswolds. They had even enjoyed exploring the wool churches built with the money from the wool sold at the markets in several of the villages, much to Jacko's vexation.

After a week, Carlo and Marcilio dragged Jacko, kicking and screaming, south with them toward Salisbury, Winchester, and several other towns. They stayed several days at the Glastonbury Abbey in the quarters set aside for travelers. They were amazed at the immensity of the complex and the beautiful church.

They passed several areas of huge stones arranged in what was a circle before some of them fell down. They were told those stones were put there by an ancient people long before the Romans came to England. Were these like the Etruscans in Italy that had build some of the temples still to be found in the countryside? One time Lucrezia had dragged Carlo to see one of those ruins up in Fiesole.

They—Carlo and Marcilio—enjoyed the cathedrals in Winchester and Salisbury, and many of the quaint churches they visited along the way. Although Winchester Cathedral was undergoing some revisions, they were impressed at the immensity of the gothic structure. Yet when they compared those cathedrals to the Duomo and San Lorenzo and others, they realized they much preferred the graceful, simple lines of their Florence churches.

Most of the cottages they passed were wattle and dab with thatched roofs. The towns were mostly wooden structures, all very cramped, with small rooms and very little light. Although they were beautiful in their setting and so very quaint, when they compared what they were seeing with Brunelleschi's beautiful arches, his airy loggia, large rooms, large windows, gracious pillars, high ceilings, and the use of outside space, they knew theirs was truly an advanced culture.

They saw a huge castle with a moat, high walls, and battlements, and they would have liked to have seen inside. It appeared quite austere with tiny slits for windows. There was no comparison with the grand palazzos of Florence, even though the castle was immense.

They were amazed at how few people were literate. Almost no one could read or write their native English language, and only a few of the priests they met could read or write Latin. None of the three had ever stopped to think about it before, but now they realized how amazing it was that almost everyone, even the poor, in Florence could read Latin and their volgare Italian as well, thanks to Dante, Boccaccio, and Petrarch. Carlo said a silent thank you to Amalia and Lucrezia for

forcing him to do his lessons for all those years. He promised himself it would not be a silent thank you if he ever saw them again.

Carlo was appalled at the artwork, if there even was any, in the boxy, dark local churches. When he thought of the beautiful frescoes painted on the walls and all the beautiful framed paintings in the Duomo, Santa Croce, Santa Maria Novella, San Marco, and all the rest of even the smallest of the churches just in Florence alone, he thought his chest would simply explode with a sense of pride he had never felt before. Why, even the receiving room in Amalia's house had a large painting on the one wall. He could not say if it was beautiful or not, because, in truth, he had never paid it the least attention. He got to thinking about the times he would lie on the pillows in front of their fireplace and look up at the ceiling with the beautifully carved painted wood beams in Amalia's receiving room. Here there were only rough-hewn beams.

They did enjoy the grandeur of the cathedral in Salisbury, and they appreciated the intricacies of the construction; but the cold stone held little attraction when they compared it to Brunelleschi's designs that were a part of so many of the Florentine churches. Again and again, they made those comparisons.

While staying at an inn in one small village, Carlo talked to a man who was making a delivery to the inn. The axle of the man's cart was made in such a way that it impeded the movement of the cart and made it more difficult for the horse to pull the load. Carlo explained to the man how he could improve his axle, but the man simply stared at him as if he were a little "tetched in the head."

On board ship, Mister Powers had used the expression, "tetched in the head" one time, and he had explained its meaning to them. Later, when Carlo told Marcilio and Jacko what had happened with the carter, they had a good laugh. It became a favorite joke between them. Each of them would see things that to them seemed very primitive, but each would keep his own counsel and then simply relay his observations to the other two later, concluding that someone must be "tetched in the head." Then they would have a good laugh.

Carlo was in no hurry to return to town, but eventually he ran out of excuses to delay the inevitable, and shortly before Christmas, Jacko prevailed. Once again settled in at The Bull and Rooster, the weather being cold but clear and calm, Marcilio and Carlo spent a lot of their time seeing what sights there were to be seen in London. In the course of their travels, they made some contacts they felt would be beneficial for Jacopo and Marco, Master Manetti and Messer Bisticci.

While Marcilio was working for his employer and hoped his efforts would be appreciated and ultimately rewarded by Jacopo, Carlo was doing all this for a friend. Yes, he would do very well financially with the arrangement he and Marco had worked out, but also he felt he had done well by a friend who was the husband of the most important person in his life. Nothing was enough or ever would be good enough for Amalia.

Carlo spent a lot of time going first to the area of town where the bookshops were clustered, talking to the owners, jotting down names and addresses, and making notes. Then he went over to the section of town where there were more crafters, and he would talk to the various artisans. He went in all the shops that sold metal ware, kitchen wares, or anything related to copper.

After a week of roaming the city talking to artisans and shopkeepers, he narrowed the copper ware sale possibilities down to four shops. He took a couple pots and one pan with him. He never got to the last two shops. The owner of the second shop was willing to buy all Carlo had in the warehouse and at an excellent price. The shop owner, Mister Farnsworth, needed two days to arrange for payment, but then, Marcilio, Jacko, and Carlo made the delivery of all the copper ware to the shop, and Mr. Farnsworth paid Carlo in cash. There was considerable talk of future dealings, and Carlo gave Mister Farnsworth the information so he could contact Marco directly.

Once the three had visited the bank, Marcilio and Jacko went their way, and Carlo started revisiting the several book stores, this time intending to talk business. Only two of them were interested or capable of stocking Master Manetti's books, but between them they took all he had and were hungry for more. It took him several days to deliver each of the various books to the prospective book dealers, but finally each dealer was satisfied with all of his selections. Carlo was paid, and another trip was made to the Medici bank on Lombard Street.

Again, Carlo put both of the book dealers in direct contact with Master Manetti. One had had dealings with him previously, but from now on, Carlo believed the relationship would be on a more personal level. He was confident trade would flourish between them in the future.

In their talks, one of the book dealers told Carlo of some very old manuscripts he knew of that might be of interest to the Italian scribes. Being familiar with that world, Carlo thought it might be worth a trip out to the monastery near Oxford that had the collection.

Marcilio agreed to ride out to Oxford with him. Since it was cold, they had no desire to be riding on horseback, and they had sold their horses back to the livery where they bought them anyway. Thus, they took the Oxford stage, intending to rent horses in Oxford for the short ride out to the monastery if necessary.

The university town greatly impressed both of them, and the actual university buildings did also. The weather was cold but clear and still, so they walked all through the town at their leisure. There was a vibrancy in the town, perhaps because of so many young people. They talked with many of the students, which was very easy to do, for the many pubs in the town were filled with them any time the students weren't at lectures. They even had some interesting conversations with a few of the dons. This greatly improved their impression of England, for although the countryside and small villages and towns might seem backward, this center of learning seemed excellent.

Carlo had a lengthy conversation with one don who was very familiar with the Italian humanists and more particularly the movement in Florence. When he learned that Carlo actually knew Poggio Bracciolini, he was very impressed and asked Carlo if they might meet again late the next day, as the don was to lecture in a short while and had to leave.

The following morning Carlo and Marcilio rode out to inquire about any manuscripts or books the monastery might have available for purchase. They were told the abbot was away, that nothing could be accomplished without him, and that he would return later that day.

Just by way of chatting, what information Carlo was able to gather led him to believe Master Manetti and Messer Bisticci might very well be interested in what he was not going to be able to view this day. Arrangements were made for them to meet with the abbot and the monk in charge of their library tomorrow after ten bells. The abbot's secretary explained that the monastery was a very busy place In the early morning, and not to come earlier.

That afternoon when Carlo returned to the pub where he had chatted with the don, he was greeted by four dons, all anxious to talk about Poggio, the manuscripts, and the humanist movement. The front area was very crowded and noisy, so the five of them retired to a private room in the back of the pub, carrying with them two large jugs of ale. The conversations continued late into the evening.

As they questioned him, Carlo was amazed at how much he knew in answer to their many questions. The men all laughed at his stories about Poggio, and they were amazed when he told them about Amalia. A woman scribe? They were aghast, astounded, and shocked. How could that be? Carlo told them of the NeoPlato Academy formed by Cosimo de' Medici. He even remembered many of the names of the several humanists that gathered at Careggi: Niccolo de Niccoli, Bruni, Traversari in the past; Messers Vespasiano, and Ficino now to study and try to understand the teachings of the Greeks and the ancient Romans.

Carlo described that many book dealers hired scribes to copy the ancient books and manuscripts. He told them one he knew named Vespasiano da Bisticci sometimes had forty scribes working for him, and Cosimo de'Medici sometimes employed a thousand scribes to copy the ancient manuscripts from Latin, Greek, Hebrew, or other languages into Latin or their Italian volgare. The dons were shocked. The dons knew several of the largest English monasteries had scriptoriums, but they were surprised to learn that individual men would undertake such a thing. The vastness of the network throughout the Mediterranean to find more antiquated books amazed them.

Carlo explained that every Florentine book dealer had agents throughout Europe, Greece, the Levant, and the entire Mediterranean searching for old, forgotten books and manuscripts. All the major bankers of Florence authorized the directors of each of their foreign branches to buy anything that came their way.

Carlo tried to explain how these books had changed the thinking and the art in Florence, how the humanists had made nature and the world around them more relevant in their lives.

He also tried to explain the concept of perspective as Riccardo and Michelozzo had explained it to him, but they only stared at him with glazed eyes. When he saw Marcilio and Jacko again, it would be a "tetched" story.

After these men were done with him, he felt like a dish rag that had been wrung and squeezed dry of every ounce of information that was in him. The dons thanked him profusely, and as they left, they went away talking to each other in a very animated fashion as they headed back toward the university.

Carlo poured himself a mug of the last of the ale from the last jug, then found himself a quiet corner to sit and think about what had just happened. He knew he had confidence in abundance—that is what had always gotten him by in so many difficult situations all his life—but tonight made him wonder if he had more than just confidence. Carlo was amazed at his store of information. How did he know all this? Where had he learned it? He knew he was "street smart" because he had to be in order to survive those early years growing up on the streets of Florence; but this wasn't street smarts. This was more. His life was so rich, so varied, and he began to come to an awareness that he had capacities he had never realized before.

Because of Amalia, he knew Latin in addition to their volgare. He knew the teachings of Cicero and Livy, Lucretius and the Greeks. What was more, he had been pulled into the world of Riccardo and lawyers, Michelozzo and architects, Poggio and the humanists, Manetti and book dealers, and he knew and worked with Donatello, Lippi, and Verrocchio. He knew Marco and the world of the artisans, plus the world of each of their neighbors, the guilds, trades—even dress designing, for whatever good that would do him.

Once he got home—if he got home—there were people he had to thank and things he had to pursue that he had never considered before. It was now going to be very difficult to wait for May to arrive, and the voyage home was going to be interminable.

It snowed during the night and by the next morning there was four inches of fresh snow over the land. Fortunately, there was no wind, so the ride out to the monastery was like riding though a fairyland. Marcilio and Carlo didn't rush the horses they had rented at a stable near their inn. They just let them go at their own pace so they had sure footing.

The trees they passed stood out like skeletons, and each branch had a tower of snow standing tall on it. Each dead, withered bloom was topped with a crown of white snow, each bent blade of grass, each twig was a work of art, and the meadows were a vast expanse of glistening white with silver and rainbow sparkles everywhere like a crystal palace.

They saw a rabbit hopping across a small field, cattle trying to graze and not being able to get through to the stubbles of grass buried under the snow, and a deer on the rise of a hill over across a field. They passed a farm, the white roofs topping the brown wood walls of the barn and the grey stones of the cottage. The monastery ahead, with its dark grey rock walls against the white expanse, was a very tranquil, majestic sight.

Once inside the monastery gate, all peace and tranquility quickly evaporated, for all around them was a beehive of activity. Monks scurried in varied directions, doing their morning chores. The men weren't early; in fact they were quite late, but perhaps some of the work had been delayed by the snow.

The abbot was a fat—there is no other way to describe him—man with a florid complexion and bright red-passing-to-white hair. He had twinkling blue eyes, a round, red, cherub-like mouth, a smile that lit up his face, and a quick, easy laugh. You could almost forget he was the man in charge, for his pleasant disposition belied his responsibilities. Apparently, Carlo decided, he was able to carry those responsibilities lightly on his broad shoulders.

Abbot Boniface offered Carlo and Marcilio a tankard of ale, and a plate of bread and cheese was brought into the Abbot's study by the monk with whom Carlo had spoken the previous day.

Carlo explained why he was there, what he was looking for, and what Master Manetti and Messer Bisticci did with manuscripts and books that came their way in Florence. Abbot Boniface was familiar with the many books shipped from Florence to London and those that filtered out to Oxford. Although he thoroughly enjoyed reading any that came his way, he said he wasn't so sure that the broad dissemination of knowledge of such radical thinking would be a benefit to the church in times to come. By the same token, he was opposed to barring that information or the learning of it, even if it might change the way people thought about things.

Carlo mentioned how the knowledge had changed the attitudes of the artists, making them more aware of nature and the world all around them, and how they were incorporating those new ideas into their art, even as they painted the saints, the holy family, and the many biblical scenes. This interested the abbot, but it didn't seem to move him one way or the other.

After a while, the monk in charge of the library joined them and described to Carlo what they had available that they would be willing to sell. The book dealer in London had told Carlo that the monastery had fallen on hard times of late, and they needed the cash.

They had a few original, old manuscripts, one a secular manuscript of folk tales Carlo knew Messer Bisticci would be anxious to obtain. Two were in Gaelic, and Carlo feared no one in Italy would be able to translate the Irish Erse. Several were in Greek, and he had no idea what they were. The rest were in Latin. Several were copies the abbot's scribes had copied. A few were biblical, but some were secular books in Latin.

Carlo decided to take all the monk was offering him except for six. One was water-soaked and of no use, and the others were almost modern copies of books from the Bible that he felt were readily available in Italy.

After some negotiating, Carlo paid the abbot, and the books were wrapped in oiled cloth and loaded into the bags Carlo had brought with him. The abbot had seemed well pleased with the deal, and Carlo wondered if perhaps he had overpaid since he really wasn't sure what he had just bought. Oh, well, if Manetti and Bisticci didn't want them, he had the start of his own library, whether they were to his reading tastes or not. It hadn't been a huge layout of cash, so he was not too concerned. The real question was how was he going to learn Gaelic if those two manuscripts wound up being his.

The ride back to Oxford was as enjoyable as the ride to the monastery had been, and it was late in the day by the time they got back to their inn.

The two men decided they would leave for London on the first stage the following morning, fearful of another storm and additional snow stranding them in Oxford. Actually, they would have enjoyed being stranded in this place. Perhaps because it was a learning center, the people seemed to have more direction, and they seemed a lot happier—at least a lot more pleasant—than those they had experienced in London; but Marcilio still had people he wanted to meet regarding future trade, so it was time.

Once back in London, they all three stayed busy going their separate directions most days, and then they found a convenient pub or their own inn for dinner together each night. Marcilio had gotten quite friendly with the various fabric and leather importers, and Carlo sometimes joined him, so very often they would be talking business in the evenings.

Carlo made the rounds of the many churches to compare the architecture and the interiors in the English churches with those of Florence. Jacko was almost always out doing who knows what, and Carlo and Marcilio really didn't want to ask for fear Jacko would tell them. He did spend a lot of time down at the docks, but it was some of the other places they didn't care to hear about.

Some days, usually when the weather was dreadful, both men would hunker down with a book in Mistress Murphy's sitting room at their inn. Many days, if there was no wind, the town would be totally enshrouded in a dense fog where one could barely see one's hand in front of one's face. The coldness would penetrate to the marrow of one's bones, and the only recourse was to stay near a good fire in a comfortable chair. Luckily for Carlo and Marcilio, they were good readers, but Jacko was a prowler. When it was the sitting room that he was prowling, he would drive the other two to distraction.

On the nicer days when they could be out on the streets, Carlo found his favorite stops were at the booksellers. He loved perusing the books, almost all of them still in Latin. Some were in English, and although he could speak and understand the language, the reading of it was another matter. He often found a book to his liking and would sit in a back corner of the shop for an hour, reading.

If there was not much business, the shopkeepers were always ready and willing to chat about books, scribing, sea travel, or England, but Florence was usually the favorite topic. Carlo loved talking about his beautiful city, which was becoming more beautiful in his mind as the days and weeks slowly passed.

As he walked the dreary streets of London, Carlo's mind often turned to Florence and even more, to Via del Fiore and the people he loved. He was dreadfully homesick, and he swore to himself if he made it back, he was never going to leave Italy again and would only leave Florence, the farm, and Via del Fiore for brief, nearby journeys.

When Carlo lost his cap in the storm while they were at sea, he thought it was an omen that he was going to die. That cap had been his father's cap, and it was his only link to his family and his childhood. To lose it was like losing his past—his youth. When he didn't die, he knew he must move on. Now there were no crutches, no omens. He might have left Florence still a boy in many respects, but he would be returning as a man.

Jacko came in one night, and as they sat down for dinner, he told them he was going to leave tomorrow and go over to Bruges with Mister Powers. He had run into him down at the docks where he was booking his passage on a vessel leaving Dover in two days, and he had asked if Jacko would like to join him.

"Anything is better than sitting around here, and I've had my fill and more of the brothels and these glum, grey, foggy, wet, cold streets and dismal bars."

"When will you be back?" asked both Carlo and Marcilio, practically in unison.

"Mister Powers says it will probably be in a week to ten days. We are to take a coach down to Dover, then cross the next day. He says his business should only take three or four days, then back."

"Jacko, are you sure?" asked Carlo.

"Yes, yes. I'm going crazy here. I'll be back in plenty of time. We still have over a month before the wool arrives, and then we will still have to wait for the weather to change. I can't stand this place. If I don't get out, I'll go crazy, and I may drive both of you crazy too."

"Well," said Carlo, "I can't argue with that."

The three enjoyed a good laugh, and Carlo clapped Jacko on the back.

In thinking about it, Marcilio and Carlo decided they would join Jacko and Mister Powers for the stage ride as far as Canterbury. They would see the sights of the small cathedral town and Jacko and Mister Powers would go on to Dover. They didn't know of any sights other than the large cathedral, but the weather might be better than London, so they all left the next day.

During their stay in Canterbury, a storm blew in, and they were hopeful Jacko was already safely in Bruges by then.

On a whim, Carlo went to the Canterbury Cathedral and asked to see the abbot. He inquired about old books and manuscripts the church might have for sale, and the abbot called in the monk in charge of their library.

In a matter of three hours, a deal was made for three manuscripts of Celtic origin but in Latin, and five in Latin but of dubious origin. Carlo thought one or another of the dealers or collectors might be interested in them, so he arranged for the purchase. He left Canterbury the proud owner of additional books for his personal library if nobody wanted to buy his collection. Marcilio gave him the "tetched" look, but Carlo shrugged and said if nothing else, he had a fine remembrance of his winter in England.

As it turned out, most of his now considerable collection was rather pedestrian. Three were well worth copying, but here were two others that were jewels that excited Bisticci and the others very much.

It was several years before an Irishman came to town that could translate the Celtic books, and then they discovered that two of them were copies of old volumes from the Monastery at Kells in Ireland. They turned out to be the real treasures from the trip.

On their return to London, as they walked from the stage depot to their inn, they passed one of the royal palaces of the king. Henry VI was not there, they were told, and Carlo and Marcilio decided the king showed good judgment to escape London this time of year. Well, no. First, they were told the king was usually mad and most times had no judgment at all. Then they were told this was when all the rich people came to London. This was the height of the "season," and everyone left their country estates and came to town. This was when Parliament sat, and the king was expected back any day now. They decided maybe that was right, because it would be difficult to conduct business or attend parties in the stench of London's summer. They weren't too sure which was worse. No, summer was worse, they decided, and they knew they hadn't even seen the worst of it.

The day after their return to The Bull & Rooster, it turned very cold, and the two men were forced to remain inside. They were delighted they had the snug sitting room with its warm fire, for the weather was wretched. It varied between snow and frozen rain with blustery winds or no wind and dense fog, none of it fit for a dog.

Weeks dragged on, and the worst of the winter finally passed. Jacko had returned safely, but he returned to his old pattern of being gone most days, no matter how foul the weather. Marcilio and Carlo made a few more jaunts out of the city to surrounding towns. They thoroughly enjoyed the village of Windsor at the foot of the enormous royal palace. They did not enjoy the community south of the Thames, and they were fearful they might run into Jacko in a most compromising manner. They were very pleased when they did not.

Finally, spring arrived. The weather was splendid, and the trees, shrubs, rose bushes, and every other plant in the city popped out with lime-green leaves, turning a darker vibrant green as they aged, then the plants burst forth with a profusion of blooms of every description and color everywhere. The birds sang in a multitude of choruses, each singing his own hymn to another glorious day. Marcilio and Carlo took to the streets again, this time in search of the many parks throughout the city. They found good reason now to think and speak fondly of the City of London, for the parks, gardens, and even areas in front of many of the houses were splendid in the array of nature's grand abundance, both the floral and the bird life. Except on the windiest of days, there was a fragrance in the air that was simply intoxicating. How long did this London last, they wondered?

Now, when they were finally actually enjoying themselves, it was time to start turning their thoughts to preparing for the journey home. Marcilio and Carlo made the rounds to the various merchants and shop owners they had come to know to say their farewells. Arrangements were double-checked at the bank, the warehouse, with the wool shipper's agent, with the dock master about passage home, and a myriad of other details to attend to.

Jacko had become friendly with one of the captains, and he suggested they book their passage home on his ship. After diligently checking it all out, Marcilio agreed that Jacko's judgment seemed sound. Marcilio was surprised, but Carlo knew that, when it mattered, Jacko did have a good head on his shoulders.

All was ready, and their arrangements were complete. All they had to do now was await the arrival of the wool. As they were returning from the docks and warehouses, Carlo was taken ill. By that night, he had developed a high fever and a cough that wracked his entire body day and night and gave him no rest for several days. He couldn't leave their room. Fortunately, Mistress Murphy was able to give Marcilio and Jacko another room or they would have had no rest.

Mistress Murphy kept Carlo plied with gruels and soups that he would try to eat, sometimes just to please her, but he had no appetite. His throat was so raw, it was difficult to swallow even a broth. Finally, the fever broke, but the cough didn't abate, and Carlo found if he tried to stand up, he simply fell down. His throat was still raw, and it was agony to try to swallow; his chest ached with any movement, and each spasm of coughing was like knives being driven into his chest. He spent most days simply dreading the anticipation of the next day. He felt so poorly, he thought he might actually die; then there were the days when he wished he would.

Finally the day of the shipment from the Cotswolds arrived, and he could not get out of bed to see to its being properly stored in the warehouse.

"Don't worry," said Jacko, "I'll take care of it." And he did.

Later that day when he returned, he told Carlo it was done, and it had all gone smoothly.

"Thank you," said Carlo. "I can't tell you how much I appreciate your help. I just couldn't do it."

"Don't worry. It is all stored in the warehouse, ready to be loaded onto the ship once the final payment is concluded. Then, as soon as we get word from Captain Petrillo, we will load the wool, board the ship, and we will be on our way. Marcilio and I talked to the captain, and we should be able to sail by Thursday. Everyone believes the weather has finally broken.

Jacko continued, "Marcilio made the arrangements at the bank, and tomorrow you need to go there to execute the necessary documents for the completion of the transaction. I have hired a chaise to take us there first thing in the morning. We just have to get you downstairs and into the chaise. Marcilio is going to meet us at the bank and we will carry you in if we have to.

"Once that is done, the wool is ours. Arrangements are all made to load it onto the Sea Eagle; then we just wait for word from Captain Petrillo, and we will move out of the inn, board the ship, and we will be ready to leave this sickly, wretched place. I promise you, once you are down the Thames and out of this town, you will start to feel better."

"Thank you, Jacko. Please, please get me on that ship, and I know once we are sailing for home, I will get well. Please get me home, Jacko. I just want to see my family again."

BOOK II

XXIII   *August 1*   *1464*

"Mother, Mother, where are you?" called Alessandra as she ran up the steps into the receiving room.

"I'm here fixing our meal. What's wrong?"

"Mother, Lisabetta and I just rode in from the farm. A rider just came down the Fiesole Road, and he told us that Cosimo has finally died at Careggi. I knew you would want to know."

Amalia crossed herself and said, "God rest his soul," then she sat down. She had heard he was very sick with the gout and he was not expected to live much longer, but still, to know it was over—

Years ago she had hoped some occasion would arise where she would be able to thank him for all she knew he had done for her, and perhaps even things she still might not know about, but it never had happened. Now it was too late.

In recent years she had known there would never be an opportunity. Word had spread through Florence that Cosimo was so incapacitated, he no longer went out. He had to be carried from room to room or villa to villa, and he spent a great deal of his time in bed. He was even forced to receive foreign dignitaries in his bedroom.

A few years ago, the French ambassador had told the story that he was received by Cosimo, Lorenzo, his brother, and Piero, his son, all three propped up in Cosimo's bed. All were suffering an attack of the gout, but still they were gracious and able to conduct the business for which the ambassador was there. The ambassador said it was quite a comical sight except it was so sad.

Amalia had lived her entire life in Cosimo's Florence. What would happen now? She assumed Piero would pick up the reins, but, of course, she had no idea, and Piero was already so sick. It had been said in town there were times when the only thing he could move was his tongue because of the pain from the gout.

Amalia decided dinner could wait. She asked Francia to help her change into a different dress. Then she walked through her garden to Lucrezia's house to tell her the sad news.

Years ago, when Lucrezia and Ermanno had bought the small house on the back of Amalia's property, Amalia had wanted to give it to them, but Lucrezia and Ermanno had insisted on paying a fair price. In addition to the money Ermanno had from the sale of his house and numerous other properties in Ravenna, he was making excellent money now as one of the most renowned singers in all of Italy.

Ermanno refused to travel very far, but he would go down to Siena, over to Bologna, or even up to Milan and a few of the nearby cities for certain engagements each year. His frequent appearances in the many saints' day festival productions in Florence were always packed. He always performed with the excellent local musical production company during its season, and he often sang at private parties in some of the grand palazzos.

Eventually, he and Lucrezia bought the house next door to their house that had been Amalia's house, and then they joined the two, making it into one large house with more than enough room for their growing family. Lucrezia now used Amalia's ground level just for her numerous seamstresses. She turned the ground level of her own house, really two houses, into two shops: one for the sale of ready-made clothing, fabric, and notions, with AnnaMaria's office in the back, and the other a display area for the sale of her dresses and other designer garments. She had reserved a space in the back for her to work on her designing. This is where Amalia found Lucrezia now.

After a while, Lucrezia said, "You—we owe him so much. I wonder how many other people, common people in Florence, have stories like ours. Somehow, I don't think his benevolence stopped with you."

Amalia stood up. "I think you're probably right. I think I'll go over to Santa Maria Novella for a few minutes I'll see you for dinner. The girls are already back, and Marco and Carlo should be home soon."

Lucrezia walked over to Amalia, and they hugged in an embrace of mutual sympathy.

As they separated, Lucrezia said, "Ermanno is at a meeting with the new musical director. He should be home soon. Anna is over with the seamstresses, and

I have no idea where Manno and Ugo are, but we won't be late. I have a meeting with a customer soon. I'm sorry. I would like to go with you."

"That's all right. I think I need to be alone anyway. I will see you later."

Amalia walked into the cool, quiet church and found her favorite spot by the side alter dedicated to Our Lady. There she knelt down to pray for Cosimo's soul, then to tender her thanks to his departed spirit for all the benefices he had bestowed on her and her family.

This was her favorite alcove to visit, and she came there often, whenever she was overwhelmed with sadness or when she wanted to offer a prayer of thanksgiving for something good that happened in her life. Amalia could pray to Our Lady in hopes that she would hear and understand her supplication, but then she was always comforted by the beautiful Brunelleschi wooden crucifix off to her left.

Amalia had two healthy children, and she was very grateful for them; but she had suffered three miscarriages, each of them nearly breaking her heart. She dearly wanted to fill their home with the voices of more children. Now she was resigned that it wouldn't happen. Marco had always assured her he was overjoyed with Alessandra and Giuliano, and all that mattered to him was that she was well and happy. She was happy with her life, the life she had been given as a scribe and as a wife, thanks to Cosimo. She was also grateful for the enduring friendship she and Lucrezia had been allowed to forge because of Cosimo's intervention that day so long ago.

She turned now to Brunelleschi's crucifix and was reminded of the love Cosimo had for both Brunelleschi and for Donatello and the love those two men had for him and for each other. She hearkened back to the story she had heard many years ago about how this crucifix was created by Brunelleschi. Donatello had carved a wooden crucifix. When Brunelleschi saw it, he told Donatello it was beautiful but that it was earthy. Donatello challenged him to do a better one. Brunelleschi went back to his boddeghe and barely spoke to anyone for the next several months as he worked diligently on his new project.

Eventually, Brunelleschi invited Donatello to dine with him one day. Donatello went, carrying some eggs and other contributions for their meal in his apron. Upon entering Brunelleschi's home, he saw Brunelleschi's crucifix. He was so overwhelmed, he fell to his knees and wept at the beautiful sight before him, smashing his eggs in the process.

Now Donatello's crucifix hung in Santa Croce, and <u>Brunelleschi's hung here in Santa Maria Novella</u> where its beauty could inspire Amalia and so many others to higher thoughts. Yet it always reminded her most of the abiding friendship between these two brilliant men. Theirs was a competition born in fellowship and love; it was a rivalry for excellence, yes, but not for superiority. It was merely a challenge for each man to achieve the finest each had to offer.

Amalia loved that story. She felt it exemplified the true value of a friendship. Yes, it was important to be there to console each other in hard times and celebrate the joys of good ones, but friendship was also to urge each other to do and be the best they were capable of being. Was it not important to help a friend find the better part of him- or herself? Amalia felt she and Lucrezia had helped each other to achieve that.

Amalia sat for a long time, allowing her mind to recall those times long ago. She thought of Cosimo, yes, for what he had done for her but also of the Florence Cosimo had helped to create: the prosperous, vibrant city that had provided her family the opportunity for growth and success. Yes, she had much to be thankful for; to God and to Cosimo.

By the time she returned to her home, only a few blocks away, everyone had arrived.

~ ~ ~

Lisabetta and Alessandra had finished helping Francia prepare the meal, and Carlo had arrived. He had been in meetings all afternoon, and he was distressed to hear Lisabetta's news about Cosimo when he arrived. He knew Amalia would be very upset, as would Lucrezia, and he also knew dinner would be a subdued event.

Usually a Saturday dinner would be shared by some of their circle of friends at their house or another's, but the other three couples they were closest with had each recently suffered deaths in their families. They were devastated by their losses and were in no mood to socialize.

Beatrice and Giovanni Volini lost their six-year-old daughter, Doria, to the fever that had swept through the city the month before.

Caterina, Amalia's oldest friend, was devastated by the loss of one of her boys. He had been sick for several years, and it was almost a blessing to see the poor child finally at peace.

Riccardo lost both his parents to the fever. He was overwhelmed, not only with grief for his parents but the work load of taking over his father's legal practice in addition to maintaining his own.

So it would be a small family dinner tonight. Because of the sad news, Carlo wondered if perhaps he and Lisabetta should change their plans.

Marco arrived next and poured a glass of wine for Carlo and himself. He was full of news for Carlo, and they decided to go down the front stairs to their small office on the ground level.

Since Lucrezia had moved the ready-made clothes over to her house, Carlo and Marco had been using that little room—Amalia's old office and her father's before her—for their business. Marco had built a large office above the boddeghe once he had purchased the property and expanded his workshop. Usually they did their business there, but they kept the small office downstairs so as not to disturb Amalia and the rest of the family if they needed to have a business discussion at the house.

Carlo no longer lived at the house in Florence. He had bought the rest of the farm owned by Jacko's uncle, Nextimo Vespucci, shortly after his return from England. Nextimo bought a much larger farm with a splendid house on it on the other side of the Arno. He was of the age when he wanted to spend more of his time in leisure with his family, and this new estate suited his desires exactly.

Nextimo was a member of a very successful and politically powerful family, and he was a very successful notary and merchant with a growing family. He had taken it upon himself to look after his brother's son, Jacko, when he was orphaned early on by the death of his parents. He was fond of Jacko's friend, Carlo, and made him a very fair deal for the farm.

Once he purchased the farm, Carlo spent a great deal of time on the many improvements to the large house on that property. Nextimo had never lived in it and had let it deteriorate. Carlo lived in the house, but he came to town almost every day. All the animals he acquired for his freighting business were on the farm, as well as the many wagons and the repair shop for the wagons. By being there first thing every morning and then again in the evenings, he could see that all was run properly.

Within a year, Carlo had acquired or built about twenty wagons of varying sizes and capacities; plus, he had a large string of horses and mules in addition to six oxen. His freighting business plied the roads in and around Florence and out to the surrounding cities of Tuscany and beyond.

Carlo needed a lot of pastureland now, and he still farmed only grains on the balance of the land. He had several employees, and two families lived in the small houses on the property where Nextimo's farm hands used to live. Rather than tending the crops, his help tended the wagons and husbanded the animals.

Carlo built the buildings necessary for the repairs and construction, and spent a lot of his time working the land and enjoyed that almost as much as being on the road between Florence and any neighboring town or city.

One time, during a violent storm, a dead tree out at the far end of the pasture was blown down. Carlo found out it housed a very large bee population. Lisabetta, Bianca, and Bianca's mother, Violetta, went about gathering much of the honey and the combs and then had Carlo's men build domed boxes so they could very carefully move the bees into their new homes. It was very slow work, and if Carlo came around, they shooed him away, because his impatience distressed the bees. Violetta had learned how to handle bees as a young girl, and very soon, Lisabetta and Bianca knew all she could teach them.

Carlo had a couple of his men build a fence around the old, fallen tree and the collection of hives standing off to one side. This was considered a part of Lisabetta's farm, even though it was at the opposite end of the large farm. Carlo, who had gotten stung a couple times while out surveying the initial damage to the tree, could never understand why or how the girls could handle the bees without being stung; but he really didn't care, as he wanted no part of the buzzing creatures. He did enjoy, however, the honey that was now gathered and became another product of Lisabetta's very profitable farm.

Marco and Erudius had steadily expanded the trade between their countries. Carlo and Marco ran the importing, marketing, and the transporting business from Marco's office above his boddeghe where very often they had to coordinate all the branches of the businesses.

It turned out that Jacko loved ships, sailing, and the sea. Once the three men, Jacko, Carlo, and Marcilio, returned to Italy from England, Jacko turned right around and went to sea on Captain Petrillo's ship for two years. The second year out, they had extraordinary luck in retrieving an abandoned ship, as had happened to the three of them on their outbound journey to England. Captain Petrillo had shared the bonanza with the entire crew.

With that money and what he had saved, Jacko felt he had enough money to come to Marco and Carlo with a business proposition. Ultimately, the three of them bought a ship Jacko had his eye on, and the three of them entered the shipping business.

It turned out that Jacko actually knew what he was doing and had found something he was really good at. He hired a good crew, and he was the conscientious captain of the "Endurance." His first mate was an old hand at sailing, and they made a good team. Jacko was a quick learner and seemed to come to sailing quite naturally. He still needed years of experience, to be sure, but he seemed to have a natural instinct for how to handle the ship. He mastered the navigation skills he needed in the first years at sea while studying under Captain Petrillo.

Captain Petrillo was a good captain, sailor, and more importantly, a good businessman. He liked Jacko and give him good advice and steered a lot of business his way in the early years when Jacko captained his first ship.

When Carlo stepped off Captain Petrillo's ship all those years ago, he swore he would never again go to sea. Carlo's cap had been blown away in the storm when they almost crashed on the African coast, and he thought that was a sign he was going to die. When he didn't, he decided not to tempt the fates. Although he was now the part-owner of a ship, he never went to sea again.

Marco went to sea with Jacko a few times to Greek, Turkish, and Spanish ports—never through the straits out into the Great Sea—and he rather enjoyed it. He said it reminded him of his early years with the Greeks and Turks. One time Carlo told him he was "tetched," and the two of them and Jacko had a good laugh, but then, if he was "tetched," it seemed Jacko was also.

No one knew what the word meant except Carlo and Jacko, but it became a favorite word for all of them to use to mean exactly what it meant in English.

~ ~ ~

Lisabetta came downstairs when she heard Lucrezia and her whole family coming up the back stairs, and she was surprised not to find Carlo and Marco there. She thought she had heard them earlier.

Lisabetta had blossomed in recent years into what people said was a beautiful young lady. She looked nothing like her aunt, so everyone assumed she looked like her mother. She was bright and studious and loved doing artwork in Amalia's books, but most of all she loved working out at the farm.

True to herself when Carlo left to travel to England all those years ago, she had carried out her plan to take care of the animals and travel back and forth to and from the farm.

Amalia was furious the first time Lisabetta arrived home from the farm, and she told her she was not to go out to the farm alone ever again.

It was the worst scene to be witnessed under the roof of that house since Amalia's brother, Stefano, had arrived shortly after their father had died so many years ago. Lisabetta was nine years with a will of iron, but Amalia was right to be guarding her safety, even against the girl's own good intentions to care for the animals and the farm.

As it turned out, the problem resolved itself the next morning when they found Luppo curled up sound asleep under the back steps. Apparently Lisabetta had not been alone while riding Traveler in her journey from the farm, she just thought she was. Amalia had to admit that nobody would come near Lisabetta on the farm, traveling to and from the farm on the country roads, or in Florence with that animal beside her.

So Lisabetta went freely back and forth to the small house on the small patch of a farm she loved and claimed as her own. She scavenged furniture wherever she found it, saved scraps of fabric from Lucrezia's shop to make coverings for the windows, sewed a huge sack out of more scraps and stuffed it with fresh straw to make a mattress for the bed that stood on three legs and a stack of bricks.

She took care of Traveler, Luppo, Boots and the chickens at the farm, and brought eggs to town in abundance on each return trip and sometimes a fresh-killed chicken for their dinner.

Over the years Lisabetta started propagating plants, and she had started a lavender farm that she increased in size each year. She was always taking grape vine cuttings from the back wall of Lucrezia's garden and rooting them in one of her sheds and then planting them. Before he left for England, Carlo had often helped her prepare the soil and lay out the plan for her garden.

Lucrezia had shown her how to do the clipping and propagating one morning, not even sure the child was paying serious attention to what she was telling her. Little did Lucrezia realize just how seriously Lisabetta had listened, taken the instruction to heart, and applied it to the plants on her farm.

She planted roses around the lavender field and around the small vineyard. Wherever she was, she would smell any rose she saw, and if it was very fragrant, no matter how unattractive the blooms, she would ask if she might take a cutting from it. She would propagate a small rose bush from the cutting in her shed back behind the chicken shed. Then she would plant the young bush somewhere on the patch of farm surrounding her small house.

Once Marco took her with him to Prato where he had to go to deliver a large sale of his copper ware to a shop in the middle of town. On the way back, they came face to face with a wall of black as a large rainstorm approached rapidly from the direction in which they were heading. They rode into the nearest farm and asked if they might seek shelter in their barn until the storm passed, and they did so. The farmer had brought his female goat in from a back pasture to birth her kids a few days earlier, and Lisabetta enjoyed the time playing with the two-day old kids.

When the storm cleared, the farmer came out and chatted with Marco. Eventually, they talked about the goats. He said the two smallest ones would have to be culled. They were runts, and he didn't want to be bothered with them. The doe had three kids, which was unheard of, and he only wanted to keep the large one.

Lisabetta was devastated at the thought of the two she liked best being put down. After considerable tears, she asked if she couldn't take them home with her. The farmer said they were too young for that, that Lisabetta would have to find a source of goat's milk and feed them many times each day.

"I can do it, Marco, I know I can. I know where there are goats only a short ride from the farm. Please, Marco, please."

"It's up to Signori Perusi. They are his kids."

"I don't care," said Signori Perusi. "I was going to cull them this morning and just didn't get around to it before the storm hit. You can have them with my blessing. Less drain on my doe. Here, I have an old sack here. It should do to get them home."

And so it was that Lisabetta became a goatherd. The first week was hard on Lisabetta, and, as it turned out, on Amalia also. Since she did not like the idea of Lisabetta spending her nights alone out on the farm, and since the two baby kids needed constant care, Amalia packed up some paper, pens, ink, and a manuscript and moved out to the small farm house for the foreseeable future.

Once she saw how Lisabetta was trying to fix up the small house, she spent time each day sewing and making some window coverings and bedding. She vowed that once she got back to the city, she would make more and better ones and get Lucrezia to help her. She had not had any idea Lisabetta had been doing her best to fix up the small, old house to make it more livable. Lisabetta was a child, but it seemed she was a child with a passion and a drive far beyond her years.

Amalia had some furniture from Dona Rutia's house that she would ask Marco to bring out. Amalia knew Dona Rutia would like her old pieces to be used again, and particularly by Lisabetta. Rosa, Dona Rutia's daughter, had taken what she wanted after Dona Rutia and Anna died. When the family who bought the house said they had their own furniture, Lucrezia and Amalia bought a lot of the fine old pieces from Rosa. Lucrezia and Ermanno used many of the pieces in their home, and Amalia and Marco had used one piece in their bedroom. Then Amalia stored several more pieces in a room upstairs behind Carlo's old castle room.

Amalia was usually the one to get up to feed the kids during the night that first week, but then once they could go all night without a feeding, Amalia planned to come back into town. She knew Alessandra and Giuliano needed her, and by now Francia would be overwhelmed with taking care of them as well as doing the household chores.

Alessandra was at Caterina's school, and Giuliano was just beginning at the school with the monks at Santa Maria Novella, but once school was over, they could be a handful. Lisabetta was missing her sessions at Caterina's school with the tutors, but Amalia and she spent a few hours each day at her lessons so she wouldn't

fall behind Blanche and the other girls. Two of the three tutors were away for two months, so things were much slower, and since Lisabetta was the best student, Amalia was not concerned.

She was surprised how much she had enjoyed her time at Lisabetta's farm, now in the flush of the lavender and rose blooms. The fragrance was overpowering. Lisabetta told Amalia she would not be in for several days, that between feeding the kids and the other animals, gathering the eggs, and maintaining Traveler, she was busy, but now she also had to gather the rose petals and the lavender to take to the Profuma Farmaceutica at Santa Maria Novella.

"What are you talking about?" asked Amalia.

"I only have a small field of the lavender and a few rose bushes, but the farmaceutica will buy all I can take to them to make their scents. I don't have to crush them, just get the petals off the rose hips. Isn't that exciting? It is a lot of work, but this plus my egg money—"

"Lisabetta, you don't have to do this for money. I will give you whatever you need. You are a little girl. I don't want you—"

"No, Ama, it's all right. I know you will take care of me, but I want to save more money to buy the farm from Carlo when he gets home. He has bigger plans, I know, but I love it here. I love the farm. I want this to be mine some day."

"Lisabetta, you are so young. You will marry and—"

"No, Ama. This is what I want. This will be my life, I am sure of it."

Amalia saw no point in arguing with Lisabetta about her future life. Surely, there were years ahead to dissuade her from her silly dream, or it would just fade away in time.

The carriage that Marco had sent to bring Amalia home arrived, and once the eggs for all the neighbors were properly stashed, as well as Amalia's personal items, Amalia hugged Lisabetta, kissed her on her forehead, and wished her well with the kids. They did seem to be thriving but were right now naaing to be fed.

"If you need me to come back out, just send word."

"I will, I promise. I will come in for the night when I make the delivery to the farmaceutica. It should be in a few days. I could stay longer if I could bring the kids, but I will be on Traveler. I'll see what I can do. Maybe I will throw them back in that sack the way the farmer did when he gave them to me. He treated them like they were two turnips."

Amalia laughed, and then Lisabetta laughed with her. "My dear, you are wonderful. I will see you soon."

With that, Amalia climbed into the carriage and was headed back to town.

Furniture and an old bed covering, plates and glasses, window curtains and drapes, and several beautiful copper pots and pans started to arrive with each visit of Amalia or Marco as well as Lucrezia and Ermanno. At first, Lisabetta objected, but Amalia said if she was to visit—and she thought she might enjoy doing so—she had to have a proper bed and more comfortable chairs and a table with four matching legs. Amalia had great fun sending out the various pieces of furniture to the farm and sometimes riding out with Lisabetta for a day.

At first Lisabetta wasn't too sure she liked the intrusion, but she loved Amalia and knew she was only trying to help her. Actually, Lisabetta got the feeling it showed that Amalia approved of what she was doing and it would be wrong to refuse her generous help.

One Sunday afternoon in the fall after church, Lisabetta was in the garden at the farm and was knee deep in mud since it had rained almost continuously for two days. She was pruning back her roses, lavender, her few herbs, and the grape vines.

Suddenly Luppo jumped up and started barking as he ran toward the cart path extending from the Fiesole Road to the house. Lisabetta was surprised to see Lucrezia, Ermanno, Amalia, and Marco riding up the path in a rented wagon.

Luppo was prepared to attack them until he heard Marco's voice calling his name. Then the fierce barks changed to happy yips and whines and a wagging tail. He greeted each one as they climbed down from the wagon. His whines left no question but that he wanted to jump up on each of them. Knowing better he settled for bumping into them and insisting on being patted and rubbed. It seemed he was immensely pleased to be welcoming them for a visit to his home.

They all four arrived in work clothes, and once they had settled Luppo and greeted Lisabetta, they immediately went to work.

Marco and Ermanno cleaned out the kitchen chimney so it would no longer fill the house with smoke every time it was used, then they cleaned the other chimney at the other end of the room just to be safe. Lucrezia and Amalia cleaned every corner and surface, polished all the furniture, even the few broken pieces that were still in use, and hung some new draperies. The house was one large room downstairs and one upstairs with a spiral stairway in one corner connecting the two floors.

Marco had brought along supplies, and he patched a crack, and then he plastered the surfaces where needed. In the meantime, Ermanno went out to help Lisabetta with the pruning and helped her plant the new lavender she had been dividing that needed to be planted and take root before the colder weather arrived.

Ermanno enjoyed gardening and had taken over the care of the garden between the Valetti and Evangelista houses, much to the relief of Amalia. Lucrezia still enjoyed light weeding or trimming and, of course, harvesting, but she was very grateful for help with the pruning, preparing the beds, and the planting.

Once finished with all the chores, they all five sat down at the new table to the excellent meal Francia had prepared for them to take out with them to the farm.

When they were done eating, the four of them climbed back in the wagon, promising to come back next Sunday with dinner again. With that, they drove down the cart path, Ermanno leading the singing of a favorite frottola, as they headed back to town.

Lisabetta walked back inside, sat down on one of her new kitchen chairs, and looked around her. She recalled that she had had some lonely days while at the farm. Now, knowing her family had embraced her venture, approved of her life style, and were now a part of each nook and cranny of her house, she wasn't so lonely anymore.

She went over to her sitting area by the fireplace and sat in a chair she had sat in many times from the time she was a very little girl at Auntie Rutia's house. That filled her with a warm feeling she knew was love; love for the memory of dear Auntie Rutia but more. In her young mind, as Lisabetta looked around her clean, nicely furnished room, she realized it was all a reflection of her family's love for her. She would remember this day always.

She had truly enjoyed those alone days because she loved what she was doing, but now she had to admit she looked forward to next Sunday afternoon when her entire family would come back, bringing a large meal with them. It was how, in the future, they came to spend their Sunday afternoons on all but the coldest or rainiest of days for the rest of the time Carlo was away.

They would arrive, each with a chore in mind they thought needed to be done or something Lisabetta had mentioned during the week. After that first Sunday, they always brought all the children along. Giuliano and Alessandra, Anna and Manno, would just run around and enjoy the freedom of the farm and play with the chickens, Luppo, Boots, and the goats or going for a ride on Traveler, being led around the farm by Ermanno. Even during the winter, unless it was one of those cold or nasty days, they all came to enjoy their Sunday afternoons at Lisabetta's snug house on her wonderful little farm—which was actually Carlo's farm.

Once Carlo returned home from England, many things changed. He bought the rest of the farm from Jacko's uncle, then bought the animals, and acquired wagons and carts of all sizes as he worked tirelessly day and night to make the freighting business a success. He hired drivers, workers to build and maintain the wagons, men to care for the animals, and workmen to improve the large house on the major part of the farm—Carlo's farm.

Besides attending to her schooling, doing some artwork with Amalia in the evenings, and spending lots of time with her girl friends when she was in town, particularly in the winter, Lisabetta still went back and forth to the farm. When at the farm, she would work on her house, or tend her goats, ultimately learning how to milk them and make cheese. She also got the goats sheared in the spring and marketed their long, silky hair. In addition, she was steadily expanding her lavender and rose petal crops each year. This last summer, with Carlo's help, she had put in a vegetable and herb garden, and with all the fertilizer from her ever-expanding chicken pens and goat herd, she had a very successful crop of everything she planted.

She was doing things far beyond the capacities of other children her age, but her enthusiasm was boundless, and her energy never flagged. As she grew older and her crops and goat herd and the number of chickens expanded, Carlo hired a man to help her. He was to do things that needed to be done on the big house and the barns and property, but a major part of his job was to be sure he did all he could to help Lisabetta in any way, including what needed to be done with the goats and chickens.

She saw a great deal of Carlo, and he often helped her with some of her tasks, plus they often rode to or from town together. Traveler was now Lisabetta's horse; there could be no question about that, so Carlo got himself a mare. For him, even Traveler was just a horse; for Lisabetta, he was her trusted traveling companion and good friend. Carlo could not have argued with that even if he had wanted to.

Even though so much had changed, the two families would still oftentimes spend a Sunday afternoon out at Lisabetta's farm.

~ ~ ~

On this day, August 1st, Lisabetta and Alessandra had gone out to the farm early to feed and water the stock quickly. They had planned then to come back home to help Francia prepare the meal and to get ready for dinner. They wound up rushing back because of the news they brought, and now Lisabetta wasn't sure how the rest of the day would go. She knew Amalia was very upset, as was Lucrezia. She didn't know if dinner would be delayed, but she went ahead and got ready. She took extra care dressing and she asked Francia to help her fix her hair.

Lisabetta and Alessandra shared the two rooms with the arch between that had been Lucrezia's rooms many years ago. They loved having their own room but still being together. Alessandra looked in and asked why Lisabetta was making such a fuss, but Lisabetta said she saw the new hair style and just wanted to try it.

"Well," said Alessandra, "it seems like a big waste of time to me. I'm going to run over to Maria's and see her new cat."

"Be back in time for dinner."

"I will. You even smell funny. Nice, I guess, but different."

"Thanks. Go."

Lisabetta went down just as Lucrezia and her family came into the gathering room. Giuliano was with them, having been playing with Manno and Ugo, and Alessandra had never made it to Maria's. Anna ran to Alessandra, and the two of them were quickly off to the far corner of the room to share those secrets shared by young girls. Moments later, Amalia came up the front steps, and, having heard her enter the front door, Carlo and Marco came back upstairs behind her.

The three young boys found another corner to talk about the latest Paleo race results from Siena and the next calcio game over at Santa Croce between their gonfalons, the Unicorns, and a team from San Lorenzo, the Golden Lions.

The six adults sat by the unlit fireplace once the three men got a glass of wine for themselves, and each brought a glass back for the ladies.

They talked about Cosimo at length, all he had done for them and for the city of Florence, how life was so different now from when they were young. On and on they went.

Finally, it was clear Carlo could restrain himself no longer. He might be a grown man now, but he could still be impetuous when he had news to share. He stood up and walked over to where Lisabetta was seated, and he began:

"Amalia, I know this is not the best time to bring this up because of the news about Cosimo, but this news cannot wait any longer. This last year, since Lisabetta has reached her womanhood, has been very difficult for both of us. I would like to ask your permission for Lisabetta and me to marry. We—"

He never got any further. Amalia and Marco, and Lucrezia and Ermanno stood up as one.

"I had no idea"

"You're so young."

"Why did you not tell us all this time?"

"Good man."

"This is such a surprise."

"How did you keep it a secret?"

All talked at once as Carlo was extending his hand to Lisabetta, who rose from her chair and into his embrace on very shaky legs.

The five younger ones, upon hearing the commotion, came over to join in the revelry.

"Of course," said Amalia, "I am so happy for you both. Are you sure, dearest? You are still so young," she asked Lisabetta.

"Oh, yes, Ama. This has been my dearest wish since I was a little girl. There has never been nor will there ever be anyone else I could possibly marry. Don't you remember, when Carlo sailed away for England, I told you then I would marry him?"

Marco laughed and said, "Yes, I do remember that. You were, what, eight years?"

"Nine," interjected Lisabetta, laughing.

"Are you really going to marry this old man?" he said, clapping Carlo on the back.

Carlo laughed and retorted, "How else was I to become a member of this family?"

"Carlo," said Amalia, "you have always been a member of this family, you know that. Since my father died and we all lived together, we have been a true family."

"Remember, I wanted to be Lisabetta's godfather so that I had a title? Now it will be a true union."

Hugs were shared by Lisabetta and Lucrezia, Lisabetta and Amalia, and Amalia and Lucrezia. Then Alessandra and Anna joined in. There was a lot of back-slapping and hand-shaking among the men; and the boys, not to be left out, enjoyed a couple of good back-slaps of their own.

The rest of the evening—and it was a long evening extending far into the night—was spent celebrating the future marriage of Lisabetta and Carlo. Many memories were recalled, particularly by Amalia, Lucrezia, and Carlo, back to the early days before the husbands and children became a part of their lives, back to when it was just the three of them against the world, breaking all customs of how things were properly done, struggling to start their three businesses, and take care of an infant. They knew they had been able to succeed because of the help and support of their friends and neighbors but mainly because of the benevolence of one man.

They filled their glasses, and lifted them as they each quietly said, "To Cosimo."

Amalia added, "May he go to God in peace. At least now he is free of pain."

Roman Amphitheater in Fiesole

Carlo and Lisabetta's wedding was a true gonfalons event. Both were deeply involved with all the neighbors. Not since Amalia and Marco and then Lucrezia and Ermanno had married was there so much excitement about a union.

Lucrezia made Lisabetta a beautiful dress, and then she made a beautiful dress for Alessandra and Anna as well. Before she was done, she had her shop make a new outfit for each member of the two families, although the boys were not nearly as pleased with their new finery as the girls.

Once everyone was dressed and ready to walk over to the church, Amalia called Lisabetta aside and asked her to come to her bedroom. Amalia picked up a small cassone she had set on her bed and sat with it on her lap. She patted the wood apron that extended all around the mattress and bedding, inviting Lisabetta to sit beside her.

"Lisabetta, this is a small cassone Lucrezia and I found in my mother's—your grandmother's—belongings after your grandfather died. It contains her jewelry, and I would like to give you this piece today so you can wear it for your wedding."

"Oh, Ama, it is beautiful. The blue stones match the trim on my dress. Look, and the pearls match the pearls in the dress."

"Yes, I know, dear. Lucrezia planned it that way. We have been planning this since the night you and Carlo announced your wishes."

"Ama, thank you very much. Help me put it on, please."

"Lisabetta, you look beautiful in the dress Lucrezia made and now this necklace, but the most beautiful thing of all is you. You are very special, and I love you very much. I know you will be very happy, and I know my dearest friend, Carlo, will also be very happy. This is truly a joyful union not only for you and Carlo but also for Lucrezia and me. Carlo was right; it seems as if the circle is closed now."

~ ~ ~

While Amalia and Lisabetta were in Amalia's bedroom, Carlo was in Lucrezia's design workroom, pacing like one of Cosimo's caged lions.

"You are my first son, Carlo, and Amalia's too. From the time we three were brought together and became a family, it has been a joy to watch you grow into the man you are today. We had some times; oh, Carlo, we did have some times, didn't we?"

Lucrezia paused to try to get control of her emotions, and Carlo walked over, took her two hands in his, lifted her out of her chair, and hugged her to him.

After time had passed, Carlo said, "Words can't express what I feel for the two of you and all that you and—"

"No," said Lucrezia, "None of that. I know, and so does Amalia. Today it is all about you and Lisabetta. You know, sometimes I wondered if you would ever marry, but I think God has brought the two of you together. Maybe it was just always meant to be. So long ago—"

The door burst open and Manno and Ugo were yelling, "They are ready, they are leaving. Come on, Let's go, let's go. Hurry."

~ ~ ~

The receiving room was full to bursting, and the lower level loggia, where they decided to serve the food for the party after the wedding, as well. The garden, too, was overflowing with well-wishers for the young couple. The neighbors had all known Carlo since he was a little barefooted scamp, running errands for anyone who would give him a coin; and they knew Lisabetta from the day she arrived, hungry and emaciated, in her father's arms, to be nursed by neighbors, and cared for by Lucrezia and Amalia. They had seen her baptized in Carlo's arms, and had watched as she grew before their eyes into a beautiful young girl, now a woman. They would be celebrating the marriage long into the night, well after the newly married couple had departed.

Carlo and Lisabetta left just before dark in Ermanno's carriage for their journey out to the farm, where they would spend their wedding night and begin their life together. They spent the first night in Lisabetta's house. Then the next day, they moved into the big house they had been working on together for several years. Lisabetta couldn't quite explain why it was important to her to spend that first night in her little house, but she felt as if she was bringing more of herself to Carlo in that way. Carlo didn't care as long as they were together.

As time passed, Lisabetta still spent a lot of time in her little house in the daytime when tending her animals and crops on that part of the farm, her farm, but now the upstairs bedroom was to be a guest room for whenever family wanted to visit. There was plenty of room in the big house, but everyone loved Lisabetta's house, as it was called, and seemed to feel freer about visiting more often when they didn't feel they were intruding on the newlywed couple's privacy.

Very often Carlo put the three young boys to work on the farm or on the equipment. Now that Lisabetta was there full time and had expanded her crops and the number of chickens and goats, she could always put any of the five of them to work and often did. It was a busy fall with plenty of work but with lots of fun times also.

Lisabetta didn't like bringing the goat hair into her little house because of the odor, so she had the men clean out the back shed behind her little barn back by the goat pens. They had to rebuild one wall and build a dividing wall, but the roof of the old shed was solid.

The blacksmith who worked for Carlo lived in one of the small houses on the farm with his wife, Violetta, and his daughter, Bianca. The daughter was thirteen, and she thought she would like working with the goats, so Lisabetta hired her the year before to do the milking that was done in the smaller half of the shed. Then the girl would process almost all of the milk into a cheese Lisabetta and Bianca's mother taught her to make, to be stored in the shed.

Little by little, over the years, Lisabetta had improved the herd so the goat hair was now long and silky and could be used to make very nice, silky yarn. Bianca and Lisabetta fixed up the other half of the shed to be their workshop for fulling, dying, carding, and spinning the yarn. Bianca had her father bring over two large tubs and put a cistern where the tubs were so they had a water supply to the inside tub but also an outside tub under the roof where they could do the fulling and dying.

Lisabetta had worked with Lucrezia in the beginning to learn about the dying process and the use of the mordants to dye the yarn. Lisabetta, in turn, taught Bianca.

Eventually, other than some carding and spinning in the wintertime, Lisabetta was able to turn everything to do with the goats over to Bianca, and she was happy to do so because, if the truth be told, she did not care for the smell of the goats—nor did Carlo. They didn't keep any mature male goats at the farm, so the smell wasn't overwhelming, but there was still some odor. She was surprised Bianca didn't mind, and she couldn't understand why Bianca never smelled. Finally, she found out that was what the second tub was for. Bianca put on special work clothes when she got to the goat shed to do all her work. When she was ready to leave, she took a bath in the second tub she had her father install inside, and then she changed back into her proper clothes. In the summertime, she would often just walk down to the river and swim; but in the colder weather, the tub was her salvation to keep her from smelling like a goat.

Lisabetta came to like the idea of the bath very much, and she had Carlo have the men build a small fireplace in the shed so they would have hot water and a warm room. It became a convenient, efficient, comfortable workplace for the two women. Carlo improved the shed, and it also became a favorite spot for Luppo and Boots and a couple of Boots's offspring. The cats all loved curling up in a nest of the goat hair once it had been thoroughly cleaned.

Bianca's mother worked in Carlo's house as the housekeeper and cook. She was a good cook, so that left Lisabetta free for all her other endeavors. Whenever they had to slaughter one of the goats, they made a goat stew that they would take to town with them when they contributed to the Buonomini at San Martino or the soup kitchen over at Santa Maria Novella.

As soon as he returned home from England, Carlo resumed his involvement with Marco and the Buonomini and the soup kitchen at Santa Maria Novella with Padre Bernardo. He would almost always take at least one wagonload in with whatever he had to contribute or had collected from some of the other local farmers to be distributed to the poor each Wednesday in town. If there was a lot, Marco would drive another wagon, and they would bring two wagonloads of produce into town, usually in the summer and fall months, and then firewood or late crops into the winter.

Ermanno and Giovanni would oftentimes go along if they could arrange the timing, because the four men truly enjoyed what they were doing, as well as the opportunity to be together. They were each in such different walks of life and pulled in such different directions, they felt this was an opportunity for them to just enjoy each other's company while doing something worthwhile.

They always tried to bring in some used clothing or old, discarded furniture: whatever they felt could be used by someone at Santa Maria Novella and the Misericordia.

Eventually, Carlo added a herd of sheep on his farm. Then in the winter, he might slaughter a lamb, and the meat would be distributed along with the soup.

Lisabetta often contributed a chicken or two, particularly in the winter, and there were always plenty of eggs. Lucrezia sometimes managed to find a pre-made garment that needed an owner.

For the Buonomini, the guilds would furnish tickets so those named people could go and get their share on a Wednesday to help them through the week. Marco worked with the committee of all of the guilds for many years now to help organize who got the tickets in any given week. His reputation for fairness and hard work grew as the years passed.

It was all governed by the confraternity, and Messer Palle, Cosimo's secretary, helped organize it each week. One time Master Palle mentioned to Marco that he and Carlo seemed very devoted to what they were doing on behalf of the group. He noted that although they might be well off, they certainly were not wealthy.

Marco told Palle that his wife was deeply indebted to Cosimo for everything, for which he and all of his extended family were very grateful. Since this seemed to be something that had meant a lot to Cosimo, they were pleased to contribute.

~ ~ ~

Amalia spent a lot of her time teaching over at Caterina's school. She taught the younger students reading and most particularly, writing—scribing—so they would have a strong Florentine script. She still did her scribing at home, but since they no longer needed the money to survive, she did it at a much more leisurely pace and incorporated a lot more artwork.

A new machine brought to Italy from the north of Europe could produce books mechanically at a rapid pace, but Italians still preferred the hand-scribed books, and it was a very long time before the printing machine became popular in Italy. Amalia's special artwork was now what still made her books desirable for a more elite clientele.

She was very sorry to lose her dear friend and staunch supporter, Master Manetti, who had died two years earlier. He had retired several years before and sold the shop to a new man, but since Amalia now worked for Messer Bisticci, she never formed a real relationship with the new man, a Master Santini. If truth be told, she didn't much care for him She went in sometimes for supplies, but after just a few manuscripts, that was all; she was never more than just another customer.

Once they were married and Amalia was working for Messer Bisticci, Marco and she invited Giorgio and his wife, Margarita, oftentimes for parties or small dinner gatherings at their home, and the Manetti's reciprocated.

They often joked about the early days and what had happened. Giorgio told Amalia that Cosimo himself came into the shop that next day, and he related what had happened. Cosimo said he had seen the manuscript Amalia had tried to sell to Master Manetti and that it was very well done; that if Master Manetti was adamant about not wishing to work with her—a girl, then—that he could understand, but he thought the girl deserved a chance since her work was so fine. He said he would see to it that Master Manetti always got a share of his manuscripts if Master Manetti saw to it the girl was kept busy and well paid.

Amalia had long ago figured that was pretty much how it happened, but had expected Cosimo had simply sent his man with a message or maybe a note, but to know he went to Master Manetti's shop himself astonished her.

Giorgio told her she had always been his most trusted scribe, even if she was a girl—and they had a good laugh—but he wondered if she missed the life of a young girl just being "a young girl?" Amalia told him she thought about that years later, but from the time her father died, she didn't have the time to think about what her life might have been or even could or should have been. She was much too busy living the life she was given, and grateful for it; that she and Lucrezia loved what they each did in those early years. Then they were given the opportunity to marry men of their choosing, which neither of them ever expected would happen; and more, each was blessed with wonderful families. What would the lives of a silly girl and her maid have been compared to what their lives actually were? Regrets? No, she thanked God every day for her wonderful life, thanks to Giorgio—and Cosimo.

She missed Giorgio—Master Manetti—her old friend, but not as much as she missed Poggio.

Poggio had lived a long life in Fiesole with his wife and large family, now grown even though he had gotten such a late start as a husband and legitimate father.

Amalia and Lucrezia came to know several of his many illegitimate children over the years, and they knew Poggio did all he could for that family and took care of their mother as well. They never asked any questions, and he never offered any explanations. He was so open about his adventures with Cosimo in the early days and his travels to Fulda and all the other monasteries, it puzzled both girls why he never really spoke about his past personal life. He didn't, though. When he married, it was as if that chapter in his life was closed.

Very often, Ermanno would be asked to go up to Fiesole during the summer months to perform at the ancient amphitheater, part of the old Roman ruins on the back side of the village but still right near the center of town. Oftentimes, Marco, Amalia, and Lucrezia would ride there and take Poggio and his wife to the performance. Then they might all go to one of the inns in town for a late dinner, or perhaps all go back to Poggio's house.

The ruins faced the west and offered a beautiful view of the mountains and valleys, especially in those early evening hours. It was incredible how little repair work had been done to those fifteen-hundred-year-old ruins to make them perfectly serviceable for the large crowd that would comprise Ermanno's audience. The acoustics were excellent and enhanced Ermanno's magnificent voice, if that was possible.

Very often, they would arrive early so they could walk around the Etruscan ruins and the ruins of the old Roman bath and village. These ruins surrounded the amphitheater ruins on three sides, just below the ridge line that formed the dividing line between the old Roman village and modern Fiesole. It was always an enjoyable visit, and Amalia missed going there.

Lucrezia had taken all five children up there several times in recent years to hear Ermanno sing and visit the ruins since Poggio died, but Amalia didn't have the heart to go along with Poggio not there. She knew Poggio's widow well, and she knew it was time she moved on. Amalia promised herself she would go next year.

~ ~ ~

Ermanno was the most famous singer in Florence, perhaps in all of Italy. He always had a starring role in whatever musical productions were performed during the season. The new company director had a great appreciation for his talent and used it wisely.

The passion plays and other saints' day festival productions had begun in Florence over a hundred years before, maybe much longer, and everyone in town knew that Giovanni de Bicci de' Medici's father and uncle had built many of the instruments used in those early years for the performances. Then, during the years when Florence was often at war and the city struggled, attention to music had faded.

Now, a new director was gathering composers, musicians, singers, writers, and dancers from all over Italy. Florence was once again known to have the finest saints' day festival productions in all of Europe, mainly because of the music. Now these composers wrote music far better than the simple frottola that was merely for amusement. The songs were now more lyrical and melodious with polyphony. They would be sung throughout the land, plus the stories told in the productions were becoming more secular.

Ermanno and Lucrezia were often invited to attend functions as a guest because of his fame, but soon those occasions became known also for the fashion statement made by Lucrezia, as she wore new creations of her own making. As it happened, very often now, other ladies would be wearing other creations by Lucrezia or other designers, and the parties were often a splendid display of the fashions of the day.

Everyone hoped the Guards of the Night, the Onesta, were busy with the prostitutes and the homosexuals and would not ask to look under the large capes of the women or the men attending those social evenings. They might have been too opulent in their appearance for the conservative tastes of the Signoria and the Onesta. Years ago, they did harass many women on the streets out shopping or just walking, and even harassed the men if they were wearing an opulent, fur-trimmed cloak. Lately, the darker side of Florence managed to keep the Onesta occupied sufficiently, and they weren't too concerned about buttons and furs and fancy trimmings on the ladies' dresses.

There were always many arrests each year for homosexual activities, but usually the penalty was light. If the accused knew someone with enough influence, the charges were often dropped or overlooked. It was a time of great energy and free time because of the better economy, but it was still a time when young girls were kept at home, hidden away until their marriages were arranged. Sometimes they never met the man who was to become their husband, so sometimes emotions ran too high and feelings got out of hand.

As for the prostitutes, as long as they wore their bells to advertise their profession, they were usually left alone, but the Onesta saw to it that they and any petty criminals were duly pursued. Most people kept off the streets at night unless they were coming home from a party in a group accompanied by servants and their personal guards.

One night, on their way home from a late party, Lucrezia and Ermanno dropped in on Amalia when they saw her receiving room was still lighted. They knew that meant Amalia was scribing late and Marco was probably out of town, but Lucrezia knew she wouldn't mind the interruption.

Lucrezia wanted to show Amalia the dress she was wearing and discuss arrangements for the outing tomorrow to the farm.

Amalia heard them coming up the stairs and put her ink away.

"I hope you don't mind. We just wanted to come by for a quick visit so I could show you my—Amalia, what is wrong?"

"Oh, Lucrezia, Ermanno; it's Maria. She is gone. She was reading to the little ones, and she told little Filippo to get his grandmother quickly. By the time Francesca got to her, she was already struggling, and then she died. I can't believe it."

The two women hugged, and then Ermanno embraced the two of them. Lucrezia said, "She was like a mother to us both when we needed her.

How old must she be? She was older than your mother, I know that, and Francesca is a lot older than we are."

"I have no idea."

Eventually, Ermanno went home, but Lucrezia and Amalia sat for an hour, discussing plans for the outing, what they would be doing for Maria and her family, and reminiscing about some of the times they had with Maria and Filippo, Dona Rutia, and many more neighbors and friends. So many of them were gone now.

When Amalia's father was killed so many years ago, their youth had ended. Now, with the death of Maria, it seemed their world had shifted, swerved beneath their feet like a clay slick in the road. They were now the older generation. Nothing had really changed, but it seemed as though everything had changed. Perhaps, if they could color their life, everything was shaded just a bit in a slightly grayer tone. There was still so much to live for and enjoy, and they would enjoy all of it, but now it was tempered by the weight of the past, the memories that were now theirs to carry. They were now the ones responsible to carry on the traditions and pass those memories and traditions on to their children and eventually their children's children. This they would do faithfully and with deep affection.

The Duomo

The entire family was preparing for Sunday Mass at Santa Maria Novella. It would be a High Mass, because they were still celebrating the holy Easter season. Then they would all gather at Amalia and Marco's home to celebrate Lucrezia's birthday. Carlo and Lisabetta and their family rode into town to join the rest of the family at Mass, and everyone was distributed between the two houses and spilling out into the garden. A boy, an orphan named Piero, was with them. Carlo had recently taken him in to help Lisabetta on her farm with her various crops and herding, processing and marketing. He seemed a bright boy, and Carlo had hopes he would prove valuable to Lisabetta. He had given the boy a proper shirt and invited him to ride along and enjoy the festivities in town with the family.

There was to be a big feast once the family returned home from the church, but for now it was all about the dressing and the excitement of the entire family going to Mass. Ermanno would be singing with the choir, and he would also sing several solos, part of his birthday gift to Lucrezia, so that increased the level of anticipation for the entire family.

All went splendidly. Of course, for the family, that was all because of Ermanno and his voice; but then, other people, as they began leaving the church, voiced a similar sentiment. Then they began to turn their thoughts toward the fun of their family gathering and the feast awaiting them at home. They were all famished from having fasted for Mass.

Once outside the church, things weren't quite right, though. People were running through the large piazza, one yelling, "People and Liberty." Another was yelling, "Lorenzo is dead." Yet another yelled, "The Medici are dead." Another said, "The Pazzi." A man on horseback rode through the piazza, also yelling, "People and Liberty," the cry of those for rebellion.

Amalia grabbed Marco's arm. "What is happening?"

"I don't know, but it doesn't sound good. Let's get everyone home in a hurry until we find out what's going on."

They gathered everyone and urged them all to hurry. Everyone entered Amalia and Marco's front door. Then Lucrezia and Ermanno went through the garden back to their house to secure the shutters and barricade their front door.

Carlo went along with them, then out their front door and over to the boddeghe/office where he had left the wagon and horses. He brought the horses inside the boddeghe and locked it securely, and then he returned to the family compound.

On his way back he heard more yelling about the Pazzi, but now many were yelling that Lorenzo and the Medicis had been killed.

When he returned, he could not find Piero, the young orphan, and no one could remember having seen him since Mass ended. Carlo thought about going back to the church to see if he had gotten separated from them and maybe gone back inside, but Lisabetta begged him to stay home.

Marco wanted to go out and find out what was happening, but Lucrezia prevailed upon him to stay at home to protect Amalia and the rest of the family. Whatever was happening, they were not and should not be a part of it, at least not until they knew exactly what was actually happening. On his return run, Carlo had heard one man yelling that troops were outside the gates preparing to invade. Giuliano and Manno went up on the roof; and when they came down, they reported there were fires over in the direction of Santa Croce.

They gathered all the weapons they could find in the two houses in case it came to that, and Giuliano and Manno each took up a post by their respective front doors so they could warn the family gathered in Amalia and Marco's receiving room and spilling down to the ground level.

The feast was all laid out on the large table in the middle of the receiving room, but no one sat down to enjoy it. They had all been famished, but now everyone just nibbled as they passed by the table full of the delicacies Francia had prepared.

Later on, the bell, the "Vaca," was rung endlessly, signifying for the city gates to be closed and that the city was in a grievous state. It might signify a political crisis or an invasion, but everyone knew it was a sign of crisis for Florence. Riders were galloping past the house, then more people running, then more riders. Guiliano looked out through the holes in the shutters on the ground floor, but he couldn't figure out what was happening. He heard one man yell "Pelle," which was the cry for the Medici, meaning the balls on their escutcheon used to identify everything Medici. Franco came from the Evangelista house and said all seemed quiet on the other street.

Two hours passed; then there was a loud banging on the front door, and a voice yelled, "Let me in, let me in. It's Piero, let me in."

Guiliano and Ermanno rushed over and unbolted the door and opened it wide enough for the boy to squeeze through, then bolted it again behind him.

Carlo came running, followed by several other members of the three households.

"Piero, where have you been? I was worried about you."

"I went to find out what was happening. I knew no one would notice a kid slipping through the alleys."

"Tell us," said Ermanno. "What's happening?"

"The Pazzi attacked the Medici during the High Mass at the Duomo. Giuliano was stabbed to death right by the altar along with some others just as they lifted the host, but Lorenzo got away. He was injured, but he got away.

The Pazzi Chapel at Santa Croce

"The Pazzi thought they had won, so they went to take over at the Palazzo Vecchio and to signal for their troops to invade the city, but then Lorenzo showed himself to the people. He is wounded with a big gash on his neck, but he's alive.

That's when the people turned on the Pazzi, and the Gonfaloniere rang the bell for the gates to be closed so no one could get in or get out and the cry of the people in the streets changed to "Pelle."

"Now the Pazzi are on the run, and the officials and the Medici men are searching them down. Three of the instigators were hanged from the top of the Palazzo Vecchio, then they were cut down, and their bodies are being dragged through the streets by horses. It's crazy out there. It was terrible trying to get back here."

"I'm glad you made it back safely, Piero," said Carlo. "But you shouldn't have gone off like that, you could have been killed. You are just a boy."

"I didn't even think about that when I took off. It was only toward the end when I was headed back here that things got risky. Then I was scared. I was really glad when you opened that door."

"It seems to me, Carlo, that I remember a boy slipping in, around, and among adults and gaining knowledge that changed my life," said Ermanno.

"Yes, but that was different. There was no danger then."

"True, but would it have made a difference? I think you found yourself in that orphanage when you brought this young boy home with you, and I think this young boy just found himself a family.

"We are grateful for the information, Piero, however risky it was for you to go off like that. If the Medici are back in control, we can rest easier. Things are back to normal."

But things were never back to normal for their city. The aftermath of the Pazzi conspiracy cost over eighty lives: Pazzi family members and their supporters, as well as Lorenzo's brother, Guiliano, and another Medici man killed in the Duomo during the initial assault died. There was much tumult in Florence. All the rest of the Pazzis and their supporters were eventually exiled, including Lorenzo's own sister, who was married to a Pazzi.

The pope himself was involved in the attempt to assassinate Lorenzo and Giuliano, and when he heard it had failed to kill both of them, he was furious. He used the execution of the priest, a favorite of his, who had been deeply involved in the plot, as an excuse to place the city of Florence under an interdict. The priests in Florence refused to enforce the interdict, and the pope was threatening to invade.

Once he recovered from his wound and the city was safely back under his control, Lorenzo felt the only way to get the pope to stop his invasion was to convince the King of Naples to force Pope Sixtus to change his position.

Lorenzo sailed alone to Naples with no troops, just many cassoni full of florins. After three months, he finally prevailed upon the King of Naples to convince the pope to relent. With that, Lorenzo returned to Florence, now politically stronger than ever before, but he was not the same man.

Where before he had been open and free with the people, he now went everywhere with six guards surrounding him at all times. He used to spend time each day walking around the inside of the Duomo, and any person could approach him and talk to him. That was no more.

After many of the frequent festivals and carnivals for the many saints' days, Lorenzo would ride through the streets of Florence with other horsemen and many walkers. They first sang hymns associated with the saint of the day, but then later in the night they would sing the frottola, the songs written by the people and for the people, often accompanied by lutes, pipes, horns, drums, or any other instrument that could be played while walking in the parade.

Often, in the past, Lorenzo would be singing songs he had composed for the event. Sometimes these parades went on deep into the night, and it was something Lorenzo truly enjoyed, for he loved the music. No more.

San Martino was a gathering place on Sunday afternoons for poets, storytellers, Gregorian chanters, musicians playing an assortment of newly-created instruments like the mandola and the chitarra, or for singers to come to entertain anyone who gathered by the steps of the church. All were welcome, from the humblest of its citizenry to the grandest of nobles, to perform and/or to listen.

Many years ago, Cosimo had read his poetry there, and Lorenzo had often read his poetry. Many would recite sections of Dante's beloved classic. Dante had brought poetry out of the darkness and back into the light by writing in the volgare thereby making poetry a viable part of everyone's lives.

The Decameron by Boccaccio was recited on the steps of San Martino; Plutarch and Leon Battista Alberti were read in the volgare, and this all became the foundation of the emerging Italian language. The Greek plays were enacted. There were often readings from Cicero and Livy or Plato and Aristotle, even Seneca, and Sallust. The humblest man on the street was exposed to the ideas of the humanists by reading and hearing such as this.

Ermanno sang on those steps often in his early years in Florence, and still did once in a while, particularly if a friend had recently written a new song that he liked.

San Marino was not the only site. San Marco was the site of the performance of a play called The Prodigal Son written by Piero di Mariano Muzi, a purse maker. It was presented at the celebration of Cosimo's renovation of San Marco. In the earliest years, these were religious presentations, but as time went on, they became more secular as the people became more familiar with the ideas of the humanists.

Florence loved her poetry, and she told her history through her poets. Piero, Lorenzo's father, had once staged a contest for anyone and everyone to submit an entry for the finest poem about friendship. It was years ago that it had happened, but the fervor of the people for poetry and song had never slackened. Lorenzo had written poetry in the volgare and in Latin, much of it very fine, ever since he was a young boy. He had been encouraged by his mother, Lucrezia, who was in her own right a renowned poet, but he wrote no more, and he appeared on the steps of San Martino no more.

Santa Croce was the center for more physical type activities. The many calcio games were staged there, and the jousts that the people loved to watch were still performed. Lorenzo and Guiliano had been avid participants in the jousts in the past, but no more.

Lorenzo never attempted to curb the enthusiasm of the people for these things, and he was still an enthusiastic supporter. He just was not the intimate participant he had been before the Pazzi tumult, and he stayed aloof from the people now. Politically, he had been strengthened once the Pazzi were exiled and the pope was brought back into accord by the King of Naples. The Medici strength was never again threatened during Lorenzo's lifetime.

All the arts were given free rein. All the buildings by Brunelleschi, Michelozzo, Alberti, all the magnificent churches built by Lorenzo's grandfather and others were now being beautified on the inside by the artists supported, hired, and encouraged by Lorenzo and the other rich bankers and merchants of his day.

Botticelli had been raised in the Medici home alongside Lorenzo as a boy, and even Leonardo in his earlier years lived there and sat at the Medici dining table with Lorenzo and all the great minds of the day, and later Michelangelo. They dined with rich bankers, merchants, and traders, who were all future patrons. They met humanists, who would influence their thinking; they met other artists, sculptors and architects, all of whom would influence their art. All this art was created out of the competitive spirit so alive in Florence.

Botticelli, Gozzoli, Verrocchio, Ucello, even Raphael, and later, Michelangelo, all were employed by Lorenzo and others to create the art in Florence and beyond.

Public buildings were being beautified by huge murals painted by the finest painters and by magnificent sculptures. As Donatello had created his Habakkuk, Mary Magdalene, and his Davids in the past, now others were creating and would create great masterpieces in the future: Michelangelo's Dawn and Dusk, Night and Day, and David were but a few.

Michelangelo's earliest sculptures were created in Lorenzo's garden behind the Medici Palazzo where he lived as a boy. Lorenzo even criticized one of them, a gnome, because Michelangelo had sculpted him with a fine set of teeth. Lorenzo commented that an old gnome wouldn't have all his teeth. By the time Lorenzo returned from his stroll Michelangelo had knocked out the offending teeth.

All this pleased the eyes of the people of Florence, but the written word was not forgotten. It flourished along with the music and art in those days of great creativity.

Poliziano had been one of Lorenzo's teachers and then for a time was a teacher for his children. Clarice, Lorenzo's wife, felt he might not be a proper influence on her children so that ended, but Lorenzo provided him with a home from which to work, because he valued the man's abilities. He was a humanist, appreciating the things Lorenzo so treasured, plus he was a brilliant composer.

When he wrote "Orfeo," music was composed to accompany it. It was performed by Ermanno, to the amazement and delight of the audience whenever and wherever it was staged. There was an orchestra, with a large assortment of instruments, words were recited, there was chant, words were sung, songs were sung by Ermanno and others to the tunes played by the numerous different instruments. There were dancers, too. It was brilliant, and by all reports, Lorenzo loved it. They all felt they were a part of something new: a secular drama set to music. It was truly special; they just didn't have a name for it yet. Ermanno always considered it to be his finest moment as a performer.

Lorenzo's life had been dramatically and forever changed by the Pazzi Conspiracy. Of that there was no doubt; but once the tumult was over—the executions ended, the Pazzis all exiled and their properties confiscated, and Lorenzo returned from Naples—the life of the ordinary citizen of Florence did slowly return to normal, including the lives of the Valetti, Evangelista, and Cavalcanti families.

~ ~ ~

When Carlo and Lisabetta returned to the farm on the day after the tumult, they learned that workers on the farm knew nothing of what had happened in town during the Pazzi Conspiracy until they heard the bell ring endlessly. Finally, word had filtered out from the city. The pope's troops were mobilizing for their attack of Florence from the south and east, but the farm workers knew nothing of that.

Piero, the young orphan boy, became a huge favorite of all the farm workers as he told the story of his adventure whenever asked—and often volunteered the telling even when not asked—in a more dramatic fashion with each telling, to the delight of everyone.

He also proved to be an excellent worker and a quick learner, and Lisabetta came to depend upon him as he grew up to become a likable, reliable employee, and much more. Amalia and Lucrezia had a particular fondness for him because he reminded them so much of the young Carlo. He often did or said things in a way that took each of the women back to their early days when the three of them were struggling together.

BOOK III

XXVI   *The Last Wedding*   *1490*

While waiting for the Lamandolas to arrive, Amalia sat under the old pear tree in the back of the garden, enjoying the sounds of the birds, distinguishing the various chirps of the several different kinds of bird inhabiting her garden and other gardens in the neighborhood. She had a book in her lap, but had closed it as she allowed her mind to wander.

It was a cloudless day, and the evening promised to be clear and cool. Amalia was confident tomorrow would be sunny, but no matter, tomorrow would be a happy day whatever the weather. Amalia and Lucrezia had been waiting for this day for a very long time. Ugo was the last of his generation to marry. He was also the youngest, so that in and of itself was not so unusual, but all the rest of his generation had been married now for over ten years. Ugo had listened to Marco's stories of his travels as a young man and had caught the wanderlust.

They heard from him often and every couple of years he would appear at Lucrezia and Ermanno's front door, move back into his old bedroom and give the appearance of settling into working with Marco and Carlo in one of the several businesses they ran, or working out at the farm. Then the day would come when he would sit down with Lucrezia and Ermanno to tell them he would be leaving the next day.

Once he went to Milan and worked assisting a notary; then he went to Genoa and worked on the docks, supervising the loading of the ships. He went on to Venice to work in the factory building gondolas, to Naples as a driver for a freighter plying the roads of southern Italy, over to Greece to work for a shipping company that sent wool to Florence, and more. He always made good money and was frugal, so he came home each time with a pocketful of money that he gave to his father for safe keeping.

Now, an old man of thirty-two, he had a nice nest egg, thanks to his father's investments in his behalf, and he was desperately needed by Carlo to help in the freighting business.

Ugo had met Lucia the last time he was home, and while gone this last time, she was ever-present in his head. As soon as he got home from what was to be his last odyssey, he went to her house to seek her out. It seemed her thoughts had been of him during that same period, so the whirlwind courtship was consummated quickly by a proposal and a wedding.

Lucrezia and Amalia liked Lucia. She was bright and quick mentally with a good sense of humor, but she had many interests and was always looking for new and exciting things to do. She was not short but shorter than Ugo, and perhaps a little too thin. No matter, thought Amalia, babies and time would take care of that. She was not a pretty girl by the standards of beauty in that time, but she had large, warm eyes, and her energy and her happy disposition drew everyone in. Her hair was a light auburn with beautiful golden highlights. She was perceived as a person far more attractive than she would appear if you just stood back and studied her features. Amalia thought she just might keep Ugo interested enough to not want to wander off too far or for too long in the future.

Lucrezia, as usual, had her girls make new dresses for all the ladies in the family and new outfits for the men as well, and she designed a beautiful dress for Lucia. Amalia had extended an invitation to the bride's parents to come to her house for dinner tonight, the night before the wedding—just the Lamandolas, Lucia and Ugo, and Lucrezia and Amalia.

Neither Marco or Ermanno would be there. This would be the first wedding without them, because both men had died since Manno's wedding almost ten years before.

Fevers of many origins were always the worst threat to life in Florence, and three years ago, a summer fever had swept through the city. Many died that summer: several friends and children of friends died, but several family members also were taken. Ermanno was the first to get sick, and he fought to live as long and as valiantly as he could, but he finally succumbed the night after Alessandra's husband, Bernardo, and her daughter both died. Two of Carlo and Lisabetta's children were stricken, but they both survived, as did Anna's daughter as well as Alessandra's son. It was a dreadful time with death all around them in the blistering, stagnant heat of the hottest summer anyone in Florence could remember.

Alessandra was so burdened when all three were sick, Amalia moved in to try to help. Bernardo, little Alessandra, and even little Bernardo were all suffering the throes of the high fever. Bernardo and little Sandra died within hours of each other the following day, and little Bernardo vacillated between life and death for two days before the fever finally broke and they had some confidence he would survive. Alessandra was devastated, in the daze of a deep grief, and she was never to be her old happy self. Everyone was either nursing the sick or at the church for a funeral Mass for a friend or relative every day for weeks. Lucrezia was devastated by the loss of Ermanno and didn't go to her shop for over a month. Fortunately, she had a good staff. AnnaMaria kept things running smoothly, stalling off ladies interested in design work only Lucrezia could handle. Two of the young seamstresses with some designing abilities stepped up and did an excellent job in numerous situations, for which Lucrezia would later show her gratitude.

The next summer Marco had a heart attack that left him quite disabled. He returned to work as best he could, but over that following year, he grew weaker and weaker until finally he was housebound. He slipped away one night with Amalia by his side. He had been a powerful, positive presence for the extended family right to the end. That positive drive and spirit was picked up, like a baton in an old Greek marathon, by all the children and the grandchildren.

Amalia was devastated by the loss, and she became a much quieter, more inward version of herself. She could enjoy the children and grandchildren, but only Lucrezia and her daughter, Alessandra saw her in the moments when she was not buoyed by the presence of others.

They were alone again, the two of them, but now they were in the embraces of the three large families: the children and their children's children, full of the irrepressible life of the living—the survivors. They would carry the two women forward until each in her own way could see the sun rise again over the horizon, urging her out of the blackness of her isolating grief.

On the evening before the wedding, Francia had prepared an excellent dinner for the visiting Lamandola family: veal and some fresh produce from Lisabetta's farm, some of Bianca's special cheeses, some of Carlo's excellent wine, and fresh fruit from their own fruit trees Lucrezia now tended again in the garden between their homes. Some of the greens served were from Lucrezia's garden. For dessert, there was a special zafferano, a pudding of almond milk, saffron, and other spices with a drizzle of Lisabetta's honey.

Carlo saw to it that his men did all the heavy work in Lucrezia's garden, but she sometimes enjoyed spending time doing whatever chores were necessary, depending on the season, now that it was back in her capable hands.

Amalia also spent time in the garden. She saw to it that the birdbath was always full of fresh water, that seeds, bugs, and dead caterpillars from the farm were available for her birds, plus maybe an overripe fig or pear was cut up. There were also several puddling ponds for the many butterflies that enjoyed the assortment of flowers she made certain were always grown.

A young orphan boy that Lisabetta had hired on her farm had instructions to gather any fresh dead bugs and caterpillars he found and have them sent to town for her aunt. When such a fuss was made by Lisabetta that this be done, the boy, Antonio, thought it really strange and at first wondered if the old lady ate them. He was greatly relieved to find out they were for her birds. Well, he thought that was weird also but at least not as weird as the other.

Young Antonio lived on the farm and became a great favorite of Lisabetta's and Bianca's, and Amalia grew fond of him also as she spent time out at the farm, always insisting on staying out in Lisabetta's small guest house. Antonio would see to it she had everything she needed and would bring out to her any treats that were being made in the kitchen in the big house by Bianca's mother, Violetta. Violetta still oversaw everything that happened at that house, especially the cooking for the family. In addition, once a week she supervised the preparation of a large meal for all the help on the farm, and it would be served on improvised tables running down the center of the big barn Carlo had built shortly after he and Lisabetta were married.

When the knock came at the front door, Ugo rushed down to greet the Lamandolas. He showed them out into the garden where Francia had set out some light refreshments and beverages. Amalia joined them, and Franco, now an old man but still healthy with good legs to navigate the stairs, was helping Francia and was prepared to serve the guests. Once they were settled, he walked back to Lucrezia's house to let her know the guests had arrived.

The six of them sat in the loggia by the edge of the garden, talking about a myriad of topics until it started to get dark. Lucrezia knew Rosetta, Lucia's mother, slightly from various church confraternity activities between their churches. Amalia knew Roberto, but not as well, because he had had business dealings with Marco in years past. Memories were shared and plans were discussed. Lucia mentioned the many statues in the different sections of the garden. Ugo reminded them of when he was a child and the vegetable vines grew all over the statues,

290

particularly the one year a zucchini hung in a most inappropriate place on one of the male nudes.

"Yes," said Lucrezia, laughing, "Franco had to be sure that never happened again. All of you children had a wonderful time with that. It was certainly quite obscene."

They all enjoyed a good laugh, and then Lucrezia told them the story of wonderful old Dona Rutia and her garden that had given her the idea for their garden.

Ugo said he had never met her, and Amalia and Lucrezia laughed and told him she had died long before he was born, but she had been a guardian angel with the devil's tongue in the Dontarino receiving room for many years when the girls were young.

Speaking of the receiving room, it was decided it was time to retire to the house. As she often did for these more formal occasions or when there was a large family gathering, Amalia had the meal served in the receiving room in front of the fireplace. She would roll up her mother's beautiful rug, and the table would be set on the tile floor for the event.

The meal was consumed to the tune of stories, memories, and laughter as the families got to know each other. Once the plates had been cleared away, Amalia reached for the small cassone in front of her and turned to Lucia, who was sitting beside her.

"Lucia, you are the last daughter-in-law we will be welcoming into our family, and there is something I wish to give you. My mother died when I was a young girl, and after my father died, Lucrezia and I found this cassone in her belongings. Lucrezia and I were very fortunate, and we never had to use any of the contents to survive in the old days, so we have given each daughter and each daughter-in-law a necklace when they married. Now we give this one to you."

"Oh, Ama, it is beautiful. Thank you very much. I can't wait to see it with my dress. It actually seems a perfect match."

"That is no accident, dear. Lucrezia designed your dress with the necklace in mind. That is why when you first wanted the V-necked dress, she kept urging you to have the rounded neckline. We are terrible plotters."

"I can't wait to try it on."

"No, child, wait until tomorrow once you have your dress on. That is when it was given to each of the others, so please continue that tradition even though we are giving it to you tonight."

"Of course. Will you be there?"

"No, dear; that is a pleasure you will share with your mother. Since you are her only daughter, I know it will be very special for both of you." Lucrezia and Amalia both looked over at Rosetta, and the three ladies shared a knowing smile.

Lucrezia said, "We are very fortunate that you will be joining our family tomorrow, and we are very pleased with Ugo's choice of a bride. We were always fearful he would bring home some Greek girl that couldn't speak Italian, or some barefoot Spanish girl, or who knew what from who knew where in his travels."

At this, everyone laughed, and Lucrezia leaned over and kissed her son on the cheek.

"We are so happy he came home to stay and that he found you here in our beloved city."

Amalia lifted her glass: "To Ugo and Lucia, and Florence," and all joined in.

Lucrezia continued, "Now it is my turn. Ugo, I wish with all my heart that your father was here today to see his son marry such a lovely girl. Yours is the only wedding Marco and Ermanno missed, so it is up to us," as she reached over and patted Amalia's arm, "to close this circle without them. You are the last of our children to marry, and we feel that our job is now completed. The next generations are in the hands of God, and we will be merely spectators and then ultimately memories.

"Don't get your hopes up; we are not going anywhere any time soon, and we will be meddling in your lives for a long time to come—" and they all laughed— "but we can now step back and enjoy the picture rather than feel we have to do the painting.

"Giuliano was given Ama's father's ring that he had inherited from his father and him from his father. That is the ring Giuliano wears every day.

"Your father had a ring he inherited from his father, and that is the ring we gave to Manno when he married. He was given the name and the inheritance of that family heirloom. He gave it back to me for safe keeping when he left to go to sea with Jacko after Eleanora died, and it will be his again when he returns home.

"Your father was given the gift of a magnificent voice, and he achieved great success. Once, after performing at the Palazzo Medici, Lucrezia de' Medici handed your father a small box. She told him it was from Cosimo, her father-in-law, but he was too infirm by then to deliver it to your father in person. She said that although he couldn't be present, Ermanno's voice reverberated throughout the palazzo, and Cosimo was not deprived of the pleasure of hearing your father sing. Cosimo had told her he knew Ermanno's extended family, and it was a special token of Cosimo's admiration for him and his magnificent talent, and also his regard for the achievements of the entire family."

Lucrezia reached for the small cassone in front of her on the table and handed it to Ugo, who was seated by her side. It was good she had to turn away from Amalia slightly, for she was sure tears were running down her dear friend's face. Lucrezia was already struggling to keep her composure and didn't want to fall apart now, so close to the end.

Ugo opened the box, and he was stunned.

"Mother, this is the ring father always wore during his performances."

"Yes, he kept it for only then. He always felt this was not his personal ring: this was the ring given to him for his voice and fame and more. Your father knew the story of Amalia's involvement with Cosimo, of course, and he knew of the several stories that have come to light over the years of Cosimo's involvement with this family, things we sometimes didn't even know about at the time of their happening, but your father always felt this ring represented things beyond him personally—family, Cosimo, Florence, as well as the fame he achieved here.

"So I have given it to you. I hope you will have the love for Florence that we have had—" Now Lucrezia did turn to Amalia, and again patted her arm "—and may you both find great happiness in your future lives together in our glorious city. Never forget that she has given this family everything."

Roberto lifted his glass this time. "To Florence—and Lucia and Ugo."

Amalia lifted Lucrezia's hand and kissed it.

Then they looked in each other's eyes, and Amalia said, "Thank you, Lucrezia."

The Lamandolas left shortly after, as they all wanted the bride and groom to get a good night's rest before the festivities the following day.

The wedding was in front of the Lamandola church, Santissima Annunziata, on the other side of town, and the reception was held at the home of Roberto and Rosetta. Then, following the family tradition begun by Carlo and Lisabetta so many years ago, and enjoyed by each couple since, Ermanno's old but still elegant carriage carried the couple out to the farm to spent their wedding night at Lisabetta's little house on her small farm.

Lisabetta and Bianca had filled it with fresh flowers, Lucrezia had a new set of special bed linens made, and everything had been aired and cleaned to perfection for the occasion.

~ ~ ~

The following week on Sunday afternoon, the entire family gathered on the farm at Carlo and Lisabetta's large house. They didn't gather every Sunday, as they had done while Carlo was away at sea so many years ago at Lisabetta's small house. Yet now, when the weather was fine, the family often went out to the big house on a Sunday afternoon, particularly during the summer months.

The newlyweds were the guests of honor and were invited to arrive late and do nothing, but Lucia was not to be dissuaded and was in the middle of the work from the time of their only slightly late arrival. Ugo enjoyed his special role and thoroughly enjoyed the camaraderie of his large family, all sisters and brothers, nieces and nephews, whether bound by blood or not.

His sister, Anna, was busy with the ladies, and he had seen a lot of her since he got home. Theirs was such a joyful house, he had been inclined to spend a lot of time there. Anna's husband, Ludovico, was the happiest, most fun-loving man Ugo had ever known. He could be serious and was a hard worker, but when you interrupted him in his shop, he might be covered with sawdust and struggling to lift or move a large cassone or other piece of furniture, but you were always greeted with a smiling, happy welcome followed by a clap on the shoulder and a bear hug. He suffered in sad times, but he found great joy in the little things in life, and he was always disposed to share his joy.

Many times over the years, Ludo had buoyed the spirits of various family members who might be struggling, for he had great compassion and understanding. With such a positive attitude and infectious joy, he alleviated everyone's troubles. One of his favorite expressions was that we should put our troubles in a box and then lose the key. He said Alberti had written it in one of his poems, and he liked it.

Ugo and Ludo now sat in the shade and shared a glass of wine with their feet propped up on a large overturned flower pot. They were soon to be joined by Anna and Ludo's two oldest children, Gino and Mariana.

Gino was presently working for Carlo, mostly freighting but also anything else Carlo needed. He was a good, hardworking boy of fifteen years. He liked his studies, and Giuliano, Amalia's son, was sure he could get him in the studium when the time came to further his education. For now, though, while Carlo was desperate for his help, Gino was willing to devote his time to helping his uncle.

Mariana was only thirteen but was willing to work at anything she could do to help several afternoons a week. With Marco gone, so much had fallen on Carlo's shoulders, sometimes it was overwhelming; so anyone in the family that could help did so. Carlo and Marco were both good bosses and had good people working for them, and Carlo was very grateful for their help, but right now he needed more than they could do.

But at this moment, Gino and Mariana were really there to ask if they could go horseback riding. Everyone rode, and Carlo kept a large string of horses just for that purpose, even some smaller horses for the smaller children in the family. This was one of the main activities on their Sunday afternoons at the farm.

Gino and Mariana would be off as soon as they got mounted, doing a couple of quick laps around, then riding like the wind across the large pasture, then circling around and back. There would always be one or two of the wranglers nearby to help with equipment and watch out for the safety of the smaller children. Young Antonio, the orphaned boy, enjoyed riding and often joined in to stay with the younger children as Gino and Mariana raced on ahead.

Traveler, her companion and the horse of Lisabetta's heart, had died about ten years before. Lisabetta had never had the heart to ride after that; but she saw to it that all the horses were properly trained, the equipment was kept in good repair, and the children were properly instructed. All three of her children were excellent riders, even little Lisa, who was only seven. Everyone remarked how much she was like her mother because she had the quiet defiance and determination to do things her own way in ways beyond her years, as her mother had done.

Dogs and cats were everywhere, some living in the several barns, some outside the house, and some inside, all clearly descended from Luppo and Boots. Usually one or two of the dogs loped alongside the riders, whatever size the rider or horse.

One of the dogs was almost as large as the smallest horse. For fun, very often the adults would put Giuliano's and Teresa's youngest, now almost two, on young Luppo's back and walk him around as everyone clapped and laughed, to young Fabio's delight.

When Manno's wife, Eleanora, died only six days after the birth of their first and only child eight years ago, little Amalia, called Lia, came to live with her grandmother, Lucrezia. Manno had been so overcome with grief, he left only one week after his wife's death to go to sea with Jacko.

Alessandra and her son, little Bernardo, moved back home to live with Amalia after her husband, Bernardo, and daughter died of the fever. The two children, being the same age, went back and forth between the two houses, each having a bedroom in both houses and being mothered by Alessandra, Amalia, and Lucrezia. Then, when they went out to visit at the farm, Lisabetta became the mother. Neither of them was ever sure who was their mother, but Bernardo knew Lia was his sister, and Lia knew Bernardo was her brother, and they looked to each other for emotional support in everything they did, first in play and later as they began their schooling. It was a bond they would have for life.

Alessandra, true to being Amalia's daughter, had always done some ink work. When she met Ludovico, she started painting on a few pieces of his furniture, and then more and more of it. Now they worked together regularly, and she loved what she did.

She didn't know how to mix the paints used by the artists, but she mastered using the colored inks. Many of the cassoni were inlaid with other woods in a style called marquetry. Still others were set with precious and semi-precious gems, depending on the wealth of the customer. Some of Ludovico's cassoni were finished in this manner, but by other artisans, not by Alessandra.

His cassoni, both large ones used for storage of clothing, bedding, and the like, or small ones used for jewelry, were considered to be quite special in design and wood workmanship, and then the artwork by Alessandra and the others made for good partnerships. She was the one who introduced Ludo to Anna, so then the partnership became family as well.

Ludo was very innovative in his furniture designs, and he kept one of the seamstresses in Lucrezia's shop busy full time making cushions for the large cassoni and also for the chairs and benches he designed and built in his ever-expanding shop.

At one point in the day, Ugo and Giuliano walked out by the fence overlooking the horse pasture to watch almost all the children riding in the large pasture. Giuliano wanted to update him on the finances of the family and also Ugo's personal holdings that his father had established in his behalf. Giuliano knew Carlo had told him in detail the status of the freighting and shipping businesses as well as all the farm enterprises, but there was much more. Ermanno's success had brought him considerable wealth as well as fame, and the family, Lucrezia's family, owned an estate out near Prato. There was a manager, and Carlo kept a close eye on the operations, but Ugo would now have to take some responsibility for the management of it. Guiliano was hoping Ugo would take some time in the future to develop it into a summer villa for the family.

There were two houses in Florence, the one Ugo and Lucia had moved into a block from Lucrezia's house and a large house over near Santa Croce that was rented to a reliable family. It provided a steady income. There were two houses near Marco's boddeghe that were rented out, plus some raw land in the direction of Pisa that had been let go fallow. These were owned by Lucrezia, but they would now become Ugo's responsibility until Manno returned home. It was not necessary to add "if he returned home."

Giuliano outlined the various investments Ermanno had made for Ugo with his money: land in several areas, a building in Fiesole, and another in Florence, an office building in the heart of Pisa.

He went on to explain that he handled all the legal dealings for Carlo—and now Ugo if he wanted him to—and always checked or prepared any contracts for the various businesses.

"Ugo, the shipping business with Jacko brings in a lot of revenue, and Carlo or I often have to go over to the coast when either ship is in port. We would like you to become a part of that also. You will have valuable input with your travel experience.

"Fortunately Carlo has a good manager for the freighting, so that has helped, and Piero, the young boy he took in years ago, is proving to be an excellent manager of the farm, but we are pulled in too many directions."

Giuliano explained that he managed Amalia's affairs—there was a small house on the other side of the River Arno, a building near the center of town rented to several lawyers, including him, a farm near Prato, and also more land near Carlo and Lisabetta's farm out the Fiesole Road.

"Ugo, there is land in all directions owned by some member of the family, much of it fallow. Alessandra as well as Anna and Ludo have property in addition to the very large building housing Ludo's shop. Manno has property, although he doesn't know it, Carlo and Lisabetta own other property, and there is a possible deal for more land behind this farm down by the river. "With your help, we might be able to start making better use of some of it and farming more of the land. I wanted to get the money invested, but without our fathers, Carlo and I have been stretched far too thin. Carlo and I will be very grateful for your help and input on a great many things."

Ugo said, "I have really let the family down. I should have been home helping out, particularly since father and Marco died. I have been very short-sighted and selfish."

"No, don't think that way. If you had stayed, you would have been a most unhappy man, and none of us would want that for you. I don't know what your plans are or if you have any, but I think you are here now because it is where you want to be, and we are all glad for that. That said, Carlo and I will be very grateful for your help."

At that moment, a group of the riders arrived on their side of the fence, and chaos ensued as all wanted praise for their beautiful horse or their pretty riding outfits, and especially, compliments on their riding skills.

Later in the day after the meal had been served, eaten, and cleared away, all the adults were gathered and relaxing in the shade of the large old tree behind the house. Some of the men were sipping a small glass of Carlo's special grappa.

Years ago Carlo had run into an old man in Fiesole who told him how to make it. He said it was very complicated and you needed some very special equipment. When Carlo told him he had the equipment in a cellar in Florence, the man got very excited, because he liked the idea of passing on the art of making the grappa.

A couple weeks later, after Carlo had talked to Amalia and taken the old, discarded equipment out to the farm, Carlo sent a wagon to Fiesole for the old man. He came to the farm to set up the equipment for Carlo and to teach him how to make the special grappa the family men were now sipping.

As the day began to draw to a close, Giuliano asked if he could have everyone's attention.

"I just wanted to tell everyone that I have just concluded the purchase of the farm next to Carlo and Lisabetta's. I intend to fix the house up as a retreat for the family from the summer heat, and Carlo and I have been talking. We will share in the farming, but we will be doubling the pastureland, and we are going to put in better trails and an actual track around the outside edge for all of you to ride."

All the younger generation burst into loud applause and yelling, frightening young Fabio so that he burst into tears, which caused everyone to laugh even more as he was passed from person to person for consoling.

Giuliano did not bother to tell everyone that Teresa was not in favor of the purchase. She wanted him to buy or build a larger house for them. Giuliano's house was already much larger than his mother's or even Lucrezia's, and he did not feel they needed more room yet since they only had two children so far. When this business opportunity presented itself, he snapped it up quickly since he felt it was a good bargain, but it had caused him no end of grief at home.

Teresa was a beautiful woman and she knew it, and although she did truly love Giuliano, she did not make his life easy. He loved her; he loved her self-assurance and enjoyed the social life she brought into their life together, but he did pay a high price.

By the time the carriages and wagons were brought around for the journey back into the city, everyone was very tired, very full from all the delicious food served, and some were slightly drunk from maybe a glass or two too much wine. All were very happy, though, not only after hearing Giuliano's great news but also from the joy of being together and enjoying the camaraderie of an exuberant and loving family.

Lucrezia needed to be in town early in the morning, but Amalia would spend the night at Lisabetta's house, and little Bernardo and Lia would stay in the big farm house. Auntie Lisabetta had promised to make them one of her delicious frittatas for breakfast, so their schooling would be delayed until the afternoon.

The wedding had been lovely, but both Amalia and Lucrezia liked it best when the family was together in this kind of relaxed atmosphere, just enjoying each other's company in the embrace of the love of family.

Sandro Botticelli's Primavera

One generation from the paintings of saints

Right in trio is believed to depict Caterina Sforza

Venus is believed to be Simonetta Vespucci, wife of Marco, a cousin of Amerigo. She was believed to have been mistress to Guiliano de' Medici, Lorenzo's brother killed in the Pazzi Conspiracy. Mercury, left, may be Guiliano. Painted for a Medici. The oranges believed to be a pun of Medici "Pelle," the balls of their escucheon.

XXVII *Loose Threads* *1490+*

As time passed, many things changed as the younger generations grew and moved on in their lives.

Although they all enjoyed singing, and did so very often, particularly while riding to or from the farm, there would never be another voice in the family like Ermanno's. For that matter, it would be many years before Florence would be blessed with such a voice again.

The night of the opening performance of the new season for the production company, there was a memorial tribute to Ermanno, and the entire family was present. All Florence would miss Ermanno, and Lucrezia had to share that with them as she had had to learn to share his magnificent voice with them so many years before.

~ ~ ~

Federico, Marco's loyal employee all these years in the copper shop, asked if he could continue to make the pots and pans after Marco died. Of course, because of his appearance, he could not do the marketing, but a lot of it was done by written orders anyway. One young man Marco had hired a few years ago named Bartolo had a presentable manner and a good head for business, as it turned out. He could deal with the many customers, so he and Federico formed an agreement to split the profits and the workload, Federico in charge of production and Bartolo handling the marketing tying in with Carlo's shipping, and freighting.

They rented the boddeghe from Amalia, while Carlo and Ugo and, whoever else was helping out, used the upstairs space so the importing, shipping, and freighting business could continue to be conducted from there as before.

Federico had hired a woman, Maria was her name, to clean the very nice house he had acquired years before and to cook for him. She had grown to love Federico. She was able to look beyond the badly scarred face and chest and ap-

301

preciate the man within. She always said the scars were a mask, and she loved the man behind the mask.

After their first child was born, Maria prevailed upon Federico to marry her. It was not that he didn't want to marry her or that he didn't love her, but he did not want her to be bound to him, for he found it difficult—no, impossible—to believe anyone could or would love him or want to share his warped life.

Since the children from all three families grew up with Federico and had long since grown accustomed to his appearance, his circle of relationships grew over the years, and he and Maria and their children were often included in family activities.

~ ~ ~

It had been a heavy burden for Carlo, but now he hoped Ugo would help carry a share of the load. Anna's older son, Gino, was already working in the freighting. He could have continued his studies, and Lucrezia begged him to, but he found he enjoyed what he was doing. Eventually, he would take time out to attend the Studium, but then he went back and took over managing the freighting business.

~ ~ ~

Amalia had developed a tremor in her right hand shortly after the death of Marco, so she could no longer scribe or do the artwork that had become her specialty and her very favorite thing to do. She had slowed down a lot in recent years as she allowed the other family needs to take priority in her life. Money was not a factor, she had been scribing for many years only for the joy of the doing. She took on the schooling of Bernardo and Lia while they were young, and she continued some teaching at Caterina's school, which had become one of the finest schools for girls in Florence.

Lisabetta had fun doing the scribing when she was young. Then for years, as she raised her young children and helped Carlo build the farm into a large operation, she had gotten away from it. Now, as the children's needs were less demanding and they hired all the help they needed for the farm, she converted the room on the third floor adjacent to the loggia of their large house into her workroom. She spent many afternoons, particularly in the winter months, copying a favorite book of poetry or compiling a book of her own favorites and then spent a month and maybe two doing the artwork she had come to enjoy doing.

These books became gifts for a very special event to a family member or for a treasured friend. Amalia had done this also, copying some of Lucrezia de' Medici's poems or other poems she liked and made them into her own small books to be given to friends as gifts. The artwork was always superb and extensive, as these were books of her heart, not for shipment to some foreign country for an unknown person. She was pleased that Lisabetta continued the tradition.

Over the years, Lisabetta moved into making sketches of various scenes on the farm and coloring them with inks. Then she developed a color wash with the inks. She never thought of herself as a painter, but others loved the paintings and she loved doing it. Soon, there were many of her ink paintings spread around in the various homes of the family, and they hung on and stood against all the walls of her upstairs workshop.

Whenever Lisabetta and Alessandra were together, there would always come a time they would be off together discussing various techniques of their work. Oftentimes, Amalia would join them, for although their work was very different, the work was also alike in many ways, and there was no one outside the family with whom they could share ideas.

No one thought it unusual that the women of these families worked so hard at their occupations. It was the custom for the women of Florence to work at something, depending on their skills. If nothing else, a spinning wheel stood in the home of most of the lower class Florentine women. Caterina had her school, Beatrice had her bake shop of dessert specialties, and the Valetti-Evangelista-Cavalcanti women were no different. They just wished they had more expertise in what they did.

Verrocchio's boddeghe had not been far from where Alessandra lived with Amalia, and now Botticelli's boddeghe was only a couple streets away. Those artists and all the others in Florence would only have laughed at them, they were sure, if any of the women had approached them with a question. Maybe Carlo could have gotten Donatello or Lippi to listen to the women and give them hints on technique, but they, and so many others, were now only memories of earlier times, the fledgling years of the magnificent greatness and glory of the art of Florence to come.

Now Leonardo was off in Milan working for the duke, and Michelangelo was still living at the Palazzo Medici, chipping small, insignificant statues in Lorenzo's vast garden where he invited all the artists to work.

In years past, Carlo was often called upon to help move the works of many of the artists. Because he loved being a part of that world, he had always hung around the boddeghe of each of the artists until they started using his services.

He particularly liked Donatello. He was so soft-spoken, so kind, Carlo would always go out of his way to help him in any way on any project. He loved seeing that pot of money hanging in the middle of the boddeghe. What sort of man did such a thing?

Carlo had helped Donatello move the Judith and Holofernes statue to the Medici Palazzo. One day he knew the side doors to the garden would be open, because they were bringing in several new trees, and he took Amalia by so she could look in and see the Judith statue, standing right in the middle of the garden.

Many years later, Carlo would be called upon to assist in moving a very large statue from one area of town to the other, and he always wondered what Amalia would have thought about that magnificent large, white marble Michelangelo David as compared with the smaller black bronze Donatello David that he had seen years before and had loved.

Just in Carlo's lifetime, there came a swerve, a new attitude toward all the many artists. When Cosimo hired the artists back when Carlo was young, all the glory went to Cosimo as the patron, and the artist was barely recognized. Now the artists got the fame and the glory they so richly deserved. Even though Lorenzo and the popes and other patrons got their due credit, now the artists were rightfully acknowledged.

~ ~ ~

Her farm was still Lisabetta's love. For Carlo, his farm was business; for Lisabetta, it was a passion. Carlo oversaw the farming of the hay and grains, the maintenance of the large collection of carts and wagons of all sizes for the freighting, plus the husbanding of his livestock: the horses, mules, and oxen for the freighting. Piero took over the management of it all as he became older and more able.

Bianca husbanded Lisabetta's part of the farm. She had charge of the goats, a fairly large herd of sheep, and a small herd of cows, all with the help of several farm hands. Then she would oversee the shearing of the sheep and the goats and the shipments to town for the production of the various yarns. She also oversaw the collection of the honey and the production of the cheeses, milk, and other products from all three of these animals as well as the beef from the year-old calves they would periodically slaughter.

Initially, the orphan boy Antonio had been hired by Lisabetta to tend her chickens, but he eventually took responsibility for the now very large section of the farm dedicated to her lavender fields, surrounded by a single row of rose bushes planted all the way around the lavender, as well as the section dedicated to rows upon rows of grapevines. Much of the land on any of the future farms purchased by Carlo or Giuliano or Ugo would be dedicated to the growing of grapes.

The farmaceutica at Santa Maria Novella bought all Lisabetta's lavender and rose petals for their scents and also for the floral-scented balls and other items they now produced as people came to enjoy the fragrances in their homes. Lizabetta always had a large store of rose hips for the tea they shared with friends and neighbors.

When the lavender and the roses were coming into full bloom, Lisabetta was down there, supervising the harvesting every day, all day. It was the same when the grapes were coming to ripeness. Once she determined the grapes had reached their peak, Carlo took over harvesting the grapes and the production of the family wine that eventually grew to be known as the finest in all of Tuscany. Carlo, Amalia, Lucrezia, and Lisabetta often laughed that their family was now producing a wine Dona Rutia would have been very pleased to drink.

Carlo's wine was a fine wine, but young Antonio had a talent for determining the exact moment each step in the wine production should be taken and a palate to determine the finest taste. It was then, under his guidance as the years progressed, that the wine became truly excellent.

~ ~ ~

Lucrezia now had other designers working for her—well, really with her—with new, fresh ideas, and she gave them free rein. She knew if she didn't, they would go out on their own and be competition. By urging each girl into slightly different paths from each other and from her, they formed the finest design house in Florence and much more.

One of the girls specialized in the jackets and capes for men; capes of all lengths, above, to, or below the knees, trimmed in furs or not, simple woolen capes or the red worn by bankers, or maybe a pink cape that was the signature cape of Leonardo da Vinci. They made others in brocades and velvets of all colors. Plus, they employed workers just for the embroidering and trapunto on other capes and jackets.

Now orders from other cities poured in and kept all her seamstresses—those working on the ground floor of her house, Amalia's house, and other seamstresses in their own homes—busy year round. On the rare occasion there were no orders for the original designer dresses or coats or capes, there was always a large stack of fabrics to be made into the ready-made garments she stocked for the more economical shoppers.

One time Carlo freighted home a shipment for Lucrezia from her son, Manno, who had been in Constantinople at the time. It had been waiting for Carlo at the Venice dock. It seems a ship and all its cargo had been confiscated by the authorities in Constantinople—a not uncommon occurrence in that city during those times—and everything was being sold off for whatever price the officials could get. Knowing his way around the docks, Manno obtained good information concerning the contents of one of the bundles, offered a very low bid, and to his surprise, his offer was accepted. He sent the bundle on to his mother by a ship leaving the next day, and for the next several years, the capes and jackets and even dresses of the men and women of Florence were all trimmed with beautiful Russian sable and other furs from that shipment received by Lucrezia.

It was on this same journey that Marco went along on Manno's ship to Constantinople. He and Erudius had made plans to meet there and bring along a representative of the next generation of each family so their trading could go on and the two families would still be united in friendship as well as business. Erudius had two sons, and Marco was using this as an opportunity, hoping to pull Manno back into the family fold, even if not immediately.

It worked even better than Erudius and Marco had hoped. The two brothers and Manno enjoyed each other's company, and Manno even invited the brothers to Florence, explaining he was never there but he said he had a brother and sister and cousins that would fill in for him, make them welcome, and entertain them.

It was several years before the brothers made the journey to Florence, and by the time they did, Manno was himself living back home. The visit was cause for great celebrations by the two families. Manno and Erudius's oldest son, Rudi, formed a friendship that would last the remainder of their lives. Business was the root of the relationship, but the letters soon went beyond business, and extended visits were exchanged over the years between the families. All regretted that the first wonderful gathering in Florence had not taken place while Erudius and Marco were still alive, but everyone knew the union of the two families was their doing.

As Erudius had done, Rudi always kept his eyes open for any old manuscripts he might come across in Constantinople, and he would always send to Amalia anything he thought she might enjoy. Once he sent a beautiful atlas on astronomy and astrology by Suetonius, *De Viris Illustribus*, and Amalia immediately took it to Messer Bisticci. Vespasiano was immensely pleased, and he set about having special scribes copy it.

Alum had been discovered in Volterra, and there was no longer a need to import it, but the two families still traded in copper, and Erudius had long before branched into many other markets. The pope and the Medici controlled the alum now, and it caused great political rifts between them at various times, so Marco and Carlo were glad they were out of that market entirely.

~ ~ ~

Anna had worked in her mother's shop since she was a very young girl. She loved the world of fashion, but also she had an appreciative and critical eye and came to have an understanding for the technical aspects of the fabrics and particularly the business side of things. She never did any designing, but she could look at a sketch by someone else and tell whether it would work technically and whether it would sell, and she was rarely wrong. She controlled all the foreign sales and shipments, ordered the fabrics and supplies, everything that had to be done to leave AnnaMaria free to run the shop and Lucrezia free to do the designing she so enjoyed.

~ ~ ~

After Lucrezia had staged her "performance" (the parade of her fashions during the June 24th celebration of St. John the Baptist Day so many years ago), there had been an outcry that it was too unseemly, too outrageous, too this and too that. She would never do it again. She had made her statement and set the mark so high, she never would have had the need.

The twin girls did come to work in her shop. One had been admired by a young man on the day of the "performance," and she ultimately married him. He was the son of a very rich merchant, and they presented the old man with three grandsons and a granddaughter upon whom he doted to the end of his very long life. She loved her husband and adored her father-in-law, and other than not seeing her sister as often as she would have liked, her life was truly complete.

Her sister met and married a young carpenter's helper. It is through them that Alessandra later met Ludovico, who owned the carpentry shop where the young man worked. Then through Alessandra, Anna met and then married Ludovico.

That second twin continued to work for Lucrezia for many years, raised a large family with her loving husband, who ultimately managed Ludovico's ever-expanding furniture factory. She even worked many years after arthritis had crippled her hands and she was no longer able to sew. She would oversee the young seamstresses, and there were always other tasks to be done. She knew and loved the work.

~ ~ ~

Amalia's son, Giuliano, had always been a good student, and when he was very young he began working in Riccardo's law office as a secretary/clerk since, of course, he had excellent scribing skills, having been well-trained by his mother. He had gone to one of the finest schools in Florence, but even before that, he had been schooled by his mother in Latin and the volgare, and he could have been an excellent scribe.

One day, as he and Marco were riding back from the farm together, Marco reminded him that his grandfather had been a notary, but perhaps he would enjoy being a lawyer. Giuliano said it was his fondest wish, but he thought Marco wanted him to go into the importing, freighting, and shipping business with him and Carlo.

"No, son. Those were the roads down which life took Carlo and me, that and my copper ware. I want you to follow your own desires and seek out what you want to do with your life. Your mother and I, as well as Aunt Lucrezia and Uncle Ermanno and even Lisabetta and Carlo have been very fortunate to do exactly what we chose to do, and none of us have had a moment's regret. I want that for you.

"I hope you marry well, but you are still young and that will be in your future. But how you earn your livelihood will mean how you spend your days, and if you can enjoy what you do each of those days, it will go far to making you a very happy man. Riccardo says you have a lawyer's mind, and he can open doors for you if that is your wish."

"Yes, father, it is what I wish. I just didn't want to disappoint you."

"Son, the only way you could disappoint me would be to do something foolish with your life, like follow my path. Understand, I have enjoyed my life. I love working with the copper when I get the chance to do it. Carlo and I have had a good time with Carlo's freighting and the shipping with Jacko and Manno and importing with Erudius, but I would wish for something different for you, if that is your wish. I think a father always wants better for his son, and we live in a time when that is possible."

"Thank you, Father. I think you just made this the happiest day of my life."

Marco laughed. "Well, I hope there will be many happier days, but if you can now swerve in the road of your life and head down your own path with full but lighter heart, then I'm very glad we have had this conversation. Talk to Riccardo, and when it is time, we will make arrangements for you to go to Bologna for the best schooling in the law.

"Find a moment tonight to tell your mother. I can promise you, she will be very pleased."

~ ~ ~

Jacko Vespucci was never home for long and was only happy when he was at the helm of one of his ships. He, Marco, and Carlo had bought two more ships over the years. Manno was captain of one of them, having spent the first year learning navigation and sailing from Jacko. They plied the Mediterranean ports wherever their shipments took them. Jacko had been back to London often over the years, as well as Bruges, and other ports outside the straits. They had company men in Venice, Genoa, and Pisa, and agents in many other cities.

Jacko's cousin, Amerigo, often sailed with either Jacko or Manno. He was a good deal younger than Jacko and only a few years older than Manno, but the three had the sea as a common interest that bound them together.

Later, after Jacko and Manno finally came home and turned the ships over to other captains, Amerigo would go on to greater things, making his mark in history sailing off to a new, yet unexplored world far beyond the straits, out across the Great Sea. Before that, for several years he did come back to Florence to work in the Medici bank, thanks to his family's close connections with that family. When the time came for him to return to the sea on his great adventure, he went with the backing of the Medici bank.

~ ~ ~

Shortly after Ugo's marriage, Manno came home, and he did not come empty-handed.

Six weeks before, his ship had taken him to the Tenerife Islands off the coast of Africa. While they were docked in the Santa Cruz harbor, he had an opportunity to go to the community of San Cristobal de La Laguna in the hills above the port. It was an old and very poor community that had only a couple churches that were of any interest.

After visiting two churches, Manno was sitting outside at a street cafe, and was reflecting on a line he had read last night in Dante's book: "In the middle of the journey of our life, I came to myself in a dark wood where the direct way was lost." He felt his life was lost in that dark wood now, and it disturbed him.

There were some children playing in the deserted street next to the cafe, and two of the girls were about the age of his daughter, the daughter he had not seen since she was only two weeks old. He didn't know what his daughter looked like, and suddenly that burned a hole in his heart.

He had run away from Florence, the memories, his life, for so long now, and it had gained him nothing. He was tired of running away, tired of being alone; and a consuming desire engulfed him that he wanted to go home. He knew it wouldn't be easy. He had a large family that he knew loved him, but he had a daughter he didn't know. No, it wouldn't be easy, but the life he was leading was no longer a solution. Whatever memories still haunted him, the sea had not and could not wash those memories away. Maybe the pain would never go away, but at least at home he might find other compensations.

Once back in Santa Cruz at the ship, he learned it would still be two days before the two shipments they were to take, the first to Spain and then the second on to Naples, would be ready to be loaded on his ship.

The next day, once his duties were done on the ship, he roamed the streets near the docks. He thought about his family but mainly he thought about his daughter. He didn't know her but more importantly, she didn't know him. He was not a part of her life; she had lived her entire life without his presence. He was a total stranger. Had he destroyed any chance for a relationship with her?

"What a fool I've been. I ran away from one problem only to create another," Manno thought. Manno spent a restless night that night, tossing and turning, fretting and chastising himself over and over again. Whatever he had to face, he would no longer avoid it. He now felt the last eight years had been lost years, but now he had to get out of that dark woods and come into the light of his life.

The last day in port would seem endless. He couldn't wait for it to be over so they could begin the journey home, but the day had to be endured. He again prowled the streets near the docks and finally found a quiet cafe away from the center of town where he could sit under a shade tree and watch some children playing. He noticed two young girls playing with three puppies off to the side of the other children. Again, they were close to his daughter's age. It seemed he was to be brutally reminded at every turn now that his decision was made. He was lost in his own thoughts and paid them no more attention.

"Please, signori," said one of the girls in Spanish, "would you buy one of my puppies?"

"No, I can't," said Manno. "I leave on a ship tomorrow. I am sorry."

"Oh," said the girl, as she slowly turned away, tears welling up in her eyes. He overheard the two girls talking.

"What can we do now? Is Papa going to kill them?"

"Yes, he said we weren't to bring them home again. He said he doesn't want three dogs running around the house now that Blanca has died."

"But Blanca was his dog. I wish we could keep them as our own."

"I do too, Maria, but he killed all four of Blanca's last litter. He will do it again."

"Maybe Signora Martinez would take one."

"No, I asked her yesterday."

"I would so love to have a puppy of my own," Maria said through her tears. "Maybe we could talk him into one but not all three."

Manno called Maria over and asked her how much she wanted for one of the puppies. She smiled a sheepish smile and told him she really didn't want any money, she just wanted to find a home for her puppies.

"I will take two of them if your father will let you keep one. Go tell him I will give you this for the two, but only if he lets you keep the third," and he held out more money than the girls could believe. "Leave the puppies here, and go ask your father if he will agree."

While they were gone, he had time to consider what he had just done. The journey home would be complicated with two puppies on board, but since it was his ship, that was not an insurmountable complication. He knew exactly what he would do with one of the pups, for watching the two girls with the puppies made him aware that nothing would melt his daughter's heart toward him more than such a gift. Was he bribing his daughter? Yes, but he would do whatever it took to win her over, and he thought this just might be a good beginning. What he would do with the other puppy, he had no idea. Maybe give it to his mother or Amalia.

While he waited for the girls to return, he observed the puppies, maybe five or six weeks old, very small white balls of curly hair. They were dirty from playing in the street, but they were all three tumbling and then one chased another's tail, then they tumbled some more. By the time Maria and her sister returned, Manno would have been disappointed if the exchange had not gone through. He was not disappointed. Maria wanted the larger male puppy, and Manno headed back to the ship with the two smaller female pups, one in each hand against his chest.

As he approached his ship, he passed one of the local ships docked next to his ship, and the captain called to him, "Ah, you like our little Tenerife Frise? They are good ship dogs, smart and happy."

"I'm taking one home to my daughter."

"She will love you for it."

"That is exactly what I'm hoping," he said and laughed. He waved to the captain, one of the pups in hand, as he neared the boarding plank to "The Golden Hawk."

Once home, Manno moved back into his old bedroom in Lucrezia's large house, got involved with Carlo and Ugo in shipping and freighting—mainly the shipping, since that was the world he understood—but most importantly, he began building a relationship with Lia, now eight years old, the daughter he had abandoned when she was only two weeks old. Since she was more comfortable when Bernardo was with her, they were a threesome for most of their many activities together. Bernardo missed his father, whom he could no longer remember, and having a man in his life instead of the ever-present four mothers was a boon.

The puppies had been a big hit. Manno never actually made a present of the second pup. It was just assumed from the start that one was for Lia and one was for Bernardo, but no one could tell which one. So as it turned out, they were a five-some for most of their many outings together over the years that followed.

Lucrezia once asked Manno what eventually brought him home, and he told her that he had run away because of his love for Eleanora, but love for his family and daughter is what brought him home again. As it turns out, he said he had learned love is all we have against the screams of life.

At Lia's wedding, ten years later, Manno met a cousin of the groom's mother, would court her, and eventually they would marry. Until then, he lived with Lucrezia, worked with the family in the various family businesses, devoted much time to his daughter and "nephew," and became a very contented man.

~ ~ ~

Jacko came home a year after Manno. He bought a very nice home near Ognissanti from his very elderly uncle where other Vespucci families lived, and was prepared to live the good live he felt he had earned after so many years at sea away from Florence.

He had loved his life at sea, and told Carlo on several occasions that had they not gone on that trip to England, he had no idea what he would have done with his life. He was pretty sure it would have been a rocky path and perhaps not one he would be proud of or pleased to recall. Sailing and the sea had been his love, and now he just wanted to enjoy the fruits of his labors.

Several weeks after Jacko moved into his new house, Carlo went by to invite him to one of the family Sunday afternoon gatherings. The servant met him at the door to tell him that she had found Jacko in his bed only a short time ago, and he was dead.

Carlo was beside himself. It was so unfair. All those dangers Jacko had faced at sea—all the life-threatening storms, the battering by a whale, the rocks and shoals—and Jacko came home to die in his bed only two months later. Carlo had lost his first and best friend. They had befriended each other as children when they each lost their mother and then their father. Jacko had his uncle, and Carlo had Amalia and Lucrezia, but they were brothers, just not of the blood.

What were family ties? Jacko had been orphaned when his parents both died, and Carlo had been abandoned when his mother left his father and him, never to be heard from again. Then his father, Barto, left town and abandoned him.

It was over twenty years later that Barto returned to Florence, a broken, dying man. Carlo took Barto in and provided for him, but no kind words were ever uttered by the old man, and he died without extending a caring thought to Carlo. Carlo had no regrets. He had done what he could for the shell of a man because it was his father, his blood. He had shown him kindness, and when it was over, it was done.

Jacko had been a different story, not blood but more. And now Carlo had a large family, his own precious Lisabetta and their three children plus all of Amalia's and Lucrezia's children. Some of these relationships were blood and most were not, but one tie was not more or less important to him than another. This was a topic Carlo raised often whenever any of his extended family was together. His true family was Amalia and Lucrezia, not his mother or father; Lisabetta's family was her aunt and Lucrezia; Manno had been taken under the wing of Carlo's non-brother, Jacko; Bernardo and Lia were sister and brother, but not; Amalia and Lucrezia were sisters but not. What is family? Only blood? Or maybe it was something even stronger than that: love, a bond forged by life, a devotion that is perhaps even stronger than the bonds of blood.

~ ~ ~

Amalia and Lucrezia had always hoped two of their children would marry and join the two families, but they had all been so close as they grew up, their relationships were more as sisters and brothers. It was something that would have to wait for the next generation when there would be two marriages that would bridge and join the three families together forever in love and blood.

314

Lorenzo

Amalia was on her way home from Messer Zaccaro's office, a doctor she had visited over the years, and the news had not been good. It was just beginning to rain a cold rain that might turn to snow, so she thought she would step into the Duomo and visit with Our Lady before heading home. As she opened the door, three men were exiting and the middle, tallest man almost knocked her over. She stumbled, and the man to the right grabbed her to keep her from falling.

As she was righting herself, the man in the middle said, "Madonna, I am so sorry. Are you all right? I was talking and was not looking where I was going. Truly, are you injured?" This was all said in a very high, nasal tone.

By then she had gathered herself and she looked up at him—into that glorious, ugly face with its smashed, flat nose, but those captivating eyes. She knew immediately who it was by the voice and the face. She knew he had an engaging, happy smile and laugh, but he was not laughing now. He was frowning with concern for her well-being.

She laughed and said, "I am fine, yes, yes." He had reached out to take her arm as he spoke, and now she put her hand gently on his chest. "I met your grandfather at this same door in the same way over forty years ago. Only he did not have a man with him to keep me from falling, so he had to help me up instead. Surely, this is God's will. God bless you, sire."

Amalia moved to enter the church, and the man who had kept her from falling held the door open for her to pass.

"Thank you," she said.

"Madonna," he said; and as the door began to close, she looked back.

Her eyes met with Lorenzo's again for but an instant before the door closed.

She had a lot to think about, and none of it was good, but instead, her mind went back to that fateful day so many years ago when she met Cosimo for those few brief moments. That encounter had changed her life, sometimes in ways she did not become aware of until years later.

He had arranged for her copies of the manuscripts to be bought when she and

Lucrezia were so desperate. Later, as her reputation grew—she did not know until years later—but he had arranged for her to copy some of the special manuscripts coming out of the monasteries. By then, her penmanship had become exquisite, but more important, her colored artwork on the special pages made them more valuable for sale throughout Europe.

When Messer D'Alessandro was threatening to come to visit her to tell her she would have to sell her house and go into a convent, that she and Lucrezia could not continue to live alone in her father's house, Cosimo had again intervened, through his man, Palle, though she had not known it at the time. They heard no more from Master D'Alessandro. When they would see him at gonfalons gatherings, he was always very attentive and courteous toward them both and never again mentioned the convent or selling the house.

Then in the court, when the simple cough of an anonymous man had changed the minds of the judges, and they had ruled she could keep her house: that had been Cosimo's man.

When Marco returned from Turkey, came to Florence, and they ultimately wanted to get married, not being a member of the guild, he could not get permission from the guild to work. Cosimo found out—she did not know how —and arranged for the guild to allow Marco to work in Florence.

How many more times had he intervened in her life that she did not know of? How did he always know when she was in trouble? She had finally found out that Cosimo's secretary, Messer Palle, had been instructed to keep a close watch over her safety and to protect her. This he was able to do through his network of informants and contacts throughout Florence and most particularly in Amalia's own gonfalons.

Now Cosimo was gone, Marco was gone, and soon she would be gone also. How she and Lucrezia would have fared had it not been for Cosimo, she knew not. She only wished she had had the opportunity to thank him for all his kindnesses to her.

Well, enough. It was getting late, and she thought the rain had stopped. Her daughter would wonder what had happened to her, so she gathered her things, walked over to take a long look up into the heights of Brunelleschi's magnificent dome, and then left her beloved Duomo to return home.

Her thoughts on her walk home were about what the doctor had told her. The streets were as familiar to her as the back of her hand, and the walk didn't require her attention. Even though she was now a slow walker, she was at her front door in a very short time.

As she went to enter the house, a man crossed the street and came up beside her. She was startled but not frightened for she immediately recognized him as one of the men that had been with Lorenzo, the one who had kept her from falling when Lorenzo had bumped into her.

"Excusa, madonna, but Messer Medici asks that I bring you to his palazzo, if you would be willing to accompany me."

"Of course," she replied without any hesitation. "Just let me tell my daughter where I'm going. I am already late getting home, and she will be worried."

"I will wait here, madonna. Please, take your time."

Amalia entered and climbed the stairs to the receiving room, and Alessandra came rushing toward her from the kitchen area.

"Mama, where have you been? You have been gone all morning. I thought you would be home an hour ago."

"It is all right, dear. I stopped by the Duomo to have a visit with Our Lady, and I met the grandson of an old friend. His man is waiting outside to take me to the Palazzo Medici. I don't know why, but this is a man you don't refuse; and certainly, I wouldn't, even if I could." She smiled, leaned over, and whispered to her daughter, "He is as ugly up close as he is from a distance, but when you are near him, his eyes are so compelling, you are immediately drawn to his charm like a moth to a flame."

"Mama," her daughter said in a shocked voice. Then they both chuckled. "But Mama, you can't go alone."

"My dear, I will not be alone. A Medici man will be escorting me, and I will be in the home of the man to whom I owe everything: my house, my work, my husband—everything that brought me happiness in my life except for you, my precious. For that, I owe your father and God."

They both laughed.

Amalia went into the kitchen to get a drink of the water from a jug they kept on the table. Thanks to Cosimo, years ago a viaduct had been built, bringing fresh, clean water from the mountains to Florence, so they no longer had to drink their cheap, watered wine.

She went upstairs to her bedroom briefly, and when she came back down, she fussed with her hair and her veil a bit. Then she kissed her daughter warmly and hugged her to her.

"Is there any word from Lucia about the baby?"

"The fever has broken, so that is good. I made a lamb stew to take over. Lucia is exhausted. She was up all night."

"I'll walk over with you when I get home. I'll read to the baby and let Lucia rest."

~ ~ ~

"Madonna, thank you for coming. I wasn't sure that you would." Lorenzo bowed slightly to Amalia and indicated the chairs in front of a large table that was obviously his work place.

"Messer Medici, yours is an invitation one does not refuse. Besides, how could I refuse an invitation to visit the home not only of the leader of Florence but also the home of my benefactor, your grandfather?" They both laughed. "How do you know my name and where I live?"

"When we left you at the church, I had my man follow you to find out who you were and ask you to come here. I was intrigued by what you said. Please, sit down."

Amalia had been ushered into a room that was obviously Lorenzo's studiolo. There were statues all around, scale models of buildings on tables and on the floor, stacks of books on the many shelves around the room and on the floor, a globe in one corner, a telescope standing nearby the open window, a statue in another corner, paintings on the walls and standing against the book shelves everywhere. The room was cluttered with so many wonderful things, Amalia had the feeling they had been accumulating there since Cosimo's day.

"What a wonderful room," she said.

Lorenzo laughed his nasal, raspy laugh, and said, "My wife would never enter here because it is such a mess. No one has been allowed to clean it since my grandfather's day. A lot of these things were his."

"I thought as much. Are any of the old, original manuscripts here?" she asked.

"Yes, over there. A lot of them are in the library Grandfather started with Signore Niccolo de Niccoli's collection at San Marco. They are all well cared for there, but a couple of them he always kept here.

"I remember when I was a boy, he would allow me to accompany him when Ficino and the others were gathering to discuss some newly discovered book or

Greek play whenever we were out at Villa Careggi. Those gatherings were magical for me. It was when I started to write my poetry."

"Yes," Amalia said, "I remember those early days well. My father was a scribe, and I learned from him. He would read the Latin manuscripts to us in the evenings after he had copied them. He didn't know Greek, so he never copied any of those. I was so young then, but I loved those books and still do."

Lorenzo was seated in the chair opposite her, and she could feel his intense charisma. He did have a high, nasal voice—probably so because of his smashed nose—but what a magnificent man he was. The nasal tone wasn't even a distraction now that she was getting used to it.

She asked, "I have read some of your poetry, and I enjoyed it very much. Do you still find time to write?"

"Not much anymore. My mother always urged me to do it. Of course, her poetry was truly beautiful. Have you ever read any of it?"

"Yes, many years ago a book dealer who worked with your grandfather had a copy of her book, and he gave it to me to copy. He suggested I might want to make a copy of it for myself, and, of course, I was thrilled to do so. It was a most unusual gesture, but he had come to like me, and over the years we became good friends. I keep her little book by my bedside always and often read it in the evening to gentle my nerves if I've had an unsettling day."

"I am glad you like it. It is certainly not to everyone's taste, but it is beautiful. Madonna, you say you met my grandfather at the Duomo years ago and that he also almost knocked you down?"

"No," she laughed, "he did knock me down. He didn't mean to, but I was running in from the rain and I was crying, and our collision was rather violent. My manuscript went flying in one direction and I went in the other. Once he had gotten me off the floor, and I had retrieved my package, he tried to calm me and asked why I was so upset.

"My father had recently died. I had no money and no means of support, but I had a copy of a manuscript to sell. The problem was, the book dealer wouldn't buy it from me because I was a woman—well, actually a girl. Your grandfather asked if he might look at the manuscript. After looking at a few pages, he asked me if I had scribed it. I told him I had, that my father had been a scribe and I had learned from him. Your grandfather told me to go back to Mr. Manetti's shop the next day. He had intervened, and from then on Mr. Manetti bought everything I could produce. Of course, he is gone now—they all are—but thanks to your grandfather, he was very good to me. As I said, ultimately he became a good friend.

"Your grandfather intervened on my behalf on several other occasions, and sometimes I didn't even know about it until years later. Thanks to him, I did not have to sell my home and go into a convent, and he helped my future husband to get approval from the guild to work in his trade so we could marry. I only learned of that years later from your grandfather's agent in our gonfalons. He intervened with the courts in my behalf when my brother was trying to disinherit me. There may be other times that I have no knowledge of even now. In essence, I owe him my life. I never had the opportunity to thank him, so I am so pleased to have this opportunity to be able to express my gratitude to you, his grandson, for all he did for me."

"Never mind about that. These are the stories I love to hear about him, and that is the man he truly was. He was always so quiet and never made a fuss or talked about the good things he did. He firmly believed his actions were more important than the words."

"Oh, there is something I need to return. While I was telling your grandfather my sad tale, I was a waterfall of tears." As she said this, she reached into the pocket on her dress, and continuing, she said, "He gave me this to dry my eyes—well, my face. He was embarrassed by my emotional state, I knew, so I tried to compose myself as best I could."

"No, he was not comfortable with emotional displays. He always managed to show his affection for us in other ways, but tears distressed him. It's a good thing my grandmother was such a happy person," Lorenzo said as he leaned back in the chair, remembering. "She could always lift his spirits. Even after a difficult day, with her in the room, he would soon be relaxed and enjoying himself. That is why our mealtimes were always so special. There was always excellent conversation, to be sure, but her warm affection for the family and her happy ways influenced everyone around her.

"Please, keep that as a token of his affection for you. He must have thought a great deal of you, from what you have told me."

"Thank you, Messer. I have always kept it on the table by my bedside with your mother's book of poems." She put the handkerchief back in her pocket, patted it gently and paused, then said, "Those mealtimes must have been very special."

"Yes, they were. We always had one or two of the artists living in the house with us. I grew up with Leonardo and Botticelli and others, but there would also always be people at our dinner table I didn't know. When I talked to them, I learned they were always interesting people from all walks of life that my grandfather had helped or was helping or someone he just enjoyed spending time with. They might be traders or businessmen, writers or humanists, professors, bankers, one of his agents, or other artists. He loved architecture and the men that did it. He could talk all day about the design of a building with Michelozzo or Donatello or even Brunelleschi, I understand, before they had their falling out.

"I have tried to continue his ways. Presently, a brilliant young man has been living with us since he was a young boy: Michelangelo Buonarroti. You will hear much about him. It is a joy to see how his mind works and know that he will do great things for Florence.

"I think the humanists were Grandfather's greatest interest. When he was at Villa Careggi, he would spend almost every evening with a group of the Greek professors and Ficino, talking about the old manuscripts and Plato and Socrates. It was so important to him to discuss the how and why of things. He believed that was what was new, and they learned it from those old books they kept finding and copying. He believed that in his time there was a rebirth of knowledge, this old knowledge.

"You know, he grew up with three books, all religious; then he had thirty books when he came back to Florence after Albizzi, and now he has two large libraries plus these." He gestured to the walls of his cluttered room. "My grandfather wanted wealth and power, to be sure, but I think he wanted knowledge even more than all that.

"He was very proud of founding the Florence Academy, his imitation of the Greek Plato Academy. We still meet when we can.

"He was a political force, to be sure, but yours is the man I like to remember. Those stories have gotten lost now, and all people remember is that they think he was suppressing the republic. Of course, I suppose I am also, but we have done what we felt was necessary for the benefit and glory of Florence and for the people. "Grandfather used to say that wealth was only good if it was used for good. He wanted to keep power out of the hands of the people who wanted to use it for personal gain. He so enjoyed his many projects for the glory of Florence; he often remarked he just wished he had started spending on those sooner.

"We were raised to love God first and family second, but to believe in the glory of Florence and to work tirelessly toward her prosperity and the benefit of all her people."

Lorenzo never lost eye contact with Amalia, and she found the intensity of that gaze very compelling, the charm of his personality overpowering.

Amalia said, "Cosimo gave us peace, stability, and prosperous times. Who knows where the Albizzi would have taken us had they had more time to force us back to their old ways for any longer than the one year they were in control. Plus, Cosimo gave us all the glorious buildings that he either built or instigated.

"You have maintained that peace so the economy could thrive, but you also brought us so much beauty with all the artists you have helped, as your grandfather and your father did. Many of the artists talk about you when they work with us on the festivals on the saints' days. I believe many of their works will live on long after you and I are both gone. You have done wonderful things. Surely your Medici name will live on through the ages."

"Have you had a good life, madonna?"

"Oh, yes. I was married for many years to a good man and have two wonderful children and four beautiful grandchildren. More than that, though, I have to say, I have lived in glorious times, and I have gotten to play a very small part in them as a scribe of those wonderful manuscripts, thanks to your grandfather.

"In my lifetime I believe there has been a swerve in the way people think. They are now more attuned to nature and its beauty and the happiness of man here on earth rather than just the hereafter and the teachings of the church."

"I agree," said Lorenzo. "I don't know that the church approves entirely of that swerve, as you call it, but I do agree that it has happened. I think our artists reflect it in the subjects of their paintings and how they paint them."

"Messer, it has been an honor to meet you, but now I must go. I have taken up far too much of your time."

"Is there anything I can do for you, madonna?"

"Thank you, messer, but I can assure you, just inviting me here to meet you and giving me the opportunity to see this wonderful room is more than I could have ever imagined could happen to me. You have made an old lady very happy, and I thank you."

While she was saying this, she glanced around the room one more time, very slowly, with intent to store away the memory of as much as her eyes and mind could take in.

"You know, I was here once before while the palazzo was still under construction. A gentleman who was to become my attorney in later years, as well as a good friend, brought me here. He was friendly with Michelozzo, so we went all through the building. I remember liking the lighting of this room when it was just stone and timbers, but I had no idea it would be Cosimo's studiolo." She said this as she continued to take in all she could of the room, cluttered with the treasures accumulated during three lifetimes devoted to the arts and literature of the Greek and Roman worlds and to Florence, her beloved—their beloved—city.

"One thing, messer, if you wouldn't mind. Might I just see and touch one of those original manuscripts? I always worked from copies since I worked at home. I knew of the originals, of course, and I knew the history behind them, but I never saw one of them."

"Of course. Come over here."

They both rose to walk over toward the book shelf Lorenzo had indicated earlier. He took down one old manuscript and laid it on the table in front of the tall shelves. As she opened it, she gasped, and her hands flew to her mouth. Amalia looked up to him, her mouth agape, and she was speechless.

Finally, gathering herself, she lowered her hands, and she said, "This is the book; this is the one that started it all: Lucretius's book that Poggio brought back from the monastery at Fulda."

She turned the pages carefully and gently ran her fingers down the page, almost, but not quite, touching the ink. She paused at some of the special passages she remembered.

"This is truly beyond belief, to see it and touch it." She turned a few more of the pages very gently. She turned and looked up at him. "You have made an old lady very happy. Oh, I said that before, didn't I?" and they both laughed.

Amalia was facing Lorenzo now, and no words would come. Instead she reached up and touched his cheek as she nodded. Then she turned and gently touched the page of Lucretius's book one last time as she closed the book.

She turned back and looked up at Lorenzo and said, "Now I must go before I make a fool of myself."

He took her hand and said, "It has been a pleasure to meet you, madonna. You have made my grandfather come alive again, if only for these few moments. Thank you for that. My man will show you out." He bent down and kissed her hand.

Amalia nodded, unable to speak, then finally she smiled and said, "Thank you, Messer Medici."

She turned and left the room. The servant ushered her into a side room by the main stairway before descending to go down and out of the palazzo. This was the Medici Chapel where all the great dignitaries were always received when arriving in Florence, usually even before going to the Palazzo Vecchio to see the Signoria or other dignitaries.

She was overwhelmed by the artwork on the three walls and the beauty of the small chapel. Then as her eyes adjusted, she began to see the details of the famous Gozzoli painting of the Journey of the Magi, the journey of the kings to visit the Christ child, but more. Here were the dignitaries that came for the Council of Florence with their monkeys and cheetahs, camels and lions, their magnificent fineries in gold and brilliant colors, and then she saw him, Cosimo, riding his father's mule beside Piero, his son, leading the procession. She stared at the painting for a very long time, never aware of the tears running down her face.

She saw Lorenzo with his flattened nose and Carlo with his Circassian skin behind Cosimo, the Archbishop from Constantinople, Sigismondo Malatesta, the Wolf of Rimini. What horrible stories they all heard about him over the years! There was Galeazzo Sforza, the Duke of Milan, son of Cosimo's good friend. So many other faces to be recognized, but she kept coming back to the one, the face of the man that had meant so much to her from that day many years ago when she collided with him at the door near Brunelleschi's dome.

This was the face of the man who had brought architecture and then art to

Florence, brought illumination into the darkness with the enlightenment by the humanist thinkers he spearheaded. This was the man who had brought the peace and prosperity Florence enjoyed for so many of Amalia's years. He had given her her career as a scribe, her home, her husband's job allowing them to marry, and who knew how much more.

"Madonna, are you all right?" asked the servant.

After a moment, she replied, "Yes, I am quite all right. Thank you for bringing me here."

"Messer thought you might enjoy seeing it."

"He was correct. Thank him for me, please."

When she did finally make her way downstairs, she paused in the loggia to look at the David she had always heard so much about. Donatello had casted it for Cosimo back shortly before she had first met Cosimo, and it had been the largest bronze statue casted of a naked man since the Roman days over a thousand years before.

Donatello's depiction of David had been most unorthodox for its time. Many people were shocked by it and some were even offended. It was almost erotic with that feather going up the inside of his leg. Looking at it now, so many years later, she could certainly understand why they felt that way back then. But they had set a new mark: Donatello and his David. They changed the way people thought about art, moving their minds from the saints and angels to man and nature, and they had helped to move an entire society in a new creative direction that would eventually help to change the world.

It was only with great difficulty that she pulled herself away from the beauty and grace of that exquisite statue. She walked over toward the passageway to the garden and could see Donatello's Judith and Holofernes bronze casting still standing in the middle of the garden. Then, after just a brief pause, she finally exited the building as the guard held the door open for her. He asked if she would like an escort home, but she declined, saying that she knew the way very well. Once outside, she paused and touched the large door with the flat of her hand. Then she laid that hand to her heart.

Amalia knew this visit had been one of the most wonderful experiences of her life, and it had happened on what was one of the worst days of her life.

Epilogue   April 9, 1492

Three months later, Amalia lay dying of the cancer Dr. Zacarro had told her would kill her very quickly. Her daughter, Alessandra, and Bernardo, her grandson were by her bedside, Giuliano and Teresa sat on the other side by Lucrezia. Lucrezia was sitting straight and strong as always, but they both knew she was failing rapidly and would not be long behind Amalia. Alessandra had been crying, but she was trying to be strong so as not to upset her mother.

"Don't cry, my dear. I am no longer in pain." But the words came so softly and slowly now. "I have had a good life. You are a good mother to dear Bernardo," and she reached over and patted Bernardo's hand. "No one could have asked for a better daughter or son," as Amalia turned and looked at her son. "I am proud of both of you, and we've had some good times together.

"I have had many friends, but one good friend," and she turned again to look at Lucrezia. "You and I have traveled this road together since we were very young girls." She reached over to take Lucrezia's hand as she looked at her and smiled. "What more can one ask for in this life?" They each smiled at the other through their tears. "Where is Lisabetta?"

"She will be back up shortly, Mother," said Giuliano. "She went downstairs when she took all the young ones down."

There were so many: Lucrezia's children and grandchildren, Amalia's grandchildren, the nieces and nephews, and even the greats. Even though Amalia and Marco's bedroom was a spacious room and could accommodate them, it was too overwhelming for the younger ones to be here now that Amalia was slipping away.

Yesterday, when she was a little stronger, all the little ones had piled up on Amalia's bed. She had spoken with each of them, giving them her loving wishes and her heartfelt thoughts she hoped each would carry forward in their long lives.

"Life goes on. With Carlo and Lisabetta, we were quite a family, weren't we, Lucrezia? Then came Marco and Ermanno, and we were still a household of orphans, but we were a family, a family built on love rather than blood, as Carlo always reminds us. Then we each built our own family of blood: children, then their husbands and wives, then their children, and more. Lucrezia, we have been well blessed. We have had our losses and heartaches, to be sure, but life has been good to us.

"Ah, I am ready to join Marco. He has been alone for far too long. He will have himself in all sorts of trouble by now, and he needs me." With that she smiled, as did the rest of them but with tears in their eyes as they did so.

Lucrezia thought, even so near death, she does not lose her sense of humor. What will I do without her? But she knew her own day would be coming very soon, and then the four of them would be together again.

Carlo had quietly come into the room. He whispered to Alessandra that Lisabetta had fixed a meal for them; it would be on the table in the kitchen for later, and she would be right up to be with Amalia. He and Lisabetta knew no one had any appetite, but they would need to eat later; and no one wanted to leave Amalia's side to be preparing food.

Carlo sat down beside Amalia on the wood apron around her bed. He kissed her gently on the cheek.

Then he said, "Amalia, I am so sorry. There is something I must tell you. Word has just reached Florence that Lorenzo de' Medici died last night at Villa Careggi."

She nodded. "So," she said, with the barest hint of a smile, "we shall travel that road together."

Historical People, Places, & Events

Medici – Cosimo – 1389-1464

    Piero – 1418-1469

    Lucrezia – 1427-1482

    Lorenzo – 1449-1492

    Palle – Cosimo's personal secretary. Responsible for his network in Florence

Pope John XXIII – Baldassarre Cossa (1370-1419 (Declared the anti-pope at Council of Constance)

Sforza, Francesco Maria – Duke of Milan and good friend of Cosimo

    son – Galeazzo; his illegitimate daughter – Caterina

Albizzi, Rinaldo degli – nobleman instigated the exile of Medicis in 1433-4, then was himself exiled for life

Manuscript world:

Vespasiano da Bisticci – 1421-1498

Poggio Bracciolini – 1380-1459

Niccolo de Niccoli – 1364-1437

Marcilio Ficino – 1433-1499

Ambrogio Traversari – 1386-1439

Marcus Aurelius – 121-80 BC

Cicero – 106-43 BC

Livy – 55 BC – 17 AD

Quintillian – 35-100

Sallust – 86-35 BC Cataline War

Lucretius – -99-55 BC wrote *On the Nature of Things*

Vitruvius (80-70 –15 BC) wrote *De architectura*

    (These last two books found at Fulda by Poggio)

Writers –

Leon Baptista Alberti – 1404-1472

Boccaccio, Giovanni – 1313-75 – Decameron

Dante, Alighiero – 1265-1321 – *Divine Comedy*

Lucrezia de' Medici – religious poems

Piero di Mariano **Muzi**, purse maker – wrote more secular play to celebrate the renovations of San Marco

Petrarch, Francesco – 1304-1374

Plutarch – 46-120

Orfeo – Pre-Opera staged event by Poliziano

Artists, Sculptors, and Architects:

Fra Angelico – 1395-1455

Botticelli – 1445-1510 (1482 – Primavera-82/Venus-85)

Brunelleschi – 1377-1446

Donatello – 1386-1466

Ghiberti – 1378-1455

Gozzoli, Benozzo – 1421-1497

Leonardo da Vinci – 1452-1519

Fra Lippi – 1406-1469

Masaccio – 1401-1428

Michelangelo – 1475-1565

Michelozzo – 1396-1472

Ucello, Paolo – 1397-1475

Verocchio, Andrea del – 1435-1488

Churches of Florence – Duomo-Santa Maria del Fiore; San Marco, San Miniato al Monte, Santa Croce, San Lorenzo, Santa Maria Novella, Santanista Annunziata, Orsanmichele,Church San Martino, Santo Spirito

Palazzos in Medici design – Rucellai, Strozzi, Guido

Palazzo del Podesta – oldest public bldg of Florence – Model for Palazzo Vecchio – Was the court, then the jail – Le Stinche, then the home of chief of police, then Bargello

Pantheon – Church in Rome predating Christianity

Campanile – bell tower of the Duomo by Giotto

Perfuma Farmaceutica at Santa Maria Novella – run by nuns of SMN

Mugello – area northwest of Florence the hereditary territory of the Medici

Careggi – Medici home toward Fiesole 3 miles outside Florence

Fiesole – hill town 10 miles from Florence with Etruscan & Roman ruins

Arno – River through the middle of Florence

Fulda Monastery – in Southern Germany Where Poggio found Lucretius's and Vitruvius's books and more

Ostia – Ruins of what was the seaport for ancient Rome

Council of Constance – 1415-1417 – Called to resolve dilemma of 3 popes. Pope John XXIII declared an anti-pope, and Pope Martin V newly elected

Council of Florence – 1439 – Pope Eugenius IV, John VIII Palaiologis, John Argyropoulos, Abram of Souzdal, Emperor Zara Yaqob of Coptic Ethiopia – Driven from Ferrara by the plague. Cosimo paid all expenses for them to come to Florence to resolve schisms in the church

Pazzi Conspiracy – 1478 – Pazzi & other families conspire with the Pope to bring down the Medicis. Kill Giovanni.

Peace of Lodi – 1454 – Milan, Naples, Florence, Venice, Genoa, Este, & other smaller states sign peace pact ending wars for many years and benefiting trade and more. Negotiated by Cosimo

NeoPlato Academy – Marciio Ficino organized it at Cosimo's direction. Met at Careggi regularly. Later Lorenzo met. Existed until Ficino's death in 1499.

Onesta – Guards of the Night

Sumptuary Laws – strict regulations against outward ostentation or extravagant ornamentation of clothing or homes – no buttons – no more than one color, MAYBE TWO SHADES

Cosimo built – or rebuilt – Holy Sepulcher in Jerusalem, San Giorgio in Venice, San Marco cloisters & church, San Lorenzo, L'Ospedale degli Innocenti Palazzo Medici in Florence and several churches and villas outside Florence,

Worst Black Death (Plague) years – 1347, 1363, 1374, 1383, 1390, 1400

Medici become Papal Bankers – 1405

Reading List

On Machiavelli, The Search for Glory	Alan Ryan
The Merchant of Prato, Daily Life in a Medieval Italian City	Iris Origo
The Swerve, How the World Became Modern	Stephen Greenblatt
Tigress of Forli, the Life of Caterina Sforza	Elizabeth Lev
History of the Florentine People	Leonardo Bruni
Cosimo de' Medici	Katherine Ewart
The Most Beautiful Woman in Florence, Botticelli	Alyssa Palombo
Decameron	Giovanni Boccaccio
Brunelleschi's Dome	Ross King
The Civilization of the Renaissance in Italy	Jacob Burckhardt
Renaissance Florence	Gene A. Brucker
Renaissance Woman	Gaia Servadio
The House of Medici, Its Rise and Fall	Christopher Hibbert
History of Forence and the Affairs of Italy	Niccolo Machiavelli
Cosimo de' Medici and the Florentine Renaissance	Dale Kent
Renaissance Florence, The Invention of a New Art	A. Richard Turner
The Family in Renaissance Florence	Leon Battista Alberti
The Medici, Power, Money, and Ambition in the Italian Renaissance	Paul Strathern
Medici Money	Tim Parks
The History of Florence	Niccolo Machiavelli
The Medici, Story of a European Dynasty	Franco Cesati
The Ugly Renaissance; Sex, Greed, Violence and Depravity in an Age of Beauty	Alexander Lee
April Blood, Florence and the Plot Against the Medici. Florence	Lauro Martines
The Renaissance, Makers of Modern Man	Michael Levey
The Lives of the Most Excellent Painters, Sculptors, and Architects	Giorgio Vasari
Catherine de Medici	Leonie Frieda
The Renaissance in Italy	John A. Symonds
Daily Life in Florence in the Time of the Medici	J. Lucas-Dubreton
On The Nature of Things	Lucretius

Special Words

Alberghetto – Little Inn (Jail at the top of the Signoria tower)

Boddeghe – Artist's or artisan's Shop

Braccia – About 24 inches

Buonomini – Cosimo charity for workers – still operating

Cassone – chests of all sizes & ornamentation

Chitarra – Newly developed instrument

Ciompi – Workers revolt in the 1300's.

Calcio – Football-Like Italian game

Erse – Common Celtic language of the Irish people

Fabbri Guild – metal workers' guild

Florens – Big bucks

Forchetta – fork

Fotella – folk song, song of the people

Gonfalons – Neighborhood

Gonfaloniere – Political title, somewhat like a mayor

Il Popolo – Nickname for Cosimo

Kermes – Red dye source – insect

Le Stinche – Florence prison

Lira – dollars

Luppo – wolf

Mandola – New style instruments

Misericordia – charity for poor in each parish – Still operating

Murex – Purple dye source – a snail

Piazza – Open area in front of several churches & Signoria

Paleo – horse race

Picciolo – Small change

Podesta – court for popolo (People)

Popolo – People

Ribollita – Italian bread soup

Studiolo – study, office

Theriaca – Pain killer medicine

Volgare – Italian word for their native tongue.

Willow bark – Pain medicine (acetaminophen)

Made in the USA
Lexington, KY
21 December 2019